THE
JENSEN
DYNASTY

THE
JENSEN
DYNASTY

WILLIAM W.
JOHNSTONE
AND
J.A. JOHNSTONE

PINNACLE BOOKS
Kensington Publishing Corp.
www.kensingtonbooks.com

CONTENTS

SMOKE JENSEN: THE BEGINNING

CHAPTER 1

Early October, Stone County, Missouri

Election season of 1860 was the most contentious election season in the history of the United States. Newspaper editorials and campaign speeches suggested that there would be major consequences, depending upon the results. Four candidates were running for President, the major two being Abraham Lincoln as a Republican and John Breckenridge as a Southern Democrat. In addition, two other candidates were in the race. Stephen Douglas was a Democrat and John Bell was running on the Constitutional Union ticket.

Several of the Southern states had already made the threat to secede if Lincoln won, and tensions were running high.

Missouri was a slave state with almost 120,000 slaves, but as of the latest count, only sixteen resided in all of Stone County. Emmett Jensen didn't have any slaves, but he did own a forty-acre farm of loam and rock adjacent to Shoal Creek. The farm required a great deal of work just to make it productive enough to feed a family of five. At twelve years old, Kirby was the youngest of Emmett and Pearl Jensen's three children. Janey was fourteen and Luke was eighteen.

The institution of slavery had an effect on the lives of almost everyone in Missouri and Kansas, a free state. The question of slave or free had gone far beyond mere debate, erupting into actual fighting between armed partisans of the two states.

The guerrillas from Kansas called themselves Jayhawkers. Their counterparts in Missouri were known as Bushwhackers, and for some time, shooting had been taking place between the groups. Led by Asa Briggs, the Missouri Bushwhackers called themselves the Ghost Riders. The Jayhawkers from southeast Kansas were led by Angus Shardeen.

Shardeen once rode with John Brown, and personally took part in the Pottawatomie Massacre in which several pro-slave sympathizers were murdered. Since John Brown's death, Shardeen had started his own group, and was making his presence known by burning homes and killing innocents in southwest Missouri, all in the name of abolition.

"There's a big war acomin'," Tom Byrd told Emmett the afternoon he went to Byrd's farm to retrieve the two mules he had rented to his neighbor for the afternoon. "You mark my words. It's acomin'."

"Maybe not," Emmett replied, his response motivated more by hope than reason. "Maybe cooler heads will prevail."

"No, they won't. The Republican, Abraham Lincoln, is going to be elected, 'n that's all it's agoin' to take. Once that ape becomes president, there's going to be war sure as a gun is iron."

Emmett shared some of the conversation with Pearl and the rest of his family over supper that night.

"If war does come, Pa, which way do you think Missouri is goin' to go?" Luke asked.

"Well, seein' as Missouri is a slave state, I don't see it goin' any other way except for the South."

"Yes, sir. That's what I was athinkin' too," Luke said.

"But Pa, you said many times, that you don't hold with ownin' slaves," Kirby said.

"I don't hold with anyone holdin' another man like that,

be the man black or white. But that ain't the only thing that's causin' the trouble. People ought to have the right to say what goes on in their state, and the federal government's got no right stickin' its nose into our business. I reckon if it comes to it, 'n all my friends and neighbors go off to join up with the South, why then that's the way I'll have to go."

"That's sort of what I was figurin' too," Kirby said. "If war comes, we'll be fighting for the South."

"There is no *we* about it, boy. You're too young to even be thinking about such things."

"I ain't always goin' to be too young," Kirby said.

"Well, you are too young now."

"Maybe Kirby is, but I ain't," Luke said. "If war comes, I'll be ridin' off to join up with the South. You can bet on that."

"I'm so tired of hearing everyone talkin' about the war," Pearl said. "Can't we at least talk about somethin' else here in our own home?"

"I hear what you're sayin', Pearl. But let's hope that it don't get no further than just talkin' about," Emmett said.

When Emmett first built the house back in 1841, it had only two bedrooms, one for him and Pearl, and one for the child he was sure they would have. Luke came along the first year, then four years later Janey was born, so Emmett put up a wall right down through the middle of the room, dividing it into two cubicles, each barely large enough to hold a bed. That arrangement gave Luke and Janey their privacy. Kirby came along two years after Janey. There was no place to put him, so Emmett built a small shelf just under the eaves of the house in order to make a sleeping loft.

It was a long time before Kirby was able to go to sleep that night. He was thinking too much about the supper conversation. Was it actually going to come to a war? Some might have said the skirmishes between the Bushwhackers and the Jayhawkers meant a war was already occurring, but that wasn't the kind of war he was wondering about. He was thinking of a real war, like the kind he had read about in books.

He knew about the Revolutionary War, the War of 1812, and the two Mexican Wars. The man that owned the leather store in town, Marvin Butrum, had been in both of the Mexican wars. He was with Sam Houston at San Jacinto during the Texas Revolution, and he had been with Robert E. Lee in the Mexican American War.

Kirby wondered what it would be like to be in a war. He pictured himself in a uniform astride a white horse, holding his saber high, and leading men into battle.

Well, it probably wouldn't really be like that. He was pretty sure that a twelve-year-old would not be entrusted to actually command an army. That realization caused the image he had projected in his mind to fade away.

He rolled over. But wait. The battle was in his imagination! While in his imagination, he could be anything he wanted, including a captain or a general or a sergeant; he wasn't sure enough about ranks to know what he wanted to be. But, whatever he was, he smiled as he remounted the white horse, lifted the saber, and gave the order to charge.

The next morning, Kirby and Janey went out to the barn to milk the two cows.

"You should be the one that does all the milkin'," Kirby complained.

"Why?"

"Because you're a girl, and milkin' cows is girl's work."

"What makes you think it's girl's work?"

"Pa don't never milk a cow, 'n neither does Luke. They plow and plant and harvest, but they don't milk cows."

"No, and they don't gather eggs either, but you do. Let's

face it, Kirby. Pa prob'ly thinks you are a girl." Janey laughed at him.

"Yeah? Well, would a girl do this?" Kirby picked up a double handful of straw and dumped it on her.

"Don't do that! You'll get straw all in my hair."

Kirby laughed.

The cows, Ada and Bridget, were back to back in a stall, waiting to be milked. Kirby and Janey put the milk stools in place, then sat down to milk.

"I bet I finish first," Kirby said.

"It isn't a contest, Kirby," Janey replied.

Kirby did finish first, then he got an idea. He had been milking Ada while Janey was with Bridget. Reaching over to grab Bridget's tail, he lifted it up, then did the same thing with Ada's tail. Using the hairy twitches at the ends of their tails, he tied them together.

Janey had been concentrating so much on the milking that she didn't notice what he had done.

"Want me to carry your bucket for you?" Kirby asked, diverting her attention.

"Well, that's very nice of you," Janey said, handing the bucket of milk to him.

They started back toward the house when the two cows began bellowing behind them.

"What in the world is wrong with those two?" Janey turned around. The two cows were trying to go in opposite directions, but couldn't because their tails were tied together. "Kirby! What did you do?"

"I don't know how it happened, Pa," Kirby tried to explain a while later. "As near as I can figure, they was just swattin' at flies 'n their tails musta got tangled up somehow. That's all I can figure."

"Are you trying to tell me they tied their own tails together?"

"Think about it, Pa. I mean, here are these two cows, just standin' there gettin' milked 'n all, and they sort of start swingin' their tails back and forth, not payin' no attention to each other. The next thing you know, why, their twitches has got all tangled up. Don't you think maybe it coulda happened that way?"

"I tell you what, Kirby. You go paint the barn, and while you're painting it, you might just come up with a lot better explanation than that cock and bull story you just tried to pass off on me."

"I thought you wasn't goin' to paint the barn till next summer."

"I changed my mind."

"All right, Pa."

Janey stuck her tongue out at Kirby.

Emmett watched his youngest son leave the house, and not until he was sure Kirby was well out of earshot did he turn to Luke. "Who would ever think to tie a couple cows together by their tails?" he asked, laughing.

"Nobody but my little brother, I'm thinking," Luke answered, laughing as well.

McMullen School was a one-room school accommodating twenty-two students in grades one through eight. Kirby was in the sixth grade. He was naturally a big boy, bigger than anyone else in the school, including the two boys in the seventh, and the one boy in the eighth grade. In addition to his natural size, hard work on the family farm had made him strong.

In the eighth grade, Janey was a beautiful girl with black hair, dark brown eyes, full lips, and prominent cheekbones. But it didn't stop there. Her body was already fully matured to the point that visitors to the school sometimes mistakenly assumed that she was the teacher. Aware that her looks and body had an effect on men, Janey wasn't above being a sexual tease when she could do so to her benefit.

After completing the fifth grade several years ago, Luke had left school to help his father work the farm. After he completed the fifth grade last spring, Kirby had petitioned his father to let him do the same thing.

On the crisp fall day, Kirby was recalling that conversation as he sat at his desk, staring through the window.

"I can already read, write, and cipher," Kirby told his father and older brother. *"I don't see any sense in me staying in school any longer, when I could be helping out on the farm."*

"You are going to stay in school," Emmett insisted.

Kirby continued staring at a distant flight of geese. Very high in the sky, the geese were maintaining a perfect V formation as they headed south for the coming winter. He imagined himself down at Shoal Creek with a shotgun. He could bring home a goose, and his mother could—

"Kirby? Kirby, have you suddenly gone deaf?"

The others in the classroom laughed, and it wasn't until that moment that Kirby was even aware he was being spoken to by his teacher.

"I beg your pardon, Miss Margrabe?"

"I just gave you an assignment. From the *McGuffey Reader*, I want you to spell, define, and tell what part of speech is the word *fluc-tuate*."

"*F-L-U-C-T-U-A-T-E*," Kirby said, spelling the word carefully.

"Very good, Kirby. And it means?"

"It means somethin' is moving back and forth, but it can also mean that somebody can't make up their mind about somethin', like if I'm tryin' to decide whether I want a piece of cherry pie or apple pie."

"And what part of speech is it?"

"It's an intransitive verb."

Miss Margrabe smiled and nodded. "Very good, Kirby. You were paying attention after all."

"Yes, ma'am," Kirby said.

"All right, children, I'm going to be working with the

first and second graders now. The rest of you know what your assignments are, so please study at your desks."

The assigned work for the sixth grade was math, and Kirby was working on a problem of long division. He hated long division, particularly when the answer never came out even. The lesson was that it had to be carried out at least four decimal points. Kirby found such problems frustrating, and he was still working on them when Miss Margrabe stopped by his desk to look at his work.

"Very good, Kirby. You wouldn't happen to know if . . . uh . . . Luke might be—" Miss Margrabe stopped in mid-sentence, then gave what could only be described as a self-deprecating chuckle.

"Might be what?"

"Never mind. It was quite inappropriate of me to ask. Keep up the good work; you have an excellent math paper here."

"Thank you." Kirby smiled as Miss Margrabe walked away. He and Janey knew that their teacher liked Luke. Kirby would never say a word about it, but Janey wasn't above teasing her brother.

Returning to his work, Kirby finished the last problem, then turned his attention outside again. A group of riders were coming toward the school, riding fast and all bunched up. That alone was enough to arouse his curiosity, but one of the men was carrying a flaming torch. Because it was the middle of the day, that made their approach even more curious.

As they drew closer, the rumble of hoofbeats became a thunder and soon everyone in the school was aware of the galloping band of horses. They looked at each other in confusion, and Kirby got up from his seat and moved to the window.

"Kirby, take your seat, please," Miss Margrabe said.

"Somethin' ain't right," Kirby said.

"*Isn't* right," Miss Margrabe corrected automatically.

The riders came within twenty yards of the school building, then stopped. The leader of the band had red hair, a red beard, and a very prominent purple scar on his face. His description was well-known. It was Angus Shardeen.

"It's Jayhawkers!" Kirby shouted.

Several of the riders began shooting toward the school, and the bullets crashed through the windows. The students started screaming.

"Get down on the floor!" Kirby shouted as he ran to his sister and pulled her down, just as a bullet slammed into the desk where she had been sitting.

"Don't they know this is a schoolhouse?" Miss Margrabe cried.

"Miss Margrabe, no! You'll get killed!" Kirby shouted. Leaving Janey lying on the floor, he ran to his teacher and pulled her down as well, though not in time to keep her from being shot in the shoulder.

"Burn in hell!" someone shouted from outside. A second later a flaming torch came in through one of the windows that had been shot out. The other students screamed and shouted and ran away from the flames. Only Kirby had the presence of mind to grab the pail of drinking water and toss the water onto the torch, extinguishing it.

"They're leavin'!" a seventh-grade boy shouted. "They're ridin' away!"

With the fire under control, Kirby hurried over to Miss Margrabe, who was on the floor, leaning up against the wall under the blackboard. She was holding her hand over the shoulder wound, and blood was coming between her fingers, though she wasn't bleeding profusely.

"Janey, come look at this, will you?" Kirby called. When Janey didn't respond right away, he called again. "Come here and take a look at Miss Margrabe's shoulder. You can get up now. The Jayhawkers is gone."

"Are gone," Miss Margrabe corrected through clenched teeth.

"Yes'm they surely are."

Janey went over to them, then knelt beside the teacher

and examined the bloody wound. The bullet hadn't actually hit her shoulder, but high up on her right arm.

"Kirby, use your knife to cut the sleeve off," Janey said.

"Must I bare my arm?" Miss Margrabe asked.

Janey nodded. "Yes'm. I'm afraid you're going to have to."

Kirby took a jackknife from his pocket and cut away the sleeve. He pulled the severed sleeve down across the teacher's hand, giving Janey an unrestricted view of the wound.

"It looks like it just cut a ridge in your arm, but I don't think the bullet is still there. Kenny, bring me some coal oil," Janey ordered one of the seventh grade boys. Boldly, she pulled up her skirt.

"Kirby, cut off enough of my chemise to make a bandage."

"Janey, that'll leave your legs bare," Kirby replied.

"Either cut enough for me to use as a bandage and bare my legs, or I'll take the whole thing off and bare my butt," Janey said. "Now do it."

Kirby took the bottom of Janey's chemise in his hands, but before he began to cut, he looked at the other boys in the room, all of whom had come closer for a look. "Every boy in here turn around, right now. If I catch any of you lookin' at my sister, I'll black your eye, and that's for sure and certain."

Reluctantly the boys turned away.

"Here's the coal oil," Kenny said, handing the can to Janey.

"You turn around, too," Kirby ordered.

A moment later, Kirby had cut a two-inch strip from all the way around the bottom of Janey's chemise.

"Now, cut a little piece off the end, so I can use it as a wiping cloth," Janey ordered.

After Kirby did so, Janey soaked the cloth in kerosene and used it to clean the wound. Then, pouring a little more kerosene over the wound, she made a bandage by wrapping the rest of the material around the teacher's arm, and tying it in place.

The sheriff and at least half a dozen other men came dashing into the school. Their sudden entrance frightened some of the other students until they realized who it was.

"We heard shooting!" the sheriff said. "What happened here?"

"It was Jayhawkers, Sheriff," one of the students said.

"Any of the kids hurt? We brought Doc Blanchard with us."

"Ain't none of the kids hurt, but they shot Miss Margrabe," Kenny said.

"*There aren't any children* hurt," Miss Margrabe corrected.

"Doc, get over here 'n look at the teacher, will you?" the sheriff asked.

"I'm real proud of both of you," Emmett said at supper that evening. "Kirby, the sheriff says that if you hadn't acted real quick, the whole school could have burned down. And Janey, Doc Blanchard said all he had to do was change the bandage. You did a fine job of nursin' Miss Margrabe."

"I stopped by to see Lettie," Luke said, speaking of Miss Margrabe. "Your teacher had nothin' but praise for the two of you."

"Praises for us, and kisses for you, I bet," Janey teased.

Luke smirked. "That's for me to know, and you to find out."

"I can't imagine any group of men so evil as to do something like that," Kirby's mother said.

"Never underestimate a man's capacity for cruelty," Emmett said.

"That's some real elegant words, Pa. Where'd you come up with 'em?" Kirby asked.

Emmett grinned. "I heard Governor Price say 'em durin' some of his speechifyin'."

"Pa, they's some fellas I know that's plannin' on joinin' up with Asa Briggs and ridin' over into Kansas to set things right," Luke said. "And I aim to go with 'em."

"No, you ain't," Emmett said.

"Pa, we can't just let 'em get away with somethin' like this."

"You ain't goin'," Emmett said again.

"It ain't like I'm plannin' on defyin' you or anythin' like that, but I'm full growed, Pa. And I reckon if I was to really take a mind to do it, there wouldn't be nothin' you could actual do about it."

"And I reckon you're right. But I would sure hope you wouldn't. It ain't our fight, boy."

"The hell it ain't! They attacked the school where Janey 'n Kirby was. They're family. They also shot Lettie. To my way of thinkin', it just don't seem right lettin' them Jayhawkers get away with doin' what they done."

"Thanks to your brother and sister, they didn't do much of anything. Kirby kept the schoolhouse from burnin' down, 'n Janey kept Miss Margrabe's wound from gettin' any worse. No need for you to be goin' over to Kansas with anyone when I need you here on the farm. Besides that, what do you mean when you say you plan to 'make things right'?"

"Just what it sounds like. Give 'em a taste of their own medicine," Luke said.

"You mean you plan to do the same thing to innocent folks over there that the Jayhawkers have been doin' over here? Are you goin' to burn a few houses, and maybe shoot some women and kids? Because it's for damn certain that you won't be runnin' into any of the ones who actually done this."

"It just don't seem right, Pa, to let 'em get away with it and do nothin' at all."

"Two wrongs don't make a right, son, and if you'll think about it, you'll see what I mean."

"All right, Pa."

"I tell you what. If you're all that anxious to shoot somethin', there's a covey o' quail down in the south pasture. I thought maybe me, you, 'n Kirby could go down there just after dawn tomorrow mornin' and shoot a few of 'em. I'd love nothin' better 'n a mess o' fried quail, gravy, and biscuits. That is, if Pearl 'n Janey would cook 'em up for us." Emmett winked at his wife.

"I'm not a very good cook, Pa. You know that," Janey complained.

"It's 'bout time you learned, don't you think? You're 'most a woman now, 'n you'll be takin' on a husband afore you know it. When you do, you're goin' to have to cook for 'im."

"I'm not ever goin' to have a husband, because I'm not ever goin' to get married," Janey said.

"Why not?"

"I have no intention of being a farmer's wife."

"What's wrong with being a farmer's wife?" Pearl asked sharply.

"Nothin' at all is wrong with it, Ma, if all you want to do is stay home, cook for your husband, and raise a passel of brats. But no, ma'am. That just ain't somethin' I want to do. I don't plan on staying around here. I'm goin' somewhere exciting, like New Orleans, or St. Louis, or maybe even Chicago."

"Well, right now you are in Stone County, Missouri," Emmett said. "And, whether you ever get married or not, you're goin' to learn to cook, if for no other reason than I told you to. And you can start tomorrow."

"What makes you think you'll get anything, anyway? Arnold Parker and a couple of others from school went quail hunting last week, and they didn't get anything."

"They aren't Jensens," Emmett said easily.

The Ozark Mountains could have been an artist's palette, alive as they were with color—yellow, orange, red, green, and brown. A crisp coolness to the morning could be felt as Kirby, his father, and brother walked across a recently harvested cornfield. Somewhere a woodpecker drummed against a tree, the rapid staccato beat of its beak echoing through the woods.

Suddenly, a brace of quail flew up in front of them, filling the air with the loud flutter of their wings. Quickly and smoothly, Kirby brought the double-barrel twelve-gauge shotgun to his shoulder and pulled first one trigger, then the other.

The double boom of the exploding cartridges caused the sounds of nature to pale in comparison. Feathers flew from two birds as they tumbled from the sky.

"Good shooting, Kirby!" Emmett shouted as the boy started forward to retrieve his two birds.

An hour later, the Jensens returned to the house with nine quail, more than enough to make a fine meal. They cleaned the birds and turned them over to Pearl and Janey to prepare.

"While your ma and sister are cookin' our dinner, how about you two boys come on out to the front porch for a few minutes," Emmett suggested.

Once they stepped out onto the porch, Emmett and Luke filled their pipes.

"Boys, we had us a real good corn crop this year. We made sixty bushels an acre, which means we've got about twenty-four hunnert bushels gathered." Emmett sucked on the pipe until the tobacco caught and a cloud of smoke wreathed. "Last I checked, we can get fifty-nine cents a bushel in Galena, which would bring in around fourteen hunnert dollars. That ain't bad for forty acres and a team of mules."

"I'll say!" Luke said enthusiastically.

"Pa, what about the seed corn for next year?" Kirby asked.

Emmett reached out and ran his hand through Kirby's hair. "Good for you, son, for thinkin' of that. I've already took out twenty bushels of the best lookin' seed corn."

"Seein' as we got only one wagon, it's goin' to take us three trips into town to get the corn delivered," Luke said.

"No it won't. Tom Byrd will rent us two wagons and two teams for ten dollars," Emmett replied.

"That still leaves us short one driver."

"Oh, I think Kirby could miss a day of school to drive one of the wagons." Smiling, Emmett looked over at Kirby. "That is, if you don't mind."

"Ha!" Kirby said with a huge grin. "I don't mind at all!"

"I didn't think you would."

"You men come on in for your dinner," Pearl called.

"There's only two men out there, Ma. Kirby's still a boy, remember." Janey smiled as she teased her younger brother.

"He does a man's work, and that makes him a man in my book," Emmett said.

"I hope you like the biscuits, Pa, because I made them," Janey said proudly.

Kirby picked one up and took a bite, even before the rest of the food was on the table. "Umm, umm. You did a great job! Yes sir, you're goin' to make some farmer a fine wife."

"You'll never see it!" Janey said, grabbing the biscuit from a laughing Kirby and throwing it at him.

CHAPTER 2

"How are you doing, Miss Margrabe?" Janey asked when she went to school Monday morning.

"Well, I'm doing just fine, dear, thanks to you and your brother," Lettie replied. She looked around. "By the way, where is Kirby?"

"Him 'n Luke 'n Pa went to Galena to sell some corn," Janey said.

"He and Luke, dear."

"He and Luke," Janey said, correcting herself.

"I don't know if you know it or not, but Luke came by to see how I was doing. Wasn't that sweet of him?"

"Yes ma'am. But, seeing as he is sweet on you, I'd expect him to come calling on you," Janey said.

"Hush, now. You shouldn't be saying such things." Lettie smiled around a blush.

"I'm just saying what's true, is all."

"Well, as much as I'm enjoying our conversation, we do need to get class started." Lettie saw one of the boys standing near the window. "Kenny, would you ring the bell, please?"

"Yes, ma'am."

* * *

"I make it two thousand, five hundred, and seventeen bushels," Fred Matthews said after the corn was unloaded and counted. "At sixty-six cents a bushel that would be—"

"Sixty-six cents?" Emmett said.

"Accordin' to the telegraph sent out by the Chicago Board of Trade ever' day, corn's tradin' at seventy-eight cents today." Matthews pointed to a sign on the wall behind him. "Like the sign says, we pay eighty-five percent of the price set in Chicago."

Emmett, Luke, and Kirby smiled at each other.

"It looks like we chose a good time to sell our corn," Emmett said.

Matthews grinned. "Yes, sir, I'd say you did. Twenty-five hundred and seventeen bushels at sixty-six cents a bushel comes to sixteen hundred and sixty-one dollars, and twenty-two cents. Do you want that in cash or by bank draft?"

"Cash, if you don't mind," Emmett replied. "I don't have a bank account, and the banks charge too much when they cash a draft."

"All right. Come on into the office and I'll count it out for you," Matthews offered.

Standing close by was a man named Roy Joiner, supposedly examining a wagon wheel. In truth, he was there to overhear conversations between the farmers who were selling their crops and the broker, hoping to happen upon an opportunity to put the information to good use.

Hearing the talk between the Jensens and Matthews was exactly the kind of information he was looking for. He watched the men enter the office, then hurried away.

"He's a dirt farmer," Joiner told Pogue Mason a few minutes later. "Him and his two sons, one of 'em nothin' more 'n a boy. Hell, just the sight of a gun would probably scare 'em so much they'd piss in their pants."

"How much money did you say they would be carryin'?" Pogue asked.

"Over sixteen hunnert dollars. And it's all in cash. We'll

hold 'em up out on the road. It'll be like takin' candy from a baby."

"Let's do it," Pogue said with a wide, nearly toothless grin.

About two miles north of Galena, Emmett, Luke, and Kirby rode in three empty wagons. Emmett was leading the little convoy, while Kirby was bringing up the rear. Aware that they were about to be overtaken by two men on horseback and thinking nothing was unusual about that, Kirby pulled over to one side of the road to give them room to pass.

They didn't pass. One of the men jumped into the wagon and put his gun against Kirby's head. "Call out to your pa, boy."

"What for?"

The man cocked the pistol, the hammer making a loud, double-clicking sound as it engaged the cylinder. "Do it, boy, or I'll blow your brains out. Maybe your brother will have more sense."

"Pa?" Kirby called. "Pa, we got a problem!"

Emmett and Luke stopped their teams and turned to look back toward Kirby. They saw the two men, one of them in the wagon with Kirby.

"Mister, if you don't want to see your boy killed, you'd best do what we tell you," ordered the man on horseback.

Setting the brake on his wagon, Emmett climbed down and started back toward Kirby. "Luke, you be ready to act if you get the chance," he said under his breath as he passed the second wagon. "Don't hurt my boy!" Emmett pleaded, making his voice sound frightened.

"Just give us the money you got from sellin' your corn, 'n ever'thing will be just fine," stated the mounted robber.

"Pa, you want me to get the money and give it to 'em?" Kirby asked.

"You may as well." Emmett kept his voice as if he was resigned.

Kirby stood up.

"Here, what are you doin'?" the man in the wagon asked.

"I'm goin' for the money. Ain't that what you said you wanted?" Kirby replied.

The two robbers were looking directly at Kirby, which meant they had taken their eyes off Emmett. Suddenly, Kirby jumped off the side of the wagon, then quickly rolled beneath it. His action left the two would-be robbers totally confused.

That was all Emmett and Luke needed. Both men drew their pistols and fired, and the two outlaws went down.

Luke jumped down from his wagon and, with his gun drawn, hurried back to where the two outlaws lay on the ground. Emmett gave both men a hard kick, but neither responded.

"Kirby, you all right?" Emmett called.

"Yeah, Pa. I'm all right."

"Come on out, then. These two ain't goin' to do you no harm now."

Kirby crawled out from beneath the wagon, then looked down at the two men his father and brother had just shot. "That's the first time I've ever seen anyone get killed," he said in awe.

"The way things is in this world, it ain't likely to be the last time you'll see it," Emmett said.

"What are we goin' to do with 'em, Pa?" Luke asked.

"Let's throw 'em in your wagon and you take 'em back into town. Me 'n Kirby will take Tom Byrd's wagons and teams back to him, then you can pick us up on your way back home."

"Take 'em to the undertaker?" Luke asked.

"No, take 'em to the sheriff. Let the county bury 'em. Besides, it's more'n likely that these two have dodgers out on 'em."

"What's a dodger?" Kirby asked.

"A reward poster. I suspect these two men may be wanted, and if they are, we'll collect some reward. And we'll split the reward money three ways." Emmett smiled. "You done real good, Kirby. I'm proud of the way you kept your head."

"Yeah," Luke added with a smile. "For a young whipper-snapper who don't have no more sense than to tie a couple cows together by their tails, you just done real good."

Kirby beamed under the praise.

A reward of three hundred dollars on each of the two men was offered and Emmett, true to his promise, gave Kirby and Luke two hundred dollars apiece. It was the most money Kirby had ever had in his entire life.

Long after midnight, Kirby heard a rider galloping toward the house, shouting at the top of his voice.

"Jensen! Jensen! Turn out! Turn out! It's Gimlin's place! They've set fire to it!"

Emmett stepped out onto the front porch, wearing his long handle underwear. "What is it, George? What's goin' on?"

"Jayhawkers, Emmett. They've set fire to Gimlin's barn and house! I'm callin' folks to go give 'em a hand."

"Good for you. On your way, then. We'll be there," Emmett promised.

Fifteen minutes later, the entire Jensen family was in a wagon headed for the Gimlin farm three miles away. They could see the glow of the fire long before they reached the farm. By the time they arrived, the house that had been home to Marvin and Gail Gimlin, and their two young children, was completely engulfed in flames. Several neighbors were gathered around, but all they could do was watch the house burn.

Standing in the yard, five-year-old Mollie was crying and shivering.

Janey went to her, carrying one of the blankets she and her mother had brought from home. "Here Mollie, wrap this around you," she said, comforting the little girl.

"Janey, why did they do this? Why did those men come burn down our house?" Mollie asked between sobs.

"Because they are evil," Janey said. "Some people are just meaner than snakes."

"My doll got all burned up."

Janey put her arms around the little girl and pulled her close for a moment. "Wait here. I have a surprise for you."

"What?"

"Well, if I told you, it wouldn't be a surprise, would it?"

Janey walked back to their wagon where blankets, quilts, cooking utensils, and extra clothing were piled, just in case the Gimlins would have need of them. Thinking of Mollie, Janey had included the doll that had been hers when she was much younger.

She took it to the little girl. "You can have my doll," Janey said, handing a China doll to the little girl.

Mollie's eyes grew big. "I can have it?"

"Yes, I don't play with her anymore, and I think she misses having someone to play with."

"I'll play with her." Mollie held the doll in a close embrace.

"That was real nice, what you done," Kirby said when Janey joined the rest of her family in front of the smoldering house.

She shrugged. "It's just an old doll. I was goin' to throw it away some day, anyway."

"Still, he's right. It was good of you to give your doll to the little Gimlin girl." Emmett walked over to Gimlin, and put his hand on the man's shoulder. "I'm real sorry about this, Dewey."

"At least we all got out without any of us gettin' hurt,"

Gimlin replied. "But we ain't got a thing left to our name. No furniture, no clothes, no dishes, nothin'. And no house to put it in, if we did have them things."

"You will, and soon." Emmett turned to the friends and neighbors who had gathered and held up both arms. "Folks!" he called. "Let me tell you what we're goin' to do."

He pointed to what was left of the house which was nothing but glowing embers and fire-blackened wood. Though the flames were mostly gone, a great deal of smoke was still pouring from it and its heat could still be felt.

"As soon as that pile of burnt wood is cool enough for us to work with it, we're goin' to clear it all out. Then we're goin' to build another house for the Gimlins just like the house that the Jayhawkers burnt down. No, we'll build it even better."

"Yeah!" one of the other men shouted. "By damn, that's exactly what we're goin' to do."

"And ladies?" Pearl called out, stepping up beside her husband. "While our men folk are rebuilding the house, we're goin' to refurnish it. I know that between us, we can come up with furniture, clothes, blankets, quilts, and whatever it takes to get the kitchen put together again."

"Looks like we won't need a cookin' stove," one of the women said, pointing to the rubble of the house. "The one they had come through just fine. All we got to do is clean it up a bit."

By mid-afternoon, a large gathering of wagons was parked at the Gimlin farm. At least fifteen families had come to help. The men were constructing a new house. Three sides of framework were already up, and they were about to put the final side into place. Kirby, doing the work of a man, scurried up one of the ladders, then got into position. Half a dozen ropes were thrown to the men on top of the frame, and Kirby grabbed one of them, pulling with the others as the end frame was raised into position.

With so many men working, the framework of the house was in place with amazing speed. After the siding and roofing was completed, everyone grabbed a brush and bucket of paint and, before supper, the house had been erected and painted, and all the furniture moved in.

The stove had been cleaned but not moved, and even before the house was completed, some of the women had started cooking. A temporary table, long enough to feed forty people, had been put together using boards and sawhorses. By the time construction clutter had all been picked up, the meal was ready and the Gimlins, Jensens, and neighbors sat on make-do benches for supper.

Kirby was watching his sister. Merlin Lewis, who had left school three years earlier, was sitting beside Janey, and it was obvious that she not only welcomed Merlin's attention, she was inviting it. Kirby couldn't help but marvel at how easy it was for her to control Lewis.

The twelve-year-old glanced over at his brother to see if he saw what was going on, but Luke was lost in his own world. Lettie Margrabe was doing the same thing to him that Janey was doing to Merlin Lewis. Kirby laughed.

"What are you laughin' at?" Emmett asked.

"Nothin', Pa. I was just laughin' is all," Kirby said as he reached for another piece of fried chicken.

"Careful, boy. Someone's goin' to see you laughin' at nothin' someday 'n they're goin' to think you've gone crazy."

Kirby turned his attention to another conversation going on near him.

"What I plan to do, 'n what I'm invitin' the rest of you to do, most especially the ones of you that ain't got a family to look after, is to join up with George Clark." The speaker was Lee Willoughby, a man who was the same age as Luke.

"Clark ain't nothin' but a murderer and an outlaw," someone said.

"That may be so, but he don't do none of his outlawin' in Missouri," Willoughby replied. "He does all of it over in Kansas. Luke, what do you say? Me 'n you was talkin' 'bout this the other day."

"We was talkin' about Asa Briggs, not George Clark."

"Briggs is an old woman compared to Clark. You want to come with me?"

Luke glanced over toward Emmett for just a moment before he replied. "I reckon not."

"Why not? You gone scared on me, have you?"

Luke stood up and glared. "Would you like to put that proposition to a test, Willoughby?"

A bit startled by Luke's response, Willoughby blinked his eyes and licked his lips for a few seconds before he responded. "No, no, I didn't mean nothin' by what I said. I don't want to fight you. I don't want to fight nobody from Missouri. All I'm lookin' to do is make things right. You folks has seen what kind of men the Jayhawkers are. They attacked the school, they come in the middle of the night to burn Mr. Gimlin and his whole family out of his house. Like I said, all I'm lookin' to do is set things right."

"I don't hardly see it as right, ridin' into Kansas and burnin' some farmer and his family out, like was done to me," Gimlin said. "I expect most folks over there are just like us. No line drawed on a map, especially one that you cain't even see, would make it right to go over there 'n start burnin' and shootin' and such."

"Yeah, well, a war's acomin', 'n I don't plan on missin' out on it," Willoughby said.

"If war comes, I expect a lot of us will get caught up in it," Emmett said. "And, in this state, I expect some, even some of us here, will choose up different sides."

"Which side would you choose, Jensen?" Willoughby asked.

"Well, sir, I don't have any slaves, 'n I don't hold with the idea of keepin' any. Besides which, I got a brother who lives up in Iowa, and he'll for sure be fightin' for the North. But the truth is, I can't see as the federal government's got 'ny right to tell a state what it can or can't do. I figure if it comes to it, I'll be pitchin' in with the South."

Emmett was normally a man of few words, and Kirby

believed that may well have been the longest speech he had ever heard his father make.

Willoughby smiled. "Well now, that's good to know. I've always looked up to you, Mr. Jensen, 'n I've always figured Luke to be my friend. I'm for sure goin' to fight for the South and I wouldn't want us to wind up bein' enemies."

"I don't consider anybody here my enemy," Emmett said, "whether they wind up fightin' for the North or the South."

One month after Gimlin's house was burned and rebuilt, Abraham Lincoln was elected President of the United States. As a result, South Carolina seceded from the Union, claiming independence. Six Southern states soon followed, eventually creating the Confederate States of America.

April 1861

A garrison of Union troops occupied Ft. Sumter in Charleston Harbor. South Carolina demanded that the troops be withdrawn, but the federal government refused to do so.

On April 10, Brigadier General Beauregard, in command of the provisional Confederate forces at Charleston, demanded the surrender of the Union garrison. Major Robert Anderson, the Union commander of Ft. Sumter, refused.

On April 12, Confederate batteries opened fire on the fort. Designed to repel invaders from the sea, Ft. Sumter was unable to maintain an effective defense against an attack from the land side.

At 2:30 PM the next day, Major Anderson surrendered and was allowed to evacuate the garrison on the following day. Not until then were there any casualties, as a Union artillerist was killed and three wounded when a cannon exploded prematurely when firing a salute during the evacuation.

Immediately after that incident, Lincoln called for 75,000 troops to be drawn from every state that had not seceded.

That action caused four more states to secede. The Confederate government matched Lincoln's move by calling for 75,000 troops of its own.

Lee Willoughby came by the Jensen farm not long after that, wearing the gray uniform of a Confederate lieutenant. "Iffen you had come with me when I asked last fall, more 'n likely you'd be an officer, too," he said to Luke. "Now, if you come in, you'll have to come in as a private. There ain't nothin' I can do for you, 'cause it's too late."

"Privates'll be fightin' the war same as officers, won't they?" Luke asked.

"Well, yes. Of course they will."

"Then the way I look at it, it don't really matter all that much whether I'm a private or an officer. Fightin' is fightin', 'n now that the war has started, I reckon I'll get into it so's I can do my part."

"When you plannin' on comin' in?" Willoughby asked.

"Right away," Luke answered. "No, wait. Give me till tomorrow. I want to tell Lettie good-bye."

"We're gettin' up a wagon to carry men to the recruitin' office in Springfield. It'll be leavin' Galena long about noon tomorrow. If you're comin' with us, be to the courthouse before the wagon leaves." Willoughby slapped his legs against the sides of his horse and rode off.

Luke looked at his father. "What about you, Pa? What are you goin' to do?"

"I don't plan to rush into anything," Emmett said. "I plan to take the night thinkin' on it. I don't like the idea of the people in Washington sendin' seventy-five thousand troops into various states to tell the folks what they can and can't do. So, if I'm bein' truthful with you, I'd say I'm leanin' hard on goin' with you." As fate would have it, he did just that.

* * *

Lettie Margrabe lay naked in bed, staring at the leaf patterns the sun was projecting onto her bedroom wall. She had slept that way for the very first time. It was also the first time she had ever slept with a man.

Lying beside her, breathing the soft, rhythmic breath of sleep, was Luke Jensen. He was also nude.

Lettie had lost her virginity.

She was in love with Luke, and what they had done was no different from what lovers had been doing since the beginning of time. He had come to tell her good-bye, to tell her that he would be leaving for the war. It was Lettie who had asked him to stay, and not until he was sure that it was truly something that she wanted, did he agree.

As she lay in bed that morning she could still feel the exquisite pleasure of the night of passion they had shared. That sensual gratification, however, was tempered by the fact that she knew that if anyone ever found out about it she would lose her teaching position. Such exposure would mean she would leave the county, and maybe even the state, in disgrace. Despite that possibility, she had no regrets about what they had done.

They had made love several times during the night, and Lettie intended to do so at least once more before she let him leave.

Emmett did not own a horse, so he hooked the team of mules up to the wagon. The entire family rode into town with him to say good-bye. When they reached the courthouse, they were surprised to see so many men were going to Springfield to join up with the Confederate army, that it took three wagons. Like the Jensen family, other families were there as well to say good-bye to their husbands, fathers, sons, and brothers.

"Pa, I don't see why I can't go with you," Kirby complained. "I've read that both armies is takin' folks my age and some even younger. Drummer boys they'll be."

"Both armies, Kirby? Are you tellin' me that if I don't approve of you joinin' with the Gray, that you'd be willin' to join the Blue? You'd fight against me 'n your brother?" Emmett was not amused.

"No, sir. I ain't atellin' you that. I'm just sayin', I don't think I'm too young to go. You said yourself that I can do a man's work."

"That is exactly what I said, and that is exactly why you need to stay here. You'll be runnin' the farm, Kirby. The responsibility of the whole thing is goin' to be on your shoulders. You're goin' to have to get the crops put in and tend to 'em. Then you're goin' to have to get 'em out and get 'em to market. I don't want to come back home to a farm that's gone and a family that's most starved 'cause nobody was takin' care of 'em. I'm countin' on you, boy. So is you ma and your sister."

Kirby didn't reply. He knew that his father was correct. Someone would need to keep the farm going. With his father and brother gone to war, he was the only one who could do it. "All right, Pa. I'll do what you say."

Emmett was not a demonstrative man. The closest thing to affection he showed was to reach out and take Kirby's hand in a firm handshake. "I know you will, son. That knowledge is what I'll keep with me the whole time I'm away."

"How long do you expect that to be, Pa?"

Emmett grunted and shook his head. "Truth is, this whole war is a foolish thing, us fightin' against each other. I expect the people in charge will come to their senses sooner than later. I'm bettin' we'll be back in time to help get the crops out, come fall."

"Emmett, you look after Luke now, you hear?" Pearl said. "He's my firstborn. It wouldn't sit good with me, if somethin' was to happen to him."

Emmett looked around. "Where is Luke?"

"He's over there, Pa," Janey said, pointing. "You didn't

expect him to leave without sayin' good-bye to his woman, did you?"

Luke and Lettie were standing close together, and though they weren't touching, the expressions on both their faces all but gave away to the discerning what had gone on between them during the night.

"I thought he told her good-bye last night," Emmett said.

"If they really are sweet on each other like Janey says, you'd expect 'em to tell each other good-bye again this mornin', wouldn't you?" Pearl said with a smile.

"I reckon so."

"Recruits!" Lee Willoughby shouted then. "Load up into these here three wagons! It's time we was leavin'!"

"Boy," Emmett said before starting toward the three wagons. "Remember what we talked about. You take care of your ma and sister while I'm gone."

"All right, Pa. I will."

Kirby had no idea how long it would be before he saw his father and brother again, or even if he ever would see them again. He could see tears in the eyes of his mother and sister and felt a lump in his throat.

But he would be damned if he would cry. He had just taken on the responsibility of a full grown man.

Two months later, Kirby had the crops planted and was watching them carefully, taking pride in what he had accomplished in such a short time. On a trip to the barn to get a new bridle for the mule called Ange, he heard a sound coming from behind a pile of hay. Not sure what it was, he looked around for a weapon of some sort, and saw an axe handle without its head. Grabbing the handle, he approached the stack.

"No. Merlin, I said no." That was Janey's voice.

"Come on, Janey. You've let me get this far. You can't stop now!" Merlin Lewis's voice was demanding and edgy.

Kirby stepped around to the other side of the stack of hay and saw his sister lying on the ground with the top of her dress and camisole pulled down so her breasts were exposed. Merlin was pulling on the dress, trying to take it all the way off.

"She said no!" Kirby said firmly.

"What the hell?" Merlin gasped, jumping up quickly. "Where did you come from? Get the hell out of here!"

Kirby drew back the axe handle. "No, Lewis. You get the hell out of here . . . before I bash your head in."

"You talk big with an axe handle in your hand." Merlin sneered.

Kirby tossed the axe handle into the hay stack, then doubled his fists and raised them. "I don't have an axe handle now."

Although Merlin was three years older, Kirby was every bit as tall and a little more muscular.

Merlin looked at him for a moment, then waved his hand dismissively. "Nah, I ain't goin' to fight you. Your sister's nothin' but a slattern anyway." Merlin turned to leave.

"Lewis?" Kirby called to him.

Merlin stopped, but he didn't turn around.

"I don't want to see you on my farm anymore."

"Your farm?"

"Yes, my farm. I'm the one living here. I'm the one working it. Don't come back."

Kirby followed Merlin out of the barn and watched to make sure that he left. He also wanted to give his sister time to cover herself up. He had never seen her like that before and was embarrassed by what he had happened on to.

"Kirby?" Janey's voice was small and frightened.

"Are you decent?" Kirby called back.

Janey was always aware that she was older and a bit more sophisticated than Kirby was, and most times she didn't mind making him aware of that fact. Her voice sounded different from normal. "Yes."

Kirby turned and saw her standing a few feet behind him. He had never seen such an expression on her face before. It showed nothing of that self-confidence. On the contrary, it was an expression of contriteness and fear.

"What was that all about?" he asked.

"I told him to stop, and he wouldn't do it. I'm just thankful that you came along when you did. If you hadn't . . . I don't know what would have happened."

"Janey, I've never been around a girl . . . like that . . . so I'm not real sure how things like what I saw here could happen. But it seems to me like it wouldn't have got that far if you hadn't let it."

"I admit I was . . . teasing him," Janey said. "But I thought I could control it. I thought that if I told him to stop, he would."

"Like I said, I ain't got that kind of experience, but I've heard enough talk to know that it don't always happen like that. You had to know that he's a lot stronger than you. You was playin' with fire."

"I was. I admit it now." She went over to Kirby and put her hand on his arm, then fixed him with a pleading gaze. "I don't know how to thank you. You came along just in time to save me. There's no telling what would have happened."

"Janey, Pa told me to look out after you 'n Ma. I'm goin' to ask you, please, don't be doin' nothin' like this again. You could get yourself in some serious trouble. And I don't know if I could even face Pa then."

"I promise I will be much more careful in the future. I've always had it in mind that I could control boys. Now I see that it isn't as easy as I thought."

"You can control boys. But you're of an age now, Janey that"—Kirby took in Janey's body with a wave of his hand—"it ain't boys you have to worry about. It's men. And you can't control men."

"You're right," Janey said contritely.

"Why don't you go on back to the house now?"

"Kirby?"

"What?"

"You won't tell Ma nothin' about this, will you?"

"I ain't goin' to say a word about it," Kirby promised.

The worry left Janey's face, and she kissed her brother on the cheek.

"Thank you, Kirby. Thank you for everything."

CHAPTER 3

Belle Robb was someone that the people of Galena euphemistically referred to as "a painted woman." She advertised her services by the very method that gave her the sobriquet by which she was called. Her red hair came from a bottle, her lips and cheeks from a paint pot. She wore fine, but revealing dresses and traveled around town in an elegant carriage driven by a free black man. She was the wealthiest person—man or woman—in the entire county.

Strange as it might seem, Belle and Lettie had developed a friendship when Belle began paying Lettie a great deal of money for private tutoring. For the last two years, Belle had been coming to the school on Saturday and Sunday afternoons for the lessons.

On this particular Saturday afternoon, Lettie was waiting most anxiously for her.

"Say, that *Pride and Prejudice* is one fine book," Belle said, returning the book to Lettie. "Thank you very much for lending it to me."

"I'm glad you enjoyed it," Lettie said, though her words were without animation.

"Lettie, what is it? What's wrong?"

"Oh, Belle, I'm so frightened. I . . . I have done something awful, and you are the only one I can talk to."

Belle reached out to put her hand on the teacher's shoulder. "Lettie, I know you, and I know that you can't do anything awful. Now, tell me what is bothering you."

"My womanly time . . . is late. I didn't worry too much about it, but . . . now I have missed it a second time. I'm two months behind, and it could only mean one thing."

"You're pregnant," Belle said matter-of-factly.

The way Belle spoke the words gave Lettie a sinking feeling. She had hoped someone like Belle might be able to come up with another reason. To hear her fears confirmed was devastating. "That's what I was afraid of."

"Does the baby's father know about it?"

"No, and I've no intention of telling him, nor anyone else."

"What are you going to do?"

"I . . . I've heard that there are ways of terminating a pregnancy," Lettie said. "I was wondering if you know anything about it. I mean, how would one go about obtaining such a thing?"

Belle shook her head. "I have known girls who did this, and I would advise against it."

"Why?"

"Because two of the girls I knew died undergoing the process. I wouldn't want to see anything like that happen to you."

"If . . . if the father was here, I would go to him and tell him. I'm sure he would marry me. But he isn't here, and I don't know when he will return, or if he ever will return."

"He has gone to war?"

"Yes. If I have the child, and he doesn't come back for a few years, how could I ever convince him that the baby is his?"

"That could be a problem," Belle agreed.

"Oh, Belle, what will I do? What is left for me besides disgrace? I'll no longer be able to hold my head up among people who had once been my friends . . . among people who respected me."

"You can leave," Belle suggested.

"Leave and go where?"

"I have a friend, a gambler, who lives in Denver. I'll write a letter for you to give him. I'll tell him that your husband was killed, and you want to get away from sad memories. He'll do right by you."

"Oh, Belle," Lettie said, her eyes filling with tears. "Thank you. From the bottom of my heart, thank you."

It was only a matter of a few weeks after Emmett and Luke joined the First Missouri State Guard Infantry, a Confederate company, that they were involved in their first battle. Union troops, under command of Brigadier General Nathaniel Lyon's Army of the West, were camped at Springfield. The Confederate troops, under the command of Brigadier General Ben McCulloch, formulated attack plans.

At 5:00 AM on the morning of August 10, the two forces met at Wilson's Creek about twelve miles southwest of the city. Rebel cavalry received the first blow and fell back, away from Bloody Hill. Confederate forces soon rushed up and stabilized their positions, attacking the Union forces. Three times they attacked that day but failed to break through the Union line.

The Union troops received a heavy blow when General Lyon was killed during the battle. Major Samuel D. Sturgis replaced him.

Meanwhile, Confederates routed Colonel Franz Sigel's column south of Skegg's Branch. Following the third Confederate attack, which ended at 11:00 AM, Sturgis ordered a retreat to Springfield. The Confederate victory buoyed Southern sympathizers in Missouri, giving the Confederates control of southwestern Missouri.

It was shortly after that battle that Emmett and Luke were split up. Emmett protested at first, but a colonel pointed something out to him that seemed to make good sense. "Suppose you and your son were in the same company. And suppose that company was engaged by such superior forces that virtually the entire company was killed. Your wife would lose a husband and a son, and your children, still at home, would lose a father and a brother. Wouldn't it be best for you to be separated, to lessen the chances of both of you being killed at the same time?"

Emmett nodded. "I reckon you're right, Colonel."

CHAPTER 4

Spring 1862

Kirby had been plowing for two weeks, averaging an acre and a half per day. By the middle of May he had the ground broken in twenty-one acres, which was just over half of the farm. What he would plant was entirely up to him, and he planned to do twenty acres of corn, ten of wheat, and ten of oats. He had already spoken with Mr. Matthews, who'd agreed to take his crops as soon as he could get them out.

"Truth is, they ought to bring a premium this year," Matthews had said. "What with the war goin' on an' all, there's a demand for the produce, and with so many men bein' off to do the fightin', not as much will be grown as in years past. It'll be a sellers' market, that's for sure."

Kirby had done some figuring and thought the chances were good that he would be able to bring in at least fifteen hundred dollars. He planned to save as much of it as he could to have for his father and brother when they came back home.

If they came back home.

Reports had already been received from a battle that happened in April at a place called Shiloh. Kirby had never heard of Shiloh, and he didn't know if his pa or Luke had fought in that battle or not. If so, he was reasonably sure that they hadn't been killed. The casualties for Stone County, including names from both participating armies, had been posted on the door of the courthouse in Galena. Neither Emmett's nor Luke's name was on the list, but Lee Willoughby's name was.

So far, the family had received only two letters from Emmett. In one of them, he told them that he and Luke had been split up, and he had no idea where Luke was. They hadn't heard from Luke.

Kirby was thinking about this when he got the whiff of an awful smell.

"Hell's bells, Ange!" he swore at the mule. "Ain't you got no better sense than to fart in a man's face? Damn. You are the fartin'ess mule I've ever seen. Why ain't you more like Rhoda? She don't hardly ever fart. I guess she's more of a lady than you are a gentleman." Kirby picked up a clod of dirt and threw it at the offending animal.

He was just reaching the end of a row when he saw Janey approaching. "Whoa," he called.

Janey was carrying a canvas bag.

"Hi, sis. You're bringing water, I hope."

Janey smiled. "No. I brought you something better." She reached into the bag and pulled out a jar of tea. "It's sweetened," she said as she handed it to him.

Kirby had worked up quite a thirst during the plowing and he took the sweetened tea with grateful hands, then took several, deep, Adam's apple bobbing swallows, until more than half of it was gone. Finally, he pulled the jar away, wiped his mouth with the back of his hand, and smiled at Janey. "Damn, that was good. If you weren't my sister, I'd marry you," he teased.

"I told you. I'm never goin' to get married. And I wouldn't marry you, even if you weren't my brother. You're too onery."

Kirby drank the rest of the tea, but saved the last mouthful, and spit it out toward his sister.

"Kirby!" Janey complained to his laughter.

"That's what you get for calling me onery." He handed the empty jar back to her. "What's Ma cookin' for supper?"

"What difference does it make? You'll gobble it down like a hog. You always do."

Ange chose that precise moment to let go another fart.

"Oh, what is that awful smell?" Janey screwed up her face and waved her hand back and forth in front of her nose.

"You ain't plowed behind a team of mules a whole lot, have you?" Kirby asked, laughing again. He slapped the reins against the back of the team. "Gee!" he called, and the team turned to the right.

Janey stood at the edge of the field, watching as Kirby started back across the field. She was thankful to him for keeping secret the incident he had happened upon between her and Merlin Lewis. She also realized that he was faithfully fulfilling his promise to their pa to "be the man of the place." She couldn't help but feel a little guilty as she lay in bed every morning when, while still dark, Kirby would go out to harness Ange and Rhoda, then start a full day of plowing. If he found the work too strenuous, he never complained. If he ever had the urge to leave the farm, he never spoke of it.

Janey wanted nothing more in the world than to leave the farm. She hated farming and everything about it. The only reason she was still there was because she felt a sense of obligation to her mother and to Kirby.

She was sixteen but could easily pass for twenty. If she left home now, that's the age she would assume. She was fully developed by the time she was twelve. Although some of the other girls had envied her, it wasn't necessarily a good thing. She sometimes felt as if she were a full grown woman trapped in a young girl's body. She began to have fewer and fewer friends because the things that most interested them seemed childish to her.

The woman she most admired in town was Belle Robb.

She had never spoken to Belle. She knew that her ma would be mortified if she did. But she had watched the woman riding by in the back of a carriage, glancing neither left nor right, either oblivious of, or unconcerned about, the stares and gossip.

What would it be like to have so much money that she didn't care what others thought? Janey wondered.

She also wondered what it would be like to be with a man . . . not a boy like Merlin Lewis, but a real man.

As Kirby started back toward the house that evening with thoughts of supper on his mind, he was surprised to see three mounted riders out front. The riders were wearing military uniforms . . . and the uniforms were blue.

"What's this about?" He hurried, not bothering to take the team to the barn, but going directly to the house. His ma and sister were standing on the porch, talking to the soldiers.

"Ma, what's going on?" he asked.

"Nothin' you have to be concerned about," Pearl replied. "They've come to try 'n take you into the army."

"Wouldn't you like to serve your country, boy?" asked the soldier who had three stripes on his sleeve.

"His father and his older brother are already serving," Pearl said. "Kirby is only fourteen years old. Is the government drafting fourteen-year-olds now?"

"Beggin' your pardon, ma'am, but he sure don't look like no fourteen-year-old."

"Can you read, Sergeant?" Pearl asked.

"Yes, I can read."

"I got his name wrote in the Bible, along with his sister's and older brother's names. That tells when they was born. If you can read and cipher, you can figure out for yourself how old he is. Do you want to see the Bible?"

"How would I know you didn't just put down when he was born so's to keep him from gettin' took into the army?"

the sergeant asked. "Is that true, boy? Are you only four-teen?"

Kirby looked the soldier in the eye. "You ain't callin' my ma a liar, are you, mister? 'Cause I don't think I'd take too kindly to that."

"Feisty, ain't he?" the sergeant said to the two soldiers with him. They laughed.

"All right, boy. We'll take your ma's word for it. But if this war's still goin' on when you come of age, you need to think about your duty and come join up with us. Come on, men, we're gettin' nothin' done here."

Kirby watched the men ride away.

"You didn't tell 'em Pa and Luke had joined up with the Gray, did you, Ma?"

Pearl shook her head. "I thought it would be best not to. Supper will be ready soon."

"I'll be in soon as I put the mules away."

Supper was pork chops, poke salad, and corn bread. As Janey had predicted, Kirby ate heartily.

The little town of Lamar, Missouri, was sleeping when Angus Shardeen approached it on the July morning. He held his hand up to stop the thirty-six men riding with him.

"What do we hit first, Angus?" Billy Bartell, Angus's second in command, asked.

"Start by burnin' the houses," Shardeen said. "That'll get ever'one drawn out to put out the fires and save the citizens, then we'll be able to ride on into town without much opposition, I'm thinkin'."

Bartell stood in his stirrups, then looked back toward the other riders. "All right men, get them torches lit!" he shouted.

A match was struck to light one torch, then it was used to pass the light on down until twenty torches were aflame.

"Let's go, men! Burn the town!" Shardeen shouted.

The group rode into town at a gallop. As they encountered the first houses, they tossed the torches toward them.

Citizens ran out into the street and were shot down without regard to age or sex. By the time Shardeen's men reached the middle of town, at least eight houses were burning and sixteen men, women, and children had been shot down.

The Jayhawkers stopped in front of the town's only hotel.

"Bartell," Shardeen ordered. "Take five men down to the marshal's office and kill anyone you find there."

"What if somebody's in jail?"

"Kill them, too," Shardeen ordered. "Tompkins, find the newspaper editor and bring him to me."

One hour later, ten women and girls were being held in one of the Lamar Hotel rooms. Shardeen was in the dining room, enjoying the breakfast he had forced the cook to prepare for him. He looked at the emergency broadsheet he had forced the newspaper to print.

PEOPLE OF LAMAR

YOUR TOWN HAS BEEN CAPTURED BY THE SHARDEEN RAIDERS. TEN OF YOUR WOMEN ARE BEING HELD PRISONER. THE TOWN IS BEING CHARGED A RANSOM OF FIVE THOUSAND DOLLARS FOR THEIR RELEASE. IF THE MONEY HAS NOT BEEN COLLECTED BY THREE O'CLOCK THIS AFTERNOON, THE WOMEN WILL BE KILLED.

BY ORDER OF COLONEL ANGUS SHARDEEN,
COMMANDING OFFICER

"Yes," Shardeen said after reading the paper. He smiled and handed it back. "This is exactly what I want. Now, print enough copies so everyone in town will be sure to see it."

"Don't hurt the women, please," the newspaper editor begged.

"If you do your job, and if the town responds, none of the women will be killed."

"Bartell?" Shardeen said after the editor left.

"Yeah?"

"Which one of the women is the best lookin' one?"

"Well, the best lookin' one would be the mayor's daughter. But you almost couldn't call her a woman, seein' as I don't think she's much over fourteen or fifteen."

"Then she's woman enough. I'm goin' upstairs to find me a room. Bring 'er to me."

"All right if I take 'er after you get 'er broke in?"

"Fine with me."

One hour later, Brenda Tadlock, fourteen-year-old daughter of the mayor of Lamar, lay dead in the alley behind the hotel. Bartell never got his chance at her. Brenda had jumped out of the window as soon as Shardeen left her alone in the room.

News of the Shardeen raid on Lamar spread throughout southwest Missouri. Small communities held meetings to discuss the possible organization of a militia to defend themselves should such an attack occur against their town.

"What good would a militia do?" Tom Byrd asked in Galena. "Most of the fightin' age men are already gone. The rest of us is on farms outside of town. Why, by the time you got us mobilized, it would be too late."

"Tom's right," another said.

After an hour of discussion, it was finally decided that raising a city militia would not be possible. The meeting disbanded without any action.

Kirby had come to town, hoping that some sort of militia would be formed, because he was sure that they would take him. He was disappointed with the results of the meeting.

Janey had come with him and, as the meeting was being conducted, had gone to Bloomberg's Mercantile to buy some jars for canning. She was surprised to see Belle Robb there. It was the first time she had ever seen the woman anywhere but riding in her carriage. Looking around to make certain that she wasn't being observed, Janey mustered up the courage to approach the notorious madam. "Hello, Miss Robb."

Belle glanced up, obviously surprised at being addressed by a local citizen. When she saw that it was a young and very beautiful girl who had spoken, and not one of the matriarchs of the town, she smiled. "Hello, dear. Can I help you with something?"

"No, I just wanted to say hello."

"How nice of you."

"Also, I was wondering how . . . I mean, suppose someone wanted to do what you do, how would—" Janey stopped in mid-sentence. "Uh, never mind. I have no right to bother you."

"What is it, exactly, that you think I do, dear?"

"I don't know, exactly, what you do," Janey admitted. "All I know is that you are the most beautiful woman I have ever seen. And you seem to be rich."

Belle laughed. "Oh, believe me, I am rich, Miss . . . what is your name?"

"Janey. Janey . . ." She started to tell her last name but at the last minute thought better of it. "Just Janey."

"Well, 'just Janey,' not everyone can do what I do."

"I suppose not. I'm sure that someone would have to be very beautiful."

"Don't you worry about that. You are certainly beautiful enough. But it takes more than beauty. It takes someone who has the ability to put aside what others may think or say about her. Do you think you could do that?"

"I . . . I don't know. I've never actually thought about it."

"But you are thinking about it now?"

"Maybe."

"Why?"

"The farm," Janey said with a dismissive wave of her

hand. "You don't know what it's like. It's nothing but work and drudgery from dawn to dusk. And the thought of marrying a farmer and living the rest of my life that way is almost more than I can take."

"You're wrong, honey. I know exactly what it's like. I was raised on a farm near New Madrid, Missouri. Not a large plantation with slaves to do our every bidding, mind you, but a small pig farm. I couldn't wait to get out of there."

"Then you *do* understand," Janey said with a broad smile.

"Oh, yes. I understand all right. How old are you, Janey?"

"I'm . . . uh . . . eighteen."

Belle smiled. "How old are you, really?"

"Seventeen," Janey lied.

"I'll tell you what. Wait a year. When you're eighteen, come visit me and we'll have a long talk."

"A talk about what?"

"Why, Janey, we'll talk about anything you want to talk about," Belle said.

"All right, and thanks. I'm sorry I bothered you."

"Oh, honey, you have been nothing but nice to me. How could that possibly be a bother?"

Later, as Janey was loading her purchases into the buckboard, a man approached her. She thought he might be the most handsome man she had ever met. His dark hair was perfectly combed, he had a neatly trimmed moustache, and he was wearing a dark green jacket with mustard-colored pants which were tucked down into highly polished boots. The vest was white, and a pearl pin was stuck in the red ascot at his throat.

"May I be of assistance, Janey?"

"Thank you, I— How do you know my name?"

"I heard you give your name to Belle."

"You . . . were listening to our conversation? Sir, you should have made your presence known."

"I feared that to do so might cause you some embarrassment. Please forgive me if I erred."

"What is your name?"

"Paul Garner at your service." He lifted his finger to his eyebrow.

"Mr. Garner . . ."

"Please, it is Paul."

"Paul, how is it that you aren't away at war?"

Garner laughed. "You do get right to the point, don't you?"

"My pa, my brother, so many of the county men are at war. I was just wondering why you weren't, is all."

"Do you believe in this war, Janey?"

"I've never given any thought to whether I believe in it or not."

"Well, I *don't* believe in it. I don't believe in the concept of holding men and women as slaves. I don't own any myself, nor have I ever, and I won't fight a war so those who do own slaves can keep them.

"On the other hand, I think if some states want to break away and go out on their own, they certainly should have the right to do so. I won't fight for an army that would force a state to belong to a union to which it no longer wishes to belong.

"So, as you see, Janey, I see nothing noble or uplifting about either belligerent party in this war. Were I to go, I would have no idea which side to support. Therefore, I have made the conscious choice to remain neutral."

"I've never heard anyone talk like you do," Janey said.

"You mean in my observation of the futility of the war?"

"No. Yes, but I mean, I've never heard anyone use pretty words the way you do. Not even my teacher talked like that. That is, when I had a teacher. She's gone now. Besides, it's been a long time since I was a schoolgirl. Are you an educated man, Paul?"

"Yes. I attended school at Westminster College in Fulton," Paul said.

"What do you do for a living?"

"I'm a peddler."

"A peddler? You mean like Mr. Gray, who goes about in a wagon selling pots, pans, notions, and the like?"

"Not exactly. I sell money."

"Money? How do you sell money?"

"I deal in investments. People invest in me and I make money for them. When I make money for them, I also make money for myself."

"I've never heard of such a thing."

"It can be quite lucrative," Paul said with a broad smile.

She tried not to smile back. "I must get back home," Janey said.

Again, Paul touched his eyebrow. "It has been a most pleasant few minutes, Janey. I do hope we see each other again."

They did see each other again, several times, at first meeting "by chance" in town, until finally, Garner took the bold step of going to the farm where Janey introduced him to her mother and brother.

"I don't like him," Kirby said after a few visits.

"He seems like a nice enough young man," Pearl said.

"I can't help but feel like he has somethin' up his sleeve. Ma, he has to be twenty-three or -four, or somethin' like that. And Janey's only sixteen. What's he doin' hangin' around her? Don't you think she's too young for him?"

"Kirby, you know that Janey ain't none like you or Luke. Ever since she was a little girl, she's been more like a feral cat than a tame kitten. Your pa and I have worried a lot about that girl, wonderin' what is going to become of her. It could be that this feller, Paul Garner, is just what Janey needs. And I warn't but seventeen when I was married."

"I hope so, Ma. But I don't mind tellin' you, he seems a

bit uppity to me. I'll keep quiet about it, though. Who am I to tell Janey who she should or shouldn't like?"

"I would appreciate you doin' that," Pearl said.

Frequent and nourishing rains throughout the long summer ensured a bumper crop and, as Fred Matthews had suggested, it was a sellers' market when Kirby took his harvest in to peddle. He was paid $2,088, which was the biggest single year, ever, for the little farm.

"What are you plannin' on doin' with that two thousand dollars you made from selling your crops?" Paul Garner asked during one of his frequent visits.

"What makes you think I made two thousand dollars?" Kirby asked, obviously irritated by the question.

"Why, Janey told me."

"She had no business telling you."

"Janey and I have no secrets between us," Garner said.

"Yeah, well this ain't just between you 'n Janey. This is the whole family, and as far as I'm concerned, you got no business knowin' anything about it."

"I can understand your concern, but my interest is more than mere curiosity. The reason I asked, is because if you will trust me, I can double your money for you in no time."

"How?"

"As I explained to your sister, I deal in money. My profession is to invest money in certain mathematical probabilities, doing so in such a way as to maximize the return."

"Sounds to me like you're usin' big words to say that you are a gamblin' man."

Garner laughed out loud. "Yes, in any investment transaction there is a degree of risk, so, I suppose you could call it gambling. But the degree of risk is inversely proportional to the skill with which the transaction is handled."

"Garner, you can use all the big words you want, I'll not be trusting you with money that I broke my back for most a year to earn. Except for what it takes my ma, my sister, 'n me to live on, I'm puttin' the rest of the money away so that when Pa comes back home, we'll have a good stake to start with."

"Have you not read the Bible?" Garner asked. "Are you not aware of the parable of the talents?"

"I don't know what you are talking about."

"In the Book of Matthew, it tells of a wealthy master who left money with three of his servants. Two of his servants invested the money so they could give even more of it to the master when he returned. But the third buried the money he was given, and when the master returned, that servant gave him only what had been left with him. 'You wicked, lazy servant! You should have put my money on deposit with the bankers, so that when I returned I would have received it back with interest.' Is that how you want to face your father when he returns, not with an increase, but only with what he left?"

"That don't apply to me," Kirby said. "Pa didn't leave me any money. He left me only a team of mules and forty acres of rock and dirt. I wasn't given the money I'm holdin' for him. I earned it."

"Yes, and you are to be commended for it," Garner said. "I only wanted to help, is all. Of course, it is your money and you should do with it as you wish."

"You were rude to Paul," Janey said to Kirby later that evening after Garner left.

"I wasn't rude. I was honest with him. He has no business bein' concerned with how much money we have, and you had no business tellin' him."

"Why not?"

"Janey, I'm going to have to agree with your brother on this," Pearl said. "Your pa always said it's best that not ever'one knows our business."

"I'm sorry," Janey said. "I didn't mean nothin' by it. I was just bragging on you, Kirby. I'm real proud of what you have done."

"I'm just askin' you not to share all our business with him. Sometimes it's good to keep secrets."

The expression on Kirby's face reminded Janey that he had kept a secret for her, and she understood exactly what he was saying. "All right, Kirby. I won't say anything else about it. Please don't be mad at me."

Kirby smiled, and kissed his sister on the cheek. "I'm not mad at you, Janey. I just want you to be careful, that's all."

After their initial meeting in Bloomberg's Mercantile, Janey had become more bold, frequently visiting Belle in her place of business. On one of her visits, one of the customers—Belle referred to them as "guests"—mistook Janey for one of the girls who worked there.

"She is not on the line," Belle said. "And I'll expect you to honor the code that we all follow here. Just as the visits of my guests are kept secret, so too shall the presence of my friend be kept secret. If I ever hear anything spoken about her, I will hold you responsible, and the consequences will be grave."

Belle's admonition to her clients had been heeded, and men that Janey recognized—married men and officials of the town—were confident that knowledge of their visits would not go beyond Belle's establishment. Janey was equally confident that her secret was safe, and she and Belle's clients developed a symbiotic relationship.

"It's called a rubber," Belle said, showing it to Janey.

She had asked how it was that the girls who worked for her didn't get pregnant.

"After it is used, it must be washed very thoroughly to

make certain that nothing is left in it. Then it should be lubricated and put back into its box."

"And that will keep me, uh, I mean the girl from getting—?"

Belle looked at Janey knowingly. She nodded. "Yes. It will. I've made every man I've ever been with use it before I will let him lie with me, and I've never gotten pregnant. You are asking about this for yourself, aren't you?"

"Yes," Janey replied rather sheepishly.

"Paul Garner?"

"Yes. I've been lucky so far but every time, I'm frightened as to what would happen if I got pregnant. How would I face my Ma and Pa?"

"It's probably smart of you to have him wear this."

"What will I say to him to make him use it?"

"All you have to do is ask him. He has used it before. Many times, I suspect. I see no reason why he wouldn't use it with you."

"He has?"

Belle put her hand on Janey's shoulder. "Honey, you didn't think you were getting a virgin, did you?"

"No. No, I guess not."

CHAPTER 5

April 1863

The day was unseasonably warm. Kirby was walking behind the plow being pulled by the two mules, Ange and Rhoda, opening the ground to plant this year's corn. He was at the far end of a row when he heard a scream coming from the house. He didn't know if the scream came from his mother or his sister, but it didn't matter. It was a scream of absolute terror. He dropped the reins and started for the house on a dead run.

He heard another scream and saw smoke curling up into the sky. Reaching the fence, he saw at least a dozen men carrying hams and sides of bacon, taken from the smokehouse before it had been set afire.

Jayhawkers!

Janey was on the ground naked. Her clothes had been torn off.

"Spread 'er legs out, boys. I'm goin' to have me a little of this." The raider was a big ugly man with only half of one ear.

"Get away from her!" Pearl attacked the man.

Their leader was standing off to one side, watching it all. He had red hair, a red beard, and a scar that started at the corner of his mouth, then zigzagged like a lightning bolt up the side of his face, ending with a deformed eye. The horse next to him had a dark blue saddle blanket. In a corner was the silver eagle insignia of a colonel outlined in gold.

Kirby knew the man was Angus Shardeen!

"What the hell, Bartell? Can't you handle a young girl and an old woman?" Shardeen asked with a demonic laugh. He raised his gun and shot Kirby's mother in the chest. She flew backward as if being yanked violently by an invisible rope, then fell and was dead before she even hit the ground.

"Ma!" Kirby shouted as he ran toward her fallen form. Before he reached her, Shardeen brought the butt of his gun down on Kirby's head, and he went down as well.

Kirby came to lying on the ground. For a long moment, he tried to understand what he was doing there. He turned his head, saw his mother lying nearby, and knew that she was dead. In that moment, he remembered what happened.

"I see you aren't dead." The words came from his sister, and they were spoken in a flat and totally unemotional tone of voice.

Looking toward her, Kirby saw that she was sitting on the front porch. She was dressed, and there was a bag sitting beside her.

"Janey." He sat up and felt a sharp pain in the back of his head. Reaching up, he felt blood.

"I didn't know if you was dead or alive," Janey said.

"I reckon I'm alive. How are you?"

"What do you mean, how am I? You know how I am. You seen me lyin' on the ground, bein' used by all of them."

Kirby was surprised to see that, rather than crying uncontrollably, she seemed to express only anger. He was oddly proud of her for showing such gumption.

"I'm sorry I didn't get here in time to stop them." Gingerly, Kirby stood up.

"What could you have done? If you woulda got here any earlier, you'd more 'n like be lyin' there dead, like Ma."

Kirby walked slowly to the porch and sat on the step. "Janey, let's don't tell Pa how Ma died. He don't need to know that while he was off fightin' in the war 'n all, that Shardeen's Raiders come here and killed her. Let's tell him that she died peacefully in her sleep. I think he'll take it somewhat easier, that way."

Janey shrugged. "You can tell him anythin' you want. I won't be here."

"What do you mean, you won't be here?"

"Paul's been tryin' to get me to run off with 'im. The only reason I ain't done so before now is because of Ma. But what with she bein' dead 'n all, I don't see nothin' to keep me here any longer."

"You can't go, Janey. You're my sister. With Ma gone, I need to look after you."

"Yeah, and you did such a good job of it, didn't you?" Janey asked sarcastically.

"I—" Kirby hung his head. "I'm sorry. You're right. I didn't do such a good job of it, did I?"

"It wasn't your fault. Like I said, there wasn't nothin' you coulda done, anyhow."

"But what will I tell Pa when he comes back and finds you're gone?"

"Tell him anything. Tell him I ran off with a peddler."

"Will you at least stay here till I get Ma buried?" Kirby asked.

"Where you goin' to bury her?"

"Up on the hill, I reckon," Kirby said, pointing. "She always liked it up there. She'd go up there to watch the sunsets."

"All right. You go dig her grave, and I'll get her changed into her best dress. I wouldn't want to see her buried in that old work dress."

"Thanks."

"Soon as she's buried, I'm leavin'. I'd like you to drive me into town, but if you don't, I'll walk. 'Cause believe me, brother, I am leaving."

It took Kirby the better part of an hour to dig the grave, but he threw himself into the work to keep from being overwhelmed by grief. He tried to hold back the tears that welled up in his eyes. His father would not have cried. Kirby would not, either. Still, he could not get the horrific image out of his mind of his mother being slaughtered. The woman had given him life, had loved him and his brother and sister with all her heart.

Halfway through the digging, Janey came up to stand beside him. She was still in a state of shock, Kirby knew.

"I got her nice dress on her, but I was thinkin' that if we don't have a box to put her in, the dress will get all messed up when you start throwin' the dirt back into the hole."

"I was thinkin' about that as well, and I got it all figured out," Kirby said.

"What are you goin' to do?"

"The trough we put the hay in to feed the mules is big enough for her. I'll put her in that, then I'll find somethin' to close off the top. It won't be nothin' fancy, but it'll make a passable coffin."

Janey nodded. "Yes. Yes, it will. But, once we get Ma in it, how will we get it up here? I think it'll be too heavy, even for the both of us to handle."

"Soon as I get her into it, I'll hook Ange up to it and let him pull her uphill."

"That's a good idea."

Kirby saw tears in Janey's eyes.

Forty-five minutes later, the feeding-trough-cum-coffin, its top closed with a door from the tack room, had been dragged up the hill, lowered in the grave, and covered.

"All right. Let's go," Janey said.

Kirby raised a hand. "Hold on a moment. Don't you think we ought to say a few words?"

"What for? There ain't neither one of us preachers."

"No, but she was our ma. Seems to me, the least we could do is say a few words over her grave."

"You're right. I'm sorry. Go ahead. Say somethin'."

Kirby took off the hat he'd been wearing to protect him from the sun and held it in front of him as he looked down at the grave. "You was a good ma. You done what you could with us, and I appreciate it, an' loved you for it. I know that I didn't tell you that I loved you as much as I should have, but I never was much for speakin' a lot of words. I reckon I just thought that you always knew.

"Listen, Ma. I ain't goin' to tell Pa how it is that you died. I mean, gettin' killed 'n all. I don't figure it's somethin' he needs to know right away. The time's goin' to come when you 'n him will be together again an' I reckon if you want to, you can tell 'im then, how it was that you died."

Kirby quit speaking, and after a moment of silence, he glanced across the grave at Janey. Tears were rolling down her face.

"You goin' to say somethin'?"

Janey nodded. "Ma, I don't know as I'll ever have any children. I know that I don't want to . . . 'cause I could never be as good a ma as you was. I know I was always a big dis-appointment to you, and I reckon that while you'll be lookin' down on me, I'll be even more of a disappointment. But, all I can say about that is that I'm sorry." Janey grew quiet then.

Kirby waited for a moment before he spoke again. "That was real good, Janey. I know Ma heard you."

"Will you take me into town now?"

Kirby nodded. "Yeah, I'll take you to town."

* * *

It was as if Janey had dropped off the face of the earth. Kirby never heard another word from her, and when he checked on Paul Garner, he learned that he was gone, too. He didn't want to ask around town about his sister, figuring it was nobody else's business that he had lost track of her.

With his mother dead and his sister gone, Kirby was all alone. That didn't actually bother him all that much. On the contrary, he learned to appreciate the solitude.

As he was sitting out on the front porch one day, wondering if he should get a dog, he heard the sound of galloping horses. His first thought was to hide, but he decided not to. It was his farm, and he'd be damned if he would be run off his own property.

Twelve mounted men followed a rider carrying a dark blue flag—the Kansas state flag. Kirby had seen it when the Jayhawkers killed his ma. The riders didn't stop, but continued on at a full gallop.

As it turned out, they were being pursued. No more than fifteen minutes later, another group came riding through, carrying a black flag with a blood red cross. Kirby knew they were part of Bloody Bill Anderson's group.

They stopped when they saw Kirby standing on his front porch. Three of the riders rode toward him. One was wearing a hat with a long, sweeping feather, one was in buckskins, and the third was a young rider who couldn't have been more than a year older than Kirby.

"Boy, did you see a bunch of riders comin' this way?" Anderson asked.

"Fifteen, maybe twenty minutes ago. Headin' west, they were," Kirby replied.

"Jayhawkers?"

"That's what I figure."

"Where's your pa?"

"He's away fightin'. Him 'n my brother."

"Which side is he fightin' for?"

"They's fightin' for the Gray. Same as you."

"What about your ma?"

"She was killed by Angus Shardeen."

"You're runnin' this place all by yourself, are you?"

"Yeah."

"That's quite a responsibility for a boy no older 'n you," said the one in buckskins.

Kirby stood tall. "I'm old enough."

Anderson chuckled. "He's got you there, Gleason."

"I reckon he does, seein' as he's doin' it. Tell me, boy, is it all right if we water our horses here?"

"Sure. Go right ahead."

Anderson and Gleason went back to water their horses, but the young man who had ridden up with them hung back. He spoke for the first time. "What's your name?"

"Jensen. Kirby Jensen."

"You got a gun, Jensen?"

"I got a shotgun."

"That ain't good enough. You need a gun you can tote." The young man had two pistols, one in a holster, and a second stuck down in his belt. He pulled the gun from his belt, and tossed it down to Kirby. Then, reaching into his pocket, he grabbed an extra cylinder and tossed it down to him, as well.

"The gun and the cylinder are already loaded. When it comes time for you to have more ammunition, it takes a .36 caliber. You think you can remember that?"

Kirby held out the pistol to examine it. The initials *JJ* were carved into the handle.

"I reckon I can remember that. You're givin' me this pistol, are you?"

"I am."

"These initials, *JJ*. What do they stand for?"

"They stand for my name. Jesse James."

"Dingus, get on back over here 'n get your horse watered. We ain't goin' to spend the night here," another man called, only slightly older than Jesse.

"Dingus?" Kirby asked.

"That's my brother, Frank. He took to callin' me that when we was kids, and it sort of stuck."

With a nod of his head, Jesse James rode over to the nearby stream to water his horse.

Kirby watched them ride off. He looked at the pistol for a moment longer, then he aimed it at a nearby tree and pulled the trigger. The pistol boomed, he felt the recoil, and he saw a chip of bark fly away. He had hit his target.

When Janey left Missouri with Paul Garner, she thought she knew him. She found out quickly that she knew virtually nothing about him. The investments and the financial risks he spoke of were nothing but wagers. Paul Garner was a gambler . . . a card shark.

"This"—he smiled a huge smile, holding up the two thousand dollars Janey had given him to invest—"is going to make us very rich."

"Not just us," Janey replied. "As soon as we can, I want to replace that money. Kirby doesn't know I took it. He doesn't even know that I knew where he had hidden it."

She'd also expected Garner to marry her, but it hadn't happened.

"You'll be a lot more valuable to me if we aren't married," Garner had said.

"What does that mean?"

"Well, just think about it, Janey. If you are my wife, nobody is going to want to flirt with you. But if you aren't married, why every drover, driver, clerk, and soldier will think you are fair game, and they'll all believe they have a chance to crawl into bed with you. And that's going to make us a lot of money."

"Paul! Are you telling me that you want me to be a prostitute for you?"

"No, you don't understand. You won't have to lie with any man. In fact, I don't want you to." Garner had reached out to put his fingers on her cheek. "You're my woman, and

I don't want to share you with anyone else. I just want you to make the others *think* you are available."

Garner gave her lessons on how to act as a distraction. She would wait for his signal and then, at an opportune time, approach a table, making certain that the player Garner had picked out would be paying more attention to her than to the game at hand.

The dresses she wore were cut so low that they left little to the imagination and though she had made friends with some of the bar girls, she wasn't one of them. At first, the other girls were a little resentful, but when they learned that she wasn't in competition with them in any way, they actually welcomed her presence. Having one more, very seductively dressed girl in the saloon increased the business traffic for all of them. They also learned that she had her own reason for being there, dressed as she was.

Neither Janey nor the others knew that Garner wasn't using her just to prevent a man from playing his best game. He was using her as a diversion in order to allow him to cheat his mark. The best plans often went awry, however. Despite Janey's most seductive attire and actions, the two thousand dollar poke they had was steadily diminishing.

"I thought you said you could double the money!" Janey had cried, concerned at how fast the money was dwindling. "We've got less than a thousand dollars left! I have to get this money back. Don't you understand? I stole it from my own father and brothers!"

Garner had been unconcerned. "Relax. In any game of chance, you are going to have your ups and downs. The secret to success is not to panic. We'll recover this sooner than you think. Then we can go on to make some real money."

At the moment, Janey was sitting at a table in the back of the Red Bull Saloon, playing a game of solitaire.

A bar girl named Callie approached the table. "Janey, would you be a dear and take this beer to that man sitting by the piano? He just ordered it, but I have to go upstairs for a while."

"Sure, I'll take it to him," Janey replied. Folding up the deck of cards she took the beer to the man Callie had pointed out.

"I was hoping you'd stop by to see me sometime," the man said. "You aren't like the other girls. You don't seem to get around to all the men."

"I don't work here," Janey replied. "I just come here as a customer, the same as you."

"Really? Well that's—"

"You cheatin' son of a—" someone shouted, followed by the sound of a gunshot.

Janey looked toward the table where Garner was playing cards and saw him sitting in his chair with a pained expression on his face. His hands were clasped across his chest and blood was spilling through his fingers.

"Paul!" she shouted, rushing across the room to him.

"Where were you?" Garner asked accusingly. "I gave you the sign and you weren't there. Now I've been—"

He was unable to finish his sentence.

Kirby bought several boxes of .36 caliber cartridges. He didn't have a holster, so he carried the pistol Jesse James had given him stuck into his waistband. With no holster, he wasn't able to practice drawing, but he was able to practice shooting. He quickly became exceptionally adept in the use of a pistol.

He had always been good with a rifle and a shotgun, and had proven that skill as a hunter almost from the time he was five. However, he had no basis of comparison as far as shooting a pistol was concerned. He knew only that he was consistently hitting anything he shot at.

Not long after an afternoon of target practice, he heard the approach of a group of riders, and quickly climbed up into the loft of the barn. He would stay out of sight, but if he was discovered and their intention was hostile, he was determined to shoot as many as he could before they got him.

When he saw that they were carrying a Confederate flag, he called out to them, then climbed down.

"Where is everyone else?" the leader of the group asked.

"There ain't nobody else."

"You're here all alone?"

"My ma was killed by Jayhawkers, my sister run away to I don't know where, and my pa and brother are off fighting in the war."

"For which side?"

Kirby pointed to the flag. "That's the flag they're fightin' for."

The leader nodded. "If your ma was killed by Jayhawkers, that's who I would expect them to be fighting for. The name is Asa Briggs."

Kirby nodded. "I've heard of you, Mr. Briggs, and I thought this might be you."

"I see you've got a pistol. What were you planning on doing with it?"

"If you had been Jayhawkers, I figured to shoot as many as I could before you got me."

Briggs chuckled. "Did you now? Can you shoot?"

"Yes sir."

"How well can you shoot?"

Kirby shrugged. "I don't know. Pretty good, I reckon."

"You want to show me?"

"All right."

Kirby picked up a pecan and handed it to him.

"That's a pretty small target. You sure you don't want to pick something a little larger?"

"No, this is big enough. Put it on that fence post over there."

"Boy, that's got to be more 'n a hundred feet," Briggs said. "You sure you don't want it a little closer?"

"No, put it there."

The other riders realized what was going on, and all conversation and watering stopped as they turned to watch the shooting demonstration.

"I got a dollar says he misses," someone said.

When nobody took the bet, Briggs spoke up. "I'll take the bet." He put the pecan on the post Kirby had pointed out to him.

Kirby raised the pistol to eye level, aimed, and pulled the trigger. Pieces of the pecan flew off the post.

The riders gasped and shouted in disbelief.

"Damn," Briggs said, a wide smile spreading across his face. "Damn! Who taught you to shoot? I ain't never seen nothin' like that."

"I just sort of taught myself," Kirby said, pleased by the accolades.

"Tell me, boy. Do you want to stay here and break dirt, and maybe get burned out again? Or would you like to go after Shardeen and take a little revenge?"

"I can't leave my mules."

"All right."

"But I'm pretty sure Mr. Byrd will look after them for me."

"Then grab your mules, and let's go."

Paul Garner had been caught cheating, so every cent he had on him—five hundred and seventeen dollars—was divided evenly among all the men who had been playing with him at the time he was killed. That represented the rest of the money Janey had brought to their partnership, which meant she was left virtually penniless . . . except for Garner's pearl stick pin and gold money clip, which she took.

She was forced to leave Ft. Worth but had money enough to go only as far as Dallas.

She tried for a little while to earn an honest living, working in a boardinghouse, but the treatment was brutal, and the pay was barely enough to keep body and soul together. Then one day she saw a woman driving a surrey. The woman was attractive, well dressed, and heavily made up. She didn't recognize the woman, but she did recognize the woman's profession.

"They call her Chicago Sue," explained one of the other women who worked at the boardinghouse. "They say she's a"—in her early fifties, the speaker was clearly embarrassed by the subject of the conversation, and she lowered her voice before completing her sentence—"an immoral woman. But I think she is somebody that immoral girls work for. She's very brazen, the way she promenades around town in her fancy dresses and her surrey. None of the other girls do that."

"Where does she live? Do you know?"

"Somewhere on Griffin Street, I think. They call it the Palace Princess Emporium, and it's the biggest and gaudiest house on the block."

That evening, just before dark, Janey put on one of the dresses she had worn when she was a *distraction* for Garner, and went to the Palace Princess Emporium. She knocked on the door.

Chicago Sue answered it. "Who are you?"

"I'm someone who is going to make you a lot of money," Janey said.

Chicago Sue looked at her and chuckled. "Honey, you just might at that. Come on in."

Janey followed Chicago Sue into her house, through an attractive foyer with a Turkish carpet, and into a drawing room. The walls were covered with a deep crimson wallpaper and the furniture was painted white with a rich gilding of gold that complemented the damask-patterned blue area rugs. The divan and the chairs were shades of greens and blues.

The women sat across from each other and Chicago Sue asked, "Now, dear, where have you worked before?"

Janey started to say that she had worked for Belle Robb but decided against it. She wouldn't be able to answer any questions if Chicago Sue started asking questions about the business. Taking a deep breath, Janey said, "I've never worked anywhere before. At least, not in a place like this."

Chicago Sue frowned. "Oh? And when you say, a place like this, what do you mean?"

"A place this elegant."

The frown left Chicago Sue's face, replaced by a smile. "How sweet of you. Yes, it is elegant, isn't it?"

"Very elegant."

"Have you ever worked as a paid woman before?"

"No."

"Then what brings you to me? It isn't as if you have the usual hard-time story. Not dressed as you are."

"I had a friend who was in the business. I spent some time with her."

"But you didn't go on the line for her? Why not? You obviously have nothing against the concept, or you wouldn't be here."

"I-I guess I just wasn't ready yet."

"But you are now?"

"Yes."

"Please tell me that you aren't a virgin."

"I'm not a virgin."

"Thank God we can get that out of the way then. What is your name?"

"My name is Janey Jensen."

Chicago Sue shook her head. "No, it isn't."

"Of course it is. I know my own name."

"You know it, and now I know it. But I'd strongly advise against using your real name in a business like this. No one does." She smiled. "You don't really think my name is Chicago Sue, do you? It isn't Sue, and hell, I've never even been to Chicago."

Janey laughed. "I didn't think that was your real name."

"Do you want to choose your own name? Or shall I give you a name to use?"

"You give me a name."

"All right." Chicago Sue crossed one arm across her chest and lifted the other to grasp her chin as she studied Janey. "Yes," she finally said. "Yes, it will be perfect for you."

"What will be perfect?"

"Your new name. I've always liked the name Lil. Your new name will be Lil." She shook her head slightly. "No, not just Lil. It will be Fancy Lil."

"Fancy Lil." Janey smiled broadly. "I like it."

"Have you eaten anything?" Chicago Sue asked.

"I had lunch," Janie said.

"Not dinner?"

"No."

"I haven't eaten, either. Come with me. Mrs. Peabody has probably already gone to bed but I'm sure I can rustle us up something."

"Thank you."

"Do you take coffee or tea?"

"Coffee normally, but it seems a little late for that."

Chicago Sue chuckled. "Oh, honey, if you plan to work here, your days and nights will be backward. My girls are just getting started. And a good strong cup of coffee will keep you going."

"All right, coffee then," Janey said.

"Where did you come from?" Sue asked as they walked to the kitchen.

"Fort Worth."

"Nobody comes from Fort Worth. You were somewhere else first. Where is that?"

"Missouri," Janey said without being more specific.

"Something brought you to me, didn't it? I mean, I don't think you grew up thinking that one day you might want to be a soiled dove."

"Soiled dove?"

"It's a rather genteel way we have of referring to ourselves. Other words are so harsh."

"No, I can't say as I grew up wanting to be a soiled dove."

"I wouldn't think so. Are you running from the law or a man?"

"I would say it is more of a situation that I'm running from."

"Are you with child?"

"No."

"That's good. In our business, babies can really complicate things." Chicago Sue took down two cups, then picked up the coffeepot.

"Do you take cream or sugar?"

"I drink it black."

"Smart move," Chicago Sue said as she poured the coffee.

CHAPTER 6

One thing about being with Briggs raiders was that Kirby didn't have to spend all his time with them. The Ghost Riders would take part in an operation or two, then they would disband and he would actually go back home for weeks at a time.

According to Briggs, doing it that way made it less likely that the Yankees would be able to catch up with them.

Late spring, 1864

Kirby returned to Galena, his first time in town in over a month. As he always did when returning home, he checked at the post office, not really expecting to get any mail. To his surprise, he *did* get a letter, but it wasn't from his father, and it was addressed to Mrs. Pearl Jensen. Kirby opened the letter before he even left the post office.

Dear Mrs. Jensen.

It is with much regret that I tell you that your son, Luke Jensen, was killed in battle on Wilderness Creek in Northern Virginia. We didn't find the body, but be-

lieve that the Yankees found him on the battlefield and buried him.

> *Sincerely,*
> *Colonel Edward Willis*
> *12th Georgia, Commanding*

Kirby folded the letter up and put it in his pocket, wondering if his pa knew about it. Perhaps not, since the last word he had received from his pa said that he and Luke had been separated.

Back outside, Kirby climbed onto Ange's back. When he was riding with Briggs, he was mounted on a horse, but the horse didn't belong to him.

Briggs had offered to give him one of the Yankee horses, but pointed out that it might be dangerous. "If the Yankee soldiers come through and find you mounted on one of their horses, they'll hang you for being a bushwhacker. If not for that, for horse stealing. On the other hand, if they see you ridin' a mule, they won't give you a second thought."

Briggs had been right. More than once Kirby had encountered Yankee soldiers, but to the soldiers, he was nothing more than a farm boy, riding a mule.

Two events occurred in Missouri that had some bearing on the fate of the war within the state. The first was on October 26 when Yankees located Bloody Bill Anderson just outside Glasgow. Though greatly outnumbered, Anderson and his men charged the Union forces, killing five or six of them before encountering heavy fire. Only Anderson and Elmer Gleason continued the attack, Gleason riding side by side with his leader. The others retreated.

Anderson was hit by a bullet behind his ear and killed instantly. Gleason immediately turned and joined the others in retreat. Four other guerrillas were also killed in the attack, but the rest of the men were able to escape.

The second significant event occurred when General Sterling Price was defeated by General James Blunt's Union cavalry in the battle of Newtonia. Price and his entire corps withdrew, effectively ending any real Confederate presence in Missouri. No longer were any regular Confederate troops in Missouri, but sporadic guerrilla operations continued.

Archie Clement led what had been Bloody Bill's guerrillas for a little while after Anderson's death, but the group splintered by mid-November, and most of the men joined Quantrill, though many, realizing that the war was lost, gave up the battle.

Elmer Gleason was the only man of Anderson's original group to join Asa Briggs. Shortly after he joined Briggs' group, he recognized Kirby by the gun he was carrying. "You're the boy Jesse give one of his guns to, ain't you? It was right after your ma was killed, as I recall."

"I'm the one," Kirby said. "I remember you. You're the one who wondered if I was old enough to run the farm."

"You've got a good memory." Gleason was at least fifteen years older, but he and Kirby became very good friends.

Briggs continued to operate as he always had, uniting his group for a particular undertaking, then having them break up and return to their homes. That ruse worked so well that the participation of most members was unknown, even to their nearest neighbors. From time to time, the men would encounter each other in town or on the road but would make no show of recognition.

The Union Army had no idea who was and who wasn't a member of the group, giving credence to the sobriquet "Ghost Riders."

* * *

Kirby's biggest disappointment during his time with Briggs was that they had not encountered Angus Shardeen. They came close once, arriving at a farm just in time to save a farmer and his wife.

Shardeen had been through an hour earlier, robbing the smoke house of the cured hams and bacon. In a macabre joke, he had tied a noose around the woman's neck and thrown the rope over a beam protruding from the hayloft of the barn. He placed her on her husband's shoulders so that she would live only as long as he could stand there supporting her.

The farmer was at the point of exhaustion when the Ghost Riders arrived.

"Kirby! Get up there and cut her down!" Asa Briggs ordered, and Kirby stood on his saddle and pulled himself up into the hayloft. He cut the rope just as her husband collapsed.

They stayed with the couple until both had recovered from the ordeal, spending the night in the barn.

"I'm going to kill him," Kirby told Elmer.

"Yeah, we would all like to get our hands on him before this war ends."

"No, not *like* to kill him. I am *going* to kill him," Kirby said. "I'm going to hunt him down, no matter where he is and no matter how long it takes. I don't care whether the war is still going or whether the war has ended. I am going to dedicate myself to finding him. And when I find him, I'm going to kill him."

January 1865

Briggs' Ghost Riders who had not taken part in the battle for Newtonia found themselves in position to, in Briggs' words, "hit the Yankees a lick." They were going to rob the payroll being transported to the Baxter Springs post.

"The best way to hurt 'em is to take their money," Briggs said. "And that's just what we're agoin' to do."

To that end, the Ghost Riders were waiting in a cornfield alongside the Columbus Road in Cherokee County. It was very cold.

Kirby shivered in the early morning chill.

"Damn. Why couldn't we wait and do this in the summer time?" Elmer Gleason complained.

"I don't know," Kirby said. "Do you think it might be because the payroll is comin' today and not this summer?"

"There you go, gettin' all practical on me," Elmer teased.

"Asa! The coach is acomin'!" one of the others called.

"All right. Get ready."

Kirby crept up to the edge of the cornfield, then lay down where he would have a good view of the road. He could hear the rumble and squeak of the approaching coach, as well as the drum of hoofbeats, not only from the team, but also from the eight men who were riding as escort.

Briggs pulled his pistol. "I'm goin' to shoot one of the coach horses. After that, all hell's goin' to break loose, so get ready."

The coach and outriders were close enough that Kirby could hear the driver's whistles and shouts to the team. He didn't like the idea of shooting an innocent horse but knew that in order for the plan to succeed, it would have to be done.

Briggs fired, and the first, off-side horse stumbled and went down, bringing the coach to an immediate halt.

Within the opening seconds, at least four of the Union soldiers were down. Others tried to return fire, but were unable to find a target. They simply fired wildly into the cornfield.

"Let's get outta here!" one of the soldiers shouted, and the others fled at a gallop.

The Ghost Riders cheered, then ran out onto the road and yelled after the retreating soldiers with cat calls and jeers.

The coach driver had been unarmed and had not taken part in the brief battle. He was still sitting on the high seat with his hands in the air.

"Throw down that strong box," Briggs called.

"What for?" the driver replied. "There ain't nothin' in it."

"What do you mean, there ain't nothin' in it? You went to pick up the payroll, didn't you?"

"Yeah, that's what we went to do all right. But the money wasn't there."

"I don't believe you," Briggs said.

"I'll throw down the strong box 'n let you see for yourself."

"All right. Do it."

The driver reached down between his legs.

Briggs pointed his gun and called out, "No, hold it. Climb down here. I'll get the strong box myself."

Nodding, and obviously frightened, the driver climbed down from the high seat.

Briggs climbed up, retrieved the strong box, then tossed it down onto the road. "Open it up."

"Kirby, you're the best shot among us," Elmer said. "Think you can shoot the lock off?"

Kirby nodded, pulled his pistol, and fired. The bullet cut the hasp.

Elmer opened the lid and looked inside. "It's empty."

"I'll be damned." Briggs jumped down from the coach and ordered, "Cut the team loose and let the horses go."

The driver, who still had his hands raised, protested. "No need for that. All I need to do is cut the dead horse free, then I can go on."

"You can go on, but it's goin' to be afoot," Briggs said. "Now, cut the team loose, unless you want to see 'em burn to death when I set fire to the coach."

"No, I wouldn't want to see no more of the horses killed." The driver set about the task Briggs had set for him.

Half an hour later, with the driver and horses gone, the dozen Ghost Riders stood near the burning coach, enjoying the heat it was putting out.

"Boys," Briggs said. "I reckon this war is all but over. I

aim to give it up. You're all free to go wherever you want." He pointed to the coach. "I had planned for this to be the last operation anyway, but I hoped we'd have some Yankee money to divide before we broke up. I'm sorry it didn't work out."

"Hell, Asa, you don't mind if some of us go ahead 'n try 'n get some of that Yankee money, do you?" Elmer asked.

"I don't mind at all, but you're on your own. I'm out of it."

"What are you going to do?" Kirby asked.

"I'm goin' to Texas," Briggs said. "You want to come along?"

"Now, why would he want to do that when he can come with me 'n get some of that Yankee money?" Elmer asked.

Kirby shook his head. "I appreciate the invite from both of you and would be honored to join either one of you, but I reckon my pa will be coming back sometime soon now. I wouldn't want him to come home 'n find nobody waitin' there for him."

"How do you know your pa is still alive?" Elmer asked.

"Truth is, Elmer, I don't know. But if he is, I aim to be there waitin' for him. Most especially since there ain't goin' to be no one else waitin' there for 'im."

Elmer nodded. "I can see that." He stuck his hand out. "Don't know as we'll ever run acrossed each other again, but don't let nobody never call you boy no more. You're a man, Kirby, and you done proved it more 'n once."

Returning to the farm, the first thing Kirby did was dig up the lidded Mason jar he had buried near the corner of the outhouse. It contained the two thousand dollars he'd received from the crops that first year. If his pa came back, he would give him the money. If he didn't come back, Kirby would have that money to start out on his own.

The stench around the outhouse was pretty intense, but it was for precisely that reason he had chosen to bury the money there. He figured nobody would think someone would choose such a place to bury money, and it was unlikely anyone would make any exploratory digs there.

It took only a few minutes to get to the jar, and with a smile, he reached down to retrieve it. The smile faded when he saw that the money was gone, replaced by a note.

Kirby,
   I took the money to invest with Paul Garner. I figure half of it is mine anyway, and I'll pay you back your half, with interest.

Janey

"Janey! You sorry-assed hellcat!" Kirby shouted at the top of his voice. He threw the jar against the side of the outhouse and watched it shatter.

By June, six months after Kirby made his last ride with the Ghost Riders, the war had been over and done for better than two months. If his father was coming home, he should be along any time.

Kirby had made the conscious decision not to tell his father about his own experiences during the war. His father had been with the regular army. Kirby wasn't sure how he would take to the idea of his son having been a Bushwhacker. He remembered his father's reaction when Luke had said he wanted to join up with George Clark, who was what his pa had said he was—a murderer and an outlaw. Briggs was an irregular, but he had not killed any innocents, nor burned any private homes or farms. Nevertheless, Kirby decided he would keep his participation in such activity to himself.

The very way Briggs had operated during the war, allowing the men to spend a lot of time at home, would help keep his secret. Tom Byrd knew of Kirby's frequent absences because he kept the mules while Kirby was gone. Kirby had told him that he was earning money by delivering messages and, as far as he knew, Byrd still believed that.

Kirby wondered what his pa would say when he learned his daughter had run off? He wondered, also, if he knew his oldest boy was dead?

Kirby was entertaining all these thoughts as he was busy plowing. Because of his guerrilla activity, he had not put in any crops in the previous two years. He didn't think he needed to; after all, there was no need for him to support anyone but himself. And he'd taken comfort from knowing that he had two thousand dollars set aside for when his pa returned.

Or at least, he thought he did.

As he thought about finding the money gone with only Janey's note in the bottle, he got angry again. Like his mother had said, Janey always was a little wild, but he never would have thought she was a thief. What bothered him more than the thought of her taking the money was her giving it to Paul Garner. It would have been bad enough had she kept it for herself. At least she was family. But to have given it to Paul Garner? That was almost more than Kirby could take.

He would like to run into Garner again, some day. Not as much as he wanted to run into Angus Shardeen, but he would like to encounter him some day, whether Janey was still with him or not.

"Where the hell are you now, Janey?" Kirby asked aloud. "Are you still with that sorry buzzard?"

The plow hit a rock and jolted Kirby out of his musing and back to his surroundings, popping his teeth together and wrenching his arms. "Damn, Ange. Didn't you see that rock?"

Kirby unhooked the plow, running the lines through the eyes of the single tree, and left the plow sitting in the middle of the field. He was late getting the crops in, but no later than anyone else in the hollows and valleys of that part of Missouri. The rains had come and stayed, making fieldwork impossible. But he wanted to get something up before his pa returned. He didn't want his pa to think that he was a wastrel.

Folding and shortening the traces, Kirby jumped onto Ange's back and kicked the mule into movement. He plodded down the turn row on the east side of the field when dust from the road caught his eye. It was one rider, pulling up to the house leading a saddled but riderless horse, a bay.

Wondering who it might be, Kirby touched the smooth butt of the Navy .36, which he now wore in a holster. As Ange plodded closer to the house, Kirby smiled when he made out the figure in the front yard.

It was his pa.

Kirby slid off the mule and walked over to his father.

"Boy," Emmett Jensen said, looking at his son, "I swear you've grown two feet."

"You've been gone for four years, Pa. Someone my age grows a lot in four years." Kirby wanted to throw his arms around his pa, but didn't. His pa didn't hold with a lot of touching between men. He stuck out his hand and Emmett shook it.

"Strong, too," Emmett commented.

"Thank you. Plowin' will do that for you."

"I expect it will. Crops is late, Kirby."

"Yes, sir. Rains come and stayed."

"I wasn't faulting you, boy." Emmett let his eyes sweep the land. He coughed, a dry hacking. "I seen a cross on the hill overlooking the creek. Would that be your ma?"

"Yes, sir."

"When did she pass?"

"Spring, three years ago," Kirby said, remembering Shardeen's raid and thinking with a twinge of regret that all the time he had been with Briggs, they had never encountered Shardeen.

"She go hard?"

She was shot down in front of her kids. Was that hard enough? He wanted to share that with his father, and maybe he would someday. There was no need to burden him with that now.

"No, sir, it wasn't hard at all. She went in her sleep. I found her the next morning when I took her coffee and grits."

"Good coffee is scarce. What did you do with the coffee?"

"I drank it," Kirby replied.

"Right nice service?"

She's buried in a feeding trough, covered by a door. Only ones here were Janey and me, and I had to talk Janey into staying until I said a few words. Kirby did not vocalize his thoughts. "Real good service. Folks come from all over to see her off."

Emmett cleared his throat and coughed. "Well, I think I'll go up to the hill and sit with your ma for a while. You put up the horses and rub them down. We'll talk over supper. I assume we got somethin' to eat in the house, don't we?"

"We got some greens. I shot 'n cleaned a squirrel no more 'n a couple hours ago. Was plannin' on fryin' it up. I'll make us some cornbread."

"Sounds good to me." Emmett's eyes flicked over the Navy .36 Colt his son was wearing in a holster. If the sight surprised him, he said nothing about it.

"Pa?"

The father looked at his son.

"I'm glad you're back."

What his pa did then couldn't have astonished Kirby any more than if he had suddenly started dancing. Stepping forward, Emmett put his arms around his son and held him. "I'm glad to be back."

Emmett turned and walked up the hill as Kirby tended to the horses.

* * *

The cross had been handmade, probably by Kirby, Emmett decided. If so, he had done a good job. The particulars were put on the cross with white paint, the words neatly printed.

PEARL VIRGINIA JENSEN
Wife of Emmett Jensen
Oct 13, 1824–April 23, 1862

Emmett wondered why Kirby hadn't mentioned that she was also a mother, but perhaps he felt he wouldn't have room to get it all onto the cross.

He took off his hat and stared down at the grave. Except for the cross, nothing indicated that anyone was buried there. The earth in front of the cross looked no different from the rest of the hill.

"Pearl, I wish I could've been here for you. I don't think this country has ever done anything more foolish than the killin' spree we just come through. I was a part of it when I shoulda been here.

"I don't reckon I need to tell you Luke got hisself killed in this war. An' the reason I don't reckon I need to tell you is, because more 'n likely, you 'n him is together right now." Despite the solemnity of the moment, Emmett smiled. "I hope the first thing you done for 'im when you seen 'im was make him some cornbread so's he could crumble it up in his milk. Lord knows, that boy did like his cornbread 'n milk.

"About Kirby 'n Janey. I didn't do right by them, neither, leavin' 'em here to look after themselves." Emmett looked around the farm. "But truth to tell, I ain't seen hide nor hair of Janey yet. Could be she's fixin' supper, but seein' as how Kirby said he would do it, I think it's more 'n likely that she's gone.

"And speakin' of bein' gone, I ain't told the boy yet, but I plan for me 'n him to get on out of here. Too many memories here. Even the good ones is painful, what with you gone 'n all. It troubles me some to be goin' off 'n leavin' you, but I know that you ain't really here now. You're up in heaven, an' the day'll come when I'll join you. So, I reckon this is the last time I'll be visitin' you like this. I need to get on in with the boy now. We've got some palaverin' to do." Emmett put his hat back on, turned, and walked down the hill.

Over greens, fried squirrel, and corn bread, the father and son ate and talked through the years that they had lost and gained. A few moments of uncomfortable silence came between them occasionally as they adjusted to the time and place, and the fact that their positions had changed.

No change had occurred in the actual relationship; they were still father and son. But Emmett had left a boy; he came home to a man.

"We done our best," Emmett said. "Can't nobody say we didn't. And there ain't nobody got nothin' to be ashamed of."

Kirby hadn't asked him anything about the war, not knowing if he should. He didn't know if his pa wanted to talk about it. But when his pa started talking, Kirby just listened.

"I thought it wrong for the Yankees to burn folks' homes like they done. But it was war, and terrible things happen in war. I didn't know there was that many Yankees in the whole world." Emmett began coughing, a deep, racking cough. It lasted for several seconds before he continued.

"Sometimes when they would come at us, why, we would mow them down like takin' a sickle to wheat. But the Blue bellies just kept on acomin'. You got to give 'em credit for courage. They saw their friends goin' down all around 'em, but they kept on acomin'. Shoot one and five more would take his place."

Emmett was quiet for a moment, and Kirby thought he was finished, but his pa continued. "They weren't near 'bout the riflemen we was, nor the riders neither, but they whupped us fair and square and now it's time to put all that behind us and get on with livin'.'"

"Yes, sir. That's what I was thinkin'."

Emmett sopped a piece of cornbread through the juice of his greens, and chewed for a time before he spoke again. "You know your brother Luke is dead, don't you?"

"Yes, sir. I didn't know if you knew it or not. I got a letter from a fella named Colonel Willis. He said Luke was killed last year in a place called The Wilderness. Fighting with Lee, wasn't he?"

Emmett nodded, but he was quiet for a moment.

Luke had always been Pa's favorite, or so Kirby had felt.

"We wasn't together, you know. I think I sent your ma a letter tellin' her that we wasn't together no more."

"Yes, sir."

"About the letters." Emmett coughed again. "I know I didn't send many, but it was hard tryin' to find some way to get the mail to go out. How was we to send 'em? The Yankees wouldn't allow any mail to pass through their lines, and they made a point of interrupting our mail as much as they could. I didn't much cotton to the idea of some Yankee reading one of my letters, so I didn't hardly write none at all.

"But, as for Luke gettin' killed, I prob'ly don't know much more 'n you do. From time to time, messengers would get through between our armies. From what I heard, he was tryin' to get back to The Wilderness. Leastwise, that's what I was told."

"Yes, sir."

"I don't see no sign of your sister Janey, and you ain't brought up her name. What are you holdin' back, Kirby?"

It was the moment Kirby had been dreading.

"She's run off, ain't she?"

"She run off with some fella, Pa. Right after Ma died."

"What kind of feller was he?"

"He was a gambler, I'd say."

"Smooth talker, I'd wager."

"Yes, sir."

"What did his hands look like?"

"Soft."

"You're right. More 'n likely was a gambler. You say this was after your ma died?"

"Yes sir."

"Prob'ly just as good. If she had run off before your ma died, it woulda more 'n likely help kill her." Emmett said it flatly, shaking his head, then rose from the table.

"I've ridden a far piece these last few weeks 'cause I wanted to get home. I was hopin' I would be comin' home to Pearl, but what is past is past 'n there's no point in chewin' on it. Now I'm home, and I'm tired. Reckon you are too, son. We'll get some sleep, then we'll have us a talk in the morning. I got a plan." He covered his mouth and coughed.

Breakfast was meager the next morning—grits and coffee that was mostly chicory, along with a piece of leftover cornbread. Kirby knew that his pa was working up to say something, and he was anxious to hear what it was, but he waited.

Finally, washing down the last piece of bread with the last swallow of coffee, Emmett began to speak. "I spent some time talkin' to your ma last night, 'n I'm goin' to tell you what I told her. I don't think it's good to stay here, boy. Too many memories and the land's got too many rocks to farm. You got 'ny money left from four years of farmin' since I been gone? I figure crops prob'ly brought in a fair price, bein' as so many farmers was off fightin' in the war."

Kirby wanted to tell his pa about the two thousand dollars he had been saving, the money that Janey took, but he held his tongue about that. "I . . . uh, ain't got no money at all."

"Ah, don't fret over it. Farmin' is a hard way to make a livin', and truth to tell, I'm proud of you just for supportin' yourself while I was gone.

"We'll sell the mules and milk cows and buy a couple o' good pack horses. The mules is getting too old for where we're goin'. Problem is, they may be too old to even sell. If we can't sell 'em, I'd hate to have to put 'em down."

"We ain't goin' to put Ange and Rhoda down, Pa," Kirby said resolutely. "If that's what it takes for us to go, you just go on without me an' I'll stay here with the mules."

Kirby's response irritated Emmett, but only for a moment, then inexplicably, he smiled. "You got grit, boy. You ain't just growed in body. All right. We'll find somethin' to do with the mules."

"I don't know if Mr. Byrd will buy 'em, but he'd take 'em, and look after 'em. He likes 'em, and the mules like him."

The expression on Emmett's face indicated surprise and curiosity. "How do you know that?"

Kirby wasn't ready to tell his pa just yet about going out with Asa Briggs and leaving the mules with Tom Byrd.

"He, uh, told me one time that if I ever wanted to get rid of the mules that he would take them." That wasn't a complete lie. Byrd had said once that, as often as Kirby brought the team over, he may as well leave them with him.

"All right. We'll leave 'em with Tom," Emmett said. "What day is this, anyway?

"It's Wednesday, Pa."

"How far you been from this holler?"

Kirby thought about his experiences with the Ghost Riders. He had been as far north as Liberty and Glasgow, Missouri, west into Kansas, east to Clark's Mill, Missouri, and south to Cane Hill, Arkansas. He felt bad about deceiving his pa, but again, that wasn't information he was ready to share just yet. "A good piece, Pa. I been to Springfield."

"Then it's about time you got out to see more of this country." Emmett stuffed his pipe and lit it, then pushed his rawhide-bottomed chair back and looked at his son.

"You got somethin' in mind, don't you, Pa?"

"Toward the end of the war, Kirby, some Texicans and

some mountain men joined up with us. Them mountain men had been all the way to the Pacific Ocean, but they talked a lot about a place the Shoshone Indians call Idee ho, or somethin' like that.

"I'd like to see it. Texas too, and some of the rest of the country between here and there, and maybe get all the way out to the Pacific Ocean." Emmett coughed again.

"I seen the Atlantic Ocean, and I tell you, boy, you never seen so much water. If I was to see the Pacific Ocean, too, why that would mean I been all the way across this country from east to west. You just got no idea how big this country is. But the West is where all the people seems to be headed now, so I figure we'll just head on out that way, too."

"Pa? How will we know when we get to where it is we're going?"

"We'll know. You got any regrets, Kirby? Leaving this place, I mean."

"Hard work, not always enough food, Jayhawks, Yankees, cold winters, and some bad memories," Kirby replied. "If that's regrets, I'm happy to leave them behind."

Emmett's reply was unusually soft. "You was just a boy when I pulled out with the Grays. I reckon I done you, your sister 'n your ma a disservice, like half a million other men done their loved ones. I didn't leave you no time for youthful foolishness, no time to be a young boy. You had to be a man at an awful young age, and I don't know if I can make up for that, but I aim to try. From now on, son, it'll be you and me."

CHAPTER 7

The Jensens pulled out the following Sunday morning just as the sun was touching the eastern rim of the Ozark Mountains of Missouri. Kirby rode the bay, sitting on a worn-out McClellan saddle, which wasn't the most comfortable saddle ever invented. Emmett had bought it from a down on his luck Confederate soldier trying to get back to Louisiana.

They left the cool valleys and hills of Missouri, with rushing creeks and shade trees, and rode into a hot Kansas summer. The pair rode slowly, the pack horses trailing from lead ropes. The father and son had no deadline to meet and no particular place to go.

They passed a small sign that read BAXTER SPRINGS 2 MILES.

"Boy, what do you say we stop in this little town ahead?"

"Why?"

"Why not? It's been a hot ride and a beer might taste pretty good about now, don't you think?"

Kirby shrugged. "I don't know. I've never drunk a beer."

"You haven't?" Emmett laughed. "I guess not. You were just a boy when I left. Well, as far as I'm concerned, you're a man now, so if you want a beer, this is as good a time and place to start as any."

Baxter Springs was one of the places Kirby had visited when he was riding with Asa Briggs. They had crossed into Kansas looking for Shardeen but didn't find him. By chance, they ran into Quantrill heading south on the Texas Road on his way to winter in Texas. A short time before the two groups met, he had happened upon and killed two Union teamsters who were from a post called Baxter Springs.

Briggs and Quantrill decided to join their bands together for an attack on the post. They encountered Union soldiers, most of whom were black, and chased them back to the earth and log fort.

There, the Rebels attacked, but the garrison, with the help of a howitzer, managed to fight them off. Quantrill decided to move on the post from a different direction, and chanced upon a small Union detachment escorting Major General James G. Blunt and wagons transporting his personal items from his former headquarters in the Department of the Frontier at Fort Scott to his new one at Fort Smith. During the engagement, nearly all of the Union soldiers were killed, though General Blunt and a few mounted men managed to escape.

As a result, what had started as a battle became known as the Baxter Springs Massacre. Neither Briggs, nor any of his men had participated in that part of the fight, but the word *massacre* had been applied to the entire campaign, which, by implication, included Kirby.

Although he had been but one of many who had participated in the fight, he was a little hesitant about going into the settlement again. He took a deep breath, thinking. It had happened almost two years ago. He could be reasonably certain that he wouldn't be recognized as one of the guerrillas who had been there that day.

Kirby nodded his agreement and they approached the little settlement which had grown up around the fort. A small building built of rip-sawed unpainted boards had already weathered gray. The roof sagged, the building leaned, and an extension was obviously newer than the rest of the building. The sign out front read:

MURPHY'S
BEER WHISKEY EATS

Kirby and his pa tied their horses and pack animals off at the hitching rail, then stepped inside. The interior light was dim, filtered as it was through the dirty windows. Beams of light projected through the cracks between the boards, the shining beams alive with hanging dust motes.

The bar, such as it was, consisted of a few boards stretched between barrels. In a white apron and a low-crowned hat, the bartender was wiping glasses and putting them on a shelf behind the bar. Above the glasses, another shelf sported a row of whiskey bottles. A barrel of beer was just to the side.

Four tables with chairs made up the seating, one of them occupied by three men.

"This is a saloon, ain't it, Pa?"

"Not the fanciest I've ever seen, but yes, it's a saloon."

The two stepped up to the bar.

"We'll each have a beer," Emmett ordered, putting a dime down on the plank bar. He started coughing again, a deep and ragged cough.

"That's some cough you got there, mister."

"It's the dust," Emmett said.

The bartender didn't respond, but filled two mugs and set them before Emmett and Kirby. The two took the mugs over to a table and sat down.

"Drink up, boy," Emmett said, holding his mug out across the table toward Kirby.

Kirby took a swallow. It wasn't the best thing he had ever tasted, but on the day of a long, hot ride, it tasted good enough.

"Ha!" Emmett said, slapping his hand on the table. "I was there when you took your first step, I was there when you spoke your first word, and now I'm here for your first beer. It tastes better when it's cold."

"Hey!" called one of the three men sitting at the other table. "Them pants you're wearin' . . . they're Rebel pants, ain't they?"

"They're just trousers," Emmett replied.

"But they're Rebel pants."

"If you don't like my pants, mister, don't look at 'em."

From under the table, the man brought his hand up holding a pistol, pointing it toward Emmett. "Take 'em off. We don't allow Rebels . . . or Rebel pants here."

"I've no intention of takin' 'em off."

"Do you know who I am? My name is Tim Shardeen. I reckon that name means somethin' to you, don't it, Reb?"

Emmett shook his head. "It don't mean a damn thing to me."

"It woulda meant somethin' if we had ever met durin' the war. The outfit I rode with was called Shardeen's Raiders. Angus Shardeen is my brother. That mean anythin' to you now?"

"Only that you was a bunch of murderin' Jayhawkers."

Tim grinned. "Then you know I ain't kiddin' when I tell you that if you don't take off them Rebel pants, I'll shoot you dead 'n take 'em off you myself."

"Let it go, Tim. What are you wantin' to get involved in this for? Hell, him 'n the boy ain't doin' nothin' but drinkin' a beer," one of the others at the table pointed out.

"I don't like Rebs."

"The war's over," said the third man at the table.

"Not for him, it ain't. I'm goin' to count to three 'n if he ain't took off them pants by the time I get to three, I'm goin' to shoot him dead. One—"

A loud boom interrupted the count, and Tim dropped his pistol and grabbed a bloody wound in his wrist. Everyone looked from Tim to Kirby, who was holding a smoking pistol, having drawn it quietly and unobserved.

"Damn! You shot me!" Tim shouted.

"Yeah, I did," Kirby replied.

A pressure bandage was quickly applied to the wound.

"How . . . how the hell did you make a shot like that?" Tim asked through clenched teeth.

Kirby shrugged. "It was an accident."

"An accident?"

"I was tryin' to kill you."

One of Tim's drinking buddies stood up. "We'd better get 'im to Doc Strafford before he bleeds to death."

Still gripping his wrist, Tim headed to the door with his friends.

"Mister?" Kirby called to him.

Tim Shardeen turned with a frown on his face. "Don't waste your time apologizin' to me."

"Oh, I ain't apologizin'. I want you to take a message to your brother for me."

"What would that message be?"

"My name is Kirby Jensen. I want you to tell your brother that if I ever run into him, I plan to kill 'im."

"Ha! You're goin' to kill my brother, are you? How old are you, boy?"

"How old do you have to be to kill a man?" Kirby pointed his pistol at Tim Shardeen again.

"No, no! Don't shoot!"

"You will deliver that message for me, won't you?"

"Yeah, yeah. I'll deliver it."

"Thank you. I appreciate that."

The three men left the saloon.

A few minutes later, Emmett and Kirby rode on, a little wary at first, but the farther away from the town they got, the less concerned they were. By the time they made camp, they were more than thirty miles west of Baxter Springs.

"Are you good enough with that handgun to get us a squirrel for our supper?" Emmett asked.

"I reckon I am, if I see one."

"What about that one?" Emmett asked, pointing to a squirrel halfway up a tree about a hundred feet away.

Kirby pulled his pistol, raised it to eye level, aimed, and fired. The squirrel fell to the ground and he hurried over to retrieve it.

"You clean the squirrel. I'll gather some wood and get us a fire goin'," Emmett said.

Half an hour later, the spitted squirrel was roasting over the fire, coffee was boiling, and the Jensens were sitting nearby.

Emmett looked at Kirby pointedly. "What happened back in the saloon . . . when you shot the gun out of that feller's hand? That warn't no accident, was it?"

"No."

"I didn't think it was." Emmett nodded toward the gun. "I been aimin' to ask you about that pistol. I know you didn't have it when I left home. How did you come by it? And how did you learn to shoot like that?"

"A bunch of Jayhawkers come through the farm one night, headin' back to Kansas like the devil was chasing them, 'n that was just about right 'cause about half an hour later Bloody Bill Anderson and his boys come ridin' up. They stopped to rest and water the horses.

"Turned out this young fellow was with them. He couldn't have been no more 'n a year or so older 'n me. He seen me there alone with nothin' but a shotgun, so he give me this Navy gun and an extra cylinder."

"That seemed like a right nice thing for him to do," Emmett replied.

"Yes, sir. I thought it was. He was nice . . . and soft-spoken, too."

"You seen him since?"

Kirby looked straight ahead. "No, sir."

In fact, he had seen him several times since then, on those occasions when the Ghost Riders and Quantrill's Raiders happened to join up for an operation. He felt bad about lying to his father, but he justified it by telling himself that the day would come when he'd tell everything.

"You thank him proper, did you?"

"Yes, sir."

"Did he tell you his name?"

"He told me. He said it was James. Jesse James. His brother Frank was with the bunch, too. Frank was somewhat older 'n Jesse."

"All right. That tells me how you got the gun. But it don't say nothin' 'bout how come it is you can shoot so well."

Kirby looked at his pa and grinned. "I practiced a lot."

"You musta spent a lot of money for bullets."

"Yes, sir, I reckon I did."

"Well, then, I can see why you didn't have no money left from the farmin', seein' as you spent it all on bullets for practicin'. As things is turnin' out, what with where we're goin' 'n all, bein' able to shoot is goin' to be a lot more important than knowin' how to plow a straight row."

"Yes, sir."

"Tell me about Angus Shardeen."

"Pa, you know about him. He's the one that burned the Gimlin farm, remember?"

Emmett frowned. "That's why you said you wanted to kill 'im?"

"That's not the only reason. He also come through on a raid and kilt Kenny Prosser 'n his ma and his little brother. Kenny was a good friend of mine, if you 'member. 'N he also kilt Merlin Lewis 'n his family."

Kirby was telling the truth. Those two county families had been killed by Angus Shardeen.

"All right. You do know that takin' a blood oath like that, which is pretty much what you just done in tellin' a man that you aim to kill his brother, is puttin' quite a load on your shoulders."

"Yes, sir."

"How fast can you get the gun out of the holster?"

"I don't know," Kirby admitted. "It ain't anythin' I've ever had to do." Being able to shoot straight had been not only a help but a necessity when he was riding the Bush-whacker trail, but a quick draw wasn't.

"If you set yourself the job of findin' someone and killin' 'im, especially someone like Angus Shardeen, bein' able to pull the gun out fast is somethin' that might come in pretty handy, don't you think? It's called a quick draw."

"A quick draw," Kirby repeated.

"Yeah. Stand up there and do a quick draw for me. Let me see what you can do."

Kirby stood up, then made a grab for his pistol. It was awkward and the draw was slow.

Emmett laughed. "Looks like we've got some work to do. You've already showed that you can shoot straight. Now you need to learn how to draw."

"You think I can learn?"

"I don't have no doubt. You have sort of a natural-born smoothness about you, so I have a feelin' you're goin' to learn pretty fast how to do a quick draw. With that and accurate shootin', I've no doubt but that you'll wind up bein' a man to be reckoned with."

"Why would I have to be reckoned with?"

"Because where we're goin', you're goin' to have to live by laws that aren't necessarily wrote down anywhere. But just 'cause they ain't wrote down, don't mean they ain't laws that need to be followed."

"What kind of laws are you talkin' about?"

Emmett had another bout of coughing before he responded. "I'm talkin' 'bout the laws of decency and good sense. Don't take what ain't yours, don't cheat at cards—for that matter, don't cheat at nothin' else, either—don't call a man a liar if he ain't, and don't be afraid to call him one if he is. And if you do, you have to be prepared to back it up."

"Back it up with a gun, you mean?"

"Yes. Where we're goin', the time is more 'n likely goin' to come when no matter how much you try and avoid it, you'll wind up gettin' pushed into a corner. When that happens, you won't have no choice but to try and defend yourself. If the one who done the evil is faster and better with a gun than the one that got the evil done to him, the wrong man might die."

"I see what you mean."

"I hope you do see what I mean, Kirby, because I'm going to teach you how to make a quick draw."

"Can you do a fast draw, Pa?"

"Fair to middlin'."

"How did you learn?"

Emmett leaned back against a big rock, thinking about what he wanted to say. "Remember me tellin' you 'bout those boys from Texas? They taught me all the skills a person needs, and I can pass those skills on to you. But it takes more than skills. It takes a natural ability like what I was tellin' you about. I've seen you move all your life, Kirby, and you got a natural way of doin' it. Things has always come easy to you, easier than it ever did to your brother. Easier than it ever did to me, easier than it has to anyone else I've ever knowed or even seen. With a little practice, you'll not only be a lot faster 'n me, few—if any—in the country will be able to stand up to you. But that'll come with a sense of responsibility."

"What kind of responsibility?"

"The responsibility to use your gun only when it's right, only to defend yourself or the innocent. Can I count on you to do that?"

"Yes, Pa."

"You promise me?"

"I promise."

"I know you will, son. I only asked you to make the promise so's it'll be somethin' you'll always keep in your mind." Emmett had another coughing spell.

"Pa, you told the bartender that it was the dust makin' you cough. Only, there ain't no dust here now. Besides which, you been acoughin' a lot ever since you got back from the war. Why is it you're coughin' so much? You ain't got what they call the consumption, do you?"

"Where did you hear about consumption?"

"Miss Margrabe said her pa died of the consumption."

"I ain't got the consumption. Now, are you ready for your first lesson?"

"Yes sir, I reckon I am."

"Good. But before I teach you the fast draw, I'm going to have to teach you to shoot."

Kirby chuckled. "Pa, I've already showed you that I can shoot."

"You have, huh?" Emmett pointed to a thumb-sized protrusion from the branch of a nearby cottonwood tree. "Take a shot at that little branch for me."

Kirby raised the pistol to eye-level and fired. His bullet snapped the branch and he turned to his father with a satisfied smile on his face. "I told you I could shoot."

"You aimed, didn't you?"

"Of course I did."

"Why?"

"Why? Because I wanted to hit what I was shootin' at. That's why."

Emmett gave instructions. "Shoot at it again, but don't aim this time."

"What do you mean, don't aim? I don't understand. How am I going to hit it, if I don't aim?"

"You are going to think the bullet onto your target."

"What?"

"Let me show you what I'm talking about." Emmett pulled his own pistol and shot at the part of the branch that was left. He didn't raise the pistol to eye level and aim, he just pulled the trigger and another piece of the branch was shot away.

Kirby's jaw dropped. "How did you do that without aiming?"

"I told you. I just thought the bullet onto the target."

"I don't understand what that means."

"Here's the thing," Emmett said as he put his pistol back in the holster. "There's no sense in drawing really fast if you have to stop and aim. You have to draw, aim, and shoot all at the same time. In order to do that, you have to think the bullet onto the target. Now, you try it."

Kirby pulled the pistol and automatically started to raise it. He stopped himself, then held the gun out in front of his body and fired. He missed.

Emmett stood up. "Here, let me help you out. Turn yourself at an angle, sort of caddy corner, so that you aren't facing the target." He positioned Kirby accordingly. "Now, don't turn your body, but look at the target by turning your head back toward it."

Kirby responded.

"Bring the pistol up to eye level and aim at the target, just as you did before, but don't shoot."

Kirby did.

"Good. Close your eyes and lower your pistol so that it is pointing straight down."

Kirby did as instructed.

"Now, with your eyes closed, aim at it again."

Kirby opened his eyes and looked at his pa. "What do you mean, aim at it again? How am I going to do that if my eyes are closed?"

"Just listen to me, boy. Close your eyes and with them still closed, bring your arm back up, thinking about where the target is. When you think you have it lined up, tell me."

Kirby closed his eyes and brought his arm up until he thought he was aligned with the target.

"Pull the trigger, but don't open your eyes."

Kirby pulled the trigger.

"Now, open your eyes and look."

He did that and saw a white chip had been taken out of the limb, just below the small branch he had been shooting at. It was a miss, but it was a very close miss.

"I almost hit it!" he said excitedly.

"That was pretty good. Now, spread your feet apart about the width of your shoulders. Keep your legs straight, but not stiff. Think you can do that?"

Kirby tried it a few times, then looked at Emmett. "Yes, I can do it."

"What are you going to do with your other arm?" Emmett asked.

Kirby looked down. "I don't know. I hadn't thought about it."

"Good."

"Good?"

"It's good that you hadn't thought about it. As far as you're concerned, the other arm isn't even there.

"Put your pistol back in the holster, then look at your target by turning your head and eyes slightly without moving from the neck down. When you know exactly where the target is, pull the pistol from the holster, but don't raise the gun to eye level. Shoot it as soon as your arm comes level."

Anxious, Kirby asked, "Should I try a quick draw?"

"No. That comes later. First learn to shoot, then learn to draw. Now, pull the gun and shoot it."

Kirby pulled the pistol and fired as soon as it came level. He had no idea where the bullet went.

Fancy Lil was easily the most beautiful dove in the covey of doves Chicago Sue employed at the Palace Princess Emporium. She had managed to avoid the dissipation so prevalent among the others. While most would lay with anywhere from three to five men a night, Fancy Lil rarely shared her bed. The others charged from two dollars to five dollars, depending on the girl and the length of the visit. It cost fifty dollars to visit Fancy Lil for a short while, and one hundred and fifty dollars to spend the night with her.

Her room, in keeping with her station as Chicago Sue's most expensive girl, was attractively furnished with lace curtains on the window and a floral carpet on the floor. The furniture was made of English oak and the headboard featured elaborate carvings.

Her clientele was of a considerably higher caliber than the average visitor to the place. She entertained wealthy cattlemen, high ranking officers who'd been in the Confederate military, and politicians, including a couple Texas state senators.

Her most frequent visitor, and the one she actually enjoyed being with, was a big man, a Confederate veteran who stood six feet seven inches tall, and weighed 330 pounds. He had given only his first name, Ben.

The well-appointed room was redolent with the scent of sex. She and Ben were lying together, naked skin against naked skin.

Though it had become a little more than routine for Janey—an act without feeling, emotionally or physically—it wasn't like that with Ben. With him, she had experienced every sensation.

Their times together were passion-filled, but she also felt a relaxed shared possessiveness between them that she had never felt with anyone else, not even Paul Garner.

She put her head on Ben's shoulder, and he wrapped his arm around her, cupping her breast in his hand. It wasn't sexual. It was comfortable.

"What is your name?" she asked. "I know there has to be more to it than just Ben."

"Some folks call me Big Ben."

Janey chuckled. "*Big* Ben? Yes, I can see that. But am I to believe that's all there is to it?"

"Am I to believe there is no more to your name than Fancy Lil?"

"I can't give my real name," Janey said.

"Why not?"

"Because girls in my . . . profession . . . never give their real names."

Big Ben smiled. "And men like me, who visit girls like you, never give our real names."

"You are a wealthy man, aren't you, Ben?"

"Why do you say that?"

"Because it costs a lot of money to visit me . . . and lately, you have been visiting me more than all my other gentlemen callers combined."

"I enjoy visiting you."

"But you can get the same thing from other girls for a lot less money."

Big Ben shook his head. "No, I can't. Lil, I would have thought that, by now, you understood. It isn't just the time we're in bed together. It's more than that. With you . . . with us . . . it's just . . . more. I thought . . . that is, I hoped . . . that it was a little more for you, as well."

Janey felt her eyes well with tears, and she leaned up to kiss him on his cheek, feeling the stubble of a day's growth of beard. "My name is Janey. Janey Garner."

She'd decided to expose herself to him, but she chose to use Garner's last name, rather than Jensen. She didn't want to bring any more shame to the Jensen name than she already had. Assuming, that is, that there were any Jensens left alive.

Big Ben turned to smile at her. "Conyers. Benjamin R. Conyers."

CHAPTER 8

Millions of soldiers who had worn the blue and the gray had laid down their arms and picked up where they had left off. Families split by the war were reunited. Friendships were renewed, crops were put in, men and women were married, children were born.

But it was not so for all men. For some, the wounds had cut too deeply and the price had been too dear. Families, fortunes, and dreams were consumed in flames and drowned in blood. So it was for Kirby and Emmett. They had only each other, along with their guns and their courage.

After leaving Baxter Springs, they headed west for a bit, then turned south through Indian Territory, heading for Texas.

"Do you think we need to be wary of the Indians, Pa?"

"No need. All the Indians here is civilized. They got their own towns, their own laws. Most even like white men. Lots of 'em even fought 'n the war. It's farther out West that we got to be wary of 'em. Out there, I hear tell that Indians is notional folks. The same bands that would leave you alone today might try to kill you tomorrow."

"Why?"

"I can't say. It's hard for the average white man to understand the Indians' way of life. But I'm sure there are white men livin' in the mountains, prob'ly been there thirty or forty years or more, who can understand them better 'n whites can now, them bein' gone so long from civilization 'n all."

Every night as they camped, Kirby would practice shooting, though he limited his practice to no more than three shots each day. They were a long way from any chance of buying new bullets.

On the seventh day, he fired three shots, *thinking* his bullets into the targets all three times. "Did you see that, Pa?"

"Can you do it again?"

Kirby repeated his performance, again hitting his targets with all three bullets.

"All right. Instead of shooting one at a time, I want you to fire three times, one shot right on top of another, and hit these three targets." Emmett put pine cones on three rocks, the two farthest rocks separated by at least ten yards. He came back to stand beside Kirby.

"Now?" Kirby asked.

"Not yet. I'm going to add something to it." Emmett took a mess skillet from his pack and put it on the ground in front of him, then he picked up a rock. "When I say, 'now,' I want you to start shooting. At the same time, I'll drop this rock, and I want to hear all three shots before the rock hits the skillet. Do you think you can do that?"

"I can get all three shots off, yes sir."

"And hit all three targets," Emmett said.

"I don't know, Pa. That's askin' quite a lot."

"Wrong answer. Do you think you can do that?"

Kirby smiled. "Yes, sir."

Emmett returned the smile. "That's my boy. Now!" he shouted without further notice.

Using his left hand to fan the hammer, Kirby fired three shots so close that it sounded like one. Then *clank*—the rock hit the skillet. All three targets had been hit.

"You didn't give me any warning," Kirby complained.

"I didn't, did I? Well, you don't always get a warning. I

think the time has come to teach you the quick draw. And this won't be costin' us any bullets at all."

"I'm ready," Kirby said with a broad smile.

"All right. Empty your pistol before we begin. I wouldn't want the damn thing to go off accidental while you're tryin' to learn."

Kirby pulled his pistol, poked all the shells out of the cylinder, and stuck it back down into the holster.

"Now, look down at the shank of your holster. That's the part that's attached to the belt. It should have a little kink in it, so that it causes the butt of the pistol to stick out just a little. You can adjust it, but we may have to make a little modification later on, so that the pistol sticks out far enough all the time so there won't be anything to get in the way of your draw."

Kirby made a few adjustments to the shank and finally, after examining it closely, Emmett announced that it was ready and continued with his instructions. "Let your arm hang down completely limp and natural along your side. Don't crook the elbow . . . don't stiffen your arm. Don't do nothin' but just let it hang there."

Kirby did as he was instructed.

"Now, without drawing the gun, bend your arm at the elbow until your hand has come up level with the ground. Stick out your trigger finger. Where is it pointing?"

"It's pointing in the same direction as my arm," Kirby said.

"All right, now what I want you to do is, move the gun belt until the gun is exactly under your hand. The butt of the pistol should be poking out away from your body just a little. That was why we adjusted the shank a while ago. Remember?"

Kirby adjusted the holster as directed, and Emmett inspected the position of the gun.

"Yes," he said, smiling. "Just like that. And the holster should be at the same angle as your arm was a while ago when you lifted it. Do that."

Kirby repositioned the holster.

"Move your hips forward real slow and bring your shoulders back, grabbing the gun as your hips and shoulders move. But don't grab it with your whole hand. Curl your middle finger, ring finger, and little finger around the butt of the gun. If you've got your holster positioned right, that will put the gun in your hand before you even start to draw it."

Kirby reacted to the directions, and as Emmett had pointed out, his hand fell naturally to the butt of the pistol. He smiled at the result. "Pa, my hand went right where you said it would."

"Good. That's very good. Keep your holster there, and do it that way every time, so that when the gun comes out of the holster, it will just naturally be pointed in the right direction. Now, when you make the draw, make sure you bring the barrel up level, 'cause if you don't, you'll shoot low ever' time."

Kirby nodded, indicating that he understood the instructions.

"All right. Good. Now, it's time to cock the gun as you draw it. What you want to do is, pull your thumb across the hammer to cock the gun at the same time you are drawing. The thumb should be moving the hammer back all the while you are bringing the gun up. You got that?"

"Yes, Pa. I got it."

Emmett chuckled. "So you say. We'll just see if you listened to anything I said. I want you to draw the gun just the way I told you. But I want you to draw it real slow, so I can see it, and make sure you're doing everything the right way. Go ahead and draw it now."

Kirby made the draw, doing it slowly and exactly as he had been instructed. Emmett smiled.

"How did you like that?" Kirby asked.

"Don't go getting all smug on me now," Emmett said.

"I did it perfectly."

"How do you know you did?"

"Because, if I hadn't done it perfectly, you wouldn't have called me smug," Kirby said with a pleased smile.

"Right. Now . . . pick out something to shoot at and draw as fast as you can."

Kirby frowned. "I don't have any bullets in the gun."

"You don't need any bullets right now. All you need to do is what I told you. Now, I want you to pick out a target."

"What about that leaf there?"

"What leaf? There are hundreds of leaves. How do I know you won't just shoot, then claim the leaf you hit is the one you wanted to hit?"

Kirby walked over to a nearby tree and put his finger on one of the leaves. "This one."

"All right. Draw your pistol as fast as you can and shoot at it."

Still confused, Kirby asked, "How can I shoot if I don't have any bullets?"

"Just do what I tell you, Kirby. If I want questions, I'll ask for them."

Kirby returned to his original position, drew his pistol, thumbed back the hammer, and pulled the trigger. The hammer fell on an empty chamber.

"Did you hit the leaf?" Emmett asked.

Kirby started to ask his father again how he could hit the leaf if he had no bullets in his gun but checked the question and smiled instead. "Yeah, I hit the leaf."

"Good. Now, put some bullets in your gun and do it again."

Kirby loaded the pistol and put it in his holster. He got ready to make his draw—

"Wait." Emmett stopped him. He picked up the rock.

"You're goin' to drop the rock on the skillet again?" Kirby asked.

"No. This time you're goin' to drop the rock. What I want you to do is hold it out in front of you. When I tell you to, drop the rock, draw your pistol, and shoot at that leaf."

Kirby held the rock out in front of him, shoulder high.

"Now!" Emmett shouted.

Kirby dropped the rock, drew his pistol, and fired. Not until after the gun fired, was there the clank of the rock hitting the skillet. The leaf, cut from the tree, fluttered down. Kirby looked over at Emmett and smiled.

"Not bad," Emmett said.

"Not bad? What do you mean, *not bad*?"

"You had your hand shoulder high. I want you to be able to do that when your hand is no higher than this." Emmett demonstrated, holding his hand lower than Kirby's waist.

"Nobody can do that." Kirby shook his head.

"You can," Emmett said. "And better."

"If you think so," Kirby said.

"No, Kirby, it's not what I think. It's what *you* think. Actually, it's not what you think, it's what you *know*. You have to *know* that you can do this."

Kirby picked up the rock and held it just below his waist. Then, with a confident grin, he moved the rock even lower. Taking a deep breath, he dropped the rock, drew the pistol, and fired . . . before the rock clanked against the skillet. And he hit the target.

As Kirby bedded down that night next to glowing embers of the fire that had cooked their supper, he let his mind pass over events that had brought him and his father near the Cherokee town of Tahlequah in the Indian Territory. He had grown up thinking he would be a farmer like his father. Once he and Luke had even discussed buying acreage just across Shoal Creek from the family farm. If they bought 40 acres apiece, they could farm all the land jointly . . . 120 acres, which would make it one of the biggest farms in Stone County. And because all the land had access to a year-round supply of water, it could be the best farm in the county.

But none of that was to be. His mother was dead. Luke was dead. Janey had run off, who knows where, and his pa had come back from the war no longer interested in farming. If Kirby was truthful with himself, he was no longer interested in it, either.

How strange life was that it could start out in one direction, then make a turn in a completely different direction.

Emmett had another bad coughing spell in his sleep.

Kirby sat up and looked over toward him. "Pa?"

Emmett coughed again. "I'm all right, son. I've just got a cough I can't shake, is all. Go back to sleep."

Kirby lay back down. He hadn't been asleep so there was no *going back to sleep*, but as he lay there, his eyelids began to grow heavy, and finally sleep pushed away all the thoughts tumbling through his mind.

Over the next several days Kirby continued to practice. His draw became so fast that it was a blur, too fast for the eye to follow. His shooting was deadly accurate, as well.

Emmett, having handled guns all his life, was a very good shooter. As he watched, he realized that Kirby was exceptionally good—already better than his pa. Emmett smiled, proud.

He had once been the city marshal of a small town in Missouri, and had found it necessary, in defense of his own life, to kill two men during his tenure in office. God alone knew how many more men he had killed during the war.

Emmett was glad that the boy could handle himself. He had not told Kirby everything—that he would have gone West whether Pearl was dead or alive, and whether or not Kirby had come with him; that his journey was not one of pure impulse; that he had given his word to Mosby that if it took him forever, he would find and kill the men who had murdered Luke and stolen the gold he was carrying to the Confederate government in Georgia.

In this, he was like his son. Kirby had taken his own oath to kill someone. Ideally, they would be together when they encountered the men they were after.

Crossing into Texas, they came across a few stage stops and trading posts along the way but didn't ride into any towns until they reached Dallas.

Emmett looked around. "This is it, boy. Dallas, Texas."

"Wow, this is purt' nigh as large as Springfield," Kirby said, taking it all in.

The main street was cut with wheel ruts and hoof marks, and covered with enough horse apples to permeate the air with strong odor. A busy town, it was filled with buck-boards, surreys, carriages, and wagons, as well as riders on horseback. Boardwalks ran the entire length of each block and were filled with the citizens of the town, many of them women who walked around holding handkerchiefs to their nose to blot out the smell.

"We might want to stop here, first," Emmett said, pointing to a gun store. "I expect you're about out of ammunition, ain't you?"

"I could sure use some more," Kirby replied.

Tying their four horses off, the two men went inside.

A clerk sitting behind the counter in a wooden chair leaning against the wall was the only person in the store. He stood up when they entered. "Yes, sir, can I help you?"

"I need some thirty-six caliber shells," Kirby said.

"Very good sir. How many do you need?"

"I'd say about two hundred."

The clerk whistled. "Two hundred? My, that's a lot of ammunition. I do hope you aren't planning on restarting the war." He laughed at his own joke.

"Got no intention of doin' that," Kirby said. "But travelin' like we are, you don't always find a place where you can get it."

"I understand." The man took four boxes from a case, then opened one of the boxes. "As you can see there are fifty bullets in each little box. Four times fifty is two hundred."

"Open all four boxes," Emmett said.

"Do you really think that is necessary?"

"Open all four boxes," Emmett said again.

The man started to put one of the boxes back in the case, but Emmett reached out to grab his wrist. "What's wrong with that box?"

"To tell the truth, it felt a little light to me, so I . . ."

Before he could finish his statement, Emmett opened the box. It was only about half full. "A little light, you said?"

"Yes. You did notice that I was putting it back," the clerk said self-righteously. He put four boxes on the counter and opened them. "Two dollars."

Satisfied that the boxes were full, Kirby paid for the ammunition, and he and Emmett went back outside.

"How'd you know he was plannin' to cheat me, Pa?"

Emmett put his finger alongside his nose. "I smelled it."

"You smelled it?" Kirby asked incredulously.

"You don't actually smell it," Emmett explained. "It's just something that you say when you have a feelin' that somethin' ain't quite right. And I had a feelin' that somethin' wasn't quite right."

"How do you learn to have them feelin's?"

"It's not somethin' you learn. It's somethin' that just sort of comes to you as you get older. I expect it'll come over you, too, eventually."

Looking around, they spotted the Lone Star Hotel.

"What do you say we spend the night in a bed instead of on the ground?" Emmett asked.

"Sounds good to me," Kirby agreed.

After checking into the hotel and boarding their horses, they walked up the wide, sunbaked street, hurrying from the shade of one building to the next, taking every opportunity to get out of the sun. After walking a few blocks, they were drenched with sweat, and the cool interior of the Yellow Dog Saloon beckoned them.

Pushing their way through the bat wing doors, they stepped inside and stood in the dark for a moment or two until their eyes adjusted to the dim light. Unlike the rather coarse establishment in Baxter Springs, this place was rather elegant. Made of burnished mahogany, the bar had a highly polished brass foot rail. Crisp, clean white towels hung from hooks on the customers' side of the bar, spaced every four feet. A mirror behind the bar was flanked on each side by a small statue of a nude woman set back in a special niche. A row of whiskey bottles sat in front of the mirror, reflected in the glass so that the row of bottles seemed to be two deep. A bartender with pomaded black hair and a waxed handlebar moustache stood behind the bar. A towel was draped across his shoulders, and his arms were folded across his chest.

"Is the beer cool?" Emmett asked.

"It's cooler than horse piss," he said in a matter-of-fact voice.

Emmett chuckled. "Good enough. We'll have a couple."

The bartender drew the beers and set them in front of Kirby and Emmett.

Kirby picked up the beer and took a drink.

"What do you think?" Emmett asked. "Is the second one better?"

"Yes, sir. It's a lot better."

"It's good to be able to enjoy a beer now 'n again but, what with you just startin' out to drink, I need to tell you to be careful about drinkin'."

"Careful? What do you mean? Why do I have to be careful?"

"I say that 'cause some folks start to likin' their liquor too much, 'n the next thing they know, 'bout the only important things in their life is the next drink 'n where it's comin' from. I sure don't want to see that happen to you."

"I don't neither. I promise you, I will take care." Kirby turned to look around the place. Nearly every table was occupied.

One of the tables was near enough to where they were standing that Emmett could quite easily listen in on the conversation that was taking place between three men.

"Her name is Lil. Fancy Lil," one of the men was saying. "She works down at the Palace Princess Emporium."

"That ain't her real name, is it, Doc?"

"I'm sure that Fancy is not a part of her sobriquet, though Lil might be. Young ladies who find themselves in such occupations, however, rarely use their real names."

"She must be somethin'," said the man in a blue shirt. "I heard that iffen you want to choose her, it's goin' to cost you a hunnert dollars. Maybe even more."

The man with a bushy mustache shook his head. "There ain't no woman worth a hunnert dollars."

"Oh, believe me, this young lady is," replied the one called Doc.

Bushy Mustache couldn't believe it. "Doc, don't tell me you spend a hunnert dollars on her."

"I have not, but only because I don't have a hundred dollars to spare. But if I did, I would do so without a moment's hesitation."

"The Palace Princess Emporium. That's Chicago Sue's place, ain't it?" Blue Shirt asked.

"Yes."

"Yeah, well, mayhaps that's why I ain't never seen this here Fancy Lil that you're talking about. I ain't never been to Chicago Sue's establishment. They ain't any of them at Chicago Sue's place that's cheap."

"Oh, I wouldn't complain. Those at the Palace Princess Emporium are different," Doc said.

"What do you mean, *different?* They's same as saloon girls, ain't they?"

"No, they are ladies that entertain."

"Does it cost money to be entertained?" Bushy Mustache wanted to know.

"Yes."

Blue Shirt wasn't convinced. "And, does that entertainment include sleepin' with 'em?"

"Yes."

Blue Shirt crossed his arms. "If a woman will go to bed

with you for money, she's same as a saloon girl, no matter how much it costs."

"I'm sure that as dissipation takes its toll, some of the young ladies who work there will slip down the scale until you can rightly throw them in with saloon girls, but not now. And you certainly can't say that for Fancy Lil. Anyone who can command one hundred dollars for her services is certainly more than a common saloon girl."

Bushy Mustache didn't believe it. "This Fancy Lil must be some kind of woman."

"She is," Doc replied. "Perhaps Christopher Marlowe expressed it best."

"Christopher Marlowe? Hmm, I don't think I know him."

"That wouldn't be likely, since he died almost two hundred years ago," Doc said.

Bushy Mustache was more confused than ever. "What? Then how could he say anything about Fancy Lil?"

"He was actually speaking of Helen of Troy, but it could have been Fancy Lil." Doc cleared his throat, then, in dramatic fashion, said the words, *"Was this the face that launch'd a thousand ships . . . And burnt the topless towers of Ilium? . . . Sweet Helen, make me immortal with a kiss."*

His table mates were stunned.

Bushy Mustache grinned. "Doc, you're the smartest man I've ever knowed. You must be. Hell, I don't understand half of what you say."

"I have established the idea that this lady, Fancy Lil, is a person of rare beauty, haven't I?"

"Oh, yeah, you've done that all right. Only I'll never get to see her. A hunnert dollars? I ain't never had that much money at one time in my whole life."

"It doesn't cost a hundred dollars just to see her. For five dollars, you can visit the parlor of the Palace Princess Emporium, enjoy food, drink, and conversation with beautiful women and a convivial atmosphere," Doc pointed out.

"Five dollars? But that don't get you no woman, does it?"

"Only in friendly conversation."

Blue Shirt looked at Bushy Mustache. "Will Fancy Lil be there?"

"She often is, when she isn't otherwise engaged."

"You mean with someone?"

"Yes."

"Hmmph. If it cost one hunnert dollars to be with her, I can't imagine she's with someone all that much."

"She is very selective," Doc replied.

Kirby had been listening intently to the conversation. He turned to Emmett, who was staring into his glass. "You know what, Pa? I'd like to see this woman they're talkin' about."

"Why?"

"You heard what Doc said. That she is the most beautiful woman he had ever seen. Wouldn't you like to see such a woman?"

"Boy, what do you know about such things? Have you ever been to such a place?" Emmett's question was pointed, but not challenging.

Kirby had never been, but he had seen one . . . once. It had been pointed out by Elmer Gleason. He couldn't share that information with his father, though, without sharing that he had ridden with Asa Briggs.

"No, sir, I ain't never been to one. But I know what one is. Some of the other boys in school was talkin' 'bout 'em one day." That was true. The subject had come up, but none of the boys who'd been discussing it knew exactly what went on there.

"Yeah, I reckon there are some things you can learn at school that ain't really all that good."

Kirby chuckled. "I never heard that till I was in the seventh grade. And remember, I wanted to quit soon as I finished the fifth grade."

Emmett chuckled, then took another drink. "Well now, ain't you glad I made you stay?"

At that moment, the back door opened and a tall, broad-shouldered, bearded man wearing a badge stepped through the door and looked around. For a long moment, he scrutinized Kirby and Emmett, obviously aware that they were new in town, then continued his perusal of the room until he saw a man who caught his attention.

"You," he said, pointing. "We got a telegram sayin' you was comin' to Dallas. I didn't think you was actually that dumb, Cox."

The man stood up slowly, then turned to face the lawman. "Yeah? Why shouldn't I come to Dallas? Am I supposed to be afraid of some piss-ant deputy?"

The situation had the look of an impending gunfight. The others at the table stood up and moved out of the way. All other conversation within the saloon ceased.

"Unbuckle your gun belt," the lawman said, making a motion with the gun he was holding. "And do it slow and easy, so's I don't get the idea you're tryin' anything."

Cox shook his head no. "I don't think so, Deputy. I think me an' you's goin' to have to settle this thing, right here and right now."

Kirby had heard stories about deadly gunfights between men, but not in all the time he had been riding with Briggs had he ever seen one. The shooting he had experienced was from a distance, and it was always one group of men against another group. He had never seen a one-on-one confrontation.

"Are you crazy, Cox?" the deputy asked. "I've already got you covered."

"Do you now?" Cox asked with a mysterious smile on his face.

Kirby was watching intently, wondering why the man called Cox didn't seem to be worrying about the gun that was pointing toward him. When he saw a man standing up in the corner, aiming his pistol at the lawman, he shouted, "Deputy, look out! There's a gun behind you!"

The man in the corner turned the pistol toward the Jensens.

Kirby acted instinctively. Dropping his beer, he pulled his pistol and fired just as the man in the corner pulled the trigger on his own gun. The would-be assailant's bullet hit the mirror behind the bar, and it fell with a crash, leaving nothing but a few jagged shards hanging in place to reflect twisting images of the dramatic scene.

Just like in all of his practicing, Kirby's bullet had gone true . . . only his target had been a man . . . who dropped his weapon and grabbed his neck. His eyes rolled up in his head and he fell backward.

The two gunshots had riveted everyone's attention to that exchange. Cox took the opportunity to go for his own gun. Suddenly, the saloon was filled with the roar of another gunshot as he fired at the deputy, whose attention had also been diverted by the gunplay between Kirby and the man in the corner. Cox's bullet struck the deputy in the back of the head.

Making a fatal mistake, Cox swung his pistol toward Kirby.

Emmett's bullet caught Cox in the center of his chest, and he went down. He sat on the floor, leaning back against the table, his gun lying on the floor beside him. "Who . . . who the hell are you?" he asked, gasping out the question. "What did you get involved for?"

"It seemed the thing to do," Emmett said.

One more gasp, and Cox was dead.

CHAPTER 9

"What's goin' on in here?" asked a loud authoritative voice. "Who's doin' all the shootin'?"

Holding smoking guns, Kirby and his pa turned toward the sound of the voice to see a man standing just inside the open door. With the brightness of the light behind him, he could be seen in silhouette only.

"Get out of the light," Emmett said, his voice a low growl.

"You don't tell me what to do, I—"

Click. Emmett pulled the hammer back and his pistol made a deadly metallic sound as the sear engaged the cylinder. "I said get out of the light," he repeated.

The figure moved out of the light. Kirby and Emmett could see that he was wearing a badge and put their pistols away.

"Marshal, I'm glad you come," said one of the men who had been sitting with Cox. "These here fellas just killed your deputy. Then they killed Haggart, 'n Cox, too, 'n they done it all in cold blood."

"That ain't true," Emmett said.

"Julius McCoy wasn't just my deputy, he was also my friend and my sister's husband. I think you two had better come down to the jail with me till I get to the bottom of this."

Although Kirby had already holstered his pistol, it suddenly appeared in his hand again, the draw so fast that it caught everyone in the saloon by surprise. He didn't shoot at the end of his draw. "I don't think we want to do that, Marshal. If you want to get to the bottom of this, you can find out what happened by askin' these people right here. I'm sure some of 'em must be honest."

Emmett had his gun out, as well, and was covering everyone else in the saloon.

"All right," the marshal said. "Let me hear what you have to say."

"I didn't have anything to do with killing your deputy, but I did kill that one." Kirby pointed to the man lying back in the corner.

"What did you shoot him for?" the marshal asked.

"He had a gun pointed at your deputy's back and was about to shoot him."

"Who killed the other two?"

"I killed that one," Emmett admitted, pointing toward Cox's body. "Unfortunately, not before he killed your deputy."

The marshal looked around until he noticed the man who had been speaking so eloquently about a woman named Fancy Lil. "Doc Dunaway, did you see what happened here?"

"I did indeed." Dr. Dunaway pointed to Kirby and Emmett. "These two men are telling the truth, Marshal. Deputy McCoy was trying to arrest Cox, when that unfortunate gentleman"—he pointed to the body lying back in the far corner—"declared his intention of interrupting the operation by pointing a pistol at McCoy. He was about to shoot, but the boy shouted a warning. At that, he turned his weapon toward those two and fired. The broken mirror behind the bar should be all the evidence you need to validate that. It was a misguided move of the part of the would-be assassin, because the young man drew his pistol and returned fire. It was quite a long shot, too.

"While all that was in progress, Cox killed the deputy when McCoy wasn't payin' attention and then he swung his gun around toward these two. By then, the older gentleman had his own pistol out. He shot Cox. If I am asked to testify in court, I will say, emphatically, that he had every right to do so."

"That's true. Ever'thing Doc said is true. That's the feller that's lyin'." Blue Shirt pointed to the man who had been sitting at the table with Cox—the one who had accused Kirby and Emmett of killing all three men.

"I, uh, just told what I thought I seen," the man said nervously.

Dr. Dunaway's testimony opened the floodgate. Nearly everyone else in the saloon began telling their own stories of the incident, and though there were a few slight variations in the telling, one theme was consistent throughout—all but one of the shootings were entirely justified.

The marshal let out a big sigh and waved his hand dismissively. "I reckon you two can put them guns away. What with ever'one in here tellin' the same story, there won't be no need in arrestin' you. But you might want to come down to my office tomorrow, anyway."

"Why would we want to do that?" Emmett asked.

"Because there's a five-hundred-dollar reward out for Cox, and I expect you'll be wantin' to stick around long enough to collect it." The marshal looked over toward the other dead man. "I don't know nothin' about him, but there may be paper on him as well."

Emmett nodded. "I reckon that's reason enough to stay around for a couple days."

"What's your name?" the marshal asked.

"I'm Emmett Jensen. This is my son, Kirby."

"I don't think I've ever heard the names before. Are you new in town?"

"We just arrived today," Emmett said.

"Just passing through, are you?"

"Sort of. Actually, I'm looking for some friends of mine. Wiley Potter, Keith Stratton, and Josh Richards. Perhaps you have run across them."

The marshal shook his head. "Nope. 'Fraid I've never heard of 'em."

"What about Angus Shardeen?" Kirby asked.

The marshal's eyes narrowed. "Would he be a friend as well?"

Kirby shook his head. "Not hardly. I've got a score to settle with him."

"Apparently a lot of people do. He's took to doin' the same he was doin' durin' the war, only now he ain't got the war as an excuse. He's a thief and a murderer."

"Is he anywhere nearby?"

"Not that I know of."

"Boy, you got quite an appetite on you, you know that?" Emmett's comment was made over supper that night at the Rustic Rock restaurant.

Kirby was eating a steak that was so large he needed a second plate for his potatoes and green beans. He had also asked for an extra serving of rolls. "Can you blame me? We ain't had nothin' but squirrel and rabbit and such for near two months. I just figured when I get a chance to eat like this, well, maybe I should."

"I don't reckon I can argue with that. By the way, Kirby, I been wantin' to say somethin' to you. The way you handled yourself today, even the way you handled yourself back in Baxter, was somethin' special. I'm just real proud of you."

"It wasn't all that much," Kirby said, embarrassed by his pa's accolades.

"Don't sell yourself short. I've been in more battles than I can count and I've seen many men get so scared that they could barely breathe when the shootin' starts."

Kirby took a bite of potatoes and nodded. "Sounds like a reasonable thing to do."

"Yes. But you've been in two shootin' scrapes, and you didn't get panicked either time."

"Didn't seem like the time for it," Kirby said.

"Still, I want you to know that I'm proud of you."

"Pa, who are these men you mentioned, Casey, Potter, Stratton, and Richards? I've never heard you mention those names before."

"Why do you ask?"

"I'm just wonderin' is all. You told the marshal they was your friends, but if they are, how come you haven't mentioned them before now?"

The response to Kirby's question was a long silence, then the silence was broken, not by Emmett's answer, but by another coughing attack. Not until the coughing fit stopped, did Emmett speak. "Why are you so interested?"

Kirby put his finger alongside his nose as his father had done back in the gun shop. "Because there's somethin' not quite right here. I can smell it."

Emmett nodded. "You're gettin' a little smarter after all. You're right. They aren't friends at all. What Angus Shardeen is to you, those men are to me. If and when I find 'em, I plan to kill 'em."

"What did they do?"

"They stole some gold that belonged to the Confederate government, and they killed a lot of good men while they was stealing it."

"Pa, the war's over. There ain't no Confederate government no more, which to my thinkin' means there ain't no Confederate gold no more."

"That's true. But it ain't the gold I'm concerned with, Kirby. It's the men they killed while they was comin' by it. One of 'em was your brother."

Kirby got a surprised expression on his face. "Are you sure, Pa? The letter I got from Colonel Willis said that Luke was killed in battle on Wilderness Creek."

"That's what the report said. But what really happened was that Casey, Potter, Stratton, and Richards shot 'im."

"Colonel Willis said Luke's body wasn't found. He thought that maybe the Yankees found him and buried him."

"I went up to Wilderness Creek lookin' for his body, but I never found it, so it could be that the Yankees did find him and bury him. It's for sure that the men who killed him didn't take the time to give him a proper burial."

"Pa, you're sure that's what happened? That he was shot by those men you mentioned?"

"Yes. I am very sure." Emmett spoke with such absolute authority, that Kirby felt no need to question it any further.

"Do you think those men might be here in Texas?"

"They could be. They might also be in New Mexico, or Colorado, or Idaho."

"Like you said, Pa, this is an awful big country. How do you plan to find them in such wide open spaces? They could be anywhere between here and the Pacific Ocean."

"I told you they stole Confederate gold. They stole a lot of it, Kirby, enough to make all of 'em rich as Croesus. Men with that much money can't hide. They're goin' to be spendin' a lot of it, and that's goin' to get them noticed. All I have to do is live long enough to find 'em."

Kirby chuckled. "Well, that'll be fifty, sixty years. I reckon we'll find 'em all right."

"Maybe not." The tone of Emmett's voice was flat and absolute.

"What are you talkin' about, Pa? What do you mean, maybe not?"

"I mean that, in all likelihood, I don't have that long left to live."

Kirby put his fork down and looked at his pa. "The cough?"

"Yeah, but the cough is the result, not the cause." As if on cue, Emmett coughed again, then he continued with his story. "I caught a ball in the lung, Kirby. Not a lot of men survived a wound like that, and I don't mind tellin' you that it laid me flat on my back for weeks. It got all festered up on me. Then lung fever hit the other lung.

"Maybe, just maybe, if I stayed in a dry climate, I might make it, according to the doctors. But they didn't sound hopeful. They also said that I should rest, and I shouldn't exert myself too much. But I can't do that. I swore I would find those men, and I aim to do it."

"That's why you wanted me to learn the fast draw, and how to shoot without aiming, isn't it?"

"Sort of," Emmett admitted. "If you are with me when I find 'em, you're goin' to just naturally get drawed into it. So, I wanted you to be able to take care of yourself. What happened tonight tells me I'm not going to have to worry."

"Pa . . . we'll find 'em. And if you don't live long enough to find all of 'em, I will. I promise you that. I owe it to you . . . and to Luke."

Emmett reached across the table and squeezed his son's hand. "I knew I could count on you."

"You think they've got dessert in this place?" Kirby asked as he took the last bite of steak, then pushed the plate to one side.

"Lord, boy. You mean you still have room for dessert?"

"Well, not a whole lot of dessert. Just enough to finish out the meal."

"What kind of dessert would you want?"

"Maybe a couple pieces of apple pie, with a slab of cheese melted on top." Kirby smiled. "We can afford it, Pa. We'll be gettin' the reward money tomorrow, don't forget."

Emmett chuckled and shook his head. "You're right. Travelin' around the way we're doin', we won't always have an opportunity to buy pie. I reckon I'll have a piece with you."

"As long as you get your own so I don't have to share," Kirby replied with a smile.

* * *

At that same moment, Dr. Tom Dunaway was standing at the buffet in the parlor of the Palace Princess Emporium, perusing the viand that was laid out for the guests—a glistening ham, a roast beef, and fried or baked chicken. In addition, mashed potatoes, baked sweet potatoes, blackeyed peas, fried and boiled okra, baked loaves of bread, rolls, biscuits, and corn bread were spread out on the long table.

Filling his plate, Dr. Dunaway found an overstuffed chair near the fireplace, which had no fire because it was summer. He began to enjoy the food.

"My goodness, Tom," Janey said. "From the looks of your plate, one would think that you hadn't eaten in a month of Sundays."

"What can I say, Lil? I come to the Palace because the food here is better than can be found at any restaurant in town."

"Oh, my. Now you have hurt my feelings. I thought you came here to enjoy my company. But now I learn it is only the food that brings you to the Palace."

"*Au contraire, mon cheri,*" Dr. Dunaway said. "It is the lovely *Mademoiselle* Lil that brings me here. *Je viens à vous prélasser dans votre beauté.*"

When it was obvious that Janey had no idea what he had just said, he translated it for her. "I come to bask in your beauty."

"Oh, what a nice thing for you to say, and to say it in such pretty words."

"Yes, French is a beautiful language." Dr. Dunaway nodded toward the plate he was holding. "The food is really a secondary reason." He took a bite of roast beef, then smiled. "But I must admit that it is a strong, secondary reason."

Janey laughed.

"Say, Doc," one of the other guests called out. "Is it true that you were in the Yellow Dog when the shootin' took place this afternoon?"

"Yes, I was there. And I testified to Marshal Wallace that the shooting, at least in two of the cases, was justified."

"McComb seen it, too, 'n he said one of them wasn't no more 'n sixteen or seventeen, and that he was really fast."

"He may have been a little older than that, but not much, I would wager," Dr. Dunaway replied. "And McComb is right, I don't believe I've ever seen anyone extract their weapon with more speed than that young man did."

The parlor was relatively crowded at the moment. Some of the men were waiting for their particular choice in girls; some had already been with a woman and hadn't left yet, while others, like Dr. Dunaway, were just visiting.

Chicago Sue had established her policy that a man could pay five dollars to visit and eat. That was very expensive for a meal that could be had for no more than a dollar at any other restaurant in town, but the food wasn't the only attraction. The five dollars allowed them to fill their plates from the buffet, and also to visit with the women who weren't currently engaged. However, their interaction with the women could go no further than visiting. If they wished to advance the temporary relationship with one of the young ladies, they were charged an additional fee.

Fancy Lil was one of the principal attractions of the parlor because she was an entertaining conversationalist . . . and the men liked being around someone as beautiful as she was. Her presence also provided the catalyst that some might need to engage one of the other girls for a more intimate visit.

"Fancy Lil," Dr. Dunaway said, holding out a wine goblet. "Would you pour me a little more wine?"

"Of course. I would be glad to," Janey replied with a practiced smile. "Red or white?"

"Red wine, of course. White wine is for women and sodomites. It isn't for real men."

Janey smiled. "Well then, by all means, it shall be red wine."

"Say, Doc, what did that feller say the gunmen's names was?" one of the other guests asked.

"I wouldn't call them gunmen," Dr. Dunaway replied. "After all, the word *gunman* has such a negative connotation."

"What would you call them, then?"

"I would call them gentlemen, who, by circumstances not of their own making, were challenged by unexpected events. And they met that challenge, quite admirably."

Janey approached Dr. Dunaway with a bottle of red wine.

"All right, *gentlemen* then. What was their names?"

Janey started to pour the wine.

"Jensen, I think. It was a father and son. Emmett and Kirby Jensen. They were—"

With a gasp, Janey poured wine onto Dr. Dunaway's trousers.

"Lil, watch what you're doing!"

"I'm . . . I'm sorry." She handed Dr. Dunaway the wine bottle, then turned and ran quickly from the parlor.

"Wait, you don't have to run away! I know it was just an accident!"

The other guest frowned. "What did you say to her, Doc?"

"Nothing that would make her run away like that. I don't know what that was all about."

Chicago Sue had never seen Janey act in such a way, so she excused herself and hurried to Janey's room. "Lil?" she called, knocking lightly on the door. She heard nothing from the other side of the door. "Lil, it's me, Sue. Please open the door, dear."

Janey opened the door, then turned and walked back into her room.

Sue followed her inside, then closed the door behind her.

"What's wrong, Janey?" she asked, using her real name. "Did Dr. Dunaway do or say something to upset you? If so, I'll make certain that he leaves tonight, and I won't let him come back until you get an apology and a guarantee that he won't do it again."

"No, no, he didn't do anything wrong. It's nothing like that," Janey said, waving her hand.

"Then what is it? What has upset you? Something has, and that's for sure."

"It's them. They are in Dallas. Oh, Sue, they've come for me. I know they have."

"Who? Who has come for you? Janey, are you in trouble with the law?"

"No."

"Then I don't understand. Who has come for you?"

"My father and my brother. I know they have come to take me back to Missouri. Oh, Sue, what can I do? I'll never go back to Missouri. I can't go back!"

"Are they downstairs now? If so, I'll go talk to them."

"No! They aren't downstairs. I'm sure that they don't know that I'm working here. At least not yet."

"Then, how do you know they are here?"

"Did you hear about the shooting in the Yellow Dog Saloon today?"

"Yes, everyone has heard about it. That's all anyone is talking about."

"That was them. The two men all the people are talking about . . . are my father and brother."

"How do you know?"

"Dr. Dunaway said that the shooters' names were Emmett and Kirby Jensen. That can't be a mere coincidence."

"Jensen? I thought your last name was Garner."

Janey sighed. "My last name is Jensen. I left Missouri with a man named Paul Garner, and even though we never got married, I took his name."

"Where is Paul Garner now? Perhaps he is the one who told your family where to find you."

"He's dead. He was caught cheating in a card game and was shot."

"Janey, if you don't want to go back with your father and your brother, there is no need for you to do so. You are certainly old enough to make up your own mind about such things."

"There's more to it than that."

"Oh?"

"Pa was away in the war and Kirby was running the farm all by himself. He did it from the time he was thirteen. And he did a real good job with it, too. He supported my ma and me. He was saving all the money he made to give to Pa when he came home from the war. Two thousand dollars. He hid the money—"

"And you took it." Sue's comment was more matter-of-fact than accusing.

"Yes. Paul talked me into doing it. He told me that he was an investor, and that if I gave him the two thousand dollars he could double it. I didn't really intend to steal it. I thought I would be able to pay the money back, with interest, before Kirby missed it. I even left a note in the empty jar when I took the money, promising to pay it back."

"But Paul didn't double the money, did he?"

"No, he lost it all. Or almost all. He still had some of the money left when he was shot, but the other card players— the ones who had been cheated by him—took the money and divided it."

"Would you like me to talk to your father and brother?"

"No! Please, no! They can't know that I'm in Dallas! And they especially can't know that I'm a . . . that I'm . . . here," she said, taking in her room with a wave of her hand.

Sue reached out to put her hand on Janey's shoulder. "Honey, you aren't the first girl to run away from home, and you aren't the first girl who took money from her family to finance her escape. And you aren't the first girl who ever wound up on the line." She smiled. "But you are the most beautiful of all the girls I have ever known in such a situation."

Janey smiled through her tears.

"Why don't you let me check around a bit? I won't mention you, and I'll see what I can find out. It may be that they are here for an entirely different reason. You didn't let anyone back in Missouri know you were coming to Dallas, did you?"

"No."

"Then, how could they possibly know you are here? I'm sure the fact that they are in Dallas is just a coincidence."

"They must not know about me, Sue," Janey said. "Please, don't say anything that would get them even suspicious."

"I promise, I'll say nothing about you."

Emmett and Kirby were having breakfast in the dining room of the Lone Star Hotel the next morning when Kirby saw a very attractive woman come into the dining room. She spoke briefly to the maître d', who pointed to their table.

Kirby leaned forward and whispered, "Pa, there's a real pretty woman comin' toward our table. I wonder if it's Fancy Lil."

"Who?"

"You know, the woman Doc and them were talkin' about yesterday. The one they said was so pretty."

Emmett chuckled. "What would make Fancy Lil, or any woman for that matter, come to our table?"

"I don't know, but here she comes."

"I'm sure you are just—" Emmett stopped in midsentence when it became evident that the woman actually was coming toward them. "Stand up."

"What for?"

"It's what a gentleman does when a lady approaches him . . . if he is sitting." Emmett stood up.

Following his father's example, Kirby stood as well.

"You would be the Jensens?" the woman asked. "Father and son, I believe." She smiled broadly.

"Yes, ma'am," Emmett replied. "What can we do for you?"

"Oh, you have already done it."

"I beg your pardon?"

"I understand that you killed Emerson Cox, yesterday."

"Yes, ma'am. It wasn't by intention. It was something that—"

"From what I hear, you had no choice. It was either kill him or be killed by him."

"Yes, ma'am. Something like that. Oh, would you join us, Miss . . ."

"Sue. Everyone just calls me Sue. Yes, I would have a cup of coffee with you, if you don't mind being seen with me."

"I don't understand. Why should we mind being seen with you?"

"I told you my name is Sue, but I'm better known as Chicago Sue." The woman smiled again. "That isn't my real name, of course. But women in my profession rarely give their real names."

"Oh." Emmett blushed just a little.

"So you can see why you might not want to embarrass yourself by being seen with me. If you wish to withdraw your invitation to sit with you, I will understand and think no ill of you because of it."

"Don't be silly, Miss Sue. The invitation stands." Emmett held the chair as Sue sat at the table, then he raised his hand to signal for a waiter.

"Yes, sir?" the waiter asked, arriving at the table. The expression on his face as he saw Sue indicated that he knew who she was and that he didn't approve of her being there.

"Coffee for the lady."

"Sir, as you are new in town, perhaps you don't know who she is. Are you sure . . ."

"That I want coffee for the lady? Yes, I'm quite sure. Please bring it."

"Yes, sir."

"I'm sorry. I shouldn't have come," Sue said.

"Don't be silly. You are welcome at our table. But I am curious. Why did you come?"

"The man you shot, Mr. Cox, beat up one of the young ladies in my employ recently. I had him arrested, and he swore that he would extract revenge. I can't be sure that is the only reason he returned to Dallas, but neither can I discount it. At any rate, thanks to you, I no longer have to be afraid of him."

"Does Fancy Lil work for you?" Kirby asked impatiently.

Sue gasped. "What? What do you know about Fancy Lil?"

"We know nothing about her," Emmett replied quickly. He smiled and shook his head. "I don't know what got into him for even asking such a thing."

"I know she is beautiful," Kirby said. "I heard someone in the saloon yesterday say that her face was so beautiful it would launch a thousand ships. I don't know what that means, but she must be some kind of beautiful for a man to say a crazy thing like that."

"Yes, Lil is a beautiful young woman, but then all my girls are . . . or they wouldn't be working for me."

Kirby smiled. "I'd sure like to see what she looks like."

"No, you wouldn't," Emmett said resolutely. "And we don't have time for such things."

"Anyway, it wouldn't be possible for you to see her now," Sue said. "She's away on a trip. I'm not sure when she'll be back."

"They asked about me?" Janey frowned.

"Not about you. The young one . . ."

"My brother."

"He asked about Fancy Lil. And he only asked because he heard someone talking about you in the Yellow Dog. Apparently, someone said that you were so beautiful that your face would launch a thousand ships." Sue laughed. "Now, who do you think would say such a thing?"

"Sounds like Dr. Dunaway."

"Of course, it's Dr. Dunaway. Apparently your brother was fascinated by the idea, and wanted to see someone whose face could do such a thing."

"What did you tell them?"

"I told them that you were away on a trip."

Janey twisted her hands in her lap. "Oh, Sue, what if they come here and see me?"

"I don't think they will. Your father strikes me as a bit of a prude."

Despite her concern, Janey laughed. "Yes, he is a prude."

"Do you really think your father would come to a place like this?"

"No, I don't think he would. But Kirby might."

CHAPTER 10

"I may not be here the next time you come," Janey said.

"What?" Big Ben raised himself up on one elbow and looked down at her lying beside him.

The cover came up only to her waist, leaving the rest of her bare body revealed to him. A bar of light slipped in around the edge of the drawn shade, falling upon her right breast and making it gleam in the light.

Ben frowned. "What do you mean you might not be here? Where would you be?"

"I don't know."

"Janey, that doesn't make sense." Since she'd told him her real name, he insisted on using it when they were together. "I mean, how can you say you aren't going to be here, but not have any idea where you will be?"

"It's just that I can't stay here any longer. I can't take the chance. They might find me."

"You can't take a chance on who finding you? Janey, are you in trouble with the law? If you are, I can afford a lawyer. Hell, I can afford an entire army of lawyers. I don't care what you did. I know I can get you out of it."

"No, it isn't that. I'm not in trouble with the law. It's my pa and my brother that I'm afraid of."

"Why are you afraid of them?"

"Ben, do you really think I want them to know that I wound up doing what I do?"

"I don't think of you in that way."

"Of course you do. How else can you think of me?"

"I can think of you as my wife."

Janey sat up in bed and looked at Ben with a surprised expression on her face. "What?" Her voice was so weak that she could barely be heard.

"I said you could be my wife."

Marshal Wallace found the Jensens in the hotel dining room. "If you two will come down to the bank, I'll see to it that you get your reward money. As it turns out, in addition to the five-hundred-dollar reward for Emerson Cox, there was another two hundred dollars bein' offered for Clarence Haggart. So the total comes to seven hundred dollars. That's a pretty good sum of money."

"Yes, sir, it is," Emmett said. "I wouldn't have killed the man for the money, but neither I nor my boy had any choice in the matter. What's done is done, and I have no regrets at taking the money."

Ben Conyers parked the surrey in front of the bank, and set the brake. "Wait here, I've got some business in the bank, but it'll only take a couple minutes," he said with a smile. "Then we'll go out to Live Oaks Ranch."

"Where is Live Oaks?" Janey asked.

"It's just north of Fort Worth. One hundred and twenty thousand acres of the finest land in Texas. You're going to love it there."

"I know that I will." She watched Ben tie off the team, then walk into the bank.

One hundred and twenty thousand acres, he had said.

She remembered making the vow never to be the wife of a farmer, but when she'd made that vow she was thinking about the forty acres she had lived on with her family.

The family that she no longer had.

As she was sitting in the carriage she saw the marshal approaching. She knew that, technically, Chicago Sue was violating a city ordinance by running a house of "entertainment," but she knew, too, that the ordinance was aimed at the rowdy, bawdy houses, more than it was at the Palace Princess Emporium, which actually passed itself off as a private club. Fights, stabbings, and even occasional shootings occurred in the bawdy houses. Such a thing had never occurred at the Palace Princess Emporium, and because of that, neither the marshal, nor any of his deputies, had ever made an official visit.

The marshal stopped at the corner and looked back as if waiting for someone. Appearing from behind the building, two other men joined him.

Recognition dawned and Janey drew a quick, alarmed breath. Her pa and brother were headed right past the surrey! No way they would not see her! She looked around in panic. What could she do?

"Marshal Wallace?" someone shouted.

Marshal Wallace held out his hand to stop her pa and her brother, then he turned his attention to the man who had called out to him. So did Emmett and Kirby.

At that moment, Ben came out of the bank, smiling up at Janey. "We're all set."

"Ben, it's them!" Janey hissed.

"What? It's who? What are you talking about?"

"Those two men down there with Marshal Wallace. That's my pa and my brother."

"Have they seen you yet?"

"No."

"Come back into the bank with me until they're gone. No, wait, they might be going to the bank." Looking around, he saw the Elite Dress Shoppe and smiled. "Come." He pulled her from the surrey. "We'll go into the dress shop. It's for sure and certain they won't be going there."

He lifted her down, then put himself between her and the men. "Stay in front of me and keep your head down."

Although it was only a few steps from the surrey to the dress shop, Janey held her breath and clenched her fists, waiting to hear her name called. She breathed a sigh of relief when they went inside.

"Yes, can I help you?" a female clerk asked.

"Do you have any ready-made dresses? Not everyday work dresses, mind you. I want something fine and beautiful, for a beautiful lady."

"Indeed we do, sir," the clerk replied.

"Good, then help her find something, would you? And you can take your time."

In the bank, the chief teller counted out seven hundred dollars and handed the money to Emmett. Emmett turned and gave half the money to Kirby.

"That is a great deal of money to be carrying with you," the bank president said. "I would be very happy to open an account for you."

Emmett nodded. "Thank you, but we won't be staying in town long enough to have an account. We'll be moving on today."

"I don't know where you are bound, but if you are looking for a good place to settle down, you won't find any place any better than Dallas."

"I'm sure Dallas is a nice town. But my son and I have itchy feet. I've seen the Atlantic Ocean. Now I have a hankering to see the Pacific."

The bank president didn't understand. "Why? Once you've seen one ocean, you've seen them all."

"The boy hasn't seen either ocean," Emmett said.

As his pa and the banker were talking, Kirby saw a newspaper lying on a table in the middle of the bank, and he walked over to glance at it.

MISSOURI BUSHWHACKER
TO BE TRIED IN SALCEDO
ELMER GLEASON RODE WITH
BLOODY BILL ANDERSON

Elmer Gleason, who is one of the most malevolent men ever to come out of the late war, has been captured in Salcedo. It is said that when he rode with Quantrill and Bloody Bill Anderson he kept a string of ears severed from the heads of his victims, be they man, woman, or child.

Although those who followed their conscience to fight for the South have been paroled, the villains who rode with Quantrill and Bloody Bill Anderson can never be forgiven. The trespasses of such men are so great that only He, who is the final arbitrator of the transgressions of those who have made their temporary journey upon this mortal coil, will be able to grant them final remission and absolution of their sins.

Trial for Elmer Gleason will commence on the 28th instant.

"Pa?" Kirby asked when they left the bank a few minutes later. "How long would it take for us to get to Salcedo?"

"I don't know. I don't know where Salcedo is or how far it is from here. Why do you ask?"

"We need to go there."

"We need to go to Salcedo? Why?"

"A friend of mine is in trouble there."

Emmett frowned impatiently. "What friend? And how come you're just now tellin' me this?"

"I didn't know about it until just now. I saw it in the paper while we was in the bank. We need to be there by the twenty-eighth of this month."

"You saw in the paper that you have a friend in trouble in Salcedo, and we have to be there by the twenty-eighth? What happens if we don't get there by the twenty-eighth?"

"It's more 'n likely, Elmer will get hung."

"All right. Who is Elmer?"

Kirby figured it was now or never. "Pa, there's somethin' me 'n you need to talk about."

"I'm sure there is." Emmett waited . . . impatiently.

"Well, I reckon it's about as good a time as any to tell you." Kirby took a deep breath. "Pa, the fella I killed yesterday . . . wasn't the first man I ever killed. I've been in some battles, quite a few of 'em, only there wasn't none of 'em big battles like the kind you fought."

Without expanding on his own role in the battles, he told of riding with Asa Briggs and being in fights at such places as Clark's Mill, Hartville, Pilot Knob, Glasgow, Lexington, and Newtonia.

"I was at Baxter Springs, too," Kirby said. "That's why I was a little hesitant about us goin' there. I was afraid someone might recognize me."

Emmett was shocked. "Boy, answer me, and I want you to tell me the truth. Did you burn any private houses or kill any innocent people?"

"No, Pa, we didn't. I will say that the Ghost Riders, that's what those of us who rode with Briggs called ourselves, from time to time joined up with Quantrill for some of the battles. And I've heard of some of the things he done, but Briggs was real particular about not killin' innocent people. And none of that ever happened on those few times Asa Briggs teamed up with Quantrill. Fact is, I don't think I woulda stayed with him if he had done anything like that."

"What you just told me has something to do with your friend Elmer?"

"Yes, sir. His name is Elmer Gleason, 'n he rode some with Quantrill and some with Bloody Bill Anderson. Then, toward the end, he rode with Asa Briggs, 'n that's when he become my friend. But now they got him on trial at Salcedo, on account of he rode with Quantrill and Anderson."

Emmett gave it some thought. "You say you want to go to Salcedo. What do you plan to do?"

"I'm not sure. But if we can figure out how to do it, I'd like to rescue him."

"It would mean violatin' the law."

"That might be true, Pa. But there's also such a thing as honor, ain't there? Seems to me, if I didn't try to save my friend, that would violate my honor."

Emmett looked at Kirby for a long moment, then nodded and put his hand on his son's shoulder. "You're right. There is such a thing as honor. But, I've got a feelin' you ain't told me ever'thing."

"No, sir. I reckon I ain't."

"Is it about your ma and your sister?"

"Yes, sir. You asked me why I wanted to kill Angus Shardeen, and what I told you about him killin' Kenny 'n his family and Merlin 'n his family is true, but that ain't the all of it. Ma didn't die in her sleep like I told you. She was killed by the Jayhawkers. Angus Shardeen is the one that shot her."

"Him in particular? Or one of his men?"

"It was him in particular, Pa, 'cause I seen him do it. I didn't have no gun or nothin', so there wasn't nothin' I could do. The only reason I joined up with Asa Briggs was 'cause

I wanted to go after Shardeen. I wanted to find him and kill him. But we never found him. That's why I say that if I find him, I'm goin' to kill 'im."

"Seems reasonable to me," Emmett said. "We'll just add his name to the list of Potter, Stratton, Casey, and Richards."

"Oh, and Pa, about the funeral for Ma? I lied to you about that, too. I told you that folks come from all over, but the truth is that the only funeral was the one that me 'n Janey give her. It was Janey that dressed her in her best dress, and I'm the one that dug the grave. Janey cleaned out the feedin' trough, the one that was used for the milk cows, and that's what we put Ma in. I'm sorry we didn't have somethin' a lot more fine for her."

Emmett nodded. "You know, I have a feelin' that your ma probably appreciated that a lot more 'n she would have if a whole lot of folks had showed up for it."

"Yes, sir. I kinda hope that's the way it is."

"What about Janey? Did she actually run off like you said?"

"Yes, sir, she did. But I can't hardly blame her. The same men that killed Ma used Janey, Pa. They used her bad. She left home right after we buried Ma."

"With the gamblin' fella?"

Kirby nodded. "Yes, sir."

"When you started tellin' the story, I thought it might be somethin' like that. I reckon now I don't hold it ag'in her so much that she left as I did. I reckon she felt like she had a good enough reason."

She might have had a good reason to leave, but she didn't have a good reason to take all our money with her, Kirby thought, but he didn't share that with his pa.

"I wonder where she is now?" Emmett asked. "I wonder if she is alive?"

* * *

"Oh, it's beautiful!" Janey was looking at herself in the mirror at the dress shop as she tried on one of the dresses.

Ben sat in a nearby chair. "Would you like it?"

"Oh, Ben, no. I mean yes, of course I like it. But I can't let you buy this for me."

"Why not? It isn't like I can't afford it."

"That's not the point."

"Of course it's the point. You like it, and I like seeing it on you." He looked at the clerk. "We'll take it."

"Wonderful. I'll just go get the ledger book and the cash box."

"They're gone," Ben said quietly after the clerk left.

Janey turned toward him. "How do you know?"

"I saw them leave the bank and walk down to the Lone Star Hotel. As soon as I pay the clerk, we'll leave town in the opposite direction."

"Oh, Ben, are you sure it will be safe? I don't know what I would do if they actually saw me."

"How long has it been since either of them saw you?"

"It's been four years since Pa last saw me, and three years since Kirby saw me."

"What were you wearing, then?"

"What? I don't know. Some sort of plain cotton dress, I think."

"Nothing like this," he said, taking in the dress she was wearing with a wave of his hand.

Janey looked down at the beautiful dress. "No, nothing like this."

Ben saw a hat with a veil, and he smiled and picked it up. "Put this on when we leave. The way you look now, you could bump right into them, and I doubt that either of them would recognize you."

Janey chuckled. "I think you might be right."

* * *

Kirby and Emmett rode into Waco on the twenty-seventh and went straight to the livery stable.

"What can I do for you gentlemen?" the liveryman asked, meeting them as they dismounted.

"We need to board our horses," Emmett said. "Is there a place we can leave our things from the pack animals?"

"Yes, sir. We got individual tack rooms you can rent for fifteen cents a night. For an extra nickel, you can rent a lock."

"Good, that's what we'll do."

"You goin' to be here long?"

"We'll be ridin' out tomorrow, but I plan to leave the two pack horses here for a while. Not sure exactly how long."

"Your horses will be a quarter apiece. That includes hay. Thirty cents if you want 'em to have oats."

"We'll want the oats," Emmett said. "How far is Salcedo from here?"

"It's about ten miles. Just follow the railroad south, and you can't miss it. Headin' that way, are you?"

"I thought we might take a look."

"It ain't that pleasant a town to visit if you want to know the truth of it. They's a bunch of Yankee soldiers down there right now reconstructin' us, 'n they've plumb took over the town. The mayor and the city marshal got no say at all. They got a Yankee captain that runs the town 'n a Yankee judge that makes the laws. The people o' the town ain't got nothin' to say about it."

"I thank you for the information."

"But you plannin' on goin' anyway, ain't you?"

"Yeah," Emmett answered. "We'll take the two saddle mounts tomorrow. Here's sixty cents for them."

"What about the pack horses?"

"I'd like to sell 'em, if you know anyone that might be interested."

The liveryman stroked his chin and examined the two

pack horses. "I might be. How much would you be askin' for 'em?"

"Fifty dollars apiece."

"I need to make a little money from 'em. I'll give you thirty dollars."

They settled on forty dollars apiece.

The liveryman gave Emmett the money. "I'll look after 'em real good until I sell 'em. Good luck in Salcedo."

Emmett nodded. "Thanks."

* * *

"What do you have in mind for tomorrow?" Emmett asked Kirby in their hotel room that night.

"I don't know, exactly, Pa. Maybe I could testify for him or somethin'."

"What would you say?"

"I'd say that I rode with him when I was with the Ghost Riders, and I never saw him do anything bad."

"I doubt that will help."

"Prob'ly not. But, Pa, he's a friend. I can't just turn my back on a friend now, can I?"

"No," Emmett said. "You're right to try and do what you can for a friend."

Emmett and Kirby followed the railroad south from Waco until they came to Salcedo, identified by a sign attached to the end of the depot, a small, red-painted, wooden building. Posted alongside the track was another sign.

CAUTION TO BRAKEMEN
NO SIDE CLEARANCE AHEAD

As they passed the depot they saw another sign that listed the passenger schedule.

NORTHBOUND TRAINS
11 AM 5 PM 11 PM
SOUTHBOUND TRAINS
9 AM 2 PM 9 PM

Leaving the track they had followed from Waco, they rode on into town where they passed a hangman's gallows in the middle of the street. They stopped to read a sign that had been nailed to the gallows.

AT TEN O'CLOCK TOMORROW MORNING
ELMER GLEASON
THE BUSHWHACKER BUTCHER
WILL BE HANGED
ON THESE GALLOWS

"You boys here for the hangin', are you?" asked a toothless old man.

"Have we missed the trial?" Kirby asked. "The paper said the trial was today."

"No, you ain't missed it. They'll be holdin' the trial at one o'clock today."

"I don't understand. This sign says Elmer will be hung tomorrow morning. How can they say that if he hasn't been found guilty."

"Oh, they'll find him guilty all right. They ain't no gettin' around that. You called him Elmer. He a friend o' yours, is he?"

"Elmer is what the name on the sign says, isn't it?" Emmett asked, speaking quickly before his son could reply.

The old-timer nodded. "Yeah, that's what the sign says, all right."

"Then that's why we called him Elmer. Where's the trial to be held?" Emmett asked.

"Onliest place it can be held." The old man pointed toward the largest building in town. "Right down there in the Scalded Cat Saloon. But iffen you're wantin' a drink, you'd best get it before one o'clock, 'cause that Yankee that's been appointed judge won't let Clyde sell any liquor while the trial is goin' on."

"Thank you for the information," Emmett said.

"Sorry 'bout your friend." The old man waved a hand as the two rode farther into town.

They passed the jail. Two armed soldiers were standing out front.

"Pa, do you think they'd let us see Elmer?"

"I don't know. But we won't know unless we try."

Dismounting, the two tied off their horses, then started across the street toward the jail.

One of the soldiers stepped out in front of them. "Where do you think you're goin'?"

"We want to talk to the prisoner," Kirby said.

"Why?"

"That would be between us and the prisoner," Emmett replied.

"Yeah? Well it don't matter what it's about, 'cause you ain't goin' to see 'im."

"Take their guns and let 'em see 'im," said the other soldier, a sergeant. "He'll be dead by a little after three today, anyway, so what's it goin' to hurt?"

"All right, Sarge. If you say so," the private said. "You boys give me your guns, 'n you can go on in."

Emmett and Kirby surrendered their pistols, then stepped into the office. Four men were playing cards around a desk, two civilians wearing badges and two soldiers. One of the soldiers had captain's bars on his shoulder board.

One of the men wearing a badge looked up. "What can I do for you?"

Kirby spoke first. "Marshal, the sergeant out front took our weapons and told us we could visit with the prisoner."

"Yeah? Why do you want to visit with him?"

"We're looking for someone and he might be able to tell us where to find him," Emmett said.

The marshal was quiet for a moment, then he nodded. "All right. Go ahead, but I'll tell you right now, he ain't much of a talker. We've been tryin' to get him to tell us if there's any more of Quantrill or Anderson's men down here, but he ain't told us nothin'."

"You goin' to talk all day or are you goin' to play cards?" one of the others asked. "I've got a good hand here, one that's goin' to get me back even."

"Go on over there and talk to him, if you want," the marshal said, pointing to the single cell at the back of the room.

Kirby walked to the cell. Elmer Gleason was lying on his bunk with his hands laced behind his head, staring up at the ceiling.

"Hi, Elmer," Kirby said.

"Damn, I thought that sounded like your voice." Elmer sat up and threw his legs over the side of his bunk. "What are you doing here?"

"I came to see you."

"Well, that was damn fine of you."

Kirby motioned to his pa. "Elmer, this is my pa."

Elmer walked over to stick his hand through the bars. "It's good to meet the boy's pa after all this time. He's always spoke high of you, but I'm sure you know that."

"He's a good boy," Emmett replied.

"Elmer, how'd you wind up here in jail?" Kirby asked.

"I got drunk."

"Drunk? They put you in jail for bein' drunk?"

"Not exactly just for bein' drunk. What happened was, I was just passin' through town 'n I stopped in at the Scalded Cat for a couple o' drinks. Well, it was a lot of drinks, 'n I got drunk 'n wound up tellin' that I rode with Quantrill. I figured, this bein' a Southern town, there wouldn't be no problem with it. Turned out they was a lot of Yankee soldiers in the saloon alistenin' to me, 'n the next thing I knew, I was arrested and brought here."

"Why would they arrest you for that? There's no paper out on any of the men who rode with Quantrill, is there?" Emmett asked.

"Not that I know of, except maybe Archie Clement," Elmer said. "But I don't think that matters. They want me, and they've got me."

"All right. You've visited with the prisoner long enough," the marshal said. "We've got to get him ready for the trial."

"We'll be at your trial," Kirby said.

"I appreciate it. And it was real nice of you two to drop by."

CHAPTER 11

"Hear ye, hear ye, hear ye! This here trial is about to commence, the honorable Daniel Gilmore, presidin'," the bailiff shouted.

The judge stepped up from the back of the saloon and took his seat behind a table being used as the judge's bench. He adjusted the glasses on the end of his nose, then cleared his throat. "Would the bailiff please bring the accused before the bench?"

The bailiff, who was leaning against the side wall, spit a quid of tobacco into the brass spittoon, then walked over to the table where Elmer was sitting. "Get up, you," he growled. "Present yourself before the judge."

Elmer approached the bench.

"Elmer Gleason, the charge against you is that you rode for that butchering, thieving, raping bushwhacker Quantrill," the judge said. "How do you plead?"

"Quantrill never raped nobody," Elmer said. "It was only them Jayhawkers that ever done any rapin', 'n they done plenty of it, I can tell you."

"You aren't here to make a speech. I'm going to ask you again, how do you plead?"

Keith Davenport, the attorney appointed to represent

Elmer, stood up behind the table he'd shared with his defendant. "Your Honor, if it please the court."

"You got somethin' to say to this court, Mr. Davenport?" the judge asked.

"Yes, Your Honor. Quantrill conducted all of his operations in Kansas and Missouri."

"What does that have to do with anything?"

"Well, Your Honor, we are in Texas. Even if Mr. Gleason is guilty of murder and looting, it didn't happen in this state. Either Kansas or Missouri is the state that should be trying this case. We don't have jurisdiction to try it here."

"Your Honor, if I may?" the prosecutor spoke up quickly. "Everybody knows that Quantrill spent a winter right here in Texas. That's all we need to give this court standing."

The judge nodded. "Your point is well taken, Mr. Taylor."

"But Your Honor, these were his own people. Even if he was here, you know that neither Quantrill, nor by extension, my client, would have done any murdering or thieving while they were here."

"None that we know of, Your Honor," Taylor countered. "But that doesn't matter anyway. We're trying this defendant for being one of Quantrill's riders, not for any specific act of murder or robbery he may have done. Therefore, the fact that Quantrill was once in Texas, and that this defendant was with him, is all that is required to put this case under your jurisdiction."

The judge slapped his gavel on the bench again. "You are right, Mr. Prosecutor. Mr. Davenport, your motion for dismissal is denied. This case shall proceed."

"Very well, Your Honor."

"How do you plead?" the judge asked again.

Before Elmer got a word out, his attorney spoke. "Your Honor, my client pleads guilty and throws himself upon the mercy of the court."

"What? Wait a minute!" Elmer shouted. "Judge, I ain't pleadin' guilty to nothin'!"

"You have already confessed your guilt, Mr. Gleason," the judge replied.

"The hell I have. That was my lawyer that just done that. It warn't me."

"I'm not talking about your lawyer's plea. I'm talking about your own declaration of guilt. Did you, or did you not, confess before several assembled men in the Scalded Cat Saloon, that you rode with Quantrill?"

"I wouldn't put it that it was a confession," Elmer said. "It was mostly just me drinkin' 'n tellin' war stories."

"In the telling of those stories, did you say you rode with Quantrill?" the judge asked again.

"I ain't confessin' to nothin'," Elmer said.

"Very well," the judge said. "Clerk, change Mr. Gleason's plea from guilty to not guilty."

"Your Honor, may I have a moment with my client?" Davenport asked.

"You may."

Elmer returned to the table and sat down.

Davenport spoke quietly. "Mr. Gleason, I think you are making a big mistake here. If you plead guilty, the judge might show some mercy in his final decision. On the other, if this goes to trial, and you're found guilty, you'll get none."

"So what if I am found guilty? What's he goin' to do to me, tell me I can't vote or somethin'? Hell, I ain't never voted for nobody nohow. I ain't got no truck with politicians."

"Do you really not know? No, how could you? You have been in jail all this time."

"What is it I don't know?"

"Mr. Gleason, I'm afraid that a gallows has already been constructed. You are scheduled to be hanged at nine o'clock tomorrow morning."

"What? How the hell can they already say I'm goin' to be hung, when I ain't even been tried yet?"

"That's the point I'm trying to make. Don't you understand? This trial is totally immaterial. The judge has already made up his mind to find you guilty. Your only hope is to plead guilty and beg for mercy."

"The hell I will. I ain't beggin' that Yankee judge for nothin'."

"Very well, Mr. Gleason. But don't say I didn't warn you." Davenport looked back toward the bench. "Your honor, the conference with my client is concluded."

"Have you reconsidered your plea, Mr. Gleason?" the judge asked.

"No, I ain't. I said I was not guilty 'n that's what I'm standin' by."

"So you say, and so it shall be. Mr. Prosecutor, are you prepared to make your case?" the judge asked.

"I am, Your Honor."

"You may call your first witness."

"You men over there," the prosecutor said, pointing to three men sitting in the front row. All three were wearing the uniform of the US Army. "You are my witnesses. Stand up and hold up your right hand."

The men did as they were instructed, and the clerk swore them in.

"Now," the prosecutor said. "Did any of you hear this man say that he had ridden for Quantrill?"

The witnesses answered in the affirmative.

"We all heard him say that," added the only sergeant within the group.

The prosecutor turned back toward the judge. "Well, there you go, Your Honor. All three of these men have just sworn that they heard the defendant admit to being one of Quantrill's riders during the war."

"Mr. Davenport, do you wish to question any of these men?" Judge Gilmore asked.

"Yes, Your Honor. You, Sergeant"—Davenport pointed to the soldier who was wearing three stripes on his sleeves—"what, exactly, did you hear my client say?"

"He said that he rode with Quantrill 'n Bloody Bill Anderson, 'n that him 'n others that rode with 'em kilt a bunch of Yankee ba— Aw, Judge, I don't want to say what he called 'em. Not where women might hear."

"I think we can figure it out. He said that?" Judge Gilmore asked.

The sergeant nodded. "Yes, sir. That's what he said."

"You may continue your cross, Mr. Davenport."

Davenport asked the witness, "Did he say, specifically, that he had killed civilians?"

"Like I told you, all he said was that he had kilt a bunch of Yankee . . . you know."

"Sergeant, did you take part in any battles in the late war?" Davenport asked.

"Yes, sir."

"And did you kill anyone?"

The sergeant smiled. "Oh, I reckon I musta kilt me at least five or six of the Secesh sons of bit—" He halted in mid-word, then corrected himself. "Uh, that is, I figure I kilt five or six of the enemy soldiers."

"Five or six, by your own count?"

"Yeah."

"Sergeant, do you consider yourself a murderer?"

"What? No, it was war. If you kill someone in a war, that ain't murder."

"If you kill someone in a war, it isn't murder. Is that what you are saying?"

"You're damn right that's what I'm sayin'."

Davenport looked pointedly at Elmer. "That's good to hear. No further questions."

"Redirect, Mr. Taylor?" the judge asked.

"Sergeant, did you kill any civilians during the war?" Taylor asked.

"No, sir. Ever'one I kilt was a soldier."

"Thank you. I'm through with this witness."

"Does defense wish to call any witnesses?"

"Your Honor, I have no—" Davenport started, but he was interrupted.

The entire court was surprised when Kirby suddenly stood up and shouted, "Me, Your Honor!"

Angrily, the judge rapped his gavel on the table. "Order in the court! Here, what do you mean by interrupting my court in such a way?"

"I'd like to be a witness on behalf of the defendant."

"Do you know anything about this, Counselor?" the judge asked Davenport.

"No, sir."

"Do you have anything that would qualify you to bear witness to this case?" the judge asked Kirby.

"I do, Your Honor."

"Get to the bottom of this, Mr. Davenport," the judge ordered.

The defense attorney walked to where Kirby was still standing. "Young man, do you know the defendant?"

"Yes, sir, I know him."

The marshal waved his hand. "Your Honor, this man came to visit the prisoner in the jail last night."

"Why didn't you say anything about it?" Judge Gilmore asked.

"I didn't say nothin' 'cause I didn't have no idea he was goin' to want to be a witness. He never told me anythin' about that last night. He and another man just visited with the prisoner, is all."

The judge looked at the gallery. "Is the other man who was with him present in this court?"

"Yes, sir. He's sittin' right there beside him." The marshal pointed toward Emmett.

"Is it your wish to be a witness as well?" Judge Gilmore asked.

"No, sir. I never met the man before last night," Emmett replied. "I couldn't say one way or the other whether or not he's guilty."

"You." Gilmore pointed toward Kirby. "Who are you, and what information do you have that you think might be pertinent to this case?"

"My name is Kirby Jensen, Your Honor. And, during the war, I rode with the defendant."

Several gasps of surprise came from those who were present to watch the trial.

The judge rapped his gavel. "Are you telling the court that you rode with Quantrill?"

"I rode with Quantrill, Bloody Bill Anderson, and Asa Briggs," Kirby replied.

"Bailiff, swear this man in," the judge ordered.

The bailiff signaled for Kirby to come forward, then he held forth a Bible. "Do you swear to tell the truth, the whole truth, and nothing but the truth, so help you God?"

"I do."

"Now, Mr. Jensen, I ask you again," Judge Gilmore said. "And this time you are under oath. Did you ride with Quantrill, Anderson, Briggs, and this man, Elmer Gleason?"

Kirby knew that he hadn't ridden with Quantrill or Anderson in the scope of the question as it was being posed by the judge. But at times a merging of the guerrilla groups had occurred, and from that perspective, he could, truthfully, answer the question in the affirmative. "I did, Your Honor."

"Marshal Ferrell, take this man's gun, and place him under arrest."

"I'm not wearin' a gun," Kirby said.

"Make certain," the judge said.

The marshal checked him closely. "He's tellin' the truth, Judge. He ain't got no gun."

"Very well. He may testify as a witness, but he is also a defendant. This has become a double trial. Mr. Jensen is being tried along with Mr. Gleason, and any verdict reached for one shall apply to both. Put him at the defendant's table alongside Gleason."

"Yes, sir," the marshal said.

"Mr. Davenport, you may present your case now," the judge said.

"I call my first witness, Mister—" Davenport looked directly at Kirby. "Excuse me, what did you say your name was?"

"Jensen. Kirby Jensen."

"Would you take the stand, Mr. Jensen?"

As Kirby sat in the witness chair, the judge looked over toward him. "I would remind the witness that you are already sworn in."

"Yes, sir," Kirby replied.

"Mr. Jensen, you have stated that you rode with the Southern guerrillas."

"Yes, sir."

"How old are you?"

"I'm seventeen."

"Seventeen? Isn't that a little young? How old were you when you began riding with the guerrillas?"

"I was fifteen."

"And you have ridden, specifically, with Mr. Gleason?"

"Yes, sir."

"Did you ever see Mr. Gleason kill an innocent civilian, or a woman, or a child?"

"No, sir, I never did."

"Thank you. Your witness, counselor."

Taylor stood up. "Have you ever killed anyone, Jensen?"

"Yes, sir."

"No further questions."

"The witness is dismissed."

Kirby started, "Your Honor, the only ones I ever killed—"

Rap! The judge cut him short with the sharp rap of his gavel. "I said you are dismissed."

"Your Honor, redirect?" Davenport called quickly.

Judge Gilmore sighed audibly. "Very well, Counselor, you may redirect."

Davenport stood in front of Kirby. "You were about to make a statement. You may make it now."

"I was just goin' to say that the only men I've ever killed were trying to kill me," Kirby said.

"Have you ever killed any women or children?"

"No, sir."

"Thank you. No further questions."

"Marshal Ferrell, return this man to the defendant's table," the judge ordered.

The marshal stepped up to Kirby and walked him to the defense table.

"Mr. Davenport, will Mr. Gleason take the stand in his own defense?"

"You're damn right I will," Elmer said.

Davenport sighed. It was obvious that he would have rather his client not take the stand.

"Can I say somethin' before you start askin' questions?" Elmer asked.

"You may."

Elmer pointed to Kirby. "Kirby warn't nothin' but a boy when I first seen 'im. Hell, he ain't more 'n a boy now. But boy or not, he's a good man. I never seen him do nothin' wrong. Even comin' here, he come to help me 'cause he read about it in the paper. That's the kind of person he is. He coulda just kept on agoin', 'n none of you woulda ever even heerd of 'im. So I'm askin' you now, whatever happens to me, I want you to leave the boy out of it. Like I said, he never done nothin' wrong." Elmer nodded at Davenport. "All right, you can ask your questions now."

"Mr. Gleason, why did you ride with such men as Quantrill and Anderson?" Davenport asked.

"We was at war," Elmer said. "And I felt like it was the right thing to do."

"Did you gain personally from riding with the guerrillas? By that, I mean did you enrich yourself by looting and pillaging?"

"I'm not sure what pillagin' means. But if you're askin' did I ever keep any of the money we took from time to time, the answer is no."

"In your mind, would you say that the only reason you participated in the war was from a sense of duty to your state?"

"Yes. I was just a soldier doin' my duty," Elmer said. "I know they was lots of men that rode for the Blue who done just as bad, and some of 'em done worse 'n we did. I ain't holdin' that against 'em, now that all the fightin' is over. It was a war, 'n I reckon they was thinkin' it was their duty, just like them of us that rode with Quantrill or Anderson. But they ain't none of them looked on as criminals like we are, 'n there ain't nothin' right about that. Nothin' at all."

"Thank you, Mr. Gleason. I have no further questions, Your Honor."

"Cross, Mr. Taylor?"

Taylor stood up, then walked over to stand in front of Elmer. He folded his arms across his chest, leaned forward, and stared directly at Elmer. "You were just a soldier doing your duty, you say?" he asked sarcastically.

"Yes, sir. That's what I done, all right. I done my duty."

"Tell me, Mr. Gleason, would you consider the burning and sacking, and the murder of civilians in the town of Lawrence, Kansas, as just doing your duty? You do recall that, don't you?"

Elmer didn't respond.

"Were you present when Quantrill attacked Lawrence?"

Elmer still didn't answer.

Taylor turned to the judge. "Your Honor, I request you order the defendant to answer the question."

The judge nodded. "The defendant will answer the question."

"Were you present on that day, Mr. Gleason?" the prosecutor asked again.

"Yes, sir, I was there," Elmer replied, the words so quiet that they could barely be heard.

"Speak up please. Loudly enough so that everyone can hear you. Were you present for the sacking of Lawrence, Kansas?"

"Yes!" Elmer said loudly.

"Old men and young boys were rounded up and murdered. Houses and businesses were burned," Taylor said. "Is that duty, Mr. Gleason?"

"It was war. I ain't proud of it, but it was war."

"Your Honor, I am finished with this man," Taylor said.

"Redirect, Mr. Davenport?" the judge asked.

"No, Your Honor."

"Then defense may make a closing argument."

"Your Honor, Marshal Ferrell is a Texan. But he's the only person of authority who is a Texan. I know that you and the appointed mayor and the prosecutor, and just about everyone else with any power in this town, in this state, and throughout the South, are Yankees, sent here for reconstruction.

"But if you would just look out into the gallery you'll see men and women who were born and raised here. They are good people, Your Honor, Southerners by birth, and, during the late unpleasantness, they were Southerners by loyalty. If you ask them to pass judgment against these men, simply because they fought for what they believed in, they're goin' to tell you that Mr. Gleason 'n the boy sittin' there beside him, were no more than soldiers doing their duty in a war that, by its very existence, pitted friend against friend, brother against brother, and in some cases, father against son. Because of that, the war was particularly brutal. It's going to take several generations before all hard feelings go away. As you have come to live among us, I ask that you pass judgment on this matter with some feeling for the sensitivities of those who, by appointment and not by election, you now represent."

The gallery broke into cheers and applause.

Judge Gilmore was surprised by the spontaneous reaction of the gallery and, angrily, he banged his gavel until they were quiet.

"You forget, Mr. Davenport, that the state of Texas is in subjugation to the laws of the United States. I do not give a whit about the laws or the sensitivities of the people of

Texas. I am here to perform the duty for which I was appointed." He looked over toward the jury. "You gentlemen of the jury. Do you go along with these folks in the gallery? Do you think these men who rode with Quantrill were nothing more than soldiers doing their duty?"

The men of the jury looked at each other, spoke quietly among themselves, then one of them spoke out. "Yes, sir, Your Honor. That's exactly what we think."

"Are you telling me that if I asked this jury for a verdict right now, it would be not guilty?"

"Yes, sir. We've spoke about it, 'n we've already come to a verdict. The verdict is they ain't neither one of 'em guilty."

Again, everyone cheered. Kirby, Elmer, and Davenport smiled broadly.

Judge Gilmore pounded his gavel on the makeshift bench until the gallery was quiet. "Your celebration is premature. I have not called for a verdict, nor shall I call for a verdict. This jury is dismissed," the judge said angrily.

Davenport objected. "Your Honor, if you empanel another jury, and hold this trial again, you are going to get the same result. No jury of this man's peers is going to find him guilty for doing his duty."

"You don't understand, Mr. Davenport," the judge said with an evil grin. "I have no intention of calling another jury. I will make the decision myself."

"What?" Davenport bellowed. "Your Honor, you can't do that! That's not legal."

"I can and I will. I find both defendants guilty as charged. You are free, Mr. Davenport, to appeal my decision, but in all candor I must tell you that an appeal would be nothing but a waste of time, for the sentence will have been long carried out before any decision can be made on the appeal. Elmer Gleason and—" He glanced toward the prosecutor. "What's the boy's name?"

"Jensen, Your Honor. Kirby Jensen," Taylor said.

"Elmer Gleason and Kirby Jensen, please present yourselves before my bench while I administer the sentence."

"Your Honor, we beg for mercy," Davenport said quickly.

"No, we don't, by God!" Elmer said sharply. He glanced over at Kirby. "I don't know about the boy. I'll let him make his own decision."

"I'll not be beggin' for mercy," Kirby said.

Judge Gilmore took off his glasses and began polishing them. He put them back on, hooking them carefully over his ears. He looked at the two defendants standing before him and cleared his throat. "Elmer Gleason and . . ." Again he paused.

"Kirby Jensen," Taylor added quietly.

"Elmer Gleason and Kirby Jensen, you have been tried before me and have been found guilty of the crime of riding with the butcher Quantrill, and aiding and abetting in the atrocities of murder, arson, and robbery that he visited upon innocent people. It is the sentence of this court that you be taken from this courthouse and put in jail where you will spend your last night on this mortal coil. At ten o'clock of the morrow, you will be taken to the gallows already constructed, and there, both of you will be suspended by your necks until you are dead."

"No!" someone in the court shouted. "You can't hang them, you Yankee crook! They ain't guilty of nothin' but bein' soldiers!"

"Marshal," the judge said. "Arrest the man who just made that outburst, and hold him in contempt of court!"

Marshal Ferrell stood and looked out over the gallery. "Arrest which man, Judge? I didn't see who it was."

To a man, every person in the courtroom was quiet.

"Who was it?" the judge asked. "Who made that outburst?"

There was no response to his inquiry.

"All right, all right!" the judge said. "You Rebels think you are putting one over on me, do you? But we'll see who has the last laugh tomorrow when these men are legally executed. Court is adjourned." He rapped the gavel once more.

The judge, the bailiff, and the prosecutor left the saloon by the back door.

"Damn, Marshal Ferrell, you ain't really goin' to hang 'em, are you?" someone called.

"You heard the judge. He give me the order. There ain't nothin' I can do about it."

"Kirby, what 'n hell did you do that for?" Elmer asked after the two men were taken back to the cell.

"I wanted to do what I could to help."

Elmer shook his head. "Well, you didn't have to go so far. Damn, boy, just showin' up woulda been enough. But what you done is got yourself caught up into the same mess I'm in."

To Elmer's surprise, Kirby flashed a big smile. "Yeah, I did, didn't I?"

Elmer frowned at him. "Boy, have you gone daft on me? Ain't you got no idea as to what's goin' to happen?"

"I know exactly what's going to happen," Kirby said. "That's why I got myself put in here."

"You got yourself put in here? Of a pure purpose?"

Kirby nodded. "Of a pure purpose."

CHAPTER 12

At that same moment, Emmett was at the livery, looking at a horse advertised for sale.

"He's a real good ridin' horse," the liveryman said. "It was rode by one of the officers in John Bell Hood's Division. Iffen you know'd anything about Hood, you know he had only the best horses."

"Yes, I know all about General Hood," Emmett replied. Hood, though an aggressive and effective officer for most of the war, had gotten many of his men slaughtered in an ill-advised frontal attack at Franklin, but Emmett didn't mention it.

"Do you have a saddle for sale as well?"

"I do, sir. I do indeed."

"Saddle him up, then ride him around the corral for me. I'd like to see him work, if you don't mind," Emmett said.

"Yes, sir. I would be happy to."

A few minutes later, the horse was saddled, and the liveryman rode him in compliance with Emmett's request. During the ride, Emmett observed the horse closely, listening to the rhythm of the gait and checking for equal striding in distance and time on the ground. He watched how the horse held his head and observed the footfalls to see if the animal showed any indication of sore feet. The horse passed his rather thorough examination.

Satisfied, Emmett said, "I'll take him. Please have this horse, and the two that I am now boarding with you, saddled and ready for me to pick up by seven o'clock this evening."

"Yes, sir. They'll be ready for you." The liveryman was happy to have made the sale.

"In the meantime, I need to rent a horse and a buckboard for a couple hours."

"All right. I'll get that ready for you right now."

A few minutes later, Emmett drove the buckboard from the livery down to the depot where he examined the rather high growth of weeds along the track. He decided they were in just the right place as they stretched just far enough to be perfect for his purpose.

Checking the time, he saw that it was just before five o'clock, which meant a train would be arriving shortly. He walked onto the depot platform and waited until the north-bound train arrived. The arrivals and departures of the trains in the small railroad town of Salcedo caused much excitement and were always well attended. Emmett aroused no attention as he stood in the crowd, watching the disembarking and boarding passengers. Pulling his watch from his pocket again, he timed exactly how long the train stood in the station before it departed.

Four minutes and thirty-five seconds after the train arrived, it was on its way again. That was good. If the train's stay was much shorter, he wouldn't have time to do what he planned to do. Staying any longer would increase the possibility of being discovered.

He would time the nine o'clock train as well, then do an average of the two times, but for now, he had another stop to make.

Returning to the buckboard parked with several others, surreys, and wagons, he drove to the opposite end of town to Sikes' Hardware Store. A small bell attached to the door rang as he pushed it open and entered the store. "What is the longest chain you have?" he asked the clerk who'd hustled over to see what he needed.

"They are all the same length, twenty feet. But it doesn't really matter. You can make the chain as long as you need it to be," the clerk replied. He picked up the end of one of the chains and showed it to Emmett. "There are hooks on each end, so all you have to do is connect them together. How long a chain do you need?"

"I'm going to snake some sunken logs out of the Colorado River, so I'm thinkin' I'm goin' to be needin' at least a hunnert and fifty feet."

"That won't be any problem. I can give you eight, twenty foot lengths. It's going to cost you forty dollars, though. Do you think those sunken logs are worth forty dollars?"

"I know some people up North who'll buy 'em. The lumber from 'em makes real shiny floors."

Emmett made the purchase, then loaded the chains onto the buckboard.

Shortly after nine o'clock, Emmett worked alongside the track in the dark. The train that just left had been in the station for six minutes and ten seconds. He could hear a dog barking. From somewhere a bit more distant, a baby began to cry. The most prominent sounds, however, came from the Scalded Cat Saloon—the tinkling of a piano, the shriek of a woman, followed by the loud guffaw of several men. From the corral of the freight wagon company came the bray of a mule.

A cat came walking up, looking at him curiously, its eyes shining in the dark.

Emmett looked back into the weeds, but could see no evidence of the work he had just done. So far, not one person had seen him and that was very good. He didn't need to be arousing any suspicions.

Once his work was finished, he walked back to the jail and went inside.

One man, a soldier, was sitting at the desk. He looked up from the game of solitaire he was playing. "If you're lookin' for the marshal, he ain't here. Him and the deputy is out makin' the rounds." He wasn't one of the three witnesses at the trial, nor had he been there when Emmett and Kirby had come to see Elmer.

"I'm not here to see him. I'm here to see my son."

"Your son?"

"Kirby Jensen, one of your prisoners, is my son," Emmett said. "I'd like to visit him."

The soldier examined one of the stacks of cards, then turned up a card, and seeing that he could use it, applied it to another stack.

"That's cheatin' you know."

"Yeah, but I ain't cheatin' no one but myself. Leave your gun here 'n go on back. Seein' as he's goin' to get his neck stretched tomorrow, I don't see no reason why you can't tell him good-bye."

"Thanks."

Emmett lay his gun on the desk, then stepped into the back. Elmer was sitting on one of the bunks, and Kirby was on the other. They looked up as Emmett approached the cell.

"Hi, Pa," Kirby said easily.

"Kirby, Elmer, I've got somethin' I'm goin' to need you to do. First of all, make certain that you are awake at eleven o'clock tonight."

"Hell, there ain't goin' to be no problem with that," Elmer said. "If this here is to be my last night on earth, I sure don't plan to be awastin' it by sleepin'."

Emmett chuckled. "This won't be your last night."

"You've got it all worked out?" Kirby asked. "Is it just the way we planned?"

"Yes."

"We'll be ready."

*   *   *

At a quarter till eleven that night, Emmett took the three saddled horses to the back of the apothecary, two buildings down the alley from the jail. From there, he walked out to the track, hoisted one end of the chain he had stretched out along the track two hours earlier, and pulled it over to the back of the jail.

He looked in through the barred window. "Kirby?"

"Yeah, Pa. We're here."

Emmett poked the chain in through the bars. "Take this, wrap it around all four bars, then pass it back out to me."

Kirby did as Emmett instructed, and taking the end his son had given him, Emmett connected the hook through one of the links. "Now, when you hear the train whistle, get over there to the corner, as far away from the wall as you can."

"All right."

With the chain wrapped around the bars, Emmett hurried back to the depot and waited.

He could hear the train before he could see it, first the whistle, then the chugging sound. As it came around the bend, about a quarter mile down the track, he could see the light, the sheltered gas flame set in a polished reflector to cast a beam before the engine. It was little over a minute before the engine reached him, so heavy that the ground shook as it rolled by. Steam was gushing from the drive cylinders and glowing coals were falling from the firebox. The engineer, with a pipe clenched tightly between his teeth, was leaning out of the open window of the cab, staring straight ahead.

After the engine came the tender, the express car, the baggage car, then the four passenger cars, lit from inside. The train squealed and screeched to a stop. It was still, but it wasn't silent as overheated journals snapped and popped, the water in the boiler bubbled, and escaping steam made a quiet hiss.

Grabbing the end of the chain and bending low, Emmett stayed in the shadows as he hurried up to the rear of the train. There, he wrapped the chain through the coupling, connecting it back on itself. That done, he ran back to the apothecary and, untying the horses, held the three sets of reins in his hand and waited.

The engineer gave two short toots on the whistle, and a gush of steam spewed forth as he opened the throttle.

Emmett watched the chain lift from the ground and grow taut. He heard the loud crashing sound as half of the back wall of the jail was pulled down and hurried up the alley with the three horses. "Let's go!" he called, as he saw Kirby and Elmer climbing out through the hole.

"Hey! What's going on back here!" the soldier shouted, coming from the front. Seeing the two men escaping through the collapsed wall, he pulled his gun and fired, but Kirby and Elmer were already out of harm's way.

"Here's your gun." Emmett handed Kirby's pistol and gun belt to him.

"And here's your horse." Emmett handed Elmer a set of reins.

The three men galloped down the alley, onto the main road, and out of town.

"Did you steal this horse?" Elmer asked the next morning. "The reason I ask is, do I need to be worryin' 'bout someone hangin' me for horse stealin'?"

"Here's the bill of sale," Emmett said. "I've already signed it over to you."

Elmer shook his head. "I ain't got no money to pay you for it. Fact is, I ain't got no money at all."

"Here." Emmett gave him fifty dollars in cash.

"No, sir." Elmer shook his head, pushing the money away. "I didn't say that hopin' for some money."

"I know you didn't, Elmer. But the way I look at it, it's my way of sayin' thanks for lookin' after my boy while I was gone."

"It warn't exactly that way. When we was ridin' together,

he was lookin' out for me half the time 'n I was lookin' out for him the other half the time."

"All right. Then this is for the times you was lookin' out for him."

Reluctantly, Elmer took the money. "You've kept me from gettin' hung, you've given me a horse, 'n you give me some money. I don't know what to say. Like as not, we ain't never goin' to run into each other again. I don't know how I'm ever goin' to be able to pay you back."

"Then don't try," Emmett said.

Elmer nodded, then got mounted. "I do have a piece of information you might be interested in. I heerd where Shardeen is."

"What?" Kirby asked excitedly. "Where?"

"I only heerd where he is. I cain't say for sure 'cause I didn't see him for my ownself. And I don't know if he's still there or not. But, last I heard, he was in Dorena."

"Pa?"

Emmett nodded. "All right. We'll go to Dorena."

Emmett and Kirby surveyed the town as they rode in. Kirby had seen many small towns like this since he left Missouri. At this point in his life he didn't realize it, but he would see many hundreds more in the years to come.

Dorena wasn't that unlike Salcedo, except there was no railroad. The single street was faced by false-fronted shanties, a few sod buildings, and even a handful of tents, straggling along for nearly a quarter mile. Just as abruptly as the town started, it quit, and nothing but open road and empty prairie existed ahead.

The street was baked hard as a rock from the summer heat. The sun was still yellow and hot in early September. In the winter and spring, the street would be a muddy mire, worked by the horses' hooves and mixed with their droppings so that it became a stinking, sucking pool of ooze.

The biggest and grandest structure in town was a building with a sign stretching across the front that read EL CABALLO Y EL TORO CANTINA. It also had a picture of a beer mug on one end of the sign and a liquor bottle on the other. Across the street from the building, they saw a man leaning up against the post that was supporting the roof of a leather store.

"Tell me, mister," Emmett said, pointing to the building. "Would that be a saloon?"

"It's a cantina," the man said. "That's Mex for a saloon."

"What does the name mean?"

"The horse and the bull."

"Thanks."

They rode over to the cantina, dismounted, and tied their horses off at a hitching rail. The shadows gave an illusion of coolness inside, but it was an illusion only. The dozen and a half drinking customers had to keep their bandanas handy to wipe the sweat from their faces.

Over the last few months, Emmett had taught Kirby how to enter a saloon. "We're lookin' for men we aim to kill," Emmett had explained. "As time goes on 'n more and more people find out what we are about, we're likely to have men looking for us as well, for one reason or another. So you need to know how to enter a saloon, and it needs to become a habit with you so's that you do it without even thinkin' about it."

Following the lesson his pa taught him, Kirby was on the alert as they stepped inside. He and Emmett surveyed the place with such calmness that the average person would think it no more than a glance of idle curiosity. In reality, it was a very thorough appraisal of the room. They checked out who was armed, what type of weapons they were carrying, and if they were wearing their guns in the way that showed they knew how to use them.

Less than half of the drinkers were even wearing guns, though there was a man standing at the other end of the bar who was armed. His gun was in a holster that was kicked-out in the way that indicated he might know how to use it.

The walls of the saloon were decorated with game heads and pictures, including one of a reclining nude woman. Some marksman had improved the painting by putting a single bullet hole in a most appropriate place.

Several large jars of boiled eggs and pickled pigs' feet sat on the bar. A stairway led to an upstairs section at the back. Kirby could see rooms opening off the second-floor landing as he watched a heavily painted saloon girl take a cowboy up the stairs with her.

The upstairs area didn't extend all the way to the front of the building, which meant that the main room of the saloon was big, with exposed rafters below the high, peaked ceiling. Nearly a dozen tables were full of drinking customers.

The piano player wore a small, round derby hat and kept his sleeves up with garters. He was pounding away at the piano, though the music was practically lost amidst the noise of a dozen or more conversations.

"What'll it be, gents?" the barkeep asked as he moved down toward them. He wiped up a spill with a wet, smelly rag before draping the rag over his shoulder.

"A couple beers," Emmett said.

"That'll be ten cents," the bartender said as he put two mugs on the bar before them. Emmett slid a dime across to him.

A bar girl sidled up to Kirby. She was heavily painted and showed the dissipation of her profession. "Oh, honey, you are a sweet one, you are."

He was embarrassed by her attention. It wasn't the first time he had ever been in a saloon, but it was the first time he had ever actually been approached by one of the bar girls.

"Whoa, Becky," said a man at one of the tables. "You sure you know what you're doin' there? You don't want to be robbin' the cradle, do you? Seems to me like you'd be better off goin' after the old one."

Several customers laughed.

"Yeah," one of the others said. "The old one looks like he ain't had a woman in near twenty years, and the young 'un there, why, I bet he ain't never had no woman."

"Would you like a drink?" Kirby asked Becky.

"A drink? Well, yes, honey, I think I would like a drink."

Kirby turned to the bartender. "Sir, would you give the lady whatever it is she would like to drink?"

The bartender took a bottle from beneath the bar and poured it into a short glass. "That'll be a quarter."

"Kirby, it would appear that your lady friend has expensive taste," Emmett said with a smile as Kirby put a quarter on the bar.

Becky picked the glass up and tossed the drink down in one gulp. Then, smiling, she put her hand on Kirby's shoulder. "Why don't you come upstairs with me, honey, and let me make a man out of you?" she suggested.

Kirby had no idea how old she was, but he was sure that she was older than Miss Margrabe would be.

Wherever Miss Margrabe was.

"No, thank you, ma'am," Kirby said. "I bought you a drink because you were being nice to me. But, I don't want to do anything else."

"Now, just a minute here, boy." The man at the other end of the bar stood up straight. "I think you just insulted my woman."

"I'm sorry, ma'am, if I insulted you," Kirby said.

"Honey, you didn't insult me." Becky turned her head back toward the man who had spoken. "And Streeter, I ain't your woman."

"Sure you are," Streeter replied with an evil grin. "You're anybody's woman that pays you. I've paid you, so that makes you my woman."

"Well you ain't payin' me now."

"Are you sassin' me, woman? 'Cause I ain't goin' to stand for no sassin'."

Becky put her hands on her hips. "I'm not sassin' you. I just told you that I'm not your woman, and I'm not."

"I say you're sassin' me, 'n if you don't apologize to me right now, why I might just have to knock some manners into you."

"I'm sorry," Becky said, showing genuine fright.

"You're sorry all right. You are sorry, washed up, and ought to be glad that anyone at all would talk to you."

"Mr. Streeter, why don't you leave the lady alone?" Kirby said. "She told you she's sorry."

"What?" Streeter nearly shouted the word in surprise that the young boy would talk to him like that. "What did you just say to me?"

"I asked you politely to leave the lady alone."

"First of all, she ain't no lady. But I reckon you're too dumb to know the difference." Streeter's tone of voice had gotten very challenging. With such a sharp edge to it, all other conversation in the bar had stopped. Everyone watched to see what was going to happen next.

"Miss Becky, I'd be real pleased if you would have another drink with me." Kirby put another quarter on the bar.

"Boy, you're beginnin' to put a burr under my saddle, you know that? But I'm goin' to let it pass for now. Because you're new in town, maybe you don't know who I am."

"The lady called you Streeter, so I reckon that's your name."

"That's it. Emile Streeter. I reckon you've heard of Emile Streeter."

Kirby shook his head. "No, sir, I can't say as I have."

"Tell 'im who I am, Jake," Streeter said to the bartender.

"Mr. Streeter, why don't you leave him alone. He's just a boy."

"He's a boy with a smart mouth, and he needs to be taught a lesson," Streeter said. "Tell 'im who I am."

"Young man, Mr. Streeter is a man of some notoriety in these parts. He is quite good with a gun." Jake pointed to the nude painting. "You might have noticed the bullet hole between the young lady's legs. Streeter put it there."

"You shoot paintings, do you?" Kirby asked. "Do they ever shoot back?"

"Boy, I've had about enough of you!" Streeter said.

Kirby smiled at the man. "Mr. Streeter, it looks like me 'n you got off on the wrong foot. If I've put a burr under your saddle, I apologize. Bartender, I would like to buy a drink for Mr. Streeter."

"Uh-uh," Streeter said, shaking his head slowly. "This has come too far for you to back out now."

"Streeter, for God's sake, leave him alone. Can't you see he's tryin' to apologize?" the bartender said as he put another whiskey in front of Streeter.

"You stay out of this, Jake, or I'll be settlin' with you after I'm finished with the boy here."

"Streeter, that's enough! What has gotten into you? Leave the boy alone!" Becky turned to Kirby. "Honey, I'm sorry I come up to you like I did. Believe me, I would have never done so, if I had had any idea that this fool was going to carry on like this."

"Well now, boy, ever'one seems awful worried about you, so I tell you what. If you'll get down on your knees and ask me, please, not to shoot you, this can all be over. Otherwise, me 'n you's goin' to have us a little dance." Streeter laughed, a high-pitched, insane sound. "Me 'n you's goin' to dance. I like that."

"Please do it," Becky begged. "He'll kill you."

"Don't worry. He's not going to kill me," Kirby said, his voice flat and amazingly calm.

"You don't understand," Becky said desperately.

Kirby had had just about enough. "No. Streeter doesn't understand. And one of the things he doesn't understand is that I'm not a boy."

"Hey you, old man," Streeter called to Emmett.

For the entire interplay between Streeter and Kirby, Emmett had done nothing but sip his beer and watch, almost dispassionately. He looked Streeter in the eye. "Are you talking to me?"

"Yeah. Looks like me 'n this boy is about to have us that little dance we was talkin' about. And you're in the way."

"I'm not in the way." Emmett coughed.

"What do you mean, you're not in the way? You're standin' right there behind the boy, ain't you?"

"I suppose I am, but it doesn't matter. You heard what he said. He's not a boy. And you won't get a shot off."

"What? What do you mean I won't get a shot off, you old fool?"

"Kirby?" Emmett said.

"Yes, Pa?"

"Pa? You mean this is your boy?" Streeter asked, laughing.

Emmett didn't move. "This bragging fool seems to be pretty proud of what he done to that painting. But it looks to me like there's room for a couple additions."

Kirby glanced up at the painting of the nude woman and smiled. "Yes, sir. I know what you mean."

"Why don't you finish the job he started?"

In a flash, Kirby pulled his pistol, fired twice, and put the pistol back in its holster. Both breasts in the painting had been punched through by perfectly placed bullet holes.

"What the hell?" someone gasped. "I didn't even see him draw!"

"That's impossible!" another said. "There cain't nobody shoot that good and that fast!"

"Now, Streeter—I believe that's what you told me your name was—shall we get this over with?" Kirby asked.

Eyes wide and mouth open, Streeter reached out with a shaking hand, picked up the glass of whiskey still on the bar, and drained it. He put the empty glass down, then turned to look at Kirby.

Kirby smiled at him, but absolutely nothing young nor innocent was in the smile. It was old as time and as dangerous as the open mouth of a hissing rattlesnake.

"I . . . uh . . . I," Streeter stammered. Glancing at the others in the room, his face mirroring his absolute fear, he held an empty hand out toward Kirby. "Don't shoot. Don't shoot." He started toward the door.

"Come back, Streeter. Next time you want to show off!" Becky called to him, and everyone in the saloon laughed.

Streeter pulled his hat down more firmly on his head and pushed through the swinging batwing doors without so much as a look back.

"Lord almighty! I ain't never seen nothin' like that!" someone said.

"I wouldn't be surprised if Streeter don't never come back here," another said.

"If he don't never come back, it'll be the town's gain, and we owe this young fella a vote of thanks." Jake drew two more mugs of beer and set them on the bar. "These are on the house. What brings you two to town?"

Kirby turned back to the bar. "I'm looking for Angus Shardeen."

The smile left the bartender's face. It wasn't only the expression that changed. The tone of his voice changed, as well. "A friend of yours, is he?"

Kirby shook his head. "Believe me, Angus Shardeen is no friend."

Jake relaxed, and the smile returned. "Good. If he was your friend, I'd be thinkin' a lot less of you than I am now."

"Where is he?"

"Nobody knows. He kilt a young cowboy about a month ago, then he skedaddled out of here."

"Most likely, he went back up to Kansas," Becky said. "I believe that's where he come from."

"Yes ma'am. That is where he came from," Kirby said.

"Why are you lookin' for him, if I might ask?" Jake inquired.

"He killed my ma," Kirby replied.

Jake nodded. "I reckon I can see why you're lookin' for him then. How long do you plan to stay in town?"

Emmett answered the question. "Long enough to finish this beer."

Kirby and his father left Texas and rode north through Indian Territory, following the Washita River. Changing colors, it snaked out across the gently undulating prairie before them—shining gold in the setting sun, sometimes white where it broke over rocks, at other times shimmering a deep blue-green in the swirling eddies and trapped pools, and sometimes running red with clay silt.

Late in the afternoon, a rabbit hopped up and bounded down the trail ahead of him.

"There's supper," Emmett said.

Kirby drew his pistol and fired. A puff of fur and spray of blood flew up as the rabbit made a head-first somersault, then lay perfectly still.

They stopped for the day and made camp under a growth of cottonwoods. Emmett started a fire while Kirby skinned and cleaned the rabbit, then skewered it on a green willow branch and suspended it over the fire between two forked limbs.

Except for Emmett's occasional coughing, they were quiet, staring at the cooking rabbit.

Finally, Kirby broke the silence. "Pa, it's been five days, 'n you ain't said nothin' about what happened back there in Dorena with that Streeter fella."

"No, I reckon I haven't," Emmett replied.

"How come you ain't said nothin'?"

Emmett coughed again before he answered. "I thought you were handlin' things pretty well."

"I figured you musta thought that, else you woulda been tellin' me what I shoulda done."

"Kirby, I'm not goin' to be here forever. Fact is, I ain't

goin' to be here much longer at all, 'n you're goin' to be on your own. A fella with a skill like yours, word's goin' to get around. When that happens, people will be comin' for you, wantin' to try you out to make a name for killing Kirby Jensen."

"How can that be, Pa? There ain't anybody even knows my name."

"They will know your name, and soon. I pretty much gave you your head back there because you need to know how to handle yourself. And like I said, you did pretty well."

"I woulda killed him if it hadn't been for you comin' up with a way that let me avoid it," Kirby said.

Emmett coughed again, then reached out to turn the skewer, allowing another side of the rabbit to face the fire. The aroma of the cooking meat permeated the campsite.

"I reckon you might have," Emmett said. "And truth to tell, you woulda been justified. But, anytime you can find a way to do what needs to be done without killin', it's best."

"Yeah, I can see that. I'm glad you come up with the idea about shootin' holes in the woman's . . . you know."

Emmett laughed.

"Pa, that woman . . . Becky. She wanted me to go upstairs with her."

"Yes, I heard her ask."

"I thought about it."

"Did you?"

"What would you have said if I had done it?"

"I wouldn'ta said nothin' at all. They's some things so private that nobody else can tell you one way or the other what to do. Why didn't you go upstairs with her?"

"I ain't never been with a woman before," Kirby said. "Leastwise, I ain't never been with a woman in . . . that . . . way . . . the way she wanted to be. I sorta figure that if you're goin' to do somethin' like that with a woman, then maybe it ought to mean somethin'."

"That's a good way of lookin' at it. Rabbit's done."

Emmett lifted the golden brown piece of meat off the fire, seasoned it with their dwindling supply of salt, then lay it on a flat rock and split it right down the middle, head to tail. He gave half of it to Kirby.

Kirby began eating, pulling the meat away with his teeth even when it was almost too hot to hold.

After his supper, he stirred the fire, then lay down alongside it, using his saddle as a pillow. He stared into the coals, watching the red sparks ride a heated column of air high up into the night sky. Still glowing red and orange, they joined the jewel-like scattering of stars.

"Pa?"

"Yes, son?"

"Just so you know, when I find Shardeen, I won't be lookin' for a way to avoid it, no more 'n I reckon you'll be lookin' for a way not to kill them men you're after."

"I wouldn't expect you to," Emmett said.

CHAPTER 13

Three months of dusty cow towns and wide open spaces proved fruitless. The Jensens had not found Shardeen, nor had they located any of the men Emmett was looking for. At the moment, they were in the middle of nowhere, with no particular place to go. Well, it wasn't actually *nowhere*. They knew they were somewhere in Kansas. Or at least, they *thought* they were in Kansas.

It was a cold and very gray day.

"Pa, what's the date?"

"I don't rightly know," Emmett admitted. "Late October, early November, maybe?"

"It's got to be later than that. I don't think it would be this cold unless it was at least December."

"Could be that you're right," Emmett agreed. "You know what I'm thinkin'?"

"What's that?"

"I'm thinkin' that the next town we see, we might want to put in for the winter."

Kirby frowned. "You got 'ny idea where that next town might be?"

"Not the slightest. But that fella we run into a couple days ago said the Arkansas River was in front of us, and it can't be more 'n a day's ride away. Once we get to the river, all we'll have to do is follow it. It's goin' to eventually take us to a town."

"All right," Kirby agreed. "Let's find the river."

During the night, snow began to fall. It came down softly, silently. It was quite a surprise when Kirby awoke the next morning to find himself almost completely buried in snow. He looked around for his father but didn't see him.

"Pa?" Kirby called. "Pa? Where are you?"

"Hrmmph!" Emmett grunted and suddenly sat up from under a blanket of snow. The white stuff was in his hair, his eyebrows, and hanging from his beard.

Kirby laughed.

"What's so funny?"

"You look like a snowman."

Emmett looked around. "We had quite a snowfall, didn't we?"

"Yes, sir, I would say that we did."

"Have you checked on the horses?"

"No, sir. Seemed like the first thing I should check on was you."

Emmett chuckled and nodded. "Good idea. Let's find the horses."

Both men stood, stomped and shook the snow from themselves, and dug through the snow to find their saddles. They walked to where the horses stood, knee deep in snow. They looked cold and miserable.

"Wow, these are going to feel awfully cold to the horses when we put them on," Kirby said as he held up the saddle, still dripping with snow.

Emmett laughed. "It's going to be just as cold on our butts."

Kirby laughed as well. "Yeah, I hadn't thought about that."

Big Ben Conyers' ranch, Live Oaks, lay just north of Ft. Worth. The gently rolling grassland and scores of year-round streams and creeks made it ideal for cattle ranching. Two dozen cowboys were part-time employees, and another two dozen were full-time employees. Those who weren't married lived in a couple long, low bunkhouses, white with red roofs. The married couples lived in small houses adjacent to the bunkhouses, all of them painted green with red roofs. A cookhouse large enough to feed all the single men, a barn, a machine shed, a granary, and a large stable were also on the property.

The most dominating feature of the ranch was what the cowboys called "The Big House." A stucco-sided example of Spanish Colonial Revival, it had an arcaded portico on the southeast corner, stained-glass windows, and an elaborate arched entryway.

In the parlor, Ben watched as Janey decorated the Christmas tree, adding gaily colored pine cones to the red and green ribbon laced all through it. The many small candles would be lit once all the decorations were in place.

"I do believe that is the prettiest Christmas tree I have ever seen," Ben said.

Janey turned toward him. "It's easy for me to say that. This is the first Christmas tree I've ever seen, anywhere."

"Well then, I'm glad that your first tree is so fine. It'll be even prettier when all the gifts are under it."

"Ben, please, no gifts for me," Janey said.

"What do you mean, no gifts for you? Of course there will be gifts for you. Why, what is Christmas without the presents?"

"But, I have no present for you."

"You know what I want from you. It would be the most wonderful present I can imagine."

Janey didn't respond.

"Marry me, Janey. I couldn't ask for a greater present than to have you as my bride."

"Ben, I can't."

"Why can't you? You aren't already married, are you?"

"No, I'm not married. But you know why I can't. You are a very important man here. Maybe if we lived somewhere else . . . someplace where there is less a chance that I would be recognized, I could consider it. But you know, without a doubt, that there are people who know who I am . . . and what I am . . . was. If word would get around, it would be terribly embarrassing. I couldn't do that to you."

"Some may recognize you, that is true. But how would they recognize you unless they, too, had visited the Palace Princess Emporium? If that was the case, it would be just as embarrassing to them as it would be to me. At any rate, I assure you, Janey, nobody will ever dare say anything about it to my face, nor would they even take a chance on me learning that they had spoken of it behind my back."

"But what if they do? What would you do? Would you kill them?"

"If I had to."

"That's what I'm afraid of."

Ben walked over to Janey and pulled her to him in an embrace. "I don't want you to ever be afraid of anything. As long as you are with me, you don't have to be. If you don't want to get married yet, I'll just enjoy whatever part of you, you are willing to share. I love you, Janey. I don't care about your background."

"Oh, Ben, why couldn't I have met you before?" Janey asked, her eyes welling with tears.

"Nothing that happened before now matters. Only *now* matters, and we are together now. So we'll just enjoy what we have, and we'll see where it leads. If I'm the luckiest man in the world, it will lead to matrimony."

As Janey lay in bed that night, she thought of their conversation. Ben had told her that he didn't want her to ever be afraid of anything, but she was afraid. She was pregnant. Ben had accepted the idea that it was his baby, but she couldn't be certain. She wasn't sure exactly how long she had been pregnant, but she had been with at least two other men a few days before she had left Dallas with Ben.

That had been in August. If the baby was born any later than April, she would know that it was Ben's. If it was born in April, or earlier, it might not be.

January 1866

Emmett and Kirby were wintering in Delphi, Kansas, a small town on the Arkansas River near the border of Kansas and the territory of Colorado. Although they still had most of the bounty money that had been paid for Cox and Haggart, they opted to take jobs through the winter to preserve what money they had.

Emmett worked for the company that operated the ferry across the river, while Kirby had agreed to become a deputy for City Marshal Darrell Wright.

"We don't have much call for lawin' here," Marshal Wright told him when he was hired. "About all we ever have to do is pick up a drunk now 'n then. Most of the time, the onliest reason we pick 'em up is 'cause they sometimes pass out on the street. In the winter time, they could likely freeze if we didn't bring 'em in."

It was the cold that worried Kirby the most—not for himself, but for his pa, who was exposed to the weather on the ferry boat. He tried to get his father to quit. "It's not costin' us all that much to live. I'm makin' enough as a deputy to pay the boardin'house . . . and the boardin'house is feedin' us. With your lung 'n all, it can't be good for you to be out in the cold all the time."

"I ain't so damn feeble that my own son has to take care of me," Emmett said. "The work ain't hard, 'n I can wrap up in a buffalo robe that keeps me warm. You don't be worryin' about me."

"I just wish you'd quit, is all."

"And do what? Sit around with my thumb up my ass all the time?"

Kirby laughed out loud. "Well, I don't guess I'd want to see you doin' that, exactly."

"I would damn sure hope not. Now, you do your work 'n I'll do mine, if you'll just let me be."

"All right, Pa. But if it gets too much for you, remember, it ain't somethin' you have to do."

The boardinghouse where they stayed was the Homestead House, owned and run by Mrs. Pauline Foley, an attractive widow in her mid-forties.

"I made biscuits this morning, Emmett," she said when Emmett and Kirby came down for breakfast. "I know how you like to sop them through sour cream and sugar."

"You're too kind to me, Mrs. Foley."

"Oh please, won't you call me Pauline?"

"I would be honored to, Pauline. I just don't want to be too forward."

"You could never be too forward," she said, smiling as she poured coffee into Emmett's cup.

As they left the boardinghouse to go to their respective jobs, Kirby smiled at his father. "Pa, I think Mrs. Foley likes you."

"She's a business woman. She's just being nice to her customers, that's all."

"Uh-huh. But she's nicer to you than she is to Mrs. Simmons or Mr. Clark."

"Boy, you know what your problem is?"

"What?"

"You see too many things that aren't there."

"She likes you, Pa. You know she does," Kirby said with a broad smile.

Emmett sighed. "She might, but I'm not encouragin' it. We'll be leavin' here, come spring. I don't want to do anythin' that might cause her some hurt. She's a good and decent woman, and she don't fit in with my plans. You do understand that, don't you, boy?"

Kirby nodded. "Yeah, Pa, I do."

"Then please, don't do or say anything to her that might give her the wrong idea."

"I won't, Pa."

"I'll see you at supper."

Kirby nodded. "Try 'n stay warm out there on the water today."

One of the advantages of working as a deputy was Kirby's access to WANTED posters. He had mixed feelings about those he had seen on Angus Shardeen. On the one hand, he was glad that Shardeen was being regarded as a wanted outlaw . . . and not a hero as was James Henry Lane. On the other hand, because Shardeen was a wanted man with a price on his head, it was quite possible that someone else might find and kill him before Kirby had the satisfaction of doing so.

As he was looking through the WANTED posters, he was surprised to see his and his father's names, not on a reward poster, but on a document that rescinded their wanted status.

> *Notice is hereby given that the Wanted status of Elmer Gleason, Emmett Jensen, and Kirby Jensen has been withdrawn. Reason for revocation: an appeal filed on their behalf by Keith Davenport has been granted, and Daniel Gilmore has been removed from the federal bench due to malfeasance.*

Kirby smiled as he read the document, and he gave a silent thanks for the honesty and integrity of the lawyer who, even though he would probably never see his clients again, had done the right thing.

On an early spring day, Kirby was in the bank to deposit a county check for the sheriff's office when his landlady came in with two men. "Hello, Mrs. Foley."

As soon as he spoke to her, he saw that the expression on her face was one of terror. He also saw the reason for her terror. Both men who had come into the bank were armed, and one of them had his gun stuck into her back.

"This is a holdup!" shouted one of the two men.

"Here, what are you doing?" the bank teller called. "You let that woman go!"

"We will, soon as you fill this bag with money." The second armed man stepped up to the teller's cage, passing a cloth bag over the counter.

With shaking hands, the teller began taking money from his drawer, and sticking it into the cloth bag.

"Hurry up!" the robber urged.

"There's no need for you to hurry, Mr. Montgomery," Kirby said easily. "These two men are under arrest. I'm going to ask you to let Mrs. Foley go . . . now."

"What did you say?"

"You may have noticed the star on my jacket. I'm the deputy marshal here, and I'm putting both of you under arrest."

The outlaws laughed.

"Are you tryin' to be funny, mister?" one asked.

"No, I'm quite serious."

"You may have a deputy's star, but you ain't got no sense. Maybe you're too dumb to notice, but you don't have a gun in your hand, and we do."

"That's true," Kirby agreed. "But you're pointing your gun at Mrs. Foley, and your friend is pointing his gun at the bank teller. Neither one of you are pointing your guns toward me. And that's where you have made your mistake."

The one holding his gun to Mrs. Foley glanced at his partner. "Can you believe this guy?"

"I'm going to ask you one more time to let Mrs. Foley go," Kirby said, his voice quiet and calm as it was the first time he'd addressed them.

"What the hell! Let's just shoot him and get it over with!" The one holding Mrs. Foley seemed to be the leader.

Kirby was watching both men very carefully. The instant the man holding Mrs. Foley moved his pistol, Kirby drew and fired twice, one on top of the other. Both would-be bank robbers went down, each of them with a bullet in his forehead, dead before realizing they were in danger.

Shocked by the sudden and unexpected turn of events, the scream that Mrs. Foley tried to make died in her throat. By the time she looked toward Kirby, he had already returned his pistol to his holster. The bank teller, with an expression of utter shock on his face, was still holding the half-filled bag of money.

"You can put the money back in the drawer now, Mr. Montgomery," Kirby said. "Oh, and the sheriff would like to deposit this county check."

The two bank robbers were identified as Frank Morris and Seth Crandall, former Jayhawkers. Within a week, word of Kirby Jensen's unbelievable performance had traveled up and down the Arkansas River and beyond.

Some declared the story fanciful since only two eyewitnesses could claim that they had seen it happen. It didn't seem possible that anyone could have actually done what was being told.

"I'm proud of you, son," Emmett said. "You are already getting a taste of what I told you was going to happen. You are beginning to build a name for yourself. I do believe there's goin' to come the time when ever'one in the West knows who you are."

"I'm not sure that's somethin' I want, Pa," Kirby said.

"I'm not goin' to lie to you. It's goin' to be a burden. But as long as you use this skill and talent for the good, you'll go to bed ever' night with a clear conscience."

Had Kirby known how close he was to Angus Shardeen, he would have turned in his badge and gone after him. The raiding Jayhawker was camped less than fifteen miles west of Delphi, just across the line in Colorado.

"Both of them?" Shardeen replied after being told about what had happened in the bank in Delphi. "Morris and Crandall were both killed?"

"Yes," Bartell said. "By that same kid that shot Tim in the hand."

"Why didn't you do somethin'?" Shardeen asked.

"I was outside with the horses. When I heard the shootin' 'n Frank 'n Seth didn't come out, I figured it was best I not give myself away. I just went across the street into the saloon. That's when I heard what happened."

"He said he was comin' for you, Angus," Tim said.

"One man? And a kid at that?"

"Yeah, but he ain't like any other kid I've ever heard of. Frank 'n Seth both had their guns already drawed when they went into the bank," Bartell said. "Jensen shot 'em both."

"A tiny bank in a one-horse town, 'n Morris and Crandall get themselves kilt. Next time I'll send better men."

Rebecca Jean Conyers was born on April 15, 1866. The date of her birth did not preclude Ben being her father, but neither did it absolutely establish that he was. She had red hair, and Ben was quick to point out that his mother's sister had been redheaded.

Janey promised that she would marry him but asked for a little time to recover from the birth.

* * *

On the day that Becca was three months old, Janey was standing in the nursery holding her.

"Do you want me to give the baby a bath?" asked Juanita Gomez, the nanny Ben had hired to look after the baby.

"Not yet," Janey said. "Juanita, I'm going to be gone for a while. I want you to look after Becca while I'm gone."

"El bebé hermoso que yo velo," Juanita said. Then she repeated it in English. "The beautiful baby, I will watch."

"I know you will. Oh, would you have Mr. McNally bring the surrey around? I'm ready to leave."

"Sí, Señora." Juanita knew that Janey and Ben weren't married, but she called her Señora anyway.

Janey waited until Juanita was gone, then she kissed the baby again. Her eyes shining brightly, Becca smiled up at Janey.

"Good-bye, my sweet child. I know you don't understand now, and you may never understand. But what I'm doing is best for you and for your father. I'll never see you again, but I swear to you, I'll never forget you."

Janey put the baby in her crib, then raised up with tears streaming down her cheeks.

When Ben returned later in the day, he went into Rebecca's room, picked her up, and kissed her on the forehead. "If you aren't the most beautiful baby in the entire state of Texas, I'll eat my hat. Without salt," he added with a laugh. He put her back in her crib and looked over toward the nanny. "Juanita, where is Janey?"

"She said she will be gone for *unos pocos días.*"

"She's going to be gone for a few days? Where did she go? Did she say?"

"No, Señor."

"That's damn odd," Ben said.

Puzzled by Janey's strange and unexpected disappearance, Ben went into the parlor. On the fireplace mantel was an envelope that bore his name.

Even more puzzled and a little worried, he hurried over to retrieve the envelope, then tore it open to read it:

> *Dear Ben,*
>
> *Please forgive me, but I cannot stay here. I am afraid that to do so can do nothing but cause you embarrassment and pain. I'm leaving Becca with you. You have enough love and means to give her a wonderful life. I have nothing to offer her but my love, and on the day she learns of my past, my love won't be enough. Then, I will be an embarrassment to her, as well, and I don't think I'd be able to bear that. Tell her that I died, for it would be much better if she grows up believing that.*
>
> *I do love you, Ben, but it is a love that cannot be. If you love me, I beg of you, make no effort to find me. Instead, give all your love to our daughter.*
>
> *Janey*

Ben went back into the nursery and picked up the baby again. He took her into the library, locked the door behind him, and walked over to sit in the big leather chair. There, the six-foot-four, 330-pound man held his baby close to him and wept.

The days had grown warmer and it was time to move on. Emmett and Kirby said good-bye to the friends they had made in Delphi.

"I wish you would stay," Pauline said. "You wouldn't have to work on the ferry boat anymore. You could help me run the boardinghouse."

Emmett took her hands in his, raised them to his lips, and kissed them. "Pauline, you are a very sweet woman. My son and I were lucky to have met you, and are very grateful for the way you made us feel so welcome. But we can't stay here. We have to go on."

"But why, Emmett?"

"I'm not sure I can answer that. At least, not in the way you could understand."

"Is it because you are dying?"

"What?"

"I've heard that kind of cough before, Emmett. I don't know how much longer you have, but I know I could make you happy in what time you do have left."

"Pauline, you don't know how much I want to do this. But I have sworn to do something, and I must do it. If I stayed here, I wouldn't actually be with you, not really. The part of me that needs to do this thing would take over my heart and soul, and I would have nothing left. You are too good a woman to have to live with that."

With tears in her eyes, Pauline nodded. "I'll always remember you, Emmett. And I'll keep you in my prayers."

"I'm blessed to have met someone like you. It's just too bad that we didn't meet under different circumstances."

"Pa, would you have stayed there?" Kirby asked as they rode out of town. "I mean if you wasn't lookin' for them men, and I wasn't lookin' for Shardeen. Would you have stayed with Mrs. Foley?"

"I don't know, Kirby. I might have," Emmett admitted. "She's a very good woman, and a man can't ask for more than to have a very good woman." He was quiet for a while, then added, "Your ma was a very good woman, too, and I didn't do right by her. I had no business goin' off to war. I was old enough that I didn't really have to go. If I had been home when the Jayhawkers came through—"

"You'd more 'n likely be dead now," Kirby said, interrupting him in mid-sentence. "There were too many of 'em, Pa."

"Maybe. But about Pauline. She deserves a man who will stay with her, and look after her. You 'n I both know that I can't do that. Not with this lung fever I got."

"Maybe when we get farther west and into dry country, it'll get better like the doc said," Kirby suggested.

"Maybe," Emmett said, but there was very little conviction in his voice.

CHAPTER 14

They rode west and north for several days across seemingly endless plains of tall grass with no sign of human habitation, then they came across a pile of rocks that had not been arranged by nature.

"Pa, look," Kirby said, pointing to the rocks.

They pulled up.

"Some of the mountain men I met told me about them," Emmett said. "That's what I been looking for."

"What's it here for?"

"It's a sign telling travelers that this here is the Santa Fe Trail. North and west of here will be Fort Larned, and north of that will be Pawnee Rock."

"Pawnee Rock? What's that, Pa?"

"Pawnee Rock would be a landmark, Pilgrim." The voice came from behind them.

Turning toward the one who had spoken, Kirby saw, without a doubt, the dirtiest man he had ever seen. The man was dressed entirely in buckskin, from the moccasins on his feet to his wide-brimmed leather hat. A white, tobacco-stained beard covered his face. His nose was red and his eyes twinkled with mischief. He was mounted on a spotted pony and had two pack animals with him.

"Ain't no pilgrim, old-timer," Emmett said, low menace in his tone.

"Reckon you're right, at that."

"Where did you come from?" Emmett asked.

"I been watching you two pilgrims from that ravine yonder," he said with a jerk of his head. "You don't know much about traveling in Injun country, do you? It's best to stay off the ridges. You two been standin' out like a third titty." The old mountain man shifted his gaze to Kirby. "What are you staring at, boy?"

The boy leaned forward in his saddle. "Be darned if I rightly know."

The old man laughed. "You got sand to your bottom, all right." He looked at Emmett. "He your'n?"

"My son."

"I'll trade you for 'im," he said, the old eyes sparkling. "Injuns will pay right smart for a strong boy like this 'n."

"My son is not for trade, old-timer."

"Tell you what. I won't call you pilgrim, you don't call me old-timer. Deal?"

Emmett smiled and nodded. "Deal."

"You don't know where you are, do you?"

"Yeah, I know."

"Do you now? And just where would that be?"

"We're somewhere west of the state of Missouri, and east of the Pacific Ocean."

The old man chuckled. "In other words, you're lost as a lizard."

"If you got no particular place to go, you ain't never lost," Emmett said.

Again, the old man laughed. "Well now, you do have a point there. You got names?"

"I'm Emmett. This is my son, Kirby."

"Folks call me Preacher."

"You're a preacher?" Kirby asked, surprised at the response.

"Didn't say I was a preacher. I said that's my handle. That's what folks call me."

Kirby laughed out loud.

"What you laughin' at, boy?"

"I'm laughin' at your name."

"Don't scoff. It ain't nice to scoff at a man's name. If I wasn't a gentle type man, I might let the hairs on my neck get stiff."

"Preacher can't be your real name."

"Well, no, you right about that, but I been called Preacher for so long, that I've near 'bout forgot my Christian name. So, Preacher it'll be. That or nothin'."

"Well, it was nice talkin' with you, but I reckon we'll be goin' on now, Preacher," Emmett said. "Maybe we'll see you again."

Preacher's eyes shifted to the northwest, then narrowed, his lips tightening in a weird smile. "Yep. I reckon you will."

Emmett turned his horse and pointed its nose west-north-west. Kirby reluctantly followed. He would have liked to stay and talk with the old man.

When they were out of earshot, Kirby said, "Pa, that old man was so dirty he smelled."

"He's a mountain man, some way from home base, I'm figuring. More 'n likely trying to get back. Cantankerous old boys, they are. Some of them mean as snakes. I think they get together once a year and bathe."

"But you said you soldiered with some mountain men."

"I did, but they didn't stay that long. They had to get back to the high lonesome."

"Where is the high lonesome?"

"It's more of a condition, than a place. Men like Preacher stay up in the high country for years. Don't do nothing but trap and such. They won't see another human being for a year or more, and not a white man more 'n once ever' two years or so. All they've got is their horses and guns and the whistling wind and the silence of the mountains. They're all alone, and it does something to them. They get notional, funny acting."

"You mean they go crazy?"

"In a way, I'm thinking. I don't know much about them. Nobody does, I don't reckon. But I think maybe that most of the folks who would go off 'n live like that, don't like people all that much to begin with. They crave the lawlessness of open space.

"The mountain men I was with, now, they were some different. They told me about that old man's kind. They're very brave men, son, don't ever doubt that. Probably the bravest in the world. They got to be to live like they do."

Kirby looked behind them. "Pa? That old man is following us, and he's shucked his rifle out of its boot."

Preacher galloped up to the pair, his rifle in his hand. "Don't get nervous. I ain't the one you need to be afeared of, but I do believe we fixin' to get ambushed."

"Ambushed by who?" Emmett asked.

"Kiowa would be my thinkin'. But they could be Pawnee. My eyes ain't as sharp as they once was. But I seen one of 'em stick his head up out of a wash over yonder. He's young or he wouldn't have done that. But that don't mean that the others with him is young."

"How many?"

"Don't know. In this country, one is too many. Do know this—we better be agettin'. If memory serves me, right over yonder, over that ridge, they's a little crick behind the stand of cottonwoods, with a old Buffalo waller in front of it." He looked up, stood up in his stirrups, and cocked his shaggy head. "Here they come, boys. Get agoin'."

Even as he was speaking, the old man slapped Kirby's bay on the rump, and they were galloping off. With the mountain man taking the lead, the three of them rode for the ridge. Cresting the ridge, the riders slid down the incline and galloped into the timber, down into the wallow. Whoops and cries of the Indians were close behind them.

Preacher might well have been past his good years, but the mountain man leaped off his spotted pony, rifle in hand, and was in position and firing as quickly as Emmett and Kirby. Preacher had a Sharps .52. It fired a paper cartridge, but was deadly up to 700 yards or more.

Kirby looked up in time to see a brave fly off his pony, a crimson gash on his naked chest. The Indian hit the ground and didn't move.

Emmett got a buck in the sights, led him on his fast running pony, then fired the Spencer in his hands. The buck was knocked off his pony, bounced once on the ground, then leaped to his feet, dodging for cover. He didn't make it. Preacher shot him in the side and lifted him off his feet, dropping him dead.

Emmett fired six more rounds in a thunderous barrage of black smoke, and the Indians scattered to cover, disappearing behind a ridge, horses and all.

"Scared 'em off," Preacher said. "They ain't used to repeaters. All they know is single shots. Let me get something out of my pack, 'n I'll show you a thing or two."

He went to one of his pack animals, which, along with the other horses, was standing just inside the tree line. He untied one of the side packs and let it fall to the ground, then pulled out the most beautiful rifle Kirby had ever seen.

"Damn!" Emmett said. "The Blue bellies had some of those toward the end of the war. But I never could get my hands on one."

Preacher smiled and pulled another Henry repeating rifle from the pack. Unpredictable as mountain men were, he tossed the second Henry to Emmett, along with a sack of cartridges.

"Now we be friends." Preacher laughed, exposing tobacco-stained stubs of teeth.

"I'll pay you for this," Emmett said, running his hands over the sleek barrel.

"What for? I didn't pay nothin' for either one of 'em," Preacher replied. "I won both of 'em in some shootin'.

Besides, somebody's got to look out for the two of you. You're liable to wander around out here and get hurt. It appears to be, you don't neither of you know tip from tat 'bout staying alive in Injun country."

"You may be right," Emmett admitted. He loaded the Henry. "So I thank you kindly."

Preacher looked at Kirby. "Boy, you plannin' on gettin' into this fight? Wait a minute, maybe I better ask you, can you shoot? Iffen you cain't shoot, better stay out of it. Don't want to worry none 'bout you maybe shootin' one of us."

Proud of his son, Emmett answered. "He can shoot. Kirby, pick up the Spencer."

"Better do it quick. Here they come," Preacher said.

"How do you know that, Preacher?" Kirby asked. "I don't see anything."

"Wind just shifted, and I smelled 'em. They close, so get ready."

Kirby wondered how the old man could smell anything over the fumes from his own body.

Emmett, a veteran of four years of continuous war, could not believe an enemy could slip up on him in open daylight. At the sound of Preacher jacking back the hammer of his Henry .44, Emmett saw a big painted up buck almost on top of him. Suddenly, the open meadow was filled with screaming, charging Indians. Emmett brought the buck down with a slug through the chest, flinging the Indian backward, the yelling abruptly cut off in his throat.

The area changed from the peacefulness of summer quiet, to a screaming, gun-smoke-filled hell.

Kirby jerked his gaze to the small creek in front of them. He had seen movement on the right side of the stream. For what seemed an eternity, he watched the young brave, a boy about his own age, leap and thrash through the water. Then he pulled back the hammer of the Spencer, aimed at the brave, and pulled the trigger.

Kirby heard a wild screaming and spun around. His father was locked in hand-to-hand combat with two knife wielding braves. Too close to use the rifle, Kirby jerked the pistol from the holster and fired in one smooth motion. He hit one of the braves in the head, just as his father buried his Arkansas toothpick to the hilt in the chest of the other.

Then as abruptly as they came, the Indians were gone. Two braves lay dead in front of Preacher, two more lay dead in the shallow ravine. The boy Kirby had shot was facedown in the creek, arms outstretched, the waters a deep crimson, the body slowly floating downstream.

A thin finger of smoke lifted from the barrel of the Navy .36 Kirby held in his hand.

Preacher smiled and spat tobacco juice. "You're some swift with that hogleg. Yep. Smoke will suit you just fine. So Smoke it'll be."

"Sir?" Kirby asked.

"Smoke," the old man repeated. "That'll be your name from now on. That's what I aim to call you. Smoke."

Preacher took another .36 Navy Colt from one of the dead Indians, then tossed it to Kirby. "I seen the way you handled that pistol. Ain't never seen no one your age that good with a handgun, and not sure that I've seen anyone full growed who was any better. Now you got yourself two guns."

From another Indian, Preacher took a long-bladed knife in a beaded sheath and handed that to him, as well. "Any man worth his salt out here needs hisself a good knife, too. Most especial someone who calls hisself Smoke."

"I don't call myself Smoke."

"You will."

"Why should I?"

"All famous men needs 'em a moniker, a name other 'n the one they was borned with. I've knowed some right famous men in my day, and Smoke sounds good to me."

"But I ain't famous."

"You're goin' to be, Smoke. Ain't no doubt in my mind. No doubt at all. You're goin' to be a famous man someday, the kind of man folks writes books about."

"I doubt that," Kirby said, but already he was beginning to think of himself as Smoke. He smiled. Yes, he liked that name.

Kirby and Emmett were shocked at what happened next. Preacher scalped the Indians they had killed.

"Good God, man, what are you doing?" Emmett asked.

"What's it look like I'm a' doin'? I'm takin' hair. I know a tradin' post that'll pay a dollar a scalp for ever'one I bring in. I won't do this with a Ute or a Crow. I've lived with them for too long. But I pure dee can't abide a Kiowa or a Pawnee." Carrying the scalps with him, Preacher started back toward the horses. "What we need to do is get out of here now . . . put as much distance between us and the Injuns as we can." He put the scalps into a buckskin bag that hung from one of the pack animals.

"Won't those stink?" Kirby asked.

"They do get ripe," Preacher replied as he mounted his pony.

The three men left the site of the battle at a gallop. Holding the gallop for several miles, they then walked their horses, then galloped them again, then walked them again, so that by late afternoon, Emmett believed they may have ridden as far as thirty miles. They made a quick camp by a creek.

"Get a fire goin'," Preacher said. "I'll get us some grub."

"I'll go hunting if you want," Kirby offered.

"'Preciate the offer, Smoke, but you'd more 'n likely have to shoot our food. Don't know who might be lurkin' around here listenin', so whatever game we take tonight has to be took quiet."

"I guess Smoke's my new name," Kirby said after the old man left the camp afoot. While there was still light, he carefully cleaned and oiled the Navy Colt taken from the dead Indian.

Emmett looked at him. "What do you think about that?"

"You know what? I kinda like it."

They ate an early supper, then doused the fire, carefully

checking for any live coals that might touch off a prairie fire, something as feared as any Indian attack, for a racing fire could outrun a galloping horse. They moved on, riding for an hour before pulling into a small stand of timber to make camp for the night.

Preacher spread out his blankets, used his saddle for a pillow, and promptly closed his eyes.

"I'll stand the first watch, *Smoke*," Emmett said, grinning at Kirby. "Then I'll wake Preacher for the second, and you can take the last watch, from two until daylight. Best you go on to sleep now until you're needed."

"All right, Pa."

Just as Kirby was drifting off to sleep, Emmett said, "If you don't like that nickname, son, we can change it."

"It's all right, Pa," the boy murmured, warmed by the wool of the blanket. "Pa? You know what? I kind of like Preacher."

"So do I," Emmett replied.

"That makes both of you good judges of character," the mountain man spoke from his blankets. "Now why don't you two quit all that jawin', 'n let an old man get some rest?"

"Night, Pa, Preacher."

"Night, Smoke," they both replied.

Preacher rolled the boy out of his blankets at two in the morning, into the summer coolness of the plains. The night was hung with the brilliance of a million stars.

"Stay sharp, now, Smoke," Preacher cautioned. "Injuns don't usually attack at night 'cause they think it's bad medicine for them. A brave gets killed at night, his spirit wanders forever, don't never get to the hereafter in peace. But Injuns is notional kind of folk, 'n not all tribes believe the same. Never can tell what they're goin' to do. More 'n likely, if they're out there, they'll hit us at first light, but you don't never know for sure." He rolled over into his blankets and was soon snoring.

The boy poured himself a cup of scalding hot coffee, strong enough to support a horseshoe, then replaced the pot on the rock grate. The fire was fueled by buffalo chips, hot and smokeless, and it couldn't be seen from ten feet away. Preacher had given him a holster for his second weapon and a wide belt from his seemingly never empty packs. Smoke adjusted it so that he was wearing a brace of pistols.

He had no way of knowing—with what had happened in Salcedo and especially in Delphi—that he had already taken the first steps toward creating a legend that would endure as long as writers would write of the West. Men would fear and respect him, women would desire him, children would play games imitating the man called Smoke. Songs would be written and sung about him in the Indian's villages and in the white man's cities.

On this pleasant night, Smoke—he was already thinking of himself as Smoke—was still some time away from being a living legend. He was just a young man in the middle of a vast open plain watching for savage Indians. He almost dozed off, caught himself, and jerked back awake. He bent forward for another cup of coffee, rubbing his sleepy eyes.

That movement saved his life.

A quivering arrow drove into the tree where, just a second before, he had been resting. Had he not leaned forward *at that precise moment*, the arrow would have driven through his chest.

Smoke drew first the right-hand Colt, then the left-hand gun, his motions almost liquid in their smoothness. The twin Colts were in the hands of one of the few men to whom guns were but an extension of the body. Two Pawnee braves went down under the first two shots. He shifted position. The muzzle flashes were like lightning, and the gunshots like thunder as the Colts roared. Two more bucks were cut down by the .36 caliber balls.

The night, filled with acrid smelling gun smoke, was silent except for the fading sounds of ponies racing away. The Indians wanted no more of that camp. They had lost too many braves.

"I ain't never seen nothing like this!" Preacher explained, walking around the dead and dying Indians. "I knowed Jim Bridger, Kit Carson, Broken Hand Fitzpatrick, uncle Dick Watt, 'n as many as a hunnert other salty old boys, but I ain't never seen nothing to top this here show you just put on. I tell you what, Smoke, you may be a youngster in years, but you'll damn sure do to ride to the river with."

Smoke did not yet know it, but that was the highest compliment a mountain man could ever give to another man.

"Thank you," Smoke said to Preacher as he reloaded the empty cylinders.

July 1867

Early morning, and though most self-respecting roosters had announced the fact long ago, half-a-dozen cocks were still trying to stake a claim on the day. The sun had been up for quite a while but the disc was still hidden by the mountains in the east. The light had already turned from red to white and here and there were signs that Westport Landing was starting another day.

A pump creaked as a housewife began pumping water for her daily chores and somewhere a carpenter was hammering. Janey was awakened by the sounds of commerce. She could scarcely believe that she was living in Kansas, given the hard feelings between Kansas and Missouri during the recent war. But she was in the place that was sometimes called the City of Kansas and sometimes called Kansas City, though it wouldn't acquire that name for a few years to come. It was known as Westport Landing, Kansas.

Getting up, she poured a basin of water and washed her face and hands. She stood by the open window and looked out on the town. She had been there for almost a year. Her baby would be fifteen months old, and she wondered if Becca was speaking. Did Becca know she had a mother? Did she wonder about her mother?

Scarcely a day went by without Janey thinking about Rebecca. Sometimes she considered going back—when she thought she couldn't stand being away any longer—begging Ben for forgiveness and spending time with her daughter. But she never followed through on it. Maybe after the first few weeks, maybe even after the first couple of months, she could have done so. But it was far too late for that.

Westport Landing was considerably more unruly than anyplace she had been. The customers of the house where she worked were rugged men who were more at home in the saddle than in a parlor. Some were hell-raisers when they came to town. Often they let off steam by shooting their guns, if not at each other in some spontaneous fight, then at any target that might catch their fancy.

The most troublesome of all the visitors to the place was a man named Cole Brennen. Twice in the last month, he had abused the woman he was with, and Maggie had told him he wasn't welcome anymore.

As expected, he didn't take that too kindly. He was a member of the city council and threatened Maggie with closure if she ever tried to deny him services.

Maggie Mouchette owned and operated the Pretty Girl and Happy Cowboy House. Janey did not occupy quite as elite a position as she had at the Palace Princess Emporium, but she and Maggie had become very good friends over the past year. As a result, Janey operated as Maggie's second in charge.

As Janey looked outside, a couple freight wagons rolled slowly through the street. The boardwalks were full of people, and a game of horseshoes was being played between two of the buildings on the opposite side of the street.

There was a knock on her door. "Abbigail? Are you ready for some breakfast?" Maggie called.

"Sure, I'll be right down."

Janey had gotten rid of the name Fancy Lil, because just as she didn't want her father or brother to track down Janey Jensen, neither did she want Ben Conyers to find Fancy Lil. She didn't really think there was much chance of him finding her, though. Westport Landing was quite a ways from Dallas.

Most of the citizens of the town had eaten breakfast quite some time ago but, as Maggie said, "The town people have their schedule, we have ours."

The other girls were already sitting at the table when Janey came down. Penelope was holding a cat in her lap.

"Penelope, why do you bring that dirty old cat in here?" one of the girls asked.

"Hortense isn't a dirty cat. He cleans himself all the time," Penelope said. "Don't you, Hortense?"

"That's another thing. If it's a tomcat, why do you call him Hortense?"

"Because I like the name."

"You are a strange person."

An older woman wearing a black dress and a white pinafore came in. "Ladies, breakfast is served."

The days passed leisurely for Maggie's girls. Some napped, some played cards, and some read. Normally Janey was one who enjoyed reading, but she had agreed to go to town with Maggie. When any of the girls went to town, they wore no makeup of any kind and plain dresses, which made them appear no different from any of the other women of the town.

Despite the fact that they purposely dressed down, all the girls were known on sight. When they went somewhere, they were generally shunned, not only by the "good" girls of the town, but quite often by the same men who frequently came calling on them at night.

Not everyone shunned them. One who was always nice to them was Elmer Gleason. He had arrived in town at about the same time Janey did. She heard, once, that he had ridden with Asa Briggs during the war, and though she was not aware that her own brother had ridden with him, she knew that many young men from the county had. It was quite possible that if Elmer Gleason ever learned her real name that he would know who she was. But he would never connect Abbigail Fontaine "from New Orleans" to Janey Jensen.

Elmer was a shotgun guard for the Westport-Landing-to-Wichita stage line, so he was often gone. When he was in town though, he was a frequent guest of the Pretty Girl and Happy Cowboy House, and had even been with Janey a few times.

His visits with her were limited though. Her time didn't cost as much here as it did back in Dallas, but she was still the most expensive girl on the line. As he once said, "In the dark, they all look alike."

Elmer was in the hardware store when Janey and Maggie stepped inside. When he saw them, he smiled, and touched the brim of his hat. Janey smiled back at him. Unfortunately, Elmer wasn't the only one in the store. Cole Brennen was there as well.

"Mr. Deckert," Brennen said to the proprietor of the hardware store. "You do know what these two women are, don't you?"

"As far as I'm concerned, they are customers," Deckert said. "The young women from Miss Mouchette's establishment stop by here from time to time, and they have always been good customers."

"Yes, well, they may not be good customers much longer. I intend to introduce a city ordinance which will close that den of iniquity, once and for all."

"Then where will you go, Brennen?" Elmer asked.

"What? Why you insolent cur! I'll sue you for libel and slander."

"I don't know what them fancy words mean," Elmer said. "But if you're tryin' to say you ain't never before been to Miss Mouchette's place, then I'm callin' you a liar, 'cause I've seen you there."

Brennen wheezed and gasped for breath, then angrily spun around and stomped out of the building.

Maggie laughed. "Elmer, next time you come to my place, I'll set you up for a free drink."

"Just a free drink?" Elmer asked.

"And a visit with one of the girls," Maggie added.

"That's more like it. All right, missy, I'll be by tonight."

CHAPTER 15

Elmer did show up that night, and he had his drink—whiskey—then claimed Penelope for his free visit.

But he wasn't the only one who showed up. Cole Brennen also arrived with another man that neither Janey nor Maggie recognized.

"This here is Marvin Lewis with the Westport Landing City Marshal's office. I've brought him with me to be a witness to what's goin' on here. However, if you treat us right, why, nothin' will happen to you, 'n you can go on doing business just like you always have."

"You are a pathetic excuse of a man, Brennen," Maggie said.

Brennen's malevolent smile stretched the skin tight across his face, giving his head the appearance of a skull. "I may be. But it seems to me like you got no choice but to be nice to us."

By midnight, all the visitors were gone except for Elmer, who had opted to spend the night with Penelope, and Cole Brennen, who was in one of the downstairs rooms with a girl named Louise. Even Marvin Lewis, who had come with Brennen, was gone.

Janey and Maggie were alone in the parlor, sitting in front of the fireplace, drinking a glass of wine.

"I don't usually pry into the past lives of my girls," Maggie said. "Almost all of them have a story as to why they got into this business. Some of them share it and some don't. Before I ask you to share your story, I'll tell you mine.

"I'm the daughter of a preacher man. I married the son of a very rich Boston banker, but he treated me like dirt, so I left him. No divorce. I just left him. Because of who he was, I had to leave Boston." She smiled. "But I took ten thousand dollars with me when I left. That's how I was able to buy this house and start my business here."

Janey thought of the two thousand dollars she had taken from Kirby, but before she responded, they heard a blood-curdling scream coming from Louise's room.

"What is going on in there?" Maggie asked, jumping up quickly, with an expression of anger and concern on her face. "Louise, what is it? What's happening?"

Maggie ran to Louise's room with Janey close behind her. She opened the door and they saw Brennen, his naked body shining gold in the light of the lamp. He was holding a bloody knife in his hand. Louise had her hand across a bloody cheek.

"He cut me!" Louise cried.

Maggie picked up a vase and held it over her head as she approached Brennen. "Get out of here!" she shouted angrily. "Get out of here now! And don't you ever come back!"

Brennen suddenly thrust his hand forward, burying the knife up to its hilt in Maggie's chest. With an expression of pain and shock on her face, Maggie stepped back from him.

"You've killed her!" Janey screamed.

Brennen turned to face her. He was nearly covered in blood, and the reflected flame in his eyes could have been the fires of hell. The smile was demonic, and he held the knife out toward her. "You're next," he said in a low hiss.

Janey backed away from him, stumbling into the chair where Brennen had put his clothes. She stuck her hand back to keep from falling and felt his pistol!

Instantly and instinctively, she pulled the pistol out of its holster and brought it around, firing just as Brennen lunged for her. The bullet hit him in the chest. The impact knocked him back against the fireplace, and he slid down to the hearth, leaving a smear of blood on the bricks behind him.

Elmer Gleason raced into the room with a gun in his hand. He didn't have to ask what happened. In one all-encompassing look, he took it in. "Girl, throw what clothes together as fast as you can. We're getting out of here."

"I had no choice!" Janey said. "He killed Maggie and he was coming after me."

"That's true," Louise said. "Abbigail didn't have any choice!"

"I believe you, Louise," Elmer said. "I believe both of you. But this feller is on the city council, 'n the man who come here earlier is a deputy marshal. They ain't nobody goin' to believe you. That's why we got to get out of here now."

"Elmer, no. If you run with me, they'll be after you, too."

"I need to get out of here, anyway," Elmer said. "I made a few rides with a feller over in Missouri called Jesse James. So I expect my welcome here is goin' to be wore out pretty quick."

Smoke and Emmett were about to partake in an event that would be one of the last of its kind. It was called Rendezvous, a gathering of the breed of men civilization sometimes raised a dubious head toward and pushed the mountain men into history. The smoke of scores of camp-fires could be seen from some distance away. As Smoke and his father drew closer, they became aware of the sounds of

Rendezvous and the aromas of roasting meat from the many cooking fires.

In the early days of trapping, before the war and the Western migration, Rendezvous would be the biggest city between the Pacific Ocean and St. Louis. Those days were over. The mountain men that remained were, for the most part, advanced in years, heading for the sunset of their lives. They had spent their youth, their best years, and the mid-point of their lives, in elements where one careless move could result in either sudden death or slow torture from hostiles.

Mountain men were not easily impressed, but those gathered were standing and watching as Smoke and his father rode slowly into the ruins of the old post, rifles across their saddles. Preacher had already spread the word about the boy called Smoke.

As did many boys of that hard era, he looked older than his years. His face was deeply tanned. His shoulders and arms were lean, but hard with muscle.

"I don't know. He don't look all that much to me," an aging mountain man said to a friend.

"Neither did Kit Carson if you recall," his friend replied. "Hell, he warn't but four inches over five feet, but he were one hell of a man."

"The boy is faster than a snake, Preacher says."

The mountain man cocked his eye at his friend. "Yeah, but don't forget, Preacher has been known to spin a tall tale ever' now and then, when he thinks it might be a mite more interestin' than tellin' the truth."

"Yeah, but not this time, I wager. Look at this kid. He's got a mean look to his eyes."

Smoke and Emmett sat their horses and stared. Neither had ever seen anything like the colorful assemblage. The men, all of whom were over sixty years old, were dressed in wild, bright colors—buckskin breeches and shirts, beaded leggings, wide red, blue, or yellow sashes about their waists.

Some were wearing cord trousers with silk shirts shining in a rainbow of colors. All were beaded and booted and bearded. Some held long muzzle-loading Kentucky rifles. A few had lever-action repeating rifles. Many were decorated with color-fully dyed rawhide strings dangling from the barrel, the shot and powder bags decorated with beads.

It would not be the last, but nearly the last great gathering of the magnificent breed of men called mountain men.

When Emmett and Smoke spotted Preacher, they couldn't believe their eyes. They sat on their horses and stared.

He was clean and his beard was well trimmed. He wore new buckskins, new leggings, and a red sash around his waist. His eyes sparkled with a light they had never seen. "Howdy," he called. "Y'all light and sit, boys."

"I don't believe it," Emmett said. "His face is clean."

"There's water to wash in over there," Preacher said, pointing. "Good strong soap, too. But you'd best dump what's in the barrel and refill it. It's got fleas in it along with the ticks."

Elmer took Janey to the one-room cabin where he lived, just on the edge of town. It had been the middle of the night when they left the Pretty Girl and Happy Cowboy House. Nobody had seen him sneak her into his place.

She stayed in the cabin for two weeks, not daring to show herself outside. The wisdom of that decision was borne out when Elmer brought a newspaper by a couple days later.

MURDER SO FOUL

Cole Brennen, a sterling citizen and member of the city council, was murdered on the 19th instant. Brennen and Deputy Marshal Marvin Lewis were investigating a residence on the suspicion that activity of an illicit nature might be taking place there. It had been reported that the owner of the house, Maggie Mouchette, was running not a boarding house for young women as her city license stated, but a bawdy house.

Deputy Lewis reports that, upon confirming that such was true, Brennen informed them that he would be reporting the true nature of the business to the authorities. That was when two of the occupants of the house attacked him. Although Brennen was able to subdue Miss Mouchette, the other woman, Abbigail Fontaine, managed to secure a pistol and shot at him. The ball, thus energized, struck Brennen in the chest, taking terrible effect.

Abbigail Fontaine has since disappeared, and authorities have asked that anyone who can give information as to her location should provide such to Marshal Kilgore.

"Lewis wasn't even there," Janey said after she read the story. "But Penelope was. Why didn't they ask her what happened?"

"I'm sure she did tell them what happened, but bein' as she is what she is, why it's most likely they didn't pay her no never mind," Elmer said.

"Elmer, what am I going to do? I can't stay here in your cabin forever."

"How'd you like to go West?"

"Go West?"

"They's a riverboat leavin' first thing in the mornin', headin' up the Missouri toward a place called Montana. I figure to get us on it."

"How am I going to get to the boat without being seen?"

"You let me worry about that."

When Elmer returned to the cabin that night, he showed Janey the tickets for the riverboat *Cora Two*. "You're Mrs. John

Smith. I'm John Smith. I figured maybe we should go up river as husband and wife. Folks that's lookin' for you won't be lookin' for you to be travelin' with a husband. Most especial since we'll be usin' names that ain't our'n."

"And John Smith is so original," Janey said.

"Yeah, I thought it was pretty good my ownself. It was the first name I come up with," Elmer said, failing to catch the sarcasm in Janey's voice.

Janey smiled. Who was she to criticize this man who had made all the arrangements to get her away? And, she was pretty sure that once she was away from Westport Landing, she would be safe. The authorities would be looking for a woman named Abbigail Fontaine from New Orleans. She had never given her real last name to anyone, not even to Maggie, nor had she ever shared with anyone that she had come from Missouri, by way of Texas.

It was after dark when they left Elmer's house, and they reached the river without arousing any suspicion. The *Cora Two* was tied up at the landing, a long, white stern wheeler with three decks and a pilot house. Two chimneys sprouted from just aft of the pilot house.

Once they were aboard, Janey stepped out onto the hurricane deck, which was between the boiler deck and the Texas deck, and looked out over the town of Westport Landing. It was quiet and dark, and she could hear a dog barking way off in the distance. The city was so peaceful at that hour of the night. The loudest sounds were the gentle lapping of the river against the hull and the creaking of the boat at its hawsers as it pulled at the current while at anchor.

She walked forward and stood against the railing to look out over the bow. Down on the boiler deck she could see neat stacks of cargo, ricks of firewood, and the men, women, and even children who held steerage tickets. They would be making the journey on that deck. They had no bunks, and would have to bed down wherever they could find room, unprotected against the weather.

A cool breeze came up and Janey shivered, then hugged herself. She thought of the river they would be following, stretched out before them for many miles. It was, she decided, a metaphor, not only bridging the distance she must travel, but reaching into her future as well. What did lie before her?

Smoke stood in front of the trading post at dawn. His pa was mounted; he wasn't.

"You do understand my ridin' off alone, don't you, boy? I wouldn't be leavin' you, but I've seen you when you was up against it, 'n you come through just fine. You can handle them guns better 'n anyone I ever saw, so I ain't worried none 'bout you bein' able to take care of yourself. But there's some things you're goin' to need to learn 'bout livin' out here. I cain't think of nobody more able to teach you them things than Preacher. Problem is, it's goin' to take you some time to learn all you need to learn, 'n me 'n you know that I don't have that much time left. So, I aim to leave you here to get your learnin' while I go out lookin' for them men that kilt your brother. You got 'ny problem with that?"

"I reckon not," Smoke replied quietly. "I know you're doin' what you feel you got to do."

"You're a good boy, Kirby. No, you're a good man. I know that when you was growin' up, you might sometimes thought I was favorin' Luke. I warn't. It was just that he was older and a mite easier for me to understand. But there ain't no man ever lived who had himself a son he was more proud of than I am of you. I'm glad the Good Lord give us this time to be together, so's I could find that out.

"Bye, Kirby." Emmett smiled. "I mean, bye, Smoke. That'll be your name from now on."

He turned and rode away. He had taken only a little of the money with him, leaving the rest with Smoke. He rode for some distance, then stopped, turned his horse, and waved at his son. Then he was gone, dipping out of sight, over the rise of a small hill.

Smoke knew, at that moment, that he would never see his father again and tried to swallow the knot that was in his throat.

For the entire time of their good-bye, Preacher had sat on the porch of the trading post, watching, saying nothing.

Smoke turned away from the road and looked up at the man who was to become his mentor. "He won't be back."

Preacher spat a stream of tobacco off the porch and onto the dusty ground. "Some things, Smoke, a man's just got to do before his time on earth slips away. Your pa has things to do. If you're wantin' to cry, I want you to know that there ain't no shame in it."

Smoke squared his shoulders. "I'm a man. I lived alone, I worked the land, and I paid the taxes all by myself. And I haven't cried since Ma died."

"Ain't nobody ever goin' to question whether or not you're a man, Smoke. You're as much a man as anyone I've ever knowed."

Smoke put his foot on the steps. "Let's get outfitted." He climbed the steps and entered the trading post. He bought a new Henry repeating rifle, one hundred rounds of .44 caliber ammunition for it, and an extra cylinder for his left hand .36, then they rode out.

Preacher told him he knew of a friendly band of Indians up north of the post. He'd see to it that Smoke got himself a pair of moccasins and leggings and a buckskin jacket, fancy beaded.

"I ain't got that kind of money to waste, Preacher."

"Ain't going to cost you nothing. I know the lady who will make them for you."

"She must like you pretty well."

Preacher smiled. "She's my daughter."

On board the *Cora Two*, a long, deep throated blast blew from the boat's horn, then the captain stepped out of the pilot house. Lifting a megaphone to his lips, he called forward to the main deck bow. "Lead man!"

"Lead man, aye!" an unseen voice called back from the front of the boat.

"Sound the bottom!"

"Aye, Cap'n!"

"We must be in shallow water," Elmer said.

Janey walked up to the front of the boat. The soundings had been taken frequently during the long journey upriver, and she was familiar with the routine.

"By the mark two!" the lead man called. To make certain that his call was heard in the pilot house, it was repeated by someone up on the Texas Deck.

The lead man continued to call his soundings, which were then echoed, both calls intoned so melodically that it was almost as if the men were singing. Janey had actually grown to appreciate them, and enjoyed listening to the calls as they played against the rhythmic slap of the paddlewheel in the water.

During the trip upriver the boat had to proceed very cautiously because of shallow water. Three times they had encountered sandbars with the water so shallow that it was necessary to "grasshopper" over them with long heavy spars carried vertically on derricks near the bow. The ends of the spars were dropped to the bottom, tops slanted forward, and with block, tackle, cable, and capstan, lifted and pushed the boat forward as if on crutches while the paddle wheel thrashed furiously. After each splash down, the spars were reset for the next "hop," until the boat was free.

At the moment, they seemed to be proceeding upriver at a steady, brisk pace.

Seventy-one days after the *Cora Two* left Westport Landing, Janey stood on the hurricane deck and watched the bluffs slide by on the south bank as the boat worked its way up the Missouri River to Ft. Benton.

Elmer came over to stand beside her. "Well, our long journey is nearly over. The cap'n told me we'd reach Fort Benton today."

"Elmer, I can't thank you enough for helping me out the way you did. I mean, you gave up your job and everything."

Elmer chuckled. "Ridin' shotgun on a stagecoach ain't that much of a job. It was about time I was movin' on."

The *Cora Two* beat its way against the current as it approached around a wide, sweeping bend. Smoke was pouring from the twin chimneys and the engine steam-pipe was booming as loudly as if the town were under a cannonading. With the engine clattering and the paddle wheel slapping at the water, it approached the Ft. Benton landing.

"Deck men, fore and aft, stand by to throw out the lines!" the captain called.

"Aye, Cap'n, standing by!" the first mate called back as two men rushed to the front of the boat and stood side by side, holding the ropes.

At the last minute, the engine was reversed, and the paddle started whirling in the opposite direction, causing the water to froth at the action. The reversing paddle wheel held the speed of the boat until the movement through the water was but a slow, gentle glide up to the dock. Waiting stevedores stood ready to receive the lines.

"Heave out your lines!" the first mate shouted, and both ropes were tossed ashore. One of the men on the boat deck walked his rope back to the stern where he wrapped it securely around a stanchion. The men ashore pulled on the lines—fore and aft—so that the boat was pulled sideways until it was snug up against the dock.

"Well, missy, we're here," Elmer said. "You got 'ny ideas as to what you might do next?"

Janey smiled. "Don't worry about me, Elmer. For the next few years, at least for as long as I can keep my looks, I'll always be able to make a living."

Elmer laughed out loud. "I reckon you will."

Janey checked into the Grand Mountain Hotel. Once she was in her room she went through her dresses and selected one that left little to the imagination. Donning the dress, she got out her powders and paints, and with an artistry developed over the last few years, she transformed her face, combining subtle eye shadows with bold lashes and mascara. A crimson smear across her lips completed the transformation, and when she walked through the lobby of the hotel a short while later, not one person would have connected her with the woman who had registered as Fannie Webber.

Exiting the hotel, Janey made her way to the largest and grandest saloon in town, the Gold Strike. She went inside, strode up to the bar, and ordered a drink.

"What kind of drink?" the bartender asked.

"I expect, if I'm going to be drinking with men all day, you'd better give me something that doesn't make me drunk." Janey fixed him with a penetrating stare.

"Uh . . . drinking with men?" the bartender asked.

The well-dressed man sitting at a table close to the bar got up and walked over to stand beside her. "Henry, I do believe this young lady is applying for a job."

"I might be," Janey replied, turning her charm toward the man. "If so, who should I see?"

"That would be me. The name is Andrew McGhee. And you would be?"

Janey thought for a moment, wondering if she should use the same name she used when she checked into the hotel. "The name I use will depend upon whether or not I can get a room here in the saloon."

McGhee laughed out loud. "For you, my finest room."

Janie's smile broadened, and she stuck out her hand. "It's nice to meet you, Andrew. My name is Fannie Webber."

CHAPTER 16

July 1869

It had been two years since Emmett rode off on his own, and Smoke had not heard anything from him since. He wasn't surprised by that, given that Emmett had written only two letters the whole time he was away fighting the war.

Nothing of the boy was left. Smoke was a man, fully grown and hard in body, face, and eyes. The bay he had ridden west hadn't survived the first year after Emmett left. The horse had fallen on the ice and broken his leg. Smoke had had to put him down, but Preacher found another horse for him, a large, mean-tempered Appaloosa. The Indian had sold him cheap, because he hadn't been able to break him.

Strangely, not only to the Indian who sold him, but to other Indians who knew the animal, the horse seemed to bond immediately with Smoke. He was a stallion, and he was mean, his eyes warning any knowledgeable person away. In addition to its distinctive markings—the mottled hide, vertically striped hooves, and pale eyes—the Appaloosa had a perfectly shaped numeral seven between his eyes. And that became his name—Seven.

"Smoke, I've done learned you about as much as I know how to learn anyone," Preacher said one summer morning.

"There ain't no doubt in my mind, but that you could light in the middle of the mountains some'ers and live as good as me or any other mountain man I ever knowed could.

"But truth to tell, the time of the mountain man is gone. There warn't even no Rendezvous this year, 'n I don't know if they'll ever be another 'n. Just be glad you got to see one of 'em when you did."

"I am glad," Smoke said. "If I live to be as old a man as you are, I'll still remember gettin' to go to that Rendezvous."

"Whoa, now! Are you tellin' me that's all you're goin' to remember? That you ain't goin' to 'member nothin' else I learned you in all this time?"

Smoke laughed. "I reckon I'll be rememberin' that, as well."

Shortly after that conversation an old mountain man rode into their camp. "You just as ugly as I remembered, Preacher," he said in the form of greeting.

"I didn't think you was even still alive, Grizzly," Preacher said. "I heard you got eat up by a pack o' wolves. No, wait. That ain't right. Now that I think on it, they said you was so old and dried up that the wolves didn't want nothin' to do with you."

Smoke had already learned that mountain men insulted each other whenever possible. It was their way of showing affection.

"Can I talk in front of the boy?" Grizzly asked.

"Anythin' you can tell me, you can say in front of him," Preacher replied.

Smoke poured himself a cup of coffee and waited.

"A man rode into the Hole about two months ago. All shot up, he was. And 'sides that, he had a bad cough."

"Is he still alive?" Smoke blurted.

The old man turned cold eyes toward him. "Don't ever interrupt a man when he's palaverin'. 'Tain't polite. One thing about Indians, they know manners. They know to allow a man to speak his piece without interrupting."

"Sorry," Smoke said.

"Accepted. No, he's dead. Strange man. Dug his own grave. Come the time, I buried him. He's planted on that there little plain at the base of the high peak east side of the canyon. Zenobia Peak, it's called. You remember it, Preacher?"

Preacher nodded.

The old mountain man reached inside his war bag and pulled out a heavy sack and tossed it to Smoke. "This would be your'n, I reckon. It's from your pa, a right smart amount of gold." Again, he dipped into the war bag and pulled out a rawhide-wrapped flat object. "And this is a piece of paper with words on it. Names, your pa said, of the men who put lead in him. He said you'd know what to do, but for me to tell you, don't do nothing rash."

His business done, the old man rose to his feet. "I done what I give my word I'd do. Now I'll be goin' on."

Smoke had purposely held off reading the letter until he found his pa's grave. When he did find it, he used a rock to chisel his pa's name onto it.

EMMETT JENSEN
BORN 1815 DIED 1869

He wasn't sure that 1815 was correct, but he figured it was close enough, especially since he was the only relative left who would ever see it, or even care about it. He wasn't counting Janey.

With the words chiseled onto the stone, Smoke moved it over to the mound of earth that was the gravesite. The stone was big and hard to move, and he was glad. That meant it would be too heavy for any vandals to mess with it for no reason other than to make mischief.

Not until the tombstone was put into position did Smoke turn his attention to the letter. He opened it and read it by the fading light.

Son,

I found some of the men who killed your brother Luke and stoled the gold that belonged to the Gray. They was more of them than I first thought. I killed two of them but they got lead in me and I had to hightail it out. Ackerman is the man Luke thought was his best friend, and the one that betrade him. He got away.

Came here, but not going to make it. Son, you don't owe nothin' to the cause of the Gray. So don't get it in your mind you do.

I got word that your sis Janey left that gambler. Don't know where she is now, but I wouldn't fret much about her. She is mine, but I think she is trash. Don't know what she got that bad streek from.

I'm gettin' tared and seein is hard. I love you Smoke.

Pa

"You're goin' out after 'em now, ain't you," Preacher said. "The fella that kilt your ma, and the ones that kilt your brother and your pa." It was more a statement than a question.

"Yeah, I am," Smoke said.

"Like I said when your pa left, they's some things a man just has to do."

Over the next couple months, Smoke's justice was thorough and extreme.

Two names he learned about belonged to men who had been complicit in shooting his brother, stealing the Confederate gold, and ultimately killing his pa. Ted Casey was the fourth man who'd stolen the Confederacy gold with Stratton, Richards, and Potter—the men Emmett had set out to find and kill. Ackerman had ridden with Quantrill. Smoke didn't know Ackerman's first name, but he'd learned from someone he met that the Confederate deserter owned a ranch just outside Canon City, Colorado.

"Sounds like all them boys done right good for themselves," Preacher said. "They all come out here and commenced ranchin'."

"They started ranchin' on the gold they stole from the South after shootin' my brother," Smoke said sourly.

Casey's place—TC Ranch—was close by so they headed there first. The shootout was deadly, with the ranch hands putting up quite a fight before they were killed. Casey wasn't among those killed at the ranch, but Smoke found him, then hung him in front of a sheriff and scores of people from the nearby town. Nobody made any real effort to stop him.

"Now," Smoke said. "I'm goin' to Canon City."

"*We're* goin', you mean," Preacher said.

"All right, we're goin' to Canon City."

"Oreodelphia," Preacher said.

"What?"

"That's what they wanted to name it. Oreodelphia, but there couldn't nobody hardly even say it, let alone spell it, so they wound up callin' it Canon City."

Smoke frowned, thinking that was more information than he needed to know at the moment. "Do you know how to get there?"

"I know."

"Then why are we standing here jawboning?"

"Boy, you got to learn patience, you know that?"

"What is his name?" Ackerman asked.

"Smoke."

"Smoke? Somebody named Smoke killed Casey and all his hands?"

"His last name is Jensen. I was told that would mean somethin' to you."

Ackerman smiled. "Luke had a brother 'n a sister he used to talk about some. His sister was named Janey. Accordin' to Luke, she was a real good looker. She must be somethin' by now. His brother was named Kirby. I ain't never heard of anyone named Smoke Jensen."

"Well, from what I've heard, he's Emmett Jensen's son."

"Damn," Ackerman said. "Then it has to be the one Luke said was Kirby. Smoke must just be the name he's took for some reason. And he's comin' here, you say?"

"That's what I've been told."

"All right. We'll just take care of 'im when he gets here. Once we kill him, there won't be nobody left but the sister. An' she ain't likely to go out after nobody."

For two days, Smoke and Preacher waited and relaxed in Canon City, making a special effort to keep out of trouble. Smoke bathed twice behind the barbershop, and Preacher told him if he didn't stop that, he was going to come down with some dreadful illness.

The mountain man and the gunfighter were civil to the men and polite to the ladies. Some of the ladies batted their eyes and swished their bustled fannies as they passed by Smoke, but he paid them no attention.

"You boys are sure taking your time buying supplies," the sheriff noted on the second day.

"We like to think things through before buying," Preacher told him. "Smoke here is a right cautious man when it comes to partin' with the greenback. You might even call him tight."

The sheriff didn't find that amusing. "You boys wouldn't be waiting for Ackerman to make a move, would you?"

"Ackerman?" Smoke looked at the sheriff. "What is an Ackerman?"

The sheriff's smile was grim. "What do you boys do for a living? I have a law on the books about vagrants."

"I'm retired," Preacher told him. "Enjoying the sunset of my years, I am. Smoke here, he runs a string of horses."

"Would you like to buy a horse?" Smoke asked. "I've got some really nice ones, and bein' as you are with the law, I can give you a real good deal."

"I ought to run you both out of this town."

"Why?" Smoke asked. "On what charge? We haven't caused you any trouble."

"Yet." The sheriff's back was stiff with anger as he walked away. The man knew a set up when he saw one.

But his feelings were mixed. Ackerman and his bunch of rowdies were all troublemakers, and he owed them nothing. He swung no wide political loop in this country, and there were persistent rumors that Ackerman had been a thief and a murderer during the war, as well as a deserter. The sheriff could not abide a coward.

He sighed. If he was right in reading the young man called Smoke, Ackerman's future looked very bleak.

A hard ridden horse hammered the street into dust. A cowhand from the Bar X slid to a halt in front of the sheriff's office. "Ackerman and his bunch is ridin' in, Sheriff," the cowhand said, still panting from his ride. "They're huntin' bear. He told me to tell you he's going to kill this kid called Smoke and anyone else that gets in his way."

The sheriff's smile grudgingly filled with admiration. The kid's patience had paid off. Ackerman had made his boast and his threat, which meant that anything the kid did now could only be called self-defense.

The sheriff thanked the cowboy and told him to hunt a hole to hide in. He crossed the street and told his deputy to clear the street from the apothecary to the blacksmith shop.

In five minutes, the main street resembled a ghost town. A yellow dog was the only living thing that had not cleared out. Behind curtains, closed doors, and shuttered windows, men and women watched and waited, anticipating the roar of gunfire from the street.

At the edge of town, Ackerman, a bull of a man with small, mean eyes, stopped for a moment. With a small wave, he started the five cowhands with him down the street, riding slowly, six abreast.

Standing on the porch of the hotel with Smoke, Preacher stuffed his mouth full of chewing tobacco, then they walked out into the street to face the six men.

"I've come for you, kid," said the big man in the center of the riders.

"Oh? Who are you?" Smoke asked.

"You know who I am, kid. I'm Ackerman."

"Ah yes!" Smoke said. "I do know that. You're the man who was supposed to be my brother's best friend, but you helped kill him by shooting him in the back. Then you stole the gold he was guarding."

Inside the hotel, pressed against the wall, the desk clerk listened intently, his mouth open in anticipation of gunfire.

"You're a liar. I didn't shoot your brother. That was Potter and his bunch."

"You stood by and watched it. Then you stole the gold."

"It was war, kid."

"But you were on the same side," Smoke said. "That not only makes you a killer, it makes you a traitor and a coward."

"I'll kill you for saying that!"

"You'll burn in hell a long time before I'm dead," Smoke told him.

Ackerman grabbed for his pistol.

The street exploded in gunfire and black powder fumes. Horses screamed and bucked in fear. One rider was thrown to the dust by his lunging mustang.

Smoke took the men on the left, Preacher the men on the right. The battle lasted no more than ten or twelve seconds. When the noise and the gun smoke cleared, five men lay in the street, two of them dead. Two more would die from their wounds. The one shot in the side would live. Ackerman had been shot three times—once in the belly, once in the chest, and one ball had taken him in the side of the face as the muzzle of the .36 had lifted him with each blast. Dead, he still sat in his saddle. The big man finally leaned to one side and toppled from his horse, one booted foot hanging up in the stirrup. The horse shied, then began walking down the dusty street, dragging Ackerman and leaving a bloody trail on the ground behind him.

The excited clerk ran out the door. "I heard it all! You were right, Mr. Smoke. Yes, sir. Right all the way." He looked at Smoke. "Why, you've been wounded, sir."

A slug had nicked the young man on the cheek, another had punched a hole in the fleshy part of his left arm, high up. Both were minor wounds.

Preacher had been grazed on the leg. He spat into the street. "Damn near swallowed my terbacky."

"I never saw a draw that fast," a man spoke from the storefront. "It was a blur."

The sheriff and the deputy came out of the jail, walking down the bloody, dusty street. Both were carrying Greeners, double-barreled, twelve-gauge shotguns.

"Right down the street," the sheriff said, pointing, "is the doctor's office. Get yourselves patched up and then get out of town. You have one hour."

"Sheriff, it was a fair fight," the desk clerk said. "I seen it."

The sheriff never took his eyes off Smoke. "One hour," he repeated.

"We'll be gone." Smoke wiped a smear of blood from his cheek.

Townspeople began hauling the bodies off. The local photographer set up his cumbersome equipment and began popping flash powder, sealing the gruesome scene for posterity. He also took a picture of Smoke.

The editor of the paper walked up to stand by the sheriff. He watched the old man and the young gun hand walk down the street. He truly had seen it all. The old man had killed one man and wounded another. The young man had killed four. "What's the young man's name?"

"His name is Smoke Jensen. But if you ask me, he's the devil."

"Your pa would be pleased," Preacher said as they rode out of town within the hour assigned by the sheriff. "Do you plan to get the other men he was looking for?"

"Yes, I do. But I'm going after Shardeen first."

"Before you start out, I want you to come to Denver with me. I've got a fella there I'd like for you to meet."

"Somebody who can help me find Shardeen?"

"You might say that," Preacher replied, without being any more specific.

It took them three days to get to Denver.

Preacher led Smoke to a low-lying building made of white limestone. A United States flag flew from the flagpole out front, and as they started into the building, Smoke saw a sign chiseled above the doorway. UNITED STATES FEDERAL OFFICE BUILDING.

"What are we going in here for?"

"You're askin' questions again. Didn't I tell you a long time ago that when words is goin' outta your mouth, nothin' can be comin' in your ears? You learn quicker if you're just quiet and pay attention," Preacher said.

Smoke smiled. "Have you always been such a cantankerous old fart?"

"Pretty much," Preacher said.

Both men were wearing buckskins, and both were a little more gamey than the average citizen of Denver. When Swayne Hodge, the office clerk, looked up and saw the two men coming in, he became a little agitated. "Gentlemen, gentlemen, are you lost?"

"Pilgrim, I been out here more 'n fifty years 'n I ain't never been lost but one time. I cain't say as I was all that lost then, since it didn't take me more 'n a month to find my way back to the trail."

"But you *do* know that this is a federal office building, don't you?"

"I didn't exactly figure it to be a house of ill repute," Preacher said.

"Oh, my," Hodge said, clearly discomforted by the vulgarity.

"Preacher! What are you doing here?" Another voice spoke openly and without reservation.

"Excuse me, Marshal Holloway, do you actually *know* these, uh, gentlemen?" Hodge asked, stumbling over the word *gentlemen*.

"I don't know both of them," the marshal said. "But I certainly know the older gentleman. Preacher, come into my office and introduce me to your young friend."

Hodge remained standing, watching with his mouth agape as Uriah B. Holloway, United States Marshal for the Colorado District, holding his commission by U.S. Senate confirmation since April 10, 1866, led the two unwashed men into his office.

"Have a seat, men," Marshal Holloway offered.

"Thank ye, kindly, Uriah." Preacher held his hand out toward Smoke. "This here is Smoke Jensen."

Holloway frowned. "Smoke? His name is Smoke?"

"It's as much Smoke as my name is Preacher."

The marshal chuckled. "All right, Preacher, I'll go along with that. Smoke, it is good to meet you."

"Marshal," Smoke replied, taking the lawman's extended hand.

"Now, what can I do for you?"

"Have you ever heard of a man named Angus Shardeen?" Preacher asked.

Holloway's eyes narrowed. "Yes, I've heard of him. What about him?"

"First, let me ask what you know about him," Preacher replied.

"He has federal and state arrest warrants out on him," Holloway replied. "He's wanted for murder, robbery, arson, and probably half a dozen other things."

"Do you have any idea where he might be now?"

Holloway shook his head. "I can't say as I do. I do know, however, that he has some bad men with him."

"An army?" Smoke asked.

"You might say that. Angus Shardeen was a colonel in the Union Army during the war . . . though there are some who dispute that. He was actually a Jayhawker, operating at the head of a gang of guerrillas, supposedly riding in support of Union troops. But his tactics were so brutal, and quite frankly, so self-enriching, that if he ever did actually hold a commission, it was probably withdrawn.

"Since the end of the war, he has continued the guerrilla operations using many of the same men, only it is without regard to any cause, other than his own."

"Bein' as you are a U.S. Marshal, would you have the authority to go after 'im, no matter where he is?" Preacher asked.

Holloway nodded. "I would."

"And say there was somebody who was a Deputy U.S. Marshal, say it was someone that you appointed. Would that fella also be able to go after Shardeen, no matter where he might be?"

"Yes, he would. Tell me, Preacher, why are you asking me all these questions? Do you know where Shardeen is?"

"I don't have 'ny idee where he is, but if you was to appoint Smoke as one of your deputies, he'll find 'im for you."

Holloway looked over at Smoke. "Do you have an idea as to where Shardeen might be?"

"No, sir."

"Then what makes you think you'll be able to find him, when I haven't."

"Marshal, you bein' the law for this whole territory, I

would expect that you have a lot more things to do than just look for Angus Shardeen, don't you?"

"Well, yes, as a matter of fact, I do."

"I don't and I intend to find him," Smoke replied with grit.

"And you want me to appoint you deputy so that you can?"

"No, sir."

"No?" Holloway looked over at Preacher in surprise. "Look here, isn't this what you just asked me to do?"

"I mean no, sir, I don't want you to appoint me deputy so I can find him," Smoke said. "I intend to find 'im, whether I'm appointed as your deputy or not."

"You did hear me tell you that Shardeen was riding at the head of his own army, didn't you?"

"Yes, sir, I heard you say that."

"Well, here's the thing, Mr. Jensen. I don't have funding for another deputy."

Preacher spoke up. "Look here, Uriah. Sometimes when you form a posse to go after someone, don't you appoint them men in the posse as Deputy U.S. Marshals?"

"Yes, I do. But I don't pay them."

"You don't have to pay me," Smoke said.

"Let me get this straight. You are willing to be an unpaid deputy in order to go out, single-handed, to find Angus Shardeen, even though you know there are at least half a dozen with him?"

Smoke nodded. "Yes, sir."

"You will have to function alone. I don't have enough men to assign anybody to one specific task."

"That's all right."

Marshal Holloway looked over at Preacher again. "Preacher, you go along with this?"

"I do."

"All right, Smoke Jensen, raise your right hand."

Smoke did as he was directed.

"Now, repeat after me. I Smoke Jensen . . ."

"I Smoke Jensen . . ." He continued with the oath as administered by Marshal Holloway. "Do solemnly swear that I will faithfully execute all lawful precepts, directed to the Marshal of the United States for the District of Colorado, under the authority of the United States, and true returns make, in all things well and truly. And without malice or partiality, perform the duties of Deputy Marshal for the District of Colorado during my continuance in said office, so help me God."

That done, Holloway reached out to shake Smoke's hand. "Congratulations, Smoke. You are now a Deputy U.S. Marshal. That gives you full authority to arrest any fugitive, anywhere within the borders of the United States. That includes all states and territories." Holloway smiled. "But you won't be paid."

"I understand."

"But even though you won't be paid, you still intend to bring him in."

"No."

"I beg your pardon? I thought that was the whole reason for appointing you a Deputy U.S. Marshal."

"I won't be bringing him in," Smoke said cryptically.

Shortly afterward, Smoke took his hunt for Angus Shardeen public. He had a letter printed in newspapers all over Kansas, Colorado, Idaho, and Wyoming.

> *To the murderer and bandit, Angus Shar-deen.*
>
> *You killed many women, children, and old men during the war. You have continued your murdering and killing since the war, having abandoned all pretense of patriotism, and are doing so for selfish reasons.*
>
> *During your murderous spree, one of the women you killed was my mother, Pearl Jen-*

sen. I watched you do this, then you clubbed me down and left me for dead. You should have checked me more closely Shardeen, for I was not dead, and now I am coming for you.

I'm coming for you for my mother and for the families of all the innocents you have killed, and I am doing this, not for revenge, but for justice. That is because as an official Deputy United States Marshal, I have the power of the law on my side.

SMOKE JENSEN

"Who in the hell does this arrogant deputy marshal think he is?" Shardeen demanded angrily, after he read the letter in the newspaper.

"He tells us right there who he is," Bartell said. "He is Smoke Jensen."

"Is that name supposed to mean anything to me?"

"From what I've heard, he may be the fastest gun there is," Bartell replied. "And they say he can shoot the eye out of a squirrel from a hundred yards away."

"*They* say? Who says?" Shardeen demanded.

"People who have seen him shoot. He could give us trouble."

"How much trouble can he be if he is dead? I want him dead," Shardeen said. "And I'm willing to pay well for it."

CHAPTER 17

March 1870

In the six months since Smoke had pinned on the star of Deputy U.S. Marshal, he had been wandering around, sometimes chasing a lead, sometimes going from town to town with no particular lead but merely "casting his net," as Preacher described his travels. And like fishermen who cast their nets into the sea, his net came up empty many more times than it provided results.

Even as he rode on, he remembered what he'd learned two months ago in the small town of Sage Creek, Wyoming.

A bartender nervously handed him a piece of paper. "I don't know if you know anything about this, and I want you to know I ain't havin' nothin' to do with it. By that, I mean I ain't handin' these things out to nobody, even though somebody give me near a hunnert of 'em 'n tole me to pass 'em out to any cowboy who might want to make a little money."

"What is it?" Smoke asked, wondering what the mysterious piece of paper might be. He opened it to read.

Five Hundred Dollars
Will Be Paid By

Angus Shardeen
To Anyone Who Kills
Smoke Jensen

Smoke chuckled.

"If you don't mind my sayin' so, Mr. Jensen, that seems like an odd reaction from someone seein' his name on a flyer that's offerin' five hunnert dollars for his bein' kilt."

"I suppose so. But to me it means that I've finally got his attention. And it isn't as if these are something that's been put out by the law." Smoke folded the paper over.

"Yeah, but to an awful lot of bounty hunters it don't make no difference who is payin' the reward, long as there is one," the bartender said.

Smoke nodded. "I guess you have a point there."

Smoke stopped on a ridge just above the road leading into the town of Commerce, Idaho. The cold gray sky was spitting snow, though it wasn't falling heavily. He tried to take a drink of water from his canteen, but it was frozen. He wasn't thirsty enough to start a fire to melt it.

He watched a stagecoach a few minutes as it started down from the pass, making its way into the town. Then, corking the canteen, he put it away, hunkered down inside his buffalo coat, slapped his legs against the side of his horse, and sloped down the long ridge. Although he was actually farther away from town than the coach, he would beat it there because he was going by a more direct route.

He stopped beside a small sign just on the edge of town.

COMMERCE
POPULATION 125
A Growing Community

The weathered board and faded letters indicated that it had been there for some time, most likely erected when optimism for the town's future was still prevalent. Smoke doubted there were that many residents in the town, and he was positive the town had no future.

He continued on into town, checking the corners and rooftops of buildings, doorways, and kiosks . . . any place that might provide concealment for a would-be shooter. His pa had taught him to be cautious. Preacher had suggested that the better he became known, the more cautious he should be. The actual procedure as to when, where, and how to look out for snipers and those who would ambush him was something he had developed by experience and common sense.

A moment later, he pulled up in front of the saloon, dismounted, and made a cautious entrance inside. Taking off his hat, he brushed away the snow, then removed his heavy coat and hung it on a stop that protruded from the wall.

He examined the saloon for a moment. Two pot-bellied stoves blazed away with such intensity that they were gleaming red. The heat was disproportional with an area that was too hot close to the stoves . . . and too cold far away, but with a wide comfort zone in between. Most of the bar was within that comfort zone, and Smoke stepped up to it.

"What'll it be?" the bartender asked.

"A beer and maybe a little information," Smoke replied.

"The beer I can supply. Not sure about the information, but you can try."

Smoke waited until the beer mug was put in front of him before he asked, "Does the name Angus Shardeen mean anything to you?"

"I know who he is. I expect just about ever'one in the West knows who he is."

"But do you know where he is?"

"I don't have any idea where he is, 'n I'm not sure I'd tell you where if I knew."

"Why not?"

"If you're plannin' on joinin' up with him, far as I'm

concerned, he has enough dregs with him already. And any-one who is plannin' on joinin' up with him is a lowlife."

"And if I'm not plannin' on joinin' him?"

"Then I got two reasons not to tell you nothin'. Number one, I don't want to give you information that could get you kilt. And number two, I don't want it gettin' back to Shar-deen that I'm tellin' folks how to find him."

At the opposite end of the bar stood a man wearing a slouch hat above a weather-lined face. Hanging low in a quick-draw holster on the right side of a bullet-studded belt was a silver-plated Colt .44, its grip inlaid with mother-of-pearl.

He had been listening to the conversation and watching Smoke in the mirror. When he'd heard enough, he tossed his drink down and wiped the back of his hand across his mouth. Then he turned to look at Smoke. "Hey, you."

Smoke did not turn.

"I'm talkin' to you, boy."

Smoke looked at him and raised his beer in salute. "Good afternoon." He knew from the tone of the man's voice that it wasn't going to be a simple exchange of pleas-antries.

"You're lookin' for Angus Shardeen, are you?"

"I am."

"And would your name be Smoke Jensen?"

"I am."

"You do know, don't you, Mr. Smoke Jensen, Mr. fa-mous . . . gunfighter"—he set the last word apart from the rest of the sentence and said it with a sneer—"that there's re-ward money out for you."

"How would you know that?" Smoke asked.

"I know that because I'm a bounty hunter, 'n it's my business to know."

"Well, I hate to disappoint you, Bounty Hunter," Smoke said. "But you don't want me. That dodger isn't official. I'm not wanted by the law."

The bounty hunter laughed a harsh and dismissive laugh.

"Hell, mister, that don't matter none to me. A reward is a reward, 'n I don't really give a damn who pays it."

"What's your name?"

An evil smile spread across the bounty hunter's face. "The name would be Blackwell. Sledge Blackwell."

Smoke gave a short nod in acknowledgment. "Well, Mr. Blackwell, I would suggest that you not try to collect this particular reward."

"Don't try?" Blackwell replied.

The saloon had grown deathly still as the patrons sat quietly, nervously, and yet titillated by the life and death drama that had suddenly begun to unfold in front of them.

He turned to address the others. "You'd like for me not to try and collect the reward. Is that what you're saying? I suppose you would rather I just walk away, wouldn't you?"

Smoke put the beer down with a tired sigh and turned to face his tormentor. "It would be better for both of us if you would. But you're not going to do that, are you?"

"I can't. Why, this is how I make my livin', boy. I'm sure you've heard of Sledge Blackwell."

"Yeah, I've heard of you." In truth, Smoke had never heard of Blackwell.

"Yeah? What have you heard?" Blackwell asked, the smile on his face broadening.

"I've heard that you are a used-up old man who shoots people in the back because you don't have the guts to face them down."

Smoke's response had just the effect he wanted it to have. The smile on Blackwell's face turned to an angry snarl. "Draw, Jensen!" he shouted, going for his own gun even before he issued the challenge.

Blackwell was fast and had proved his mettle in many gunfights, but midway through his draw, he realized that he had made a big mistake. The arrogant confidence in his eyes was replaced by fear, then acceptance of the fact that he was about to be killed.

The two pistols discharged almost simultaneously, but

Smoke had been able to bring his gun to bear and his bullet plunged into Blackwell's chest, while the bounty hunter didn't even get his gun high enough to avoid punching a hole in the floor.

Looking down at himself, Blackwell put his hand over his wound, then pulled it away and examined the blood that had pooled in his palm. When he looked back at Smoke, an almost whimsical smile appeared on his face. "Damn, you're fast. I ain't never seen anyone that . . ." His sentence ended with a cough, then he fell back against the bar, making an attempt to grab onto the bar to keep himself erect. His arm moved across the top of the bar, sweeping away both drinks. His shot glass and Smoke's beer mug wound up on the floor. The slouch hat fell from his head into the half-filled spittoon. The eye-burning, acrid smoke of two discharges hung in a gray-blue cloud just below the ceiling.

Smoke turned back to the bar. "Looks like I'm going to need another beer."

"Yes, sir, another beer, and this one is on the house," the bartender said, holding a new mug under the spigot of the beer barrel.

Behind Smoke, the silence was broken as everyone discussed what they had just seen. He was only halfway through his beer when the town marshal and two of his deputies arrived.

"What happened here?" the marshal asked.

The question wasn't directed to anyone in particular, so everyone started answering at once, availing themselves of the first opportunity to tell a story they would be telling for the rest of their lives.

"Hold it, hold it!" The marshal put up his hands. "Don't everyone talk at once." He looked over toward the bartender. "Ed, did you see what happened?"

"It's this way, Marshal Moore. Blackwell tried to brace this man."

The marshal looked at Smoke. "Blackwell braced you?" the marshal asked.

"Yes."

"Blackwell's a bounty hunter. If he braced you, he must've thought you've got a wanted flyer out on you. Do you, mister?"

Smoke started to reach for his shirt pocket.

"What are you doing?" Marshal Moore demanded anxiously.

"Take it easy, Marshal," Smoke replied. "You asked if I had paper out on me, and I'm about to show it to you."

"You mean to say that you are a wanted man, and you not only admit it, but you are going to prove it?"

Smoke smiled. "Yeah, you might say something like that." He pulled a folded up piece of paper from his pocket and handed it to the marshal.

The marshal unfolded the paper, read it, then looked up at Smoke. "You're Smoke Jensen?"

"Yes, sir."

Moore folded the paper and handed it back. "Did Blackwell realize this wasn't a real reward poster?"

"Oh, it's real all right, Marshal. It just isn't a reward that was put out by the law."

"Evidently, Blackwell didn't care who put out the reward."

"That's right, Marshal," the bartender said. "Why, Blackwell stood right here and said as much."

"I've heard of you, Jensen. But I'm curious as to what brought you to our town?"

Smoke showed the marshal his Deputy U.S. Marshal badge. "I'm looking for Angus Shardeen."

"Alone?"

"Yes. Do you know where he is?"

"I'm sorry. I don't have the slightest idea."

"That's too bad. I was hoping you might have some idea."

"Look Jensen, with all the men Shardeen has around him, I hope you're just trying to locate him, and don't have any intention of bringing him in by yourself."

"I have no intention of bringing him in," Smoke said, repeating what he had told Marshal Holloway.

"That's being smart," Marshal Moore said, not understanding the intent of Smoke's reply.

Three hundred miles north of Commerce, the town of Fort Benton sat alongside the completely iced-over Missouri River. Elmer Gleason stopped by the Gold Strike Saloon to see Janey. He had taken a job as deputy city marshal and though he did drop by to see her fairly often, he had never become one of her more intimate customers. For one thing, he couldn't afford her. She was considerably more expensive than any other girl who worked the saloon. But the real reason was more complex than that.

"It's just that I sort of look at you as my sister, Abbigail," Elmer told her as they shared a table, using the name by which he had first known her. "I ain't never had me no sister, but if I did, I sure wouldn't be takin' her to bed."

Janey laughed. "No, I wouldn't think so."

"You got 'ny brothers?"

The smile left Janey's face, and Elmer held up his hand. "Never mind. Hell, I know better 'n to ask a question like that. Forget that I asked."

"No, it's all right," Janey said. "I think I will tell you. It might be nice having a friend who knows something about me. Otherwise, being this far from home, with a name that isn't mine, and with nobody who really knows me, it becomes almost like I don't exist. Do you know what I mean?"

Elmer smiled. "I'm not sure that I do. That kind of talk is sort of hard for me to get aholt of."

"It means I want somebody to know me, to really know who I am. And I'd like for that somebody to be you. That is, if you don't mind listenin' to my story.

Elmer nodded. "I think I'd be plumb honored if you'd tell me."

"To begin with, yes, I do have a brother. I had two brothers, but one of them was killed in the war. And of course, my name isn't really Fannie Webber, nor is it Abbigail Fontaine. My real name is Jane. Janey, my family always called me. Janey Jensen."

Elmer was surprised. "Jensen?"

"Yes. My father is Emmett, and my brother is—"

"Kirby," Elmer said. It wasn't a question, rather a statement of fact.

Janey gasped and put her hand to her mouth. "How long have you known?"

"I didn't know. Not till right now when you told me. But it turns out that I do know your brother. Me 'n him rode together with the Ghost Riders durin' the war."

"I didn't know Kirby had gone off to war. It must've been after I left."

"He was a good man to ride with, one you could count on when things got a little testy. Me 'n him was great friends. He 'n your pa even saved my life once."

"My pa? You also know my pa?"

"I met 'im."

Janey reached across the table and put her hand on Elmer's arm. "Elmer, please, you must swear to me that you will never tell them about me. Don't tell them where I am. Don't even tell them that you know me."

"They are good people, Abbi . . . uh, Janey. Why not tell them?"

"Do you have to ask? You're right. They are good people. But you know me for what I am. Do you really think I could compare the life I have lived with the lives they have lived?"

"Janey, you being what you are don't make you a bad person. Fact is, you're one of the best women I've ever knowed."

"Please, Elmer, if you care anything at all for me, you'll never tell them about me."

"All right. Prob'ly don't matter, anyhow. I don't expect to ever see either one of 'em again. One of the reasons I come by today was to tell you good-bye."

"Good-bye? What do mean, good-bye? Where are you goin'?"

"I've always had me a hankerin' to go sailin' acrossed the ocean so's I could see me some of the rest of the world."

"Will you write me?"

"I ain't never been much for writin'," Elmer said. "Anyhow, I don't even know how I'd go about sendin' you a letter from Australia or Siam or China, or some such place. Besides, you more 'n likely won't be here much longer, anyhow. You damn near got as much of a wanderin' around itch as I do."

Janey smiled. "I do at that. I reckon I'll leave soon as you're gone. There's bound to be some place that's warmer 'n Fort Benton."

"You got that right."

"I'm goin' to miss you, Elmer. If I never see you again, I'll keep your memory forever in my heart."

Elmer nodded and got a strange, almost yearning look in his eyes. "Abbi . . . I mean, Janey, that thought brings me more comfort than I can say."

The two hugged good-bye.

"Sally, dear, I'm so happy you decided to come to New York to visit your old aunt."

"Oh, I'd hardly call you old, Aunt Mildred." Sally Reynolds was sitting on the windowsill of the third floor of one of the Greek Revival row houses on the north side of Washington Square. The apartment belonged to her Aunt Mildred, and Sally had come to New York to spend a couple weeks with her. It was a cold and gray day in late March. The steely sunlight illuminated but did not warm the city. Spring had already begun, but the pedestrians walking on the sidewalk below wore heavy coats and scarves. From this elevation, they were a never-ending flow of black figures, rather like a stream of ants on the march.

She heard the distant rumble of an el train and the clatter of an omnibus, and wondered about so many people on the move. Who were they? Where were they going? What lay ahead of them?

What lay ahead for *her*?

Sally had already made the decision for her own future and had announced it to her family with great passion and intensity. She had recently graduated from Mary Woodson Normal College and was a qualified teacher. She was going West to teach school and to see some of the country she had only read about.

Sally's parents were completely opposed to the idea and had sent her to New York on a visit in the hope that she would, in her father's words, "come to her senses."

"Have you given any thought as to what you want for supper?" Aunt Mildred asked. "There are so many nice restaurants close by."

"Could we just have some scrambled eggs and stay home for supper?" Sally asked. "I've something I would like to speak with you about."

"Of course we can. But instead of scrambled eggs, suppose I make us an omelet? If you don't mind a little bragging, I will tell you that I make a wonderful omelet."

"That would be great," Sally replied with a smile.

A short while later, the two sat down at the kitchen table for supper.

"Oh," Sally said after her first bite. "It's not bragging if what you say is true. This really *is* a wonderful omelet."

"Why, thank you, dear. You said you had something you wanted to discuss with me. Would it be your idea about going West to teach school?"

"Oh!" Sally replied with a gasp. "How did you know that?"

"I got a letter from my brother telling me about it. He wants me to talk some sense into you."

"And are you going to try?"

"Yes."

"I see."

Mildred smiled and put her hand across the table. "I'm going to tell you to go where your heart tells you to go."

"What? Oh, Aunt Mildred, I thought . . . that is, I was afraid . . ."

"I know what you thought. You thought I was going to try and talk you out of it. May I share a secret with you?"

"Yes, of course!"

"There was a time when, more than anything else in the world, I wanted to move to San Francisco, to see what was on the other side of this country.

"I didn't go, because my older brother, your father, talked me out of it. I've wondered about that decision for my entire life. I know now that I should have gone. I don't want you to spend the rest of your life wondering. Go, Sally. Follow your heart while you are still young. If you find that you don't like it, you can always come back home, like the prodigal son, or in this case the prodigal daughter." Aunt Mildred chuckled.

"I'm going to do it," Sally said, a broad smile spreading across her face.

"Do you have any idea where you'll wind up?"

"I sent some letters out, and the only place that responded was a town called Bury, Idaho."

One month later, Elmer Gleason was standing on the waterfront in San Francisco. The ship *Pacific Dancer* was tied alongside the dock. The canvas was rolled tight against the yardarms and the lines hung loose, whistling in the breeze. The ship was taking on a cargo of buffalo hides, and it rocked gently in the waves that lapped ashore.

Elmer had just applied for a job as an able-bodied seaman.

"Have you ever sailed before?" the purser asked.

"Cain't say as I have, 'cause I ain't," Elmer said.

"Why should I sign you on, then? More 'n likely you'd wind up doin' nothin' more 'n spendin' all your time pukin' on the deck. The crew will have enough to do without cleanin' up your puke."

"Look, sonny. Sign me up or don't sign me up, I really don't give a damn which one you do. This here ain't the only ship tied up in the bay. If you don't take me on, I don't reckon it's goin' to be all that hard to find me one that will." Elmer turned and started to walk away.

"Wait," the purser called out to him. He chuckled. "It might be good to see you get seasick at that. Could be that it'll take you down a notch or two. Can you sign your name?"

Elmer wrote his name in bold, legible letters.

"Report to the First Mate."

"Who would that be?"

The purser pointed to the gangplank. "Go on aboard and stand there without doin' nothin' for a moment or two. The man that yells at you will be the first mate."

"Where's this ship bound?"

"You mean you signed on without even knowin' where the ship was goin'?"

"Yeah."

"Why would you do that?"

"Because I didn't really care where it was goin'."

"Then why do you care now?"

"'Cause now I'm actual on it," Elmer replied, starting toward the gangplank.

"China," the purser yelled at him. "We're goin' to China."

Elmer lifted his hand in recognition that he had heard, but he didn't turn his head around. He had seen his share of Chinamen. Now, he supposed, he was about to see a whole bunch of them.

* * *

The man caught Janey's attention as soon as he got on the train. He was a handsome man, tall, with black hair, dark eyes, a fine nose, and a strong chin. The clothes he was wearing indicated that he must be a wealthy man. He was wearing fawn-colored riding breeches tucked into highly polished calf-high boots, a dark jacket held closed by one brass button, and a vest that matched his trousers, across which was strung a gold watch chain. At his neck he wore a maroon cravat.

He looked as if he might be every bit as wealthy as Big Ben Conyers, but something else about him Janey found even more intriguing. She knew instinctively that he was a man who had few compunctions and little concern about what others might think of him.

She got up from her seat and walked to the front of the car to take a drink of water from the water barrel. She gave him a very close look as she passed him by, then studied him over the brim of the dipper. When she walked back to her seat, she managed to lose her balance just as she drew even with him. "Oh, my!" she exclaimed as she fell into his lap. "Oh, dear. I'm so sorry."

She made an effort to get back on her feet, but she put her hand on the inside of his thigh, then slipped again, causing her hand to slide up his thigh. "Oh! I'm so clumsy. Please forgive me!"

"Nothing to forgive, my dear," the man said, smiling at her. "It can sometimes be difficult walking on a moving train."

"So I see."

"May I suggest that you sit next to me until you have quite recovered."

"Thank you, sir. You are such a gentleman. I don't know how to thank you, mister . . .".

"Richards. Josh Richards."

"I'm Janey Garner."

"It's good to meet you, Miss Garner."

"It's Mrs. Garner."

"Oh, I beg your pardon for the mistake."

Janey smiled. "I assume Mrs. is still appropriate. Poor Paul was killed in . . . a boating accident." She'd started to say, "in the war," but since the war was some five years past, she didn't want to appear old enough to be a war widow.

"Actually, and I do hope you don't think it too forward of me, I would prefer to be called Janey."

"Then Janey it shall be," Richards said.

"Where are you going, Mr. Richards?"

"Please, if I am to call you Janey, you must call me Josh."

"Very well, Josh. Where are you going?" She put her hand across her mouth. "Oh, please, you must forgive me. I have no business in inquiring about such a personal matter."

"No forgiveness is necessary. I don't mind at all telling you where I'm going. I am an owner of the PSR, which is an obscenely large ranch just outside the town of Bury, Idaho."

"Oh! What a coincidence! I, too, am going to Bury," Janey said, making the decision at that very instant. "I am sure that your wife is looking forward quite anxiously to your return."

"I suppose she would be if I had a wife. I'm not married, Janey."

"Well now, that is very nice to know."

CHAPTER 18

Smoke heard the high, keening sound of a steam-powered saw and knew that he was close to a town. If he had followed directions, the town was Buffington. At least, he hoped it was Buffington. A couple weeks ago a man had told him that Angus Shardeen had been seen in the town.

As he rode closer, he smelled meat cooking and bread baking. His stomach churned as those aromas reminded him of just how hungry he was.

Finally, he saw a church steeple through the trees, a tall spire, topped by a brass-plated cross that glistened in the high noon sun. He reached a road running parallel to the railroad tracks and moved onto it, following it the rest of the way into the settlement.

The town impressed him with its bustling activity. In addition to the working sawmill, he saw several other examples of commerce—freight wagons lumbering down the street, carpenters erecting a new building, a store clerk in a white apron sweeping the boardwalk in front of his place of employment. Well-maintained boardwalks ran the length of the town on either side of the street. At the end of each block, planks were laid across the road to allow pedestrians to cross to the other side without having to walk in the dirt or mud.

Smoke stopped his horse and waited patiently at one of the intersections while he watched a woman cross on the plank, daintily holding her skirt up above her ankles to keep the hem from getting soiled. She nodded her appreciation to him as she stepped up onto the boardwalk on the opposite side of the street.

Smoke clucked at Seven, and the Appaloosa stepped across the plank, then headed toward the livery, a little farther down. Smoke dismounted in front of it.

An old man got up from the barrel he had been sitting on and walked, with a limp, over to Smoke. "Boardin' your horse, mister?"

"Yes."

"How long will you be stayin'?" he asked.

"I'm not sure," Smoke said.

"It'll cost you fifteen cents a night."

"Does that include feeding him?"

"Hay, only. Oats'll cost you five cents extra."

Smoke gave the man a silver dollar. "I'll be back before this is worked off."

"Wes," the old man called, and a boy of about fourteen appeared from inside the barn.

"Yes, sir?"

"Take this man's horse."

"Wait a minute," Smoke said.

"Beg your pardon?"

"I need to let Seven know that you've got my permission to be around him. I'd better introduce you."

"Mister, I been handlin' horses since I was ten years old," Wes said. "You don't need to introduce me to your horse."

Smoke smiled and stepped away. "All right, come get him."

The boy started toward the horse, and Seven lowered his head and bared his teeth.

Startled, the boy jumped back. "Uh, maybe you had better introduce us."

"Yeah, it might work out better that way," Smoke said with a smile. He put one hand on the side of the horse's face and the other hand on the boy's shoulder. "Seven, it's all right. This boy's name is Wes, and he's going to take good care of you while I'm gone."

Seven nodded his head, and Smoke reached out to take the boy's hand. He was about to put it on Seven's face, but Wes pulled back.

"It's all right," Smoke said. "Seven's going to treat you fine. Here, give him a couple pats."

Hesitantly, Wes allowed his hand to be put on Seven's face. Only when Seven moved his head against the hand did the boy smile.

"There, now you and my horse are friends. Wes, I'd suggest that before anyone else handles him, you tell Seven it'll be all right."

"You mean he'll listen to me?"

"Sure he will. Like I said, you and Seven are friends now."

The smile broadened, spreading across Wes's face. "Yes, sir, I'll be sure 'n introduce the others to 'im!" he said proudly. "Come on, Seven. Like he said, me 'n you's friends now."

Smoke turned to the livery man. "The name of this town is Buf-fington, isn't it?"

"Yes, sir, it is." The man extended his hand. "I'm Tony Heckemeyer."

"Smoke Jensen." He examined Heckemeyer's face for any sign of recognition, but he gave none. "This seems like a nice, industrious town."

"Yes, sir. We like it."

Suddenly, several gunshots interrupted their conversation. Looking toward the opposite end of the street, Smoke saw two men backing out of a building.

"That's the bank! They're robbin' the bank!" Heckemeyer said.

A third man suddenly appeared from the alley that ran between the bank and the building next to it. He was mounted and leading two horses. Leaning down, he threw the reins to the two others. Once they mounted, all three began shooting up the town in order to keep people off the street.

Their efforts were effective, in that most people were scurrying to get out of the way. But Smoke saw a little girl not more than five or six years old standing at the edge of the street, obviously in the line of fire from the shooters. She was too frightened and too confused to move.

Dropping his saddlebags, Smoke ran out into the street toward her, scooped her up in his arms, and was about to carry her to safety, but it was too late. The three bank robbers were galloping down the street toward them.

He put the girl down, then stepped out between her and the gunmen. "Stay behind me and don't move!" he shouted at her.

Smoke's initial intention had been no more than to get the little girl to safety, but in so doing he had put himself in the path of the robbers' escape route.

Pulling his pistol, Smoke aimed at the closest rider and fired. Even as that robber was tumbling from his saddle, Smoke knocked a second rider from his horse. The two riderless horses galloped by.

The third robber, suddenly realizing that he was alone, reined in his own horse, tossed his gun down and threw both arms into the air. "No, no!" he shouted. "Don't shoot, don't shoot! I quit, I quit!"

With the surrender, nearly a dozen armed men of the town came running out into the street with their guns aimed at the one remaining robber.

"Get down from there, mister," one of the men shouted in an authoritative voice. His authority, Smoke saw, came from the badge he was wearing on his vest.

A woman came running into the street and picked up the little girl. "Oh, Frances, sweetheart! Are you all right!"

"Did any of the bullets hit her?" Smoke asked anxiously.

"No, no, I don't think so," the woman said. "I don't know how to thank you."

"Just seeing that she wasn't hurt is thanks enough for me," Smoke said.

"Take him to jail," the man with the badge said, referring to the robber who had given up. Two others responded to the order, prodding their prisoner along at gunpoint.

The man with the badge came back to speak to Smoke. He stuck out his hand. "I'm Sheriff Gwaltney. Mister, I want to thank you for what you done. You not only saved the little girl there, you probably saved several others by stoppin' those men before they could shoot up the whole town. Also, because of what you done we got the bank's money back. The whole town owes you for that."

"That was a real brave thing, you standin' out in the middle of the street like that," Heckemeyer said, coming over to join them.

"I didn't have much choice," Smoke said. "I sort of got caught out there."

"You coulda just stayed out of the way."

Smoke looked at the little girl, who was examining him closely with blue eyes that were open wide in wonder. He shook his head. "No, I couldn't."

Even as Smoke and the sheriff were speaking, a man wearing a long black coat came driving up in a wagon. He stopped the wagon between the two men Smoke had shot.

"Doolin, don't you go puttin' them fellas in any of your fancy coffins, thinkin' maybe that the county's goin' to pay for it," Sheriff Gwaltney said. "'Cause I'm tellin' you right now, we ain't agoin' to do it."

"I won't use nothin' but a couple plain pine boxes," Doolin replied.

"Why waste a box? Put both of 'em in the same box," another said, and those gathered laughed rather nervously at the macabre joke.

At that moment, Smoke couldn't help but think of the feeding trough he had used as the coffin to bury his mother.

Sheriff Gwaltney looked back at Smoke. "What's your name, mister?"

"Jensen. Smoke Jensen."

"Smoke Jensen?" Gwaltney replied as a look of recognition passed across his face. He stroked his chin. "Seems to me like I've heard that name before. Do you have any paper out on you?"

"Yeah, I do."

"What?"

As he had done with Marshal Moore, Smoke took out the WANTED poster that Angus Shardeen had circulated.

"Damn. That's purdee advertisin' for someone to murder you," Gwaltney said. "It takes someone evil and arrogant to do somethin' like that. Don't he know that somethin' like this will get the law after him?"

Smoke laughed.

"What's so funny?"

"The law is already after him. What would one more thing matter?"

Sheriff Gwaltney laughed. "I guess you're right. And, to tell you the truth, it wouldn't make no never mind to me whether the law had paper out on you or not. After stoppin' the bank robbery the way you done, you have certainly made some friends in this town. I don't know what brought you here, but I'm sure glad you showed up when you did."

"Mister Jensen, have you had your lunch yet?" asked the mother of the little girl.

"No, I haven't."

"My name's Kathy York. I would love to fix lunch for you."

"Well, I—uh . . ." Smoke stuttered his response.

Kathy chuckled. "It's not what you are thinking, Mr. Jensen." She pointed to a building directly across from them.

"That's my café there, Dumplins. You come on over and have lunch, on me."

"Thanks," Smoke said.

While Smoke was having his lunch, several of the townspeople stopped by his table to thank him for what he had done in saving little Frances York, and in stopping the bank robbery.

"Most ever'one in town's got money in that bank. Why, if them men had gotten away with it, there's several of us would've fallen on hard times, and that's for sure," one of the men said.

The accolades were growing so profuse that Smoke was beginning to feel self-conscious about it.

After lunch, Frances came over to Smoke's table, very carefully carrying a small plate. "This is Mama's blackberry cobbler."

Smoke smiled. "Well, thank you." He turned serious. "But I don't know. Is it any good?"

Frances nodded. "Oh, yes. It's very good."

"You know what? When I have something that is very good, like blackberry cobbler, I like to have someone else eat with me. Do you think your mama would let you have a plate of cobbler so you could eat with me?"

"Mama! He wants me to have some, too!" Frances called out happily, and a moment later she was sitting across the table from him as they ate the cobbler together.

Smoke got a sudden image of his sister when she was a little girl. Blackberry cobbler had been her favorite dessert, and he wondered if she still liked it. He wondered, too, where she was, and if he would ever see her again.

She had run away because she obviously wanted to be on her own. If that was really what she wanted, he had no intention of disturbing her.

*   *   *

Smoke walked back down to the sheriff's office.

"Mr. Jensen, what can I do for you?" the sheriff said, greeting him effusively.

"You asked me earlier what brought me here," Smoke said. "It didn't seem the right time or place to tell you then, but I'm looking for a man." Smoke turned his vest out, so the sheriff could see that he was a Deputy U.S. Marshal.

"A Deputy U.S. Marshal, are you? Well, now I can see how you were able to handle those two men so easily. Who are you looking for?"

"Angus Shardeen."

"Angus Shardeen? You mean the one that's put out the reward to have you killed?"

"Yes."

"Well then, with the two of you lookin' for each other, you're bound to meet up with him, don't you think?"

"No, there's a difference. He's not actually looking for me. All he's done is put out Wanted posters promising to reward anyone who can kill me. I'm actually looking for him."

"Do you have a posse with you? Or are you looking for him alone?"

"I have no one with me."

"That's quite a job for one man. I know Marshal Holloway. I can't imagine him sending one man out for Shardeen."

"He didn't send me out," Smoke said. "I volunteered."

"If you're tryin' to make a name for yourself, Jensen, you don't need to go so far as to try and tackle Shardeen all by yourself. Hell, you're already gettin' known around."

"It has nothing to do with making a name for myself," Smoke said. "Truth is, I'd just as soon not have a name. What's between Shardeen and me is personal."

"Yes, but there's the problem you see. It might be personal for you, but it won't be for him. Last I heard, he had at least six or seven men ridin' with him, and maybe even more than that. Here's the thing, most of 'em is the same ones that rode with him durin' the war."

"So I've heard. I also heard that he had been seen here in Buffington."

"That's true. He and his men passed through town one day a few weeks ago. They stocked up at the general store, then rode on. But like I said, there were quite a few of 'em. They didn't give us any trouble, so we didn't give them any trouble."

"You wouldn't have any idea as to where they might be now, would you?"

The sheriff shook his head. "No, I don't know. I'm just telling you that if you go after him alone, you may be takin' on a bigger bite than you can chew."

"You may be right, but I'm determined to find him. By the way, I don't think I saw a hotel when I came into town."

"The reason you didn't see one is because we don't have one. At least, not 'ny more. The one hotel we had burned down last month, and it ain't been built back. But if you're lookin' for a place to stay, you might check in at the Salt Lick Saloon. You can get a room there if they aren't all in use."

The Salt Lick was the most substantial-looking saloon in a row of saloons. A drunk was passed out on the steps in front of the place and Smoke had to step over him in order to go inside.

The chimneys of all the lanterns were soot-covered. Dingy light filtered through drifting smoke. The place smelled of sour whiskey, stale beer, and strong tobacco. The long bar on the left with a large mirror behind it was like everything else about the saloon—so dirty Smoke could scarcely see any images in it. What he could see was distorted by imperfections in the glass.

Eight or ten tables were nearly all occupied. A half-dozen or so bar girls were flitting about, pushing drinks. A few card games were in progress, but most of the patrons were just drinking and talking.

Smoke stepped up to the bar. The bartender was pouring the residue from abandoned whiskey glasses back into a bottle. He pulled a soggy cigar butt from one glass, laid the butt aside, then poured the whiskey back into the bottle without qualms.

One of the other men standing at the bar recognized Smoke. "Hey, you're the man that stopped the bank robbery, ain't you?"

"I was here when it happened," Smoke replied.

"Here? Hell, you was a lot more than just here. Sam, give this feller whatever it is he wants to drink. I'll pay for it."

"Thanks," Smoke said.

"What'll it be?" the bartender asked.

"A beer."

Sam drew a mug of beer, then set it before him.

"I'd also like a room."

"With or without."

That was confusing. "With or without what?"

The bartender looked up in surprise. "Are you kidding me, mister? With or without a woman."

"Without."

"All right. That'll be six bits."

"Six bits? Isn't that a little expensive?"

"If we left the room empty so the girls could use it for their customers, we could make three, maybe four times that," the bartender said. "But since the hotel got burnt down we sometimes take in people who just want a room, so we gotta charge six bits for it. Take it or leave it."

It had been a while since Smoke last slept in a bed, so even though he complained about having to pay seventy-five cents for a room, he considered it well worth it. "Here," he said, slapping the coins on the bar. "Tell your girls and their customers not to come into my room by mistake. If they do, they just might get shot."

"Mister, I don't know who the hell you are, but it ain't healthy to go around making threats you can't back up," the bartender growled. He picked up the silver and took it over to the money box, then reached for a key.

"Sam," someone called from the other end of the bar. "Come here."

The bartender went over to the customer, then leaned over as the customer whispered something in his ear. The bartender looked back toward Smoke, listened a moment longer, then nodded, and hurried back down the bar with the key.

"Mr. Jensen, you don't have to worry none about anyone disturbin' you tonight. I'll make sure you're left in peace."

"I appreciate that, Sam," Smoke replied.

One of the bar girls sidled over to Smoke. Dissipation had not yet taken its toll with her, and she was actually rather attractive. "I heard you say you didn't want to be disturbed tonight," she said as flirtatiously as she could. "I don't blame you. Once you find someone that you want to be with for the rest of the night, the last thing you'd want would be for someone to come bustin' in on you. My name is Gloria, and don't you worry, if you come to my room with me, I'll make certain we aren't disturbed."

Smoke smiled at her. "You know what, Gloria? You could almost tempt me to do just that. But I'm so tired that when I finally do get up there tonight, all I'm going to want to do is sleep."

"All right, honey," Gloria said. "But you don't know what you are missing."

"Oh, I've got a pretty good idea."

"We're losing a player here!" somebody called from one of the tables. "We need another man! Anybody want to get into the game?"

Suddenly Preacher's words came back to Smoke. *"You want to get the measure of any place, you get into a friendly card game in one of the local saloons. Men gets to palaverin' in a card game 'n if you keep your mouth shut, and just listen, why you'll learn more in an hour than you could by readin' a month o' newspapers."*

"I'd like to join you, if you don't mind a stranger playing with you," Smoke said.

"You be a stranger do you? Well, tell me, stranger, are you goin' to be playin' with American money?" asked one of the others at the table.

"Yes, but what difference would it make to you whether I'm playing with American money or not? None of you will ever see it. I intend to win all the hands," Smoke teased.

"Ha! Come on in here, stranger, and sit at the table," another player said. "There ain't nothin' I like better 'n partin' an overconfident fool from his money. And anyone that thinks they're likely to not lose anythin' at all is just the kind of fool that is goin' to lose."

The others laughed, and Smoke joined them at the table. They noticed that he did not sit in a way that would compromise his ability to get to his gun quickly, if he had to.

The other players quickly learned that Smoke was the man who had stopped the bank robbery, and since all three of them had money in the bank, they were grateful to him.

One of the players was Robert Vaughan, owner and editor of the local newspaper. Seeing it as an opportunity to get a story, he began questioning Smoke rather extensively.

Smoke didn't mind the interrogation as it actually opened up avenues for conversation which allowed him to get information, as well as give it. "I understand that Angus Shardeen was in Buffington a while ago."

"He was here, all right," Vaughan said.

"I heard some folks say that it was him, but I don't know as that's true," Rick Adams replied as he picked up his cards.

"It's true, all right." Vaughan looked at the cards he'd been dealt.

"How do you know?" Smoke asked.

The conversation continued between Smoke and the

newspaper editor as he answered, "I know because I recognized two of them. Their leader had red hair, a red beard, and a scar that runs up the side of his face and looks like it damn near cuts his eye in two. That, my friends, could be no one but Angus Shardeen. I also recognized one of the others. He only has half an ear on the left side of his head. That could only be Billy Bartell."

"You wouldn't happen to know where they are holed up, would you?"

"I don't have any idea, but if I had to make an educated guess, I would say that they are holed up in the mountains where they can use the rocks and the draws as a fortress. That way they could stand off an army."

Smoke looked at his cards. "Has anyone actually ever gone into the mountains to try and find Shardeen and his men?"

"No, and they aren't likely to, either. At least, not anyone who has good sense. Why are you asking so many questions about Shardeen, anyway?"

Smoke chuckled. "I guess you could say I'm one of those people who doesn't have very good sense."

"I'll be damned! Are you planning to go after him?"

"Yes."

"I've heard about you, Smoke Jensen. They say you are quite skilled in the way you employ your pistol, in terms of speed with which you can extract your weapon and the deadly accuracy of your shooting. I also know that the reward being offered for Shardeen has reached a rather substantial amount. But no reward is worth getting yourself killed."

"The reward has nothing to do with it. I have a personal reason for going after Mr. Angus Shardeen."

For the remainder of the game, Smoke explained his personal reasons for going after Shardeen, telling how he had witnessed his mother being murdered, and his sister violated.

"And after I take care of Shardeen I intend to deal with Mr. Billy Bartell. By the way, I raise the bet by five dollars," he added, pushing five more dollars into the pot.

"All I can do is wish you luck," Vaughan said. "And call your bet," he added with a triumphant smile.

When Smoke got up from the table somewhat later, he was down by twenty dollars. "Damn. Maybe I shouldn't have played with American money," he teased, and the others laughed.

After a supper of biscuits, bacon, and beans, which he ate at the saloon, he went up the backstairs to the room the bartender had rented him. Smoke poured water into the bowl, took off his shirt, washed, then turned the covers down and crawled into bed.

He was awakened in the middle of the night by a small clicking sound. Instantly, his hand went to the pistol hanging from the headboard. He slipped out of bed and walked barefoot across the carpet, then stood with his back to the wall just beside the door.

The *click* he had heard was the latch being unlocked. He watched the doorknob turn. Holding his pistol in his right hand, arm crooked at the elbow, and pistol pointing up, he eased back on the hammer, cocking it so slowly it made practically no sound as the sear engaged the cylinder.

The door opened, moving silently on the hinges. A little wedge of light spilled into the room from the hallway, the wedge growing wider as the door opened farther until finally it stretched from the open door all the way to the bed. Every muscle in Smoke's body tensed as he waited for the confrontation.

"Hello?" a woman's voice called quietly. "Is anyone in here?"

Who was this woman, and what was she doing here? With a sigh, Smoke's tension was relieved, and he eased the hammer back down as he lowered his pistol. "I'm here," he said from the darkness behind her.

"Oh!" the woman gasped, startled by the sound from an unexpected direction. She put her hand to her chest. "Don't do that! You could scare a body to death that way."

"You *should* be frightened."

"Who are you?"

"My name is Smoke Jensen. Who are you?"

"Smoke Jensen? You're the one who stopped the bank robbers, aren't you?"

"You didn't answer my question. Who are you, and what do you mean coming into my room in the middle of the night? I could've shot you."

"My name is Ida Jean, and this is my room."

"Ida Jean, is it? Well, Ida Jean, if this really is your room, why did you ask if anyone was in here?"

"Sometimes one of the other girls uses it to entertain one of their gentlemen friends. I didn't want to come bargin' in on something."

Smoke shook his head. "I'm all alone in here."

"You rented the room for the night, did you?"

"Yes."

"You know, you don't have to be all alone."

"Yeah, I do."

"Too bad," Ida Jean said. "All right. I'll go somewhere else."

"No," Smoke offered. "If this really is your room, I'll leave."

"Honey, there's no need for you to do that. I have somewhere else I can go. You don't. Good night . . . and sleep tight."

"Thanks," Smoke said.

Ida Jean left the room and Smoke closed and locked the door. He propped a chair under the doorknob. If the woman who just came in had a key, how many more keys were out there? he wondered.

As Smoke lay in the darkness, he thought about the woman and her offer. He had not yet been with a woman . . . in that way . . . and he sometimes wondered about it. He remembered his conversation with his pa.

"I ain't never been with a woman before. Leastwise, I ain't never been with a woman in . . . that . . . way. The way she wanted to be. And I sorta figure that if you're goin' to do somethin' like that with a woman, then maybe it ought to mean somethin'."

Smoke hadn't changed his mind.

CHAPTER 19

Smoke left the saloon the next morning and headed toward Dumplins for breakfast. He had just crossed the street when he heard a voice call out to him.

"Mr. Jensen, look out!" The warning was shouted by Wes, the boy from the stable.

Almost on top of the warning, Smoke felt a blow to the side of his head. He saw stars, but even as he was being hit, he was reacting to the warning so that, while it didn't prevent the attack, it did prevent him from being knocked down.

When his attacker swung at him a second time, Smoke was able to avoid him. With his fists up, he danced quickly out to the middle of the street, avoiding any more surprises from the shadows. It wasn't until then that he saw his attacker, a large man with heavy brows and a bulbous nose.

Smoke called out, "What are you doing? Why are you attacking me?"

"Mister," the man replied with a low growl, "you kilt my brother a few weeks ago."

Almost instantly, a crowd had gathered around Smoke and the man who had come at him from the shadows. It was still fairly early in the morning. He hadn't seen anyone on the street when he first came out of the saloon. Where had all these people come from? he wondered before calling out, "Who is your brother?"

"Damn. Have you kilt so many men that you can't even keep track? It was Sledge Blackwell."

"I'm sorry about your brother. I didn't have any choice. He drew against me."

"Yeah, well, bein' sorry don't do much for bringin' 'im back, does it?" Blackwell caught up with Smoke in the middle of the street.

"Ever'body knows that Sledge Blackwell wasn't worth a bucket of spit. Why's Bull fightin' for 'im?" someone asked.

"Because Bull ain't got good sense."

Blackwell threw a long wild swing at Smoke, but it was easy for Smoke to slip away from it, then counterpunch with a quick, slashing left to Blackwell's face. It was a well-delivered blow, one that would have dropped most men, but Blackwell barely showed the effects. He laughed a low evil laugh. "That the best you got?"

"Somebody ought to stop this," said a man on the boardwalk. "Bull is almost twice as big as Jensen. He's goin' to beat 'im to death."

"Yeah? Well, Smoke ain't no little man, and what he's got is all muscle. I'm goin' with him."

With an angry roar, Blackwell rushed Smoke again, and Smoke stepped aside, avoiding the rush. The big man slammed into a hitching rail, smashing through it as if it were kindling. He turned and faced Smoke again.

A hush fell over the crowd as they watched the two men, observing the fight with a great deal of interest, wanting to see if this young man could handle Blackwell.

Smoke and Blackwell circled around for a moment, holding their fists doubled in front of them, each trying to test the mettle of the other. Blackwell swung, a club-like swing which Smoke leaned away from. Smoke counterpunched and again he scored well, but again, Blackwell laughed it off.

Smoke hit Blackwell almost at will, and though the big

man continued to shrug off the punches, the repeated blows were beginning to take effect. Blackwell's eyes began to puff up, and his lip had a nasty cut.

Smoke saw an opening and was set perfectly to deliver the blow. He sent a long, whistling right into Blackwell's nose and when he felt the nose go under his hand, he knew that he had broken it.

Blackwell's nose bled, the blood ran down across his teeth and chin. The big man continued to throw great swinging blows toward Smoke, but he was getting clumsier and more uncoordinated with each swing.

Growing exhausted from his ineffective efforts, Blackwell quit swinging and started with bull-like charges, all of which Smoke was able to easily avoid. As Blackwell rushed by with his head down, Smoke stepped to one side and sent a powerful right jab to Blackwell's neck, connecting with his Adam's apple. Grabbing his neck, Blackwell went down, gasping for breath.

Smoke stepped up to him and drew his fist back for the final blow, but he stopped when he saw the abject fear in Blackwell's eyes. "You are a lucky man. You came at me with your fists. If you had come after me with a gun, you'd be dead."

As Smoke walked away, he saw Wes standing close by. It was his warning that had enabled Smoke to duck, thus ameliorating Blackwell's first blow. "Thanks, Wes."

"I never thought you could whup him. He's a lot bigger 'n you are."

"Big doesn't always count," Smoke said.

"Yes, sir, I seen that. And I'm goin' to 'member it, too."

"How is Seven doing?"

Wes smiled. "He's a great horse, 'n he won't let anybody aroun' him unless I say it's all right."

"That's because he knows his friends." Smoke flipped a quarter to the boy. "Tell you what. Why don't you give him an extra rubdown today?"

"Yes, sir!" Wes replied enthusiastically.

Smoke stepped into Dumplins a few minutes later.

He was greeted warmly by Kathy. "I hope you like biscuits and gravy, because that's what I've made for breakfast this morning."

"My favorite," Smoke replied with a smile.

After breakfast, Smoke tried to pay for it, but Kathy refused his money.

Smoke shook his head. "No ma'am. You fed me last night. I don't intend you to lose money on me."

"I'm not losing money. Your breakfast has already been paid for."

"What? Who would do that?"

"Mr. Vaughan picked up your bill," Kathy said, pointing to the newspaper publisher.

Smoke walked over to him. "Mr. Vaughan, I want to thank you for buying my breakfast, but there was no need for you to do that."

"It was my pleasure, Smoke." Vaughan chuckled. "Anyway, it isn't costing me anything. I paid for it with money that I won from you yesterday, so you might say that you are paying for it yourself."

"Well, then I don't feel so bad."

"By the way, do make it a point to read the *Delta Metro* today."

"Delta Metro?"

"That's my newspaper. The title comes from the delta formed by the confluence of Horse and Coffee creeks," Vaughan explained. "Not quite the Mississippi River Delta, I admit. But then, *metro* isn't any more appropriate than *delta*, so you might call it poetic license."

Later that same day, while sitting at a table in the back of the Salt Lick, Smoke saw his name in print for the very first time.

Smoke Jensen, Western Hero

> *Yesterday our fair town of Buffington rang with the sound of gunfire as three outlaws attempted to hold up the bank. They were stopped and economic disaster was prevented by the heroic and timely intervention of Smoke Jensen.*
>
> *Like Leonidas at Thermopylae, Smoke stood his ground, defending a young child as he dispatched two of the would-be robbers and forced the third into an ignominious surrender.*
>
> *It is said that Smoke Jensen is seeking that most perfidious of outlaws, Angus Shardeen, with the intention of bringing him to justice. But Shardeen is a coward who surrounds himself with cowards, believing that there is bravery in numbers. This reporter has taken the measure of Smoke Jensen, and believes that he will find, and bring to justice, Angus Shardeen and his minions. Some may wish to compare Smoke Jensen with Don Quixote, dueling windmills. But I say that if it weren't for the Don Quixotes of the world, we would be overrun with windmills.*

Smoke chose the corner, which not only put his back to the wall, but limited the access to him from either side. One of the bar girls approached him, and he recognized her as the one who had come into his room last night. "Hello, Ida Jean. You aren't planning on coming into my room again tonight, are you?"

"No. You made it pretty clear last night that you aren't really interested in that sort of thing."

"Just because I didn't want to share my bed with you, doesn't mean I won't have a drink with a pretty girl." He gave her some money and she walked back over to the bar to buy the drinks.

As he watched her, Smoke noticed a man standing at the far end of the bar staring at him. The man had only half an ear on the left side of his face, and he was glaring at Smoke. An old memory flashed back.

"Spread 'er legs out, boys, I'm goin' to have me a little of this," one of the men was saying. He was a big ugly man with only half of one of his ears.

"Get away from her!" his ma said. She attacked the man.

"What the hell, Bartell, can't you handle a young girl and an old woman?" Shardeen asked with a demonic laugh.

The man at the bar was Billy Bartell, one of the men he had seen at the farm that day, and one of the men, it was said, who was still riding with Shardeen. Bartell had no way of recognizing Smoke, but must have had Smoke pointed out to him, because suddenly and without warning, Bartell reached for his pistol.

If Smoke had not recognized him, Bartell may have had an insurmountable advantage. As it was, he did have the advantage of drawing first, and his many years on the outlaw trail had made him a formidable man with a gun. He got his pistol out first, and for a brief second Bartell actually thought he had won. He smiled as he brought his pistol up.

It wasn't until then that Smoke drew and fired. The bullet hit Bartell in the chest with the impact of a hammer blow, and he was slammed back against the bar before sliding down. He sat there, leaning back against the bar, his gun hand empty and the unfired gun on the floor beside him. He watched as Smoke approached him.

"There ain't nobody that fast." Bartell coughed, a body-shaking cough.

"Don't die yet, Bartell. I want you to know why I killed you."

"I know you been alookin' for us. I reckon it's for the reward."

"It isn't for the reward. It's for Janey."

"Janey?" Bartell got a puzzled look on his face. "Are you crazy? I don't know nobody named Janey."

"I didn't say you knew her. But not knowing her didn't stop you from raping her when you and Shardeen raided my farm during the war."

"I raped a lot of women durin' the war. Some of 'em even liked it."

"She wasn't a woman. She was just a girl."

"How do you know it was me that done it?"

"Because I was there, and I saw you."

"You was there? You musta been just a kid then. How do you even know what you seen?"

Smoke's eyes glinted with retribution. "I know. Where is Angus Shardeen?"

Bartell coughed again, another body-racking cough, bringing up blood. "You know what? I think I am goin' to tell you where he's at. Only I ain't doin' you no favors, 'cause if you find 'im, he'll kill you."

"Where is he?"

"Rattlesnake Canyon." Bartell tried to laugh, but it turned into another blood-oozing cough. "Yeah, you go on out there . . . 'n after he kills you, me 'n you will be meetin' again . . . 'cause I'm goin' to be waitin' for you in hell."

There was a rattling sound deep in Bartell's throat, then his head fell to one side as his eyes, still open, glazed over.

Smoke called out, "Anybody know where Rattlesnake Canyon is?"

"It's about twenty miles west of here," one of the customers said.

"Thanks."

"Jensen, if that's really where he is, you might want to think twice 'bout goin' out there," the bartender said. "Shardeen has some bad men with 'im. You go out there alone, you'll just be committin' suicide."

"I thank you for your concern." Smoke started toward the door.

"You're goin' out there anyway, ain't you?" the man who had spoken to him earlier asked. "You're goin' out there, knowin' that in them rocks he may as well be in a fort, and knowin' how many men he's got with 'im."

Smoke stopped and turned around. "I've been after him for a long time. If he was on the moon, and there was some way I could get there, I would go after him."

"I know that area. Hell, if Shardeen is up there with his men, an army couldn't get him out of there."

"I won't be going with an army," Smoke said. "It'll just be me."

"All by yourself?"

"Yes. The problem with an army is that many men can't hide or keep quiet. Shardeen and his men would see an army comin', and they would be able get ready for them. But one man travelin' alone would more 'n likely be able slip around the rocks and through the crevices and such so as to be able to sneak up on them."

"Jensen, all I can say is, you got a lot more guts than you got brains."

Smoke left the saloon and went directly to the stable to get his horse.

Heckemeyer came over to talk to him as he was throwing the saddle over Seven. "I heered what you was plannin' on doin'. I mean, goin' after Shardeen 'n all."

"You aren't goin' to try and talk me out of it, are you, Mr. Heckemeyer? Because it won't do you any good. I'm goin'."

"I ain't goin' to try 'n talk you out of it. I just thought I might give you a little advice. When you get out there, they's two trails that go to the top," Heckemeyer said, speaking quietly. "You can stay mounted if you take the lower trail, but you'll have to leave your horse somewhere if you take the upper trail. The upper trail is a lot steeper and harder, but that's the one I'd take if I was you."

Smoke nodded as he tightened the cinch strap.

"Thing is . . . if you take the lower trail, you can be seen for a long way before you get there. You take the upper trail, you'll be on top long afore anyone has any idee that you're there."

"Thanks." Smoke handed Heckemeyer two dollar bills. "Give one of these to Wes. You keep the other one."

"Thank you," Heckemeyer said with a smile.

Smoke swung into the saddle, and with a nod, rode out through the open doors at the front of the stable.

Wes walked over then. "He won't be comin' back, will he?"

Heckemeyer gave Wes one of the two dollar bills. "More 'n likely, he won't even live to see the sun go down. 'N that's too bad. The world could use more men like him."

"He ain't goin' to get kilt," Wes said.

"What makes you so sure?"

"I just know."

Rattlesnake Canyon was unique in that it had so many perfectly formed arches that it almost looked as if they were man-made, rather than a work of nature. The interior was so well concealed by rocks and ridgelines that its entrance couldn't be seen unless someone was specifically looking for it. Inside the canyon was a source of water, which made it an ideal place for an outlaw encampment.

After Smoke dismounted, he let Seven go, but not ground tethered. He was free to graze and water. Remembering what Heckemeyer had told him about the two trails, Smoke took the upper one, staying close to the wall, and taking advantage of the many rocks and protrusions. He passed through apertures when possible, rather than going around or over the long fingers. The climb up to the top of the promontory was easy enough at first with an inclining ledge that allowed him to walk upright. The higher he got, the more narrow the ledge became until finally the only way he could stay on the ledge was by holding on to whatever rocks and protrusions he could grab. Then the ledge disappeared altogether, and at the very end of the climb, he had to go straight up, finding footholds and handholds where he could. Finally he reached the top.

From a concealed position, he saw several men sitting around a campfire about two hundred yards away. They were drinking coffee as casually as if they were in a downtown café, showing no concern about anyone approaching them, and why should they? There were five of them, and they were well fortified. Also, as Heckemeyer had promised, Smoke's approach had been totally unnoticed.

Smoke could see the men, but he couldn't approach them directly. Boulders and draws would provide them cover in any gunfight, but the two hundred yards between him and them were wide open, with very few positions along the way where he might be able to take cover.

Lying on his stomach, Smoke used a looking glass to peruse the campsite. He was able to pick out Shardeen, the prominent scar on his face making him easy to spot. Smoke counted six more men and . . . no. As he studied the faces, he realized there were only five more men. The sixth person was a woman.

At first, he thought she was one of them, then he saw that her arms and legs were bound. Whoever the woman was, she was their prisoner!

Smoke gave some consideration to just shooting Shardeen. After all, the Jayhawker was the one he wanted. If he killed him, he could just leave the others behind, then go after Potter, Stratton, and Richards—the men his pa had been after.

Smoke put the looking glass in his pocket and jacked a round into the Henry, then aimed at Shardeen. His finger rested on the trigger, but he didn't shoot. He couldn't do it. He couldn't just shoot Shardeen and leave. He couldn't leave the woman at the mercy of the others. He was sure they would kill her.

With a sigh of frustration, Smoke kept the Henry cocked,

then stood up and walked toward the encampment. For the first twenty-five yards or so, nobody noticed him. Nobody expected anyone to just walk in on them.

"When in the hell is Bartell comin' back? He's s'posed to bring me a bottle of whiskey," one of the men complained.

Smoke recognized him as Tim Shardeen, the man he and his father had encountered a few years ago, when they first started West.

"Hell, Tim. More 'n likely he's took your money and bought hisself a woman," one of the others replied, and they all laughed.

"He better not have done that."

"Bartell's not coming back," Smoke said, his voice startling those gathered around the campfire.

"What the hell?" Tim shouted. "Who the hell are you?"

"I'm the man who killed Bartell."

One of the other men, responding more quickly to the unexpected intrusion, pulled his pistol and fired. Smoke fired back, never lifting the rifle higher than his waist. The man with the pistol went down.

Smoke fired two more times, killing two others. The remaining three men ran behind cover, leaving only the woman exposed.

In the open as he was, Smoke was at a disadvantage. He ran quickly to a small rock that did little to provide cover for him. They began shooting at him, the bullets hitting the rocky ground all around him, whining as they ricocheted away.

A puff of gun smoke hung just over one of the distant boulders, indicating that someone was behind it. Smoke aimed at the corner of the boulder and waited.

A few seconds later, a man's head rose up, just far enough for the man to see where to shoot.

It was all the opening Smoke needed. He squeezed the trigger and watched a little spray of blood and brain detritus fly out from the bullet wound in the outlaw's head.

The shooting stilled. A long period of silence was finally

broken by a man's shout. "Shardeen? Shardeen, you yellow belly! Don't you leave me here all alone!"

Was Shardeen really leaving? Or was it merely a ploy? Smoke wondered.

"Shardeen! Come back here, you low-assed chicken!"

After that last shout, Smoke heard the clatter of horseshoes on the rocky surface as a horse galloped away.

The man shouted more obscenities, the tone of his voice betraying his anger and fear.

"Mister, it looks like you've been deserted. There's only one of you left," Smoke called out from behind his scant rock.

"Who the hell are you?" the disembodied voice shouted.

"My name is Smoke Jensen. Who are you?"

"The name is Hanks."

"Hanks? That name doesn't mean anything to me. I didn't come for you, Hanks. I came for Shardeen."

"Yeah, well, you mighta come for Shardeen, but you have near 'bout kilt all of us."

"Come on out into the open, and let me see you," Smoke invited. "I think we can palaver a little, then both of us go on our way."

"I ain't acomin' out lessen you do."

"We can come out at the same time."

Hanks tried a bit of negotiating. "You said you didn't come for me?"

"That's right."

"Then why don't you just ride away?"

"I'm not leavin' the woman here."

"Why not? She ain't nothin' to you."

"I'm not leavin' her here," Smoke said again a bit stronger. "Now, if you want this to end, put your gun in your holster and come on out."

"I'll come out, but I ain't puttin' my gun away."

"All right. Come on. As long you aren't shooting."

"You said we'd come out at the same time," Hanks replied.

"I'll count to three."

Smoke counted. At three, he stepped cautiously out into the open.

A small man with a narrow face and a hook nose came out from behind the boulder across from Smoke, gun in hand, though the gun was pointing down.

Smoke stood up and walked toward him, still holding the rifle. "Do you have any idea where Shardeen might have gone?"

"Why should I tell you?"

"Why shouldn't you? He ran off, didn't he? You don't owe him anything."

Hanks was obstinate. "I don't owe you nothin' neither."

Smoke walked backwards to the woman, keeping his eyes on the outlaw.

Although out in the open during the entire exchange of gunfire, she hadn't been hit, but her eyes were wide open with fear. So far, she had not uttered a sound.

"Let me get you untied. Then we'll get you back home." Smoke put the rifle down and leaned over to untie the woman.

"Look out!" she shouted suddenly.

In one motion, Smoke drew and fired at Hanks, who was raising his pistol and thumbing back the hammer.

With a bullet in his chest, he stumbled back with a look of shock and pain on his face. He dropped his gun, then slapped both hands over the wound. "How did you—?" was as far as he got before tumbling over, dead.

"Chugwater, Wyoming," the woman said as Smoke untied her.

"That's where you live?"

"No. That's where Shardeen will be going."

"How do you know?"

"He has a woman there. Lulu Barton."

"You know this woman?"

"She's my sister."

* * *

Sally Reynolds' first day in Bury, Idaho, was nearly her last. Nobody had met her at the train, so leaving her luggage at the depot to be picked up later, she started down the boardwalk toward the address that was on the acceptance letter she held in her hand.

Suddenly, she heard and felt the concussion of something whizzing by her very fast. Concurrent with her hearing the report of a gunshot, a bullet crashed through one of the square panes of the big glass window next to her. Actually, it was two gunshots, one right on top of the other. She turned and looked out into the street. Two men faced each other with smoking guns in their hands. She stared at them in shock for a moment, then one of the two men fell to the dirt.

"Miss!" A very attractive and expensively dressed woman called out to her. "Get in here, off the street! Quickly!"

Sally didn't need a second invitation to hurry into the building, which turned out to be a dress shop.

"There's likely to be more shooting. Clay, the man who was just shot, has a brother," the pretty woman said. "I expect Jeb will be coming out into the street shortly, wanting revenge."

"Heavens," Sally said. "Does this sort of thing go on often?"

"Fairly often."

True to the pretty lady's prediction a second man walked into the street, firing his pistol. The two men continued to shoot at each other until the second man, Sally assumed it was Jeb, went down. The first man put his gun back in the holster, then started toward a nearby saloon as several others rushed forward to congratulate him.

"It's over now," the pretty lady said.

"I must say, this was quite a dramatic welcome to Bury," Sally said.

"Just arrived?"

"Yes, by train a few minutes ago."

"Have you come to work at the Pink House?"

"The Pink House?"

The woman nodded. "For Miss Flora."

Sally shook her head. "I don't know who Miss Flora is." She smiled. "My name is Sally Reynolds, and I'm the new schoolteacher."

"A schoolteacher, are you? Well, Miss Reynolds, it's good to meet you. I'm Janey Garner." Janey remembered Miss Margrabe, and gave a passing wonder as to where she might be.

"Do you work at the Pink House? Whatever that is."

"No, I'm a business manager for PSR," Janey replied.

"PSR?"

"It's a ranch, the Potter, Stratton, and Richards. Only it's not just a ranch, it's a *huge* ranch."

"A lady ranch manager? That's most impressive. You must be as intelligent as you are beautiful."

Janey laughed and extended her hand. "Sally, I think you and I are going to wind up being very good friends."

CHAPTER 20

Smoke had been riding for more than six hours. Behind him, the darker color of hoof-churned earth stood out against the lighter, sunbaked ground. Before him, the desert stretched out in motionless waves, one right after another. As each wave was crested, another was exposed, and beyond that another still.

The only sounds were the jangle of the horse's bit and harness, the squeaking leather as he shifted his weight upon the saddle, and the dull thud of hoofbeats.

He had filled the canteen before he left Rattlesnake Canyon, but that was more than forty miles ago and he had come across no other water since then.

His tongue was swollen with thirst and the canteen was already down by a third, but he was allowing himself no more than one swallow of water per hour. He was also rationing the water for Seven by taking two mouthfuls, then spitting the water into his hat and holding the hat up for Seven to drink.

"I'm sorry, boy. This is all we have," he apologized, feeling sorry for the horse. "I tell you what. I won't be riding you anymore. We'll both walk the rest of the way," he promised.

Smoke had no idea how much farther he would have to go, but he was determined not to burden Seven any longer.

Just before dark, a scattering of adobe buildings rose from the desert floor, wavering in the shimmering heat waves. The buildings so matched the desert in color and texture that Smoke wasn't even sure the town was there. Gathering what strength he had remaining, he started toward it. He had no other choice. If it was real, he and Seven would live. If it was a mirage, they would probably die.

It took at least another hour to reach the town, but within thirty minutes he knew that the town was real. "It's real, Seven!" Smoke exclaimed, his voice hoarse from thirst. "It's a real town! A real town with water!"

At the edge of town he stopped to catch his breath and read the sign.

CHUGWATER, WYOMING
POP. 256
"FRIENDLY PEOPLE"

Smoke limped on into town and, seeing a pump in the town square, hurried toward it. He moved the handle a couple times and was rewarded by seeing a wide, cool stream of water pour from the pump mouth. Holding his hat under the pump, he filled his hat and let Seven drink. Seven finished that hatful and two more before Smoke allowed himself to drink. Putting his left hand in front of the spout, he caused the water to pool and, continuing to pump, drank deeply. Never, in his life, had anything tasted better to him.

With the killing thirst satisfied, Smoke stood up from the pump and patted Seven on his neck. "I'm sorry to have put you through that, Seven, but you were a good horse, and I'm proud of you."

Just down the street a door slammed, and an isinglass shade came down on the upstairs window. A sign creaked in the wind and flies buzzed loudly around a nearby pile of horse manure.

Smoke walked on down the street, leading Seven. He saw three saloons, sure that if Angus Shardeen was there, he would be in one of them.

But which one?

Smoke continued walking as he looked around. A horse in front of a saloon that identified itself as the Ace High caught his attention. Under the saddle was a distinctive saddle blanket—dark blue with a gold band around the outside edge. Nestled in the corner was the silver eagle insignia of a colonel.

He remembered seeing the very saddle blanket on one of the horses when his farm had been raided. He knew that would be Shardeen's horse. Whether he was really a colonel or not, he had passed himself off as such.

After examining the horse, Smoke started toward the saloon door.

A man stepped in front of him. "Where do you think you're goin'?"

The man blocking Smoke's way was thin and muscular, with a moustache that curved up at each end like the horns on a Texas steer. He was wearing a yellow duster, pulled back on one side to expose a Colt sheathed in a man's leg holster that was tied halfway down his leg. He had an angry, evil countenance, and looking directly at him was like staring into the eyes of an angry bull.

"Mister, you're in my way," Smoke said dryly.

"Would your name be Smoke Jensen?"

Smoke was surprised to hear himself addressed by name in a town that he had never visited.

"It is. Why? Do you have a particular interest in me?"

"Yeah, I've got an interest in you." The big man pulled his yellow duster to one side and Smoke saw a peace-officer's badge pinned to his shirt.

"I've got one of those, too." Smoke showed his own Deputy U.S. Marshal's badge. "And my badge outranks yours. Now, step out of the way. I've got business inside."

"Would that business have anything to do with Angus Shardeen?" the lawman asked.

"It would."

The lawman shook his head. "Uh-uh. Not here. Shardeen has been good to this town, so he has sanctuary in Chugwater."

"Mister, if I had to go to hell to get Shardeen, I would do it," Smoke said coldly. "As far as I'm concerned, he doesn't have sanctuary anywhere. Now, get out of my way."

The lawman went for his gun. He was exceptionally fast and his hand moved toward his Colt as quickly as a striking rattlesnake.

Smoke had not expected the lawman to draw on him and didn't even start for his gun until the man's gun was coming out. But if Smoke had been surprised by the lawman's sudden draw, the peace officer was undoubtedly surprised by the speed with which Smoke drew and fired.

The lawman staggered backward, crashing through the batwing doors, and backpedaling into the saloon, landing flat on his back, his unfired gun still in his hand.

Smoke bounded up the steps, onto the porch, then pushed through the batwing doors, following the lawman's body inside. A wisp of smoke curled up from the barrel of the pistol he still held in his hand.

"Mister, you just killed our marshal," said one of the men in the saloon.

"Yeah, I guess I did." Smoke slipped his pistol back into its holster.

"Damn. I never figured anyone would be good enough to beat Coyle."

"He drew first," Smoke said. "I didn't have any choice."

"Uh-huh. He drew first, but you still beat him. Is that what you want us to believe?"

"To tell the truth, I don't care whether any of you believe it or not," Smoke said. "I'm a Deputy United States Marshal, and I've come to arrest Angus Shardeen." He saw the nervous exchanges of glances among the customers in the saloon.

"What makes you think Shardeen is here?"

"His horse is out front." Smoke stood for a moment, studying the layout. To his left was the bar. In front of him were four tables; to the right, a potbellied stove, sitting in a box of sand. Because it was summer, the stove was cold, but the stale, acrid smell of last winter's smoke still hung in the air.

One man was behind the bar, three customers were in front of it, and a heavily painted bar girl was standing at the far end of it. At least six more men sat at the tables.

"I know he's here," Smoke said. "Now, where is he?"

No one answered.

Smoke drew his pistol from its holster. "I asked, where is he?" When still no one answered, he pointed his pistol toward the barkeep and pulled the hammer back. A deadly double *click* sounded as the sear engaged the cylinder. "You want to die protecting a murderer like Shardeen?"

"I don't know where he is, mister," the barkeep answered nervously. "I don't pay no attention to what folks come and go here."

"For God's sake, tell 'im, Gene!" the woman said. "He's right, you know. A man like Shardeen ain't worth dyin' for. Just—"

"Sue Ann, shut your mouth," the bartender ordered in sharp anger, cutting her off in mid-sentence.

"Mister, I think you had better be the one who keeps quiet." Smoke lowered his pistol. "Go ahead, Sue Ann. Where is he?"

She looked nervously toward the bartender.

"Don't be worrying about Gene. If that's all that's keeping you from talking, I'll kill him for you right now." Again, Smoke pointed his pistol toward the bartender.

"Tell 'im, Sue Ann!" Gene shouted nervously. "Tell 'im!"

"He's up there," Sue Ann said, lifting her head toward

the landing that looked out over the saloon floor. "First room on the right. He went upstairs with Lulu."

"Thanks." With his pistol still cocked, and holding it in his crooked arm, muzzle point up, Smoke started up the stairs. He had just reached the top step when the bartender shouted a warning.

"Shardeen! Look out! Someone's comin' up for you!"

Surprised that anyone would actually shout a warning, Smoke turned to look back downstairs. Gene was standing at the bottom of the stairs with a double-barrel shotgun pointing up at him.

Smoke managed to jump behind the corner at the top of the stairs, just as Gene fired. The load of buckshot tore a large hole in the door to a room just behind him. Smoke fired back before Gene could get off a second shot. His bullet hit Gene in the forehead, and he dropped the shotgun, then fell heavily to the floor.

At almost the same moment, four shots sounded from inside one of the rooms. Dust and sawdust flew as the bullets punched holes through the door. Smoke flattened himself against the wall, clear of the door. A second later, he heard the sound of crashing window glass.

Smoke ran to the door, kicked it open, and dashed into the room. A naked woman on the bed screamed as he rushed by her to the broken window. He leaned through the shattered glass to look down to the ground below. If Shardeen had jumped through the window, Smoke should still be able to see him.

He wasn't there.

Intuitively, Smoke realized that someone was behind him and he turned, leaping to one side, just as Shardeen, with a broad, triumphant grin on his face, pulled the trigger. The bullet slammed into the wall behind where Smoke had been but a split second earlier.

Smoke fired back. As his bullet struck home, Shardeen's grin of triumph turned to a look of shock and pain.

Shardeen dropped his pistol, put his hands over the

wound in his chest, then sank to his knees. He looked up at his shooter. "You must be Smoke Jensen."

"I am."

"Why? Why have you hounded me all these years? I don't even remember you."

"It doesn't matter. I remember you."

The old mountain man and the gunfighter rode slowly down the main street of Yampa, Colorado, drawing some attention. The sheriff and one of his deputies were among those watching the pair as they reined up in front of the saloon and dismounted.

The sheriff approached them. "Howdy, boys," he greeted.

"Sheriff," Smoke replied.

The lawman looked at the mountain man. "You're the one called Preacher?"

"That's what I'm called."

"And you are the gun hand called Smoke."

"That's what I'm called," Smoke replied, mimicking Preacher's response.

"You boys planning on staying long?"

Smoke turned his dark eyes on the sheriff and let them smolder for a few seconds. "Long enough to do what we plan to do."

"I've been hearing a lot about you, Smoke Jensen," the sheriff said, speaking in low tones. "I've heard how you killed Sledge Blackwell, Billy Bartell, how you wiped Shardeen's band like some one man army, and how you went up to Chugwater, Wyoming, and killed Angus Shardeen his ownself. I hope you ain't lookin' for anyone in this town. Yampa is a nice little place. I wouldn't want to see it turned into a battleground."

Smoke smiled at the sheriff. "You don't mind if we buy some supplies, have a few hot meals, and rest for a day or two, do you, Sheriff? Maybe take a hot bath?"

"Speak for yourself on that last part," Preacher said. "I

had me a bath no more 'n a month ago. I don't hold with too much bathin'. It ain't healthy, keepin' your skin all exposed like that."

"Smoke, from ever'thing I've heard, you ain't never kilt nobody that didn't need killin'," the sheriff said. "I'm just sort of hopin' that nothin' like that happens here. If you'll give me your word on it, why, that'll be good enough for me."

"Sheriff, I'm not after anybody in this town. To be truthful with you, my pa is buried at the foot of Zenobia Peak, 'n all I got in mind is just visiting his grave and payin' my respects."

The sheriff nodded. "You got ever' right to do that. I'm sorry if I come off a bit cantankerous there, 'n I hope you don't take offense, but I feel like I owe it to the folks here 'bout to keep the peace as best I can."

"I understand. No offense taken," Smoke said.

"Also, I'm sorry 'bout your pa."

"I appreciate the sentiment," Smoke replied.

The sheriff wasn't the only one who had heard about Smoke single-handedly cleaning out the Angus Shardeen gang. By the time he and Preacher stepped into the saloon, word of their arrival had spread and, in the words of one of the saloon patrons, "Your money is no good here! Anybody that's got rid of a no-account polecat like Angus Shardeen and those scoundrels who rode with him has done a good service to ever'one between St. Louis and the Pacific Ocean."

"What will you have?" the bartender asked.

"Before we get started on the drinkin', don't you think maybe we should get us a bite or two to eat?" Preacher suggested.

"We got food," the bartender said. "Our food is as good as anything you'll get over at the City Pig Café."

"What do you have?"

"Beans cooked with ham, taters, and hot peppers, with a side of turnip greens, and cornbread."

"Sounds good enough," Smoke said.

"You got coffee?" Preacher asked. "I don't mean brown water. I mean real coffee."

"You like it strong, do you?" the bartender asked.

Smoke chuckled. "If it won't float a horseshoe, it's too weak."

"I'll see what I can do."

After the meal, Smoke and Preacher enjoyed a couple beers bought for them by the patrons of the saloon. They could have had as many as they wanted, without having to pay for any, but Smoke knew better than to ever allow himself to get drunk.

"Last thing you need is to be too drunk when some young scoundrel decides to make a name for hisself by shootin' you," Preacher had told him once.

It hadn't been necessary for Preacher to warn him. He had figured that out a long time ago.

In Bury, Idaho, Sally Reynolds was having lunch with Miss Flora. They were dining in Sally's house, because Flora didn't want to embarrass Sally by being seen in public with her.

"Nonsense," Sally said. "Why should I be embarrassed to be seen with you?"

"I'm a lady of the night, honey. I own the Pink House, and the girls who work there, work for me. I don't actually bed with men, but how do you think I got the money to buy the house in the first place?"

"I want to read something to you," Sally said. She stepped over to the buffet to pick up a Bible, turned to the selection she wanted, and began to read. "'And one of the Pharisees desired that he would eat with him. And he went into the

Pharisee's house, and sat down to meat. And, behold, a woman in the city, which was a sinner, when she knew that Jesus sat at meat in the Pharisee's house, brought an alabaster box of ointment, and stood at his feet behind him weeping, and began to wash his feet with tears, and did wipe them with the hairs of her head, and kissed his feet, and anointed them with the ointment.

"'Now when the Pharisee which had bidden him saw it, he spake within himself, saying, This man, if he were a prophet, would have known who and what manner of woman this is that toucheth him: for she is a sinner.

"'And Jesus turned to the woman, and said unto Simon, Seest thou this woman? I entered into thine house, thou gavest me no water for my feet: but she hath washed my feet with tears, and wiped them with the hairs of her head. Thou gavest me no kiss: but this woman since the time I came in hath not ceased to kiss my feet. My head with oil thou didst not anoint: but this woman hath anointed my feet with ointment.

"'Wherefore I say unto thee, her sins, which are many, are forgiven; for she loved much: but to whom little is forgiven, the same loveth little.'"

Closing the Bible, Sally smiled at Miss Flora. "You are a *friend*, Flora."

"Janey said you were different from the others," Flora said. "She said you wouldn't judge her."

"You mean because she isn't just a business manager, she is also Josh Richards's mistress? No, I don't judge her at all. She was very nice to me the first day I arrived in town." Sally laughed. "She was more than nice. I'm quite sure that she saved my life."

EPILOGUE

Smoke stood at the grave of his father, holding his hat in his hands. He was pleased to see that the markings he had chiseled in the rock-turned-tombstone were still quite legible. Preacher was standing some distance away, having told Smoke that he needed some private time with his pa.

"Pa, I've settled some accounts. I've killed Billy Bartell. He was the man that raped Janey, and in my way of thinking, is probably the one that sent her down the wrong trail. I don't know where she is now, and to be honest with you, I haven't been lookin' for her. I hope she's alive, and livin' well somewhere, but I figure that's none of my doin' anymore. I set things right for her, by killin' Bartell. What happens to her from now on is up to her.

"I'm happy to say, I also found and killed Angus Shardeen. I told you he's the one that killed Ma.

"I'd like to say that ever'thing is all settled now, but I can't say that just yet. I'm goin' after the ones that killed you and Luke. I killed Ted Casey already. He was one you didn't know about. I know the names of the others—Wiley Potter, Keith Stratton, and Josh Richards. I'm goin' to find 'em, Pa, and I'm goin' to make things right. I give you that promise."

Smoke stood there in silence for another moment, then put his hat on, and started back toward Preacher.

"Got things settled with your pa?" Preacher asked.

"Yeah."

"He was real proud of you, boy. Same as I am."

The lump in Smoke's throat wouldn't let him reply.

LUKE JENSEN:
BOUNTY HUNTER

PROLOGUE

A rifle bullet smacked off the top of the log and sprayed splinters toward Luke Smith's face. He dropped his head quickly so the brim of his battered black hat protected his eyes. A splinter stung his cheek close to his neatly trimmed black mustache.

Luke looked into the sightless, staring eyes of the dead man who lay next to him. "Those amigos of yours are getting closer with their shots, José. Too bad for you that you're not alive to watch them kill me. Reckon you probably would've enjoyed that."

José Cardona didn't say anything. A bullet hole from one of Luke's Remingtons lay in the middle of his forehead, surrounded by powder burns. Most of the back of his head was gone where the slug had exploded out.

More shots rang out from the cabin about a hundred yards away, next to the little creek at the bottom of the slope. The sturdy log structure had been built for defense, with thick walls and numerous loopholes where rifle barrels could be stuck out and fired.

Luke had no idea who had built the cabin. Probably some old fur trapper or prospector. Those mountains in New Mexico Territory had seen their fair share of both.

Currently, it was being used as a hideout for the Solomon

Burke gang. Luke had been on the trail of Burke and his bunch for several weeks. There was a $1500 bounty on Burke's head and lesser amounts posted on the half-dozen owlhoots who rode with him. If Luke was able to bring in all of them, it would be a mighty nice payoff for him.

Unfortunately, it didn't look like things were going to work out that way. Luke had tracked the gang to the cabin and had been crouched in the timber up on the hill overlooking the creek, trying to figure out his next move, when someone tackled him from behind, knocking him out into the open. They rolled down the hill together, locked in a desperate struggle, even as the man screeched a warning to the others at the top of his lungs.

The big log, which had also rolled about twenty feet down the hill when it toppled sometime in the past, brought the two men to an abrupt halt as they slammed into it. Luke barely had time to recognize the bandito as Cardona from drawings he had seen on wanted posters when he realized the man was about to bring a knife almost as big as a machete down on his head and split his skull wide open.

Without having to think about what he was doing, Luke palmed out one of his Remingtons, eared back the hammer as he jammed the muzzle against Cardona's forehead, and pulled the trigger.

The point-blank shot blew Cardona away from him, and the dead outlaw flopped onto the ground behind the log. Luke rolled over and started to get up, when a bullet had whipped past his ear. Instinct made him drop belly down behind the log. A second later, more rifles opened up from the cabin and a volley of high-powered slugs smashed into the fallen tree. If it hadn't been there to give him cover, Luke would have been shot to pieces.

As it was, he was pinned down on the slope. The trees above him were too far away. If he stood up and made a dash for them, Burke and the others in the cabin would riddle him with rifle fire. Trying to crawl up there would make him an even easier target. The grass was too short to conceal him.

He was stuck, with a dead man for company and only a matter of time until some of those varmints slipped out of the cabin and circled around to catch him in a crossfire. Luke's craggy face was grim, in spite of the ghost of a smile lurking around his mouth.

In plenty of tight spots during the years he'd spent as a bounty hunter, he had always pulled through somehow. But he had known his luck was bound to run out someday.

After all, he had already cheated certain death once. A man didn't get too many breaks like that.

From time to time, he rose up long enough to throw a couple shots at the cabin, but not really expecting to do any damage—too long range for a handgun. His nature wouldn't let him die without a fight, though. He could put up a better one, if his Winchester wasn't still in the saddle boot strapped to his horse, a good hundred feet upslope. Might as well have been a hundred miles.

"Blast it, José, I must be getting old to let a clumsy galoot like you sneak up on me," Luke said, keeping his eyes on the cabin.

Cardona had been a big, burly man, built along the lines of a black bear. Like all the other men in Solomon Burke's gang, he'd had a reputation for ruthlessness and cruelty. He had killed seven men that Luke knew of during various bank and train robberies, and was probably responsible for more deaths in addition to those. But he wouldn't be killing anybody else.

Luke took some small comfort from that. He tracked down outlaws mostly for the bounties posted on them, and he wasn't going to lie about it to himself or anybody else. It pleased him to know, because of him, men such as Cardona were no longer around to spread suffering and death across the frontier.

More bullets pounded into the log. One tore all the way through it and struck a rock lying on the slope, causing the bullet to whine off in a ricochet and bringing a thoughtful frown to Luke's face. He realized the log had been lying there long enough to be half-rotten in places. He holstered the Remington he was still holding and drew a heavy-bladed knife from its sheath on his left hip. Attacking the log with the blade, he hacked and dug at the soft wood.

It didn't take him long to break through and see what he'd been hoping to see. The log was partially hollow. Luke began enlarging the opening he had made and soon realized the hollow part ran all the way to one end of the log. He could see sunlight shining through it.

It took fifteen minutes of hard work to carve out a big enough hole for him to fit his head and shoulders through. By the time he was finished, sweat was dripping down his face.

He sheathed his knife and looked over at Cardona. "Adios, José. If I see you again, I reckon it'll probably be in hell."

Luke wormed his way through the opening into the hollow log. Down below in the cabin, the outlaws hadn't been able to see what he was doing. He could only hope none of them had snuck around to where they could observe him. If they had, he was as good as dead.

He began shifting his weight back and forth as much as he could in those close confines. He felt insects crawling on him. His nerves twanged, taut as bowstrings. The log began to rock back and forth slightly. Bunching his muscles, he threw himself hard against the wood surrounding him. Over the pounding of his heart, he heard a faint grating sound as the log shifted.

Suddenly, it was rolling.

He let out a startled yell, even though rolling the log down the hill was exactly what he'd been trying to do. Up and down switched places rapidly.

With nothing between the log and the cabin to stop it, the crazy, bouncing, spinning, dizzying ride lasted only a few seconds.

The log crashed into the side of the cabin with a loud cracking sound just as he had counted on. Luke bulled his

way out of the broken trunk, pulling both Remingtons from
their cross-draw holsters as he did so.

He was on his feet when one of the outlaws appeared in
the doorway, unwisely rushing out to see what had happened.

Luke shot him in the chest with the left-hand Remington.
The slug drove the owlhoot back, making him fall. His body
tangled with the feet of the man behind him. Luke blasted
that hombre with the right-hand gun, then pressed himself
against the cabin wall and waited. The men inside couldn't
bring their guns to bear on him from those loopholes, and
the log walls were too thick to shoot through. If anybody
tried to rush out through the door, he was in position to gun
them down. And, if the door was the only way out, he had
them bottled up.

Of course, he couldn't go anywhere, either. But a stale-
mate was better than being stuck behind that log and his enemies having all the advantage.

As the echoes of the shots rolled away through the mountain valleys, a charged silence settled over the area. Luke
thought he heard harsh breathing coming from inside the
cabin.

After a few tense minutes, a man called out. "Who are
you, mister?"

"Name's Luke Smith." He wasn't giving anything away
by replying. They already knew where he was.

"I've heard of you. You're a bounty hunter!"

"Am I talking to Solomon Burke?"

"That's right."

"Who are the two boys I killed in there?"

Burke didn't answer for a moment. "How do you know
they're dead?" he finally asked.

"Wasn't time for anything fancy. They're dead, all right."

Again Burke hesitated before saying, "Phil Gaylord and
Oscar Montrose."

"José Cardona's dead up on the hillside. I blew his brains
out. That's nearly half your bunch gone over the divide, Burke.

Why don't you throw your guns out and surrender before I have to kill the rest of you?"

That brought a hoot of derisive laughter from inside.

"Mighty big talk, Smith. You step away from that wall and you'll be full of lead in a hurry. How in blazes are you gonna kill anybody else?"

"I've got my ways." Luke looked along the wall next to him. One of the loopholes, empty now, was within reach.

"We've got food, water, and plenty of ammunition. What do you have?"

"Got a cigar."

"Well, go ahead and smoke it, then," Burke told him. "It'll be the last one you ever do."

Luke kept his left-hand gun trained on the doorway. He pouched the right-hand iron and reached under his coat, bringing out a thin, black cigar. He bit off the end, spit it out, and clamped the cylinder of tobacco between his teeth. Fishing a lucifer from his pocket, he snapped it to life with his thumbnail. He held the flame to the end of the cigar and puffed until it was burning good. "Smell that?"

"Whoo-eee!" Burke mocked. "Smells like you set a wet dog on fire."

"It tastes good, though," Luke said. "I've got something else."

"What might that be?" Burke asked.

Luke took another cylinder from under his coat. Longer and thicker than the cigar, it was wrapped tightly in dark red paper. A short length of fuse dangled from one end. Luke puffed on the cigar until the end was glowing bright red, then held the fuse to it.

"This," he said around the cigar as the fuse began to sputter and spit sparks. He leaned over and shoved the cylinder through the empty loophole. It clattered on the puncheon floor inside the cabin.

One of the other men howled a curse and yelled, "Look out! That's dynamite!"

Luke drew his second gun and swung away from the wall

as he extended the revolvers and squared himself up. As the outlaws tumbled through the door, trying to get away before the dynamite exploded, he started firing.

They shot back, of course, even as Luke's lead tore through them and knocked them off their feet. He felt the impact as a bullet struck him, then another. But he stayed upright and the Remingtons in his hands continued to roar.

Solomon Burke, a fox-faced, red-haired man, went down with his guts shot to pieces. Dour, sallow Lane Hutton stumbled and fell as blood from his bullet-torn throat cascaded down the front of his shirt. Young Billy Wells died with half his jaw shot away. Paco Hernandez stayed on his feet the longest and got a final shot off even as he collapsed with blood welling from two holes in his chest.

That last bullet rocked Luke. He swayed and spit out the cigar, but didn't fall. His vision was foggy, because he'd been shot three times or because clouds of powder smoke were swirling around him, he couldn't tell. The Remingtons seemed to weigh a thousand pounds apiece, but he didn't let them droop until he was certain all the outlaws were dead.

Then he couldn't hold the guns up anymore. They slipped from his blood-slick fingers and thudded to the ground at his feet.

I might not live to collect the bounty on these men, but at least they won't hurt anybody else, he thought as he stumbled through the cabin door. The single room inside was dim and shadowy.

The cylinder he had shoved through the loophole lay on the floor near a table. The fuse had burned out harmlessly. The blasting cap on the end was just clay and the "dynamite" was nothing more than a piece of wood with red paper wrapped around it. Luke had used it a number of times before. Outlaws tended to panic when they thought they were about to be blown to kingdom come.

Ignoring the fake dynamite, he stumbled across the room. Sitting on the table was the thing he had hoped to find inside.

It took him a couple tries before he was able to snag the neck of the whiskey bottle and lift it to his mouth. Some of the liquor spilled over his chin and throat, but he got enough of the fiery stuff down his throat to brace himself.

He leaned on the rough-hewn table and tried to take stock of his injuries. He'd been hit low on his left side. There was a lot of blood. A bullet had torn a furrow along his left forearm, too, and blood ran down and dripped from his fingers. The bullet hole high on his chest was starting to make his right arm and shoulder go numb.

He needed to stop the bleeding before he did anything else. With little time before his hands quit working, he pulled the bandanna from around his neck and used his teeth to start a rip in it. He tore it in half and managed to pour some whiskey on the pieces. He pulled up his shirt, felt around until he found the hole in his side, and shoved one wadded up piece of the whiskey-soaked bandanna into the hole.

But that was just where the bullet had gone in. Wincing in pain, he located the exit wound and pushed the other piece of bandanna into it.

That left the hole in his chest. All the gun-thunder had deafened him for a few moments, but his hearing was starting to come back. He listened intently as he breathed, but didn't hear any whistling or sucking sounds. The slug hadn't pierced his lung, he decided. That was good.

The bullet hadn't come out, either. It was still in there somewhere. Not good, he thought. Fumbling, he pulled his knife from its sheath and used the blade to cut a piece from his shirt tail. Lucky he didn't slice off a finger or two in the process. He upended the bottle and poured whiskey right over the wound, then bit back a scream as he crammed the piece of cloth into the hole.

That was all he could do. His muscles refused to work the way he wanted them to. He had to lie down. He took an unsteady step toward one of the bunks built against the side walls. The world suddenly spun crazily around him. The floor seemed to tilt under his feet. His balance deserted him, and he crashed down on the puncheons, sending fresh jolts of pain stabbing through him.

He felt consciousness slipping away from him and knew if he passed out, he probably wouldn't wake up again. He tried to hold on, but a black tide swept over him.

That black surge didn't just wash him away from his primitive surroundings. To his already fevered mind, it seemed to lift him and carry him back, back, a bit of human flotsam swept along by a raging torrent, to an earlier time and a different place. The darkness surrounding him was shot through with red flashes, like artillery shells bursting in the night.

BOOK ONE

CHAPTER 1

The bombardment sounded like the worst thunderstorm in the history of the world, but unlike a thunderstorm, it went on and on and on. For long days, that devil Ulysses S. Grant and his Yankee army had squatted outside Richmond, pounding away at the capital city of the Confederacy with their big guns. Half the buildings in town had been reduced to rubble, and untold numbers of Richmond's citizens were dead, killed in the endless barrages.

And still the guns continued to roar.

Rangy, rawboned Luke Jensen felt the floor shake under his feet as shells fell not far from the building where he stood. It had been one of Richmond's genteel mansions, not far from the capital itself, but recently it had been taken over by the government. One particular part of the government, in fact: the Confederate treasury.

Luke was one of eight men summoned tonight for reasons unknown to them. They were waiting in what had been the parlor before the comfortable, overstuffed furniture was shoved aside and replaced by desks and tables.

In the light of a couple smoky lamps, he glanced around at the other men. Some of them he knew, and some he didn't. The faces of all bore the same weary, haggard look, the expression of men who had been at war for too long and suffered too many defeats despite their best efforts.

Luke knew that look all too well. He saw it in the mirror every time he got a chance to shave, which wasn't very often these days.

For nearly four long years, he had worn Confederate gray—ever since the day he had walked away from the hardscrabble farm tucked into the Ozark Mountains of southwestern Missouri and enlisted. Behind him he'd left his father Emmett and his little brother Kirby, along with his mother and sister.

It had been hard for Luke to leave his family, but he felt it was the right thing to do. Fighting for the Confederacy didn't mean a man held with slavery, although he figured that was what all those ignorant Yankees believed. Luke didn't believe at all in the notion of one man owning another.

At the same time he didn't think it was right for a bunch of Northern politicians in By-God Washington City to be telling Southern folks what they could and couldn't do, especially when it came to secession. The states had joined together voluntarily, back when they'd won their freedom from England. If some of them wanted to say "thanks, but so long" and go their own way, it seemed to Luke they had every right to do so.

Even so, if they'd just kept on wrangling about it in the halls of Congress, Luke, like a lot of other Southerners, would have pretty much ignored it and gone on about his business. But Abraham Lincoln had to go and send the army marching into Virginia, and the battle along the creek called Bull Run was the last straw as far as Luke was concerned. He'd been raised to avoid trouble if he could, but when a Jensen saw something wrong going on, he couldn't just sit back and do nothing.

So he'd been a soldier for four years, fighting against the Northern aggressors, slogging along as an infantryman for a while before his natural talents for tracking, shooting, and fighting got noticed and he was made a scout and a sharp-shooter.

He knew three of the men waiting in the parlor with him were the same sort. Remy Duquesne, Dale Cardwell, and Edgar Millgard were good men, and if he was being sent on some sort of mission with them, Luke was fine with that.

The other four had introduced themselves as Keith Stratton, Wiley Potter, Josh Richards, and Ted Casey. Luke hadn't formed an opinion about them based only on their names. He didn't blame them for being close-mouthed, though. He was the same way himself.

Remy fired up a cigar and said in his soft Cajun accent, "Anybody got an idea why they brought us here tonight?"

"Not a clue," Wiley Potter said.

"The treasury department has its office here now," Dale Cardwell pointed out. He smiled. "Maybe they're finally going to pay us all those back wages we haven't seen in months."

That comment drew grim chuckles from several of the men.

Remy said, "I wouldn't count on that, my frien'."

Luke didn't think it was very likely, either. The Confederacy was in bad shape. Financially, militarily, morale-wise . . . everything was cratering, and there didn't seem to be anything anybody could do to stop it. They would fight to the end, of course—there was no question about that—but that end seemed to be getting more and more inevitable.

The front door opened, and footsteps sounded in the foyer. Several gray-clad troopers appeared in the arched entrance to the former parlor. They carried rifles with bayonets fixed to the barrels.

A pair of officers followed the soldiers into the room. Luke and the other men snapped to attention. He recognized one of the officers as a high-ranking general. The other man was the colonel who commanded the regiment in which Luke, Remy, Dale, and Edgar served.

The two men in civilian clothes who came into the room behind the general and the colonel were the real surprise. Luke caught his breath as he recognized the President of the Confederacy, Jefferson Davis, and the Secretary of the Treasury, George Trenholm.

"At ease," the general said.

Luke and the others relaxed, but not much. It was hard to be at ease with the president in the room.

Jefferson Davis gave them a sad, tired smile and said, "Thank you for coming here tonight, gentlemen," as if they'd had a choice in the matter. "I know you'd probably rather be with your comrades in arms, facing the enemy."

Stratton and Potter grimaced slightly and exchanged a quick glance, as if that was the last thing they wanted to be doing.

"I've summoned you because I have a special job for you," Davis went on. "Secretary Trenholm will tell you about it."

Luke had wondered if they were going to be given a special assignment, but he hadn't expected it would come from the president himself. It had to be something of extreme importance. He waited eagerly to hear what the treasury secretary was going to say.

"As you know, Richmond is under siege by the Yankees," the man began rather pompously as he clasped his hands behind his back.

Luke preferred Confederate politicians to Yankees, but they all had a tendency to be windbags, as far as he was concerned.

"Although I hate to say it, it appears that our efforts to defend the city ultimately will prove to be unsuccessful," the secretary continued.

"Are you saying that Richmond's going to fall, sir?" Potter asked.

Trenholm nodded. "I'm afraid so."

"But that doesn't necessarily mean the Confederacy is about to fall as well," Davis put in. "Our glorious nation will persevere. The Yankees may overrun Richmond, but we will establish a new capital elsewhere." He smiled at the treasury secretary. "I'm sorry, I didn't mean to interrupt."

"That's quite all right, Mr. President. No one in this room has more right to speak than you." Trenholm cleared his throat and went on. "Of course, no government can continue to function without funds, so to that end, acting on the orders of President Davis, I have assembled a shipment of gold bullion that is to be spirited out of the city and taken to Georgia to await the arrival of our government. This is most of what we have left in our coffers, gentlemen. I'm not exaggerating when I say the very survival of the Confederacy itself depends on the secure transport of this gold."

Luke wasn't surprised by what he had just heard. For the past few days, rumors had been going around the city that the treasury was going to be cleaned out and the money taken elsewhere so the Yankees wouldn't get their grubby paws on it.

The secretary nodded toward Luke's commanding officer. "Colonel Lancaster will be in charge of the gold's safety."

"You're taking the whole regiment to Georgia, sir?" Dale asked.

The colonel shook his head. "Not at all, Corporal. That would only draw the Yankees' attention to what we're doing." Lancaster paused. "We're entrusting the safety of the bullion— and the future of the Confederacy—to a smaller detail. Eight men, to be exact." He looked around the room. "The eight of you who are gathered here."

CHAPTER 2

L uke had figured that out even before Lancaster said it. The idea seemed obvious. Getting the gold out of Richmond would require speed and stealth, and no one was better at moving fast and quiet than he and his fellow scouts.

It seemed like a mighty big risk, though, turning over a fortune in gold to only eight men. Of course, as long as they were loyal to the Confederacy, it didn't really matter.

"I'll be going along as well," Colonel Lancaster pointed out. "I've been relieved of my command of the regiment and given this task."

"I know you'd rather be with the men you've led in such sterling fashion, Colonel," Jefferson Davis said. "However, we all must make sacrifices for our noble cause."

"Of course, Mr. President," Lancaster said stiffly.

Davis turned back to Luke and the other scouts. "No one is going to order you enlisted men to accept this assignment. If there are any of you who don't want to go along, speak up now, and it won't be held against you. You'll be allowed to return to your units. All we ask is that you say nothing about this. Secrecy is the watchword until the bullion is safely on its way to Georgia."

Luke looked at his friends. Remy shrugged and told

Davis, "Mr. President, I don't think any of us are gonna say no to this job."

"That's right," Edgar said. "If this is something that will help the Confederacy, you can count on us, sir."

"I knew that." Davis smiled. "I knew you valiant lads wouldn't let me down, but I felt it was only right to ask. Thank you for justifying my faith in you."

"You can thank us when we get that gold where it's goin', Mr. President," Stratton said.

Luke had been quiet so far, but he asked, "When are we leaving?"

"Tonight," Colonel Lancaster said.

"That soon?" Potter was surprised.

"Do you have a problem with that, Sergeant? Something you need to do here in Richmond before you leave?"

Potter grunted and shook his head. "Permission to speak freely, sir?"

"Go ahead," Lancaster told him.

"Richmond's turned into a hellhole ever since the Yankees showed up on our doorstep, and as far as I'm concerned, the sooner we get out of here, the better."

As if to punctuate his comment, another shell fell somewhere nearby, and the blast shook the house enough that little bits of plaster sifted down from the ceiling.

The general said to Davis, "You should get back to somewhere safer, sir. The colonel and I can handle this."

"Very well, General." Davis turned to the treasury secretary. "Come on, George."

The troopers escorted the two politicians from the room. Once they were gone, Colonel Lancaster said, "The gold is being stored in a warehouse not far from here. It's packed in crates in a couple wagons and covered with canvas so they'll look like supplies."

"No offense, Colonel," Luke said, "but are you sure that's a good idea? With the city cut off like it is, people are starting to get pretty hungry. They're liable to come after food quicker than they would gold."

"How else would you suggest we transport it, Jensen?" the colonel snapped.

Luke shrugged. "I don't know, sir," he admitted. "As scarce as everything is these days, folks are going to be interested no matter what it looks like."

"That's why it's up to us to get the wagons out of the city quickly, and with as little fuss as possible. We have civilian clothes at the warehouse for all of you, as well. Hopefully that'll keep you from drawing too much attention."

Luke didn't know about that, but the idea of getting some fresh duds appealed to him. His gray uniform was worn and ragged and covered with stains from too many nights spent sleeping in the mud. The black bill of his forage cap was crooked and broken. His shoes were more hole than shoe leather.

His only possessions still in good shape were his Fayetteville rifle and his Griswold and Gunnison revolver, both of which he kept in excellent condition. His life often depended on them.

The general shook hands with all eight of the scouts and wished them luck, then Colonel Lancaster said gruffly, "Let's go. We'll dispense with military formality since we're supposed to be civilians, but don't forget who's in charge here."

Luke didn't think Lancaster was likely to let that happen.

"I don't know about you boys," Ted Casey said with a wide grin, "but I feel like a whole new man in this get-up!"

The civilian clothes they had donned when they reached the warehouse weren't new—some of them even had patches here and there—but they were clean and in much better shape than the uniforms the eight men had been wearing.

Colonel Lancaster, as befitted his rank, was dressed in the only real suit, including a flat-crowned planter's hat.

Other than his ramrod-stiff backbone, in those clothes and with his florid face and thick side-whiskers, he might have been mistaken for a plantation owner.

The other men were dressed more like overseers on that hypothetical plantation, in boots, whipcord trousers, linsey-woolsey shirts, and leather vests. They wore an assortment of headgear ranging from broad-brimmed hats to tweed caps.

Luke had snagged one of the hats he thought made him look like a plainsman. Such men rode through the Ozarks from time to time, on their way to or from the vast western frontier, and Luke had always admired them.

His revolver was tucked in the waistband of the trousers. Most enlisted men didn't carry handguns, but since scouts often had to do some close-quarters fighting, they had been issued revolvers along with their rifles. Luke considered himself pretty handy with either weapon, and with a knife, too, for that matter.

He didn't think about it very often, but he had killed quite a few men during his time in the army. It was war, of course. That was what soldiers did. He had killed more than his share up close, though, sneaking up on Yankee pickets and slitting their throats or driving his knife into their backs so the blade penetrated the heart. He had felt the hot gush of enemy blood on his hand, heard the death rattle, and borne the weight of a suddenly limp body that had to be lowered to the ground quietly. He had seen the terrible damage gunshots did to human flesh, especially at close range.

Those memories didn't haunt his sleep, but they were part of him and always would be.

Wiley Potter, Keith Stratton, Ted Casey, and Josh Richards clustered together near one of the wagons. Luke saw them casting furtive glances at the canvas-covered cargo in the back of the vehicle.

"Like dogs lickin' their chops over a big ol' soup bone, eh?" Remy said quietly as he came up beside Luke.

"You can't blame them. I sent some mighty hard looks at

those wagons myself. I've never been this close to so much gold." Luke snorted. "Hell, back home I might go as long as a year without seeing as much as a double eagle."

"I suppose I'm more accustomed to it, seeing as I spent a lot of time in the gambling halls in New Orleans. The money always flowed freely there."

"Maybe so," Luke said. "Where I come from, money flows more like quicksand."

Dale asked Lancaster, "Are we going to be riding on the wagons, Colonel?"

"We'll have a driver and a guard on each wagon," Lancaster explained. "The other four of you, plus myself, will be on horseback and serve as outriders."

"Horses sound good," Casey said. "I always hankered to ride something better than an old mule. They turned me down for the cavalry because that was all I had."

"You'll take turns at the jobs, at least starting out. I don't care who does what, though. You can settle that among yourselves."

Dale commented, "I wouldn't mind handling one of the teams. I used to drive a freight wagon before the war."

"So did I," Edgar offered. "I reckon I'll take the other driver's job starting out."

None of the other men volunteered to ride on the wagons as guards. Luke and Remy looked at each other. Luke shrugged, and Remy said, "We'll take the wagons, too, Colonel."

Lancaster nodded. "Fine." He looked to Potter, Stratton, Casey, and Richards. "You men will find your horses in the alley behind the warehouse. Bring them around front and mount up. You can fetch my mount as well." He motioned to the uniformed soldiers who had been waiting in the warehouse, guarding the gold shipment. "Open the doors."

The troopers swung the big double doors back while Luke and his friends climbed onto the wagons. Luke settled down on the seat of the first wagon beside Dale. "Sure you can handle this?"

"Oh, yeah. To tell you the truth, I've never been that comfortable in a saddle."

"I was riding almost before I could walk, at least according to my pa," Luke told him.

The mention of Emmett Jensen put a pensive look on Luke's face. Luke had joined up first, back in '61, but he had suspected his pa wouldn't be able to stay out of the fight for long. Sure enough, Emmett had enlisted, too.

Proving that the world really was a small place, the two of them had run into each other at Chancellorsville, even though they were in different regiments. Hundreds of thousands of troops rampaging around those Virginia woods, and yet father and son had practically bumped heads.

That wasn't the last time, either. Any time their units were anywhere near each other, one of them would seek out the other so they could visit in the lull between battles. Neither of them got much news from home, but Emmett was confident his youngest son Kirby was keeping things going on the farm.

"Kirby may be just a boy," Emmett had said during one visit, "but he's got something special inside him. I don't think I've ever seen a boy willing to work harder or more determined to do the right thing."

"He'll have the farm waiting for us when we come back," Luke had said.

"Shoot, he may not even need our help!" Emmett had replied with a grin.

It had been a while since Luke had seen his pa. He hoped Emmett was all right. Both were soldiers, so who knew what might happen. It was a dangerous line of work.

When the wagons rolled out of the warehouse into the darkness, Colonel Lancaster and the other four outriders were waiting on horseback.

"I'll lead the way," Lancaster declared. "I want a rider on each side of the wagons. Keep an eye out behind you as well. We don't want anybody sneaking up on us."

"Did the colonel tell any of us exactly where we're going?" Luke asked Dale as the party set out over the rough, cobblestoned streets.

"Not that I know of," Dale replied.

"I might say something to him about that the first time we stop. He's bound to have a map or something, but if anything happened to him, we wouldn't know where we were supposed to take this"—Luke stopped himself before he said the word *gold*—"cargo."

"Yeah, that's true," Dale agreed. "All we know is that we're headed for Georgia, but Georgia's a pretty big place."

It was pretty far away, too, Luke thought, and almost anything could happen between here and there. He felt the unaccustomed burden of responsibility weighing on his shoulders. He wasn't used to taking care of anybody but himself or maybe two or three of his comrades. He'd never had anything like the fate of the Confederacy riding on his back before.

The city was dark except for the few fires started by exploding artillery shells. The Yankee bombardment continued. It went on almost around the clock. Luke didn't see how the city could hold out much longer.

A shell screamed overhead and landed maybe half a mile behind them, blowing up with a huge explosion. Dale looked back over his shoulder at the pillar of flame rising into the black sky. "What do you think it'd be like if one of those things landed right on top of us?"

"We'll never know," Luke said.

"Because it won't happen?"

"Because if it does, we'll be blown to smithereens before we know what happened."

"You really know how to make a fella feel encouraged, Luke—" Dale stopped short and hauled back on the reins. Colonel Lancaster had come to an abrupt halt in front of the wagon team. Garish, flickering light spilled over the cobblestones as a large number of men, many of them carrying torches, surged around a corner up ahead.

"That looks like trouble," Dale muttered.

Luke was thinking the same thing. He knew mobs made of desperate civilians and deserters had taken to roaming the streets of Richmond. The army was trying to keep things under control, but it was getting more difficult with every passing day as the Yankee siege continued. Already there had been several riots.

And it looked like the two wagons were in the path of another one, as one of the men in the forefront of the mob yelled, "There are some wagons! There might be food in them!"

It was an easy conclusion to jump to. A starving man saw food everywhere.

The man waved his torch forward, and with a full-throated cry sounding like the howl of a wounded animal, the mob surged toward the wagons and riders.

CHAPTER 3

Luke saw Colonel Lancaster look around as if searching for a way out. In the narrow street it would be difficult and time-consuming to turn the wagons around, and there were no alleys nearby down which they could escape.

Fleeing wasn't going to do any good. As close as the mob was, the starving men would be able to overtake the wagons without much trouble.

"Get ready to fight if you have to, Dale," Luke said as he pulled the Griswold and Gunnison revolver from his waistband. He stood up and almost called Lancaster "Colonel," catching himself just in time. He took a breath and shouted, "Mr. Lancaster, get out of the way!"

The army and the Confederate government wanted the bullion shipment kept secret, along with the fact that those with the wagons were soldiers. But the secret would be out if the mob swarmed over the wagons. Although the last thing he wanted was to hurt any of his fellow Southerners, Luke would do whatever was necessary to protect the gold. He hadn't seen any firearms in the crowd, only torches and makeshift clubs. Figuring it was a small risk he raised the revolver.

As Lancaster yanked his horse to the side, out of the line of fire, Luke thumbed back the hammer and squeezed the trigger. The Griswold and Gunnison was a .36 caliber weapon modeled after the Colt Navy and not noted for its accuracy. But the range was short, and he sent the pistol ball slamming into the cobblestones just a few feet in front of the mob's leaders.

They stopped in a hurry.

The other members of the escort lifted rifles or pulled out pistols.

Luke knew hunger could make a man risk a great deal, up to and including his life. He cocked the revolver again and raised the barrel until he was aiming right between the eyes of the man who'd urged the mob into action. He didn't know if the man was one of the leaders or just someone who'd been moved to shout, but he wanted to be certain the man was aware of the danger he was facing.

"You fellas stay right where you are!" Luke warned them. "We'll shoot if we have to, make no mistake about that!"

"You can't kill all of us!" somebody yelled.

Somebody in the back of the crowd, Luke noted. "No, but we can do for half of you. Maybe more than that."

That estimate was good only if every member of the escort emptied his guns and scored a hit with every shot, which was highly unlikely, but the members of the mob probably wouldn't bother to do that ciphering.

"And you'll be the first one to die, mister," Luke went on, addressing the man he'd aimed at. "Is it worth dying for something you can't even eat?"

The man looked scared, but he asked, "What is it? What's in those wagons?"

"Manufacturing equipment," Luke said. He didn't know where that answer came from, but it struck him as a good one. "We're trying to get it out of town while we still can."

"What sort of equipment?"

Luke bit back a curse. The varmint was awfully curious for somebody who had a gun pointed at him. "Leather goods. Tool and die presses."

He wasn't sure that answer even made sense. He didn't

know anything about manufacturing, but recalled hearing that phrase once from a fellow who owned a saddle shop.

He figured the stubborn man would want to take a look at the contents of the crate, but before that could happen, somebody else called out, "You don't have any food?"

"Just our own provisions for the trip," Luke answered, putting some sympathy in his voice. "And we're going to be on mighty short rations just like everybody else."

"We might as well let 'em go," another man grumbled. "Can't eat a bunch of damn machinery."

"They've got horses," yet another man said.

"I'll be damned if I'm far enough gone that I'll eat horse meat! Let 'em pass!"

After that bit of discourse, the crowd seemed to be of two minds. Some agreed they ought to let the travelers go, while others were so angered by the fate that had befallen them they wanted to hurt somebody, anybody, for any excuse. It was a delicate balance, and Luke knew it could tip at any second to the side of violence.

He glanced at his companions. They looked tense and ready to fight, but were scared, too. Only fools would not be scared in the face of an angry mob. Luke hoped none of them panicked and got trigger-happy. All it would take was one shot to set off an orgy of killing.

Finally, the man in the lead stepped aside and swung the blazing brand. "All right, go on and get out of here." He raised his voice to the others in the mob. "Get out of the way! Let them pass!"

The men crowded to the sides of the street. As the wagons and riders passed between them it was uncomfortably like running a gauntlet. As the lead wagon rolled by the man with the torch, Luke told him, "You made a wise decision, friend. Good luck to you."

"You're the lucky ones," the man said with bitterness in his voice. "You're getting out of Richmond. Maybe the Yankees will catch you and kill you, but even if they do, it'll be quick. The ones left behind here will be a long time dying."

As he reloaded the expended chamber, Luke had a feeling the man's grim prediction was correct.

The gold escorts didn't encounter any more trouble as they made their way to the city's edge, but Luke knew they were far from being out of danger yet. The Yankees patrolled heavily around Richmond to keep the city's inhabitants bottled up while the artillery bombardment continued.

Colonel Lancaster dropped back alongside the lead wagon and said to Luke, "I appreciate your help with that mob back there, Jensen, but don't forget that I'm in command here. The way you took charge bordered on insubordination."

Well, then, you should've come up with some way to get us out of that mess, Luke thought, *instead of sitting there looking scared and confused.* He kept that opinion to himself, of course. "That's not the way I meant it, Colonel. I was just trying anything to keep those fellas from swarming over us."

"I understand," Lancaster said with a nod. "Just remember in the future that you look to me for your orders."

"Yes, sir."

The colonel rode ahead again, and Dale said quietly, "If we'd waited for him to figure out what to do, we'd all be dead now."

"More than likely," Luke agreed. "The colonel's a good commander out in the field, but I'm not sure he's really cut out for a job like this."

"That's why I'm glad you're with us, Luke. You can think on your feet about as well as anybody I ever saw."

Luke took that compliment in silence. He had never thought of himself as any sort of strategist or tactician. He was just a fellow who wanted to stay alive and was willing to do almost anything to accomplish that goal.

Their route took them north out of the city, which was opposite from where they wanted to go, but Luke understood why. The heaviest concentration of Yankee forces was south of Richmond. The scouts had to take the wagons north, then circle far to the west, well behind Union lines, and make a fast dash southward. It was the long way around, but a direct route just wasn't possible.

Lancaster called a halt. "I want to be out of the city by dawn. The farther away we can get, the better."

"How will we dodge those Yankee patrols?" Stratton asked.

"We'll have to do some good scouting." The colonel nodded toward Luke. "That's why I want one of you men to give Jensen the horse you're riding. I want a mount for Duquesne, too."

"We've done plenty of scoutin', Colonel," Richards protested. "You can send a couple of us."

Lancaster shook his head. "Jensen and Duquesne have served under my command. I know what they can do. You other men were recommended to me, but I haven't seen you in action yet. Now, dismount, a couple of you."

There was some angry muttering, but Richards and Casey swung down from their saddles.

"Keep your eyes open, Dale," Luke said to his friend.

"You bet I will," Dale promised.

Taking his rifle with him, Luke hopped down from the wagon seat. Richards handed him his reins and climbed up to take his place.

Once Luke and Remy were mounted, Lancaster told them, "Follow this road we're on and see if the way is clear up ahead to the bridge about a mile from here. If it is, one of you come back and tell us, and we'll come ahead."

"What if the Yankees have blown up the bridge, Colonel?" Luke asked.

"Then we'll have to find another way," Lancaster replied as if that were the most obvious thing in the world, and Luke supposed it was.

Crossing the river was probably going to be the most difficult part of getting out of Richmond, Luke thought. If the Yankees really wanted to keep the citizens and the Confederate government trapped in the city, the first thing they should have done was destroy all the bridges.

But that would make it more difficult for them to get in and out of the city from the north once Richmond had fallen, so maybe one or two bridges were still standing. In normal times, the small road the Confederates were on was little used and might be overlooked, along with its bridge spanning the river.

Those were anything but normal times, however.

Luke and Remy moved forward, leaving the buildings on the edge of town behind. Trees crowded in on the road from both sides as they rode northward. Although the sky behind them was bright with the orange glow of fires and the flashes of exploding shells from the Yankee barrage, the darkness grew thicker the farther they went. Luke eyed the trees warily. A Yankee cavalry patrol could be hidden in there, and he wouldn't see them until they opened fire.

But he might be able to hear them. He kept his ears open, listening for hoofbeats, the jingle of bit chains, or coughs, and he watched his horse's ears. If the animal smelled other horses, it would prick its ears in the direction of the scent.

Nothing. Only the slow thud of hoofbeats from his and Remy's mounts.

"We're fortunate," the Cajun whispered. "I don't think anybody's out there right now."

"Yeah," Luke breathed, "but I wouldn't count us lucky until we see whether the bridge is there."

The road was fairly straight, with only a few curves in it. They had just ridden around one when a large structure loomed in front of them about two hundred yards away. Luke recognized it as the covered bridge that crossed the James River.

"That's it," Remy said. "It's still there."

Luke grinned in the darkness. "Yeah." His eyes searched

the shadows around the bridge, looking for any sign of movement. "Seems to be deserted, too. But we'd better take a closer look before one of us goes back and tells the colonel the path is clear."

"Absolutely." Remy heeled his horse into a slightly faster gait. "Let's go."

Luke started to call out to his friend and tell him to slow down, but Remy was right, they didn't really have any time to waste. As Colonel Lancaster had said, the farther away from Richmond they were by morning, the better. Luke rode after Remy.

They were about fifty feet away from the bridge when a sheet of orange muzzle flame split the night.

CHAPTER 4

Luke's only warning was a sudden toss of his horse's head a split second before the shots rang out, giving him just enough time to duck.

It was a good thing he did. As it passed over his head, he heard the sinister hum of a minié ball.

He pulled the revolver from his waistband—he had five rounds ready—and cocked the gun as he brought it up, turning the cylinder from the empty chamber on which the hammer had rested.

As several men on horseback burst out of the trees just short of the bridge, Luke thumbed off a couple rounds. Even though he couldn't see their uniforms, he knew they had to be Yankee cavalrymen.

More shots blasted as muzzle flames continued to tear orange gashes in the darkness. He pulled hard on the reins to whirl his horse around and flee, but saw something that made him stop short.

A match had flared into life on the bridge. He could think of only one reason why somebody would be striking a lucifer out there.

To light the fuse attached to a keg of blasting powder.

The Yankees hadn't destroyed the bridge yet, but only because they were just getting around to it.

"Cover me, Remy!" Luke yelled, and he did something the Yankees wouldn't have expected in a million years. If he'd had time to think about it, likely he wouldn't have done it.

He charged straight at them.

Luke leaned forward over his horse's neck as he sent the animal lunging toward the cavalrymen. The revolver in his hand roared twice more. He saw one of the troopers topple loosely from the saddle. A glance over his shoulder told Luke his friend had taken cover in the trees at the side of the road and opened up with his revolver. Remy was firing, too.

The Yankees were confused. Instead of fleeing, as they had expected, the two Confederates were putting up a fight. The patrol's charge had broken up, and the horses were milling around in the road.

Luke's horse thundered between a couple Yankees. One of the cavalrymen drew a saber. Silvery moonlight winked off the blade as it started to slash toward Luke. He still had one round in the revolver. Tipping up the barrel, he triggered the gun.

The .36 caliber slug caught the saber-wielding cavalryman in the throat. A fountain of blood, black in the moonlight, sprayed from him as he went backward out of his saddle. Luke flashed past, unharmed.

With no time to reload the revolver, he jammed it back in his waistband. Up ahead, sparks flew in the darkness as the lit fuse burned toward a small keg filled with blasting powder. It would be enough to destroy the bridge. Even if the explosion didn't blow the bridge in two, the fire it was bound to start would finish the job.

The fuse lighter stood in the middle of the bridge, vaguely illuminated by the sputtering glow. Confused by the unexpected fight of the Confederates, he took too long to decide whether to flee or stay. Luke was already on the bridge, his horse's hooves ringing on the planks and echoing from the arched cover.

The Yankee lifted a rifle and fired. The ball whipped past Luke's head.

Luke kicked his feet free of the stirrups and left the saddle in a diving tackle that sent him crashing into the enemy soldier. The collision's impact drove the man backward off his feet.

Luke landed hard, too, knocking the breath out of him. He gasped for air as he scrambled to his knees. The powder keg was about ten feet from him, sitting against the wall on the left-hand side of the bridge. The fuse had only a few inches left to burn.

The Yankee wasn't interested in fighting anymore. He just wanted to get the hell out of there before the powder went off and he was blown to bits. Leaping to his feet, he raced for the north end of the bridge.

Luke threw himself at the keg, snatched it up, and plucked the fuse from it as he rolled over. As he came up again, he flung the keg after the fleeing Yankee.

It landed beside the man and bounced past him. He screamed in sheer terror and stumbled, falling and hitting the ground right at the end of the bridge. He rolled over a couple times and came to a stop with the keg resting on its side a few feet away from him.

Luke heard the swift rataplan of hoofbeats and looked back to see the cavalry patrol had regrouped. They charged toward him. Their revolvers roared as they opened fire.

Luke lunged toward the closest decorative opening in the cover of the bridge as bullets sizzled through the air right behind his back. Down at the far end of the bridge, the Yankee who'd lit the fuse screeched, "Stop shooting! Hold your—"

It was all he got out before one of the wild slugs aimed at Luke struck the powder keg. Luke saw the fierce burst of flames from the explosion out of the corner of his eye as he dived through the opening in the bridge cover.

There wouldn't be enough left of that luckless Yankee to bury.

Luke had problems of his own. He was plunging through empty air toward the black surface of the James River.

He barely had time to drag a breath into his lungs before

he struck the chilly water and went under. The river closed over him. He kept sinking for a moment before he was able to right himself.

He wasn't the best swimmer in the world, but he stroked his arms and kicked his feet, fighting his way back to the surface until his head broke out of the water.

While he tried to stay afloat, gun thunder pealed and echoed along the bridge. The Yankees weren't shooting at him, Luke realized. A separate fight was going on under the arched cover. Muzzle flashes were visible through the openings in the walls.

Since nobody seemed to be trying to kill him at the moment, he struggled toward the northern bank, which was closer. By the time he got there, the shooting had stopped and a couple horsemen emerged from under the cover near the site of the blast.

Luke didn't know how he was going to put up a fight. His revolver wasn't loaded, and getting dunked in the river probably had ruined his caps and powder. He still had his knife, but he wasn't in any shape for hand-to-hand combat against overwhelming odds.

The Yankees could just sit there and shoot him while he tried to climb out of the river.

"Luke! Luke, is that you?"

The familiar voice sent a surge of relief through him. "Remy! Down here!"

The Cajun laughed. "Come out of there, you old water rat!"

With river water streaming from his clothes, Luke clambered onto the bank and collapsed. Remy dismounted and went down to help him.

"What happened?" Luke asked as he made it to his feet with Remy's assistance.

"Lancaster and the others heard the shooting and came to see what was going on. You and I had already done enough damage to the Yankees that they were able to wipe out the rest of the patrol."

"Anybody hurt?"

"No, we were lucky. How about you?"

"I reckon I'm all right. Just wet and tired. My ammunition's probably ruined, too."

"Don't worry about that. We'll be able to scavenge plenty of powder and shot from those dead Yankees, not to mention their guns."

"And their horses," Luke suggested. "It won't hurt for us to have some extra mounts."

"Most of the horses have bolted, but we might be able to catch a few."

By the time Luke and Remy reached the road, the wagons had crossed the bridge. They had to steer around the gaping hole in the ground where the keg of blasting powder had gone off, but there was room enough at the side of the road for them to manage that.

Colonel Lancaster said, "From what Corporal Duquesne tells me, if we'd come along a little later this bridge would already be gone. The same would be true if not for your swift action, Jensen. Good job."

"Thank you, sir. And thank you for coming along and taking a hand in the fight."

"When we heard the shots, I should have ordered the drivers to turn the wagons around. We should have gone back and looked for another way out of the city. It really wasn't wise of me to risk our cargo just to see what was happening to the two of you." The colonel shrugged. "But everything seems to have worked out all right. Just don't expect me to keep on pulling your fat out of the fire, Jensen."

"No, sir, I won't." Luke managed to keep the irritation he felt out of his voice. He'd just been following orders when all hell broke loose.

"We'd better move quickly now," Lancaster went on. "There are probably more Yankee patrols in the area. They would have been expecting to hear an explosion, but when their men don't come back, they'll start to wonder what happened. We don't want to be here when they come to find out."

Luke knew that was true. He started looking for his horse and found the animal grazing peacefully on the grass at the side of the road.

He couldn't do anything about his wet clothes except wait for them to dry. That would be miserable, but he could put up with it. He found his hat on the bridge where it had fallen off when he tackled the Yankee.

The Confederates hastily helped themselves to guns and ammunition from their fallen foes. They were trying to catch some of the Yankee cavalry horses when Lancaster said, "No, leave them here."

"It never hurts to have extra mounts, Colonel," Stratton suggested, unknowingly echoing what Luke had said earlier to Remy.

"Those horses have U.S. army brands on them," Lancaster pointed out. "If we're captured, it's unlikely we'll be able to talk ourselves out of a firing squad, but it would be even more difficult if we were in possession of Yankee cavalry mounts."

"The colonel's got a point there," Luke said. "It might be better if we just make do without them."

Nobody put up an argument. A short time later, the group was on the move, following the road into the rugged, wooded countryside of northern Virginia.

Riding on the wagon with Dale again, Luke looked over at Wiley Potter, who rode alongside the vehicle. "Thanks for coming to help me back there."

"Well, sure, Jensen," Potter said. "What else could we do? We're all on the same side, ain't we?"

CHAPTER 5

After the fight at the bridge, the scouts didn't run into any more trouble. A couple times they heard hoofbeats coming along the road and quickly found places where they could pull the wagons off into the trees. Yankee cavalrymen galloped past without even slowing down, never realizing how close the Confederates were.

The riders could only be Yankees. Nobody else would be out and about at night. The people who lived in the area were huddled in their houses and cabins, hoping and praying they wouldn't be slaughtered before morning by the northern invaders.

Luke thought about his ma and Kirby and Janey back on the farm. There had been fighting in Missouri, although not as much as in the east, and widespread bloody raids by guerrilla forces on both sides. He hoped none of the violence had come near the Jensen family farm.

By morning the Confederates were several miles north of Richmond. As the sun came up, Potter and Casey found a cave-like opening under a rugged bluff topped with trees, and Dale and Edgar drove the wagons into it at Colonel Lancaster's command. There was room for the horses under the bluff, too.

"We'll stay here today," the colonel said. "Traveling in

daylight is too risky while we're still this close to Richmond. When we swing west and then south we'll be less likely to run into the Yankees, so we can stay on the road more and make better time then."

Based on what he had seen so far, Luke had doubts of Lancaster's ability to be in charge of the mission, but he agreed with the colonel's decision. They were all tired and needed some rest, and it would be better for them to lie low for a while.

They made an unappetizing breakfast of hardtack and salt jowl. No coffee. Luke wasn't sure how long it had been since he'd had real coffee, but it hadn't been any time recently, that was for sure. They took turns sleeping while two men stood guard at all times.

When it was Luke's turn to watch, he was paired with Ted Casey. They hunkered in some brush near the wagons, and the first thing Casey did was reach for a tobacco pouch and papers in his shirt pocket.

Like stopped him with a hand on his arm. "You can't roll a quirly."

"Why not?" Casey asked with a frown.

"Because the smell of tobacco smoke can travel a pretty good distance. The road's only about a quarter mile away. You don't want some smart Yankee coming along, smelling your smoke, and getting curious enough to come over here and take a look around."

Casey let out a disgusted snort, but he shrugged and put away the pouch. "If they was smart, they wouldn't be Yankees."

"They probably think the same thing about us Confederates," Luke pointed out.

"Don't start talkin' about how they just think they're doin' the right thing and how we shouldn't hate 'em because of that."

"They're *not* doing the right thing," Luke said with conviction. "They invaded our homes. Of course we have to fight them. But the ones I really hate are the politicians from both sides who kept prodding and poking at each other until they felt like they had to start a war over something that could have been settled without one."

"What are you talkin' about?" Casey asked.

"Did you know that more than twenty years ago, some congressmen from the South were already talking about ending slavery? Their plan was to get rid of it in stages, so the southern economy wouldn't be ruined in the process. If the northern politicians had just gone along with that idea, by now a lot of the slaves would be free, maybe even all of them, and there wouldn't have been any need for this war. But the Northerners turned it down flat. They'd already started making speeches about how all the slaves had to be freed at once, or they wouldn't go along with it."

Casey gave him a dubious squint. "I never heard nothin' about anything like that. You're makin' it up."

Luke shook his head. "Nope. I read about it in an old newspaper I came across once."

"You know how to read, eh?"

"My ma saw to that. And once I learned, I had a liking for it."

That was true. As a boy and a young man, he had read every book and newspaper he could get his hands on. Unfortunately, in the part of the country where he'd grown up, reading material wasn't all that common.

But some of the settlements had schools, and whenever he could, Luke would ride over to one of them, sneak in, and "borrow" whatever books he could find. He always took them back once he'd finished reading them, so he didn't consider it stealing. He was just doing whatever he had to in order to feed his thirst for knowledge.

One of the few good things about the war, churches across the South had donated Bibles for the troops, so Luke got the chance to read the Good Book from cover to cover, more than once.

Sometimes he came across other books, usually in abandoned houses. He'd nearly always had some sort of volume of prose or poetry tucked away in his gear, and he read them until they fell apart from exposure to the elements.

He didn't have a book with him at the moment, but maybe once they got to Georgia he could scrounge up a few. He had read some plays by an Englishman named Shakespeare, and he had a hankering to read more.

"I don't understand it," Casey said. "I thought those Yankees were so all-fired anxious to have the slaves freed, and now you're tellin' me they turned down a chance to have that happen and went to war instead."

"The politicians in Washington raised a big stink about slavery because they didn't want folks up north thinking too much about the way we were starting to develop more industry here in the South. All those rich men who own factories up there didn't like that. They didn't like the contracts our businessmen were starting to make with businesses in England and other places in Europe, either."

Luke grunted disdainfully, then went on. "The way they saw it, we weren't supposed to do anything except grow the crops. They'd do everything else the country needed and rake in all the money. They stirred up a bunch of well-meaning people who had real doubts about slavery and got them to fight a war over it. But if you want the truth, all you have to do is look around. You don't see any factories still standing in the South, do you?"

Casey frowned as if thinking about the question hurt his head. "It's all about states' rights. That's what we're fightin' for."

At this point, all we're really fighting for is survival, Luke thought. But he said, "It's true the North tried to trample on the rights of our sovereign states, but consider this . . . the Southern businessmen building those factories and making those contracts with the British wanted the money from those things as much as the Northern industrialists didn't want them to have it."

"So what you're sayin' is the politicians and the fellas with a lot of money on both sides have got us fightin' each other because they want to keep rakin' it in?"

Luke shrugged. "Draw your own conclusions, Casey. All I'm saying is the whole situation is a lot more complicated than what most folks think. One side yells about slavery and the other side yells about states' rights, but like nearly everything else in life, most of it always comes back to money."

Casey nodded slowly, as if the implications of what Luke had said were sinking into his brain. After a moment, he said, "You know what we need to do?"

"What's that?"

"We need to get our own hands on some of that money the varmints are fightin' over."

Luke laughed softly. "Men like you and me don't get rich, Casey. It's just not in the cards. And I don't really care. If this war was over tomorrow, I'd go back home and be mighty happy to do it. My family's farm isn't much, but if we have faith and work hard enough, it'll take care of us."

"There's better ways to get rich. Easier ways." And with that, Casey turned his head to stare hard at the wagons.

Luke stiffened as he saw where the man was looking. A harsh note came into his voice. "You can forget about that. That gold belongs to the Confederacy. Thinking otherwise is the same thing as committing treason."

Casey shook his head and said hastily, "You've got me all wrong, Jensen. I'm not thinkin' anything except I'll be glad when our turn at guard duty is over so I can get me some more sleep." He yawned, but Luke wasn't sure if it was genuine. "It was a hard night, and I'm still tired."

"It was a hard night," Luke agreed, thinking about the encounter with the mob in Richmond and then the fight with the Yankee patrol at the bridge.

Casey grinned as he poked a fist against Luke's upper arm.

"Your problem is you got too many thoughts in that head of yours. A man's brain ain't built to work that hard, Jensen. Me, all I think about is whiskey and women and killin' Yankees, and that's plenty."

"I figure it'll be a while before we get any whiskey or women," Luke said, "but it wouldn't surprise me if you get your fill of killing Yankees before this is all over."

CHAPTER 6

After talking to Casey, Luke felt the need for some solitude. He took his rifle, climbed to the top of the bluff hanging over the wagons, and stretched out among the trees so he could gaze around the countryside.

Other than numerous columns of smoke rising in the distance marking the location of Richmond, he couldn't see any signs of the war from where he lay. Here and there, the vegetation was starting to turn green with the approach of spring. A few birds winged through the blue sky.

It would have been a tranquil, beautiful scene if not for the never-ending rumble of artillery, which could be heard even so far from the capital city. The sound of the bombardment was a constant reminder of the ugliness lurking beneath the apparently peaceful surface.

He and his companions were putting that behind them, at least for the moment, Luke reminded himself. He was sure the war would catch up to them again, probably sooner rather than later, but he was going to enjoy the solitude while he could.

Weariness stole over him, begging him to close his eyes. He fought it off, knowing if he gave in to the temptation, he would fall asleep. The possibility of the Yankees sneaking up on the escort on his watch was unacceptable.

To help keep himself awake, he looked down at the brush where Ted Casey still hunkered. He caught a glimpse of the scout through the branches, but only because he knew where the man was. Luke thought it was very unlikely anybody else would spot Casey.

He recalled the way Casey had looked at the wagons while they were talking about getting rich. The memory brought a frown to Luke's face.

As soon as President Davis had explained the details of the mission the night before, Luke had worried about entrusting the safety of so much gold to such a small group of men.

It made sense from a tactical standpoint. Nine men and two wagons could move a lot faster and attract a lot less attention than a company of soldiers.

But if some of those men turned out not to be trustworthy, it could lead to trouble. Luke knew he could trust Remy, Dale, and Edgar, and Colonel Lancaster was completely devoted to the Confederacy. The other four men were unknown quantities. In the long run, how would they react to the temptation of all that bullion?

Of course, they could be wondering the exact same thing about him and his friends, Luke reminded himself. Potter, Stratton, Richards, and Casey certainly hadn't held back when it came to fighting the Yankees at the bridge. They had pitched right in, risking their lives for the cause . . . and also to save him and Remy.

Thinking about the cause made Luke ponder the future. It was pretty obvious the Confederate government couldn't survive without the funds represented by that gold. Even if they made it safely to Georgia with the wagons, and the government set up a new capital there, would it mean anything except the Confederacy would cling to existence by its fingernails for another few weeks?

General William Tecumseh Sherman had already stormed through Georgia, leaving much of it in ruins. Atlanta—what

was left of it after the Yankees had burned the city—was in
Union hands. Once Richmond fell, as seemed inevitable,
Grant could just turn around and march south, and the rem-
nants of the Confederacy would be caught between two
overwhelming forces.

The glorious cause, Luke thought bitterly. But despite his
own cynicism, he knew he would fight to the end. Jensens
didn't give up, even in the face of certain defeat. Sometimes
events had a way of taking unexpected turns.

Even so, Luke didn't hold out much hope the mission
would really change anything.

He lay on top of the bluff until it was time to wake up
Dale for a turn on guard duty. He climbed down, went into
the cave-like overhang, and reached under the lead wagon to
where Dale had wrapped up in a blanket.

A shaken shoulder brought Dale out of his slumber.
"Trouble?" he asked in a groggy voice.

"Nope," Luke told him. "Everything's quiet. But it's your
turn to stand guard."

Dale yawned and stretched.

"One thing," Luke went on quietly after glancing around
to see that no one was going to overhear. "Keep an eye on
Casey, Stratton, Potter, and Richards."

"Why?" Dale asked with a frown.

"I just think it would be a good idea, until we're sure how
much we can count on them."

Understanding dawned in Dale's eyes. "All right, Luke.
But so far they haven't given us any reason not to trust
them."

"Maybe not," Luke said, not wanting to get into the details of his conversation with Casey just yet, "but we want
things to stay that way."

Before the sun went down that evening, Edgar Millgard
built a small fire under the bluff. The overhang would dis-

perse the smoke enough that it wouldn't be noticed. He cooked more of the salt pork, and they had biscuits with the meat instead of hardtack. "Don't get used to eatin' so fancy," he warned the men with a grin. "We don't have much flour."

They washed the food down with brackish water from their canteens. Josh Richards sighed. "I sure could use a real drink right about now."

"No liquor," Lancaster snapped. "We can't afford to let our guard down, even for a minute."

"Don't worry, Colonel," Richards drawled. "I was just wishin'. We don't have any redeye, anyway." He glanced over at Stratton and winked fast.

Luke barely noticed it, but it made him wonder. A little later, while they were saddling the horses, he pretended not to see Stratton until he bumped into the man.

When Stratton turned with a scowl and said, "Hey, be careful," he was close enough that Luke caught a faint whiff of whiskey on his breath.

"Sorry, Stratton, that was my fault. I wasn't watching what I was doing."

Stratton shrugged. "Well, no harm done. So don't worry about it."

Luke was going to worry about it, though. He was going to worry that either Stratton or Richards—or one of the other two, he supposed—had managed to sneak a bottle or a flask into their gear.

Drinking itself didn't bother Luke. From time to time he liked to have a beer or a shot of corn liquor. But he'd never had the thirst for the stuff some men did, and he agreed with Colonel Lancaster. They didn't need anything to distract them from their mission. They had been given the job of taking the bullion to Georgia, and as soldiers, it was their duty to carry out those orders.

It was just one more reason to keep an eye on the four men, he told himself.

Before they left the camp, Luke went over to Lancaster. "I've been thinking about something, Colonel."

"What's that, Jensen?"

"You seem to be the only one of us who knows exactly where we're going."

Lancaster frowned. "What's your point? I'm the only officer with this detail. The rest of you are just enlisted men. I'm the only one who needs to know."

Luke ignored the man's annoying arrogance. "Begging your pardon, sir, but if anything were to happen to you, we wouldn't know where to deliver the gold. I was thinking that if you had a map or something—"

"So you'd know exactly where to avoid if you tried to abscond with these wagons?" Lancaster broke in.

Luke couldn't stop himself from responding angrily. "Colonel, I never said such a thing. I never even thought it!"

"Well, I can't take any chances. President Davis himself picked me for this mission, and I don't intend to let him, or the Confederacy, down. So you just concern yourself with your own responsibilities, Corporal, and let me worry about everything else."

There was nothing Luke could do except grit his teeth for a second. "Yes, sir, Colonel." He turned and went back to the wagons.

Remy was helping Dale hitch up the team to the lead wagon. He inclined his head toward Lancaster and asked, "What was that about, *mon ami*?"

"Remember we talked about how the colonel is the only one who knows where we're going?" Luke asked.

"Sure."

"Well, I said something to him about it . . . and he wasn't inclined to share the information . . . which he told me in no uncertain terms."

Dale chuckled. "I never minded serving under the colonel in the field. Thought he did a pretty good job, in fact.

But put him out here in command of a small group like this and he's sort of a jackass, ain't he?"

"So far," Luke agreed.

"You think he can manage to get all the way to Georgia without getting himself killed?"

"It's not him I'm worried about," Luke said. "I'd just as soon get the rest of us there without us getting killed."

CHAPTER 7

They traveled through the night without encountering any trouble, and after resting the next day Colonel Lancaster announced they would turn and head west for a night before starting south again. "We'll be well clear of Richmond, so we shouldn't run into any trouble."

"We'll be behind Yankee lines," Potter said.

"Yes, but all their attention is focused on Richmond now. As long as we avoid their supply trains and relief columns, we should be fine. I'm relying on you men for that."

Several more days passed without incident. They traveled by day, since they were off the main roads and needed light to see where they were going. Also, they were moving through country where none of them had been before, so they didn't know the terrain. Sometimes they found their way blocked by a ravine or a ridge the wagons couldn't handle, and were forced to backtrack until they found another route.

They were making progress southward, and that was encouraging to Luke. He didn't know how long it would take them to reach Georgia—a couple weeks, more than likely, he thought—but at least they were heading in the right direction finally. He just hoped the Confederacy hadn't collapsed by the time they got there.

In a way, that would be simpler, he mused as he rode ahead of the wagons, scouting with Remy. If the damned war was over, they could just surrender and be done with it. Admitting defeat to the Yankees would be a bitter pill to swallow, but at least they would all be alive.

Of course, in that case the Union would seize the gold. Off it would go to Washington. That bothered Luke, too, but the final fate of the gold was really none of his business.

He suspected Potter, Stratton, Richards, and Casey were all sneaking drinks now and then, but none of them got drunk so he didn't say anything about it. Lancaster seemed oblivious to what was going on, but that was nothing unusual. The colonel was oblivious about a lot of things.

Several times they had to take to the woods and find hiding places when Yankees were in the vicinity. Once they watched from the concealment of trees while a lone supply wagon rolled slowly past, accompanied by a handful of tired-looking blue-clad troopers. In whispers, Stratton and Potter urged Lancaster to let them attack the wagon.

"There's bound to be provisions in there we could use," Potter said.

"And we can kill all them blue bellies before they know what's goin' on," Stratton added.

Lancaster shook his head stubbornly. "We can't risk the shots drawing attention. We'll stay here until they're gone."

Stratton and Potter didn't argue, but Luke saw them looking at the colonel with a mixture of scorn and hatred. He didn't have a very high opinion of Lancaster himself, but those two looked like they wanted to murder him.

The bad feelings he had about the mission grew stronger as they continued heading south. More than a week had passed since they left Richmond when they paused to rest the horses one afternoon and suddenly heard something they hadn't heard in quite a while.

Female voices.

Casey's head came up like a bloodhound catching a scent. "Hear that, fellas? There's womenfolks somewhere close by!"

Luke heard it, all right. Several women, by the sound of it, and they were laughing. The voices were coming from the other side of a thick stand of trees.

"We'd better check that out, Colonel," Stratton said to Lancaster.

"Yeah, there's no tellin' but what they might be spyin' on us," Richards said.

It didn't sound to Luke like the women were spying on them. He thought it would be better to move on as quickly as possible.

But Lancaster nodded. "All right. Three of you go find out who they are and what they're doing here. Jensen, Casey, and Potter, you go."

Luke would have rather gone with a couple of his friends, but he nodded and got his rifle from the wagon. He and Casey and Potter slipped into the woods, moving quickly but quietly.

The stand of trees wasn't very thick. A couple minutes later, the three men came to a creek. A covered wagon was parked on the other side of the stream. A woman perched on the seat with a shotgun across her knees.

"Holy Moses," Casey breathed.

He was looking at six women standing knee-deep in the creek, stripped down to their underthings. They were taking advantage of the creek and the warm afternoon to bathe. The flimsy garments were soaked and clung to their bodies.

"You know what kind of women those are?" Potter asked in a whisper.

Luke knew. It was pretty obvious. They ranged in age from late teens to early thirties, he judged, although soiled doves led such hard lives they often looked older than they really were. Such women always followed the armies. Union, Confederate, it didn't matter. Luke figured such women could have been found with the Greeks outside the walls of Troy. "Must be Yankees around here. Otherwise those women wouldn't be here."

"I don't care about that," Casey said. "I just want to go say howdy to them."

Potter grunted. "I want to do a hell of a lot more than say howdy."

Luke understood. He was as human as the next man, and the sight of all that wet, bare, female flesh made him react just like Potter and Casey. But they had other things to worry about. "We'd better leave them alone. We'd just be asking for trouble if we start bothering with them."

"You're not in charge here, Jensen," Potter snapped.

"No, but the colonel wouldn't want—"

"The hell with the colonel! Come on, Ted."

Before Luke could stop him, Potter straightened, stepped out of the trees, and called, "Howdy there, ladies."

The women in the creek shrieked and giggled in surprise, but the older woman on the wagon seat instantly swung up her shotgun and pointed it across the stream. "Howdy yourself, you damn Rebel. You come a step closer and I'll blast you to hell!"

Potter held up his hands. "Whoa, there, ma'am. I don't mean any harm. I just came along and saw all these beautiful young fillies, and I had to say hello." As Casey stepped out of the trees, Potter went on. "My friend here feels the same way."

"That's right," Casey said with a broad grin on his face.

Still under cover, Luke saw what was about to happen. "Casey, no!" He started forward, but was too late.

Casey's hand came up with a gun in it. The revolver roared, and across the creek, the woman on the wagon rocked backward as the bullet drove into her. One barrel of the shotgun boomed as her finger jerked on the trigger, but the weapon was angled upward and the load of buckshot went harmlessly into the air.

The woman swayed forward, dropped the shotgun, and pitched off the wagon seat, landing on the creek bank in a limp sprawl. Luke could tell by looking that she was dead.

The screams that came from the whores in the creek weren't playful any longer. The girls were terrified.

Potter drew his gun and said in a loud voice, "Shut up! Nobody's gonna hurt you!" He glared at Casey. "Why the hell did you shoot the old woman?"

"I don't like people pointin' guns at me," Casey said. "Anyway, you heard her call me a Rebel. She was a Yankee madam, nothin' to be worried about."

Even though Luke had seen far, far more than his share of violence over the past four years, the callous way Casey had murdered the woman sickened him. He was about to draw his own gun and cold-cock the varmint from behind when footsteps rushed through the trees toward them. He looked over his shoulder and saw Remy and the other men coming to see what the commotion was about.

"Hold your fire!" Lancaster called, even though no one was shooting. "Damn it, what's going on here?"

As they emerged from the trees, the man all gaped at the women in the creek, who were now huddled together in frightened silence. Even Lancaster stared at them.

Casey holstered his revolver and said coolly, "That old biddy over yonder by the wagon tried to blast us with a shot-gun, Colonel. I stopped her."

"I heard those shots," Lancaster said, "and so did any Yankees within a mile of here! Come on. We have to get moving while we still have the chance."

"No offense, Colonel," Casey said, "but I'm not goin' any-where until I've had a chance to get to know one of those gals a mite better. That one with the yaller hair, I'm thinkin'."

Luke saw how things were shaping up. Stratton and Richards had drifted toward Casey and Potter. Remy, Dale, and Edgar had moved up alongside Luke. Lancaster was in the middle.

The colonel realized it wasn't a very good place to be and stepped back quickly. "I've given you men an order. By God, I expect you to carry it out!"

They were standing on the knife-edge of bad trouble, Luke sensed. He had felt such impending violence in the air many times, and seldom did it end well.

However, something intervened. From the corner of his eye, he saw one of the soiled doves break away from the others. The blonde Casey had mentioned, in fact. She scrambled out of the creek onto the bank and snatched up the shotgun the older woman had dropped.

With their attention focused on each other, none of the other men saw it happening until it was too late. Potter finally noticed the blonde and twisted toward her, his hand clawing for the gun at his waist.

Luke's revolver came out with blinding speed. He leveled the barrel at Potter and drew back the hammer. The sinister metallic sound made Potter freeze.

"Don't do it," Luke warned.

Across the creek, the blonde screamed, "Get out of here, damn you! One barrel of this scattergun's still loaded! I'll cut you all down! I ought to do it anyway, for killin' Maddy!"

Potter's gun was in his hand, already cocked, but it was still pointed at the ground. He looked at Luke through eyes slitted narrow with hate. "You're takin' the side of a bunch of damned whores over your friends?"

"I don't recall you and me being friends, Potter," Luke said. "We just have the same job to do, that's all."

"And that job's in danger the longer we stay here," Lancaster said. "We have to go. Now."

For a second Luke thought Potter was going to lift his gun and pull the trigger, anyway. If he did, the creek bank would erupt in gunfire. They might all die, especially if the blonde cut loose at the men with that shotgun. She very well might do just that, considering the other whores had scrambled out of the creek and taken shelter behind their wagon.

Potter laughed and shook his head. "I'll never figure you out, Jensen." He lowered the hammer of his revolver and stuck the gun back in his waistband. "But I reckon you and the colonel are right. There might be a Yankee patrol gallopin' toward us right now, so we better light a shuck."

"But, Wiley—" Casey began.

"I said we're goin'."

Casey cast a regretful glance at the blonde. Clearly, he might have dared that shotgun to get at her. But too much else was against him at the moment. He nodded. "Yeah, come on, fellas." He pointed a finger across the creek at the blonde and added, "I'll see you again one of these days, darlin'."

"You better hope I don't see you first," she said as her mouth twisted in a snarl.

Luke didn't put his gun away until the men had gone back to the wagons. He saw Potter glancing at him several times as they got ready to move. It was hard to read the man's expression, but Luke knew he had made an enemy.

The outriders mounted up, and the drivers and guards climbed onto the wagons. With no Yankees in sight, they moved out smartly, still heading south.

Remy brought his horse alongside the wagon where Luke and Dale were riding. "The next time those girls see Yankee soldiers, they're gonna tell them about us."

"I expect you're right," Luke said.

"And that blond belle, she be a smart one, Luke. She heard Casey and Potter call the colonel by his rank, and she heard him givin' us orders. She'll figure out that, civilian clothes or not, we're soldiers. Confederate soldiers."

Luke nodded. He knew Remy was right.

And because of what had happened at that creek, he knew their mission had just gotten harder.

CHAPTER 8

The rest of that day, everyone in the group kept looking behind them fairly often, checking their back trail. The same thought was in their minds: one time, they'd look back and see Yankee cavalry chasing them.

It didn't happen, though. By the time they camped that night, they hadn't encountered anyone else.

The next day passed without incident as well, and Luke began to hope if the whores had told somebody about what had happened, the Yankees were too busy to worry about some strange-acting Confederate soldiers dressed in civilian clothing.

They were somewhere in eastern Tennessee, Luke figured, maybe in the Smoky Mountains, and the terrain grew more rugged. The wagons followed narrow, twisting trails running between steep, heavily wooded slopes. Luke watched those mountainsides intently, knowing the dark valleys were perfect for an ambush.

The travelers avoided settlements, but every now and then they passed isolated cabins with small garden patches nearby. The people living there barely subsisted on what little food they could grow, along with any small game they could trap. Obviously, it wasn't much. The people who came out of those rickety cabins to watch them pass were gaunt and hollow-eyed. They looked like it had been months since their bellies were even half full.

The children were the worst, Luke thought. His heart went out to them as they stared up at the wagons and riders with dull, defeated eyes. He wanted to give them something to eat, but he and his companions were already short on rations. His own belly spent a lot of time growling in hunger. The soldiers couldn't do any hunting because of the attention the shots might attract.

They were approaching one such cabin when an old man with a long white beard limped onto the trail to stop them.

Lancaster called, "Get out of the way, old-timer," but the man didn't budge. Dale hauled back on the reins to bring the lead team to a halt before they ran over the old man. Lancaster cast an irritated look over his shoulder, and Luke knew it was because Dale had stopped the wagon without waiting for the colonel's order.

"What do you want, old man?" Lancaster asked.

The man raked gnarled fingers through his long white beard before answering. "I don't know who ye are or where ye be goin', but I want you to take my grandson wi' ye." He turned his head and nodded toward the shack, where a skinny boy about twelve years old stood on the leaning porch. He was barefoot and wore only a pair of ragged overalls.

"I'm sorry, we can't do that," Lancaster said.

"If he stays here, he'll starve, sure as shootin'," the old man insisted. "The only chance he's got to live is goin' somewheres else, somewheres they have more food."

A harsh laugh came from Potter. "Then he's out of luck, old-timer, because it's like this all over the South. The Yankees have burned and looted and torn down until there's nothing left. The boy might as well stay here and starve instead of starvin' somewhere else."

The old man lifted a trembling hand. "Ye can't mean that. There's got to be some place better. There's got to be a place where folks still have some hope."

"If there is, we haven't seen it," Lancaster said. "I'm sorry, sir, but we have to be moving on. Now, if you'll get out of our way . . ."

In desperation, the old man reached for the halter on the colonel's horse. "Please . . . you got supplies . . ."

"Not enough to share," Lancaster snapped. "Not even enough to last us until we get where we're going." He pulled his horse to the side, out of the old man's reach. "Get out of—"

He didn't say any more. At that moment, a shot boomed and the old man's head jerked as a sizable chunk of it was blown away by a rifle ball. Blood sprayed in the air, turning his white hair pink.

The shot came from just behind them and to the right, Luke judged. While he was turning on the wagon seat to locate the threat, the thought crossed his mind that the shot had been aimed at Lancaster. When the colonel moved his horse suddenly, it sealed the old man's fate.

More shots roared. Tongues of flame spurted in the trees almost at the edge of the trail. Luke whipped his rifle to his shoulder and fired at one of the muzzle flashes. A man in a dirty blue uniform and black forage cap staggered out from behind a tree, clutching his chest where Luke's bullet had gone. The Yankee soldier collapsed.

The rifle was good for only one shot, and Luke didn't have time to reload. He dropped it at his feet and yanked the revolver from his waistband as he used his other hand to shove Dale off the seat. He followed, diving after his friend.

The bushwhackers seemed to be on the right side of the road. As the Confederates returned the fire, they hurriedly took cover behind the wagons. The saddle mounts bolted down the trail, but that was a problem to worry about later, Luke thought . . . if any of them survived.

Crouching behind the lead wagon, he tried to make his shots count, waiting for a glimpse of blue before he pulled the trigger. Fortunately, the Yankees cooperated. There was no telling where those Union troops were from, but they didn't seem to have much experience at the sort of hill fighting the

Southerners did. Nobody grew up in the Ozarks without learning about the dangers of bushwhackers.

Three more men fell to Luke's shots, and the heavy fire from his companions was taking a toll, too. The wagons with their cargo of bullion provided good cover. No bullets could penetrate those crates full of gold bars.

Luke glanced at the other men. They were all on their feet. He couldn't tell if any were wounded, but they were all still in the fight, something that couldn't be said for the Yankees.

The officer in charge of the ambush realized the same thing. He shouted over the sound of gunfire, "We'll overrun them! Charge!"

That was just about the worst thing those Yankees could have done. As they burst out of the woods, yelling and shooting, they were met by a hail of bullets from the wagons.

The first rank went down as lead tore into them, then the second, and the charge disintegrated into a chaotic milling around, turning the soldiers into sitting ducks. A few tried to flee back into the trees, but they were gunned down.

An eerie silence fell as clouds of powder smoke drifted over the trail and around the wagons. Luke risked a look. It appeared all the Yankees were on the ground. A few were writhing around and groaning in pain, but most of them lay in the limp sprawl that signified death.

If there had been enough of them, maybe they could have overrun the wagons and finished off the Confederates with their bayonets. But the attack had fallen short

"Check those men," Lancaster ordered.

Stratton tucked away his pistol and drew a knife. He looked over at Richards and grinned. "Josh and me will take care of it, Colonel."

Richards grinned, too, and pulled out his own knife.

Luke knew they intended to cut the throats of the Yankees who were only wounded. He didn't like the idea of killing defenseless men, but this was war, after all.

A sob made him turn around. The boy who'd been on the porch had come onto the trail, falling to his knees beside the body of his grandfather. He was leaning forward over the corpse, crying.

Luke reloaded his pistol and his rifle, then walked over to the boy and rested a hand on his shoulder. "Come on, son. That won't do any good. Your gramps is gone. I'm sorry."

"The . . . the Yankees came marchin' up a while ago," the youngster managed to say. "They told Grampa that . . . that there would be some wagons comin' along . . . They said they'd been chasin' you for days . . . and wanted him to stop y'all somehow. Grampa didn't want to do it . . . but they said they'd kill us both and burn down our place if he didn't . . . He had to do it, mister. He had to."

"I reckon he did." Luke had already figured out something like that must have happened. "There's no shame in a man doing whatever he has to in order to protect his family. You remember that, son."

"But then they . . . they shot him anyway!"

"I think that was an accident. They were trying to shoot one of us."

"He's dead, though, either way."

There was no denying that. Luke didn't even try to. He couldn't do anything for the boy except squeeze his shoulder again and leave him there to mourn his grandfather.

When he went back over to the wagons, he asked Remy, "Anybody hurt in our bunch?"

"Edgar got nicked on the arm, but Dale's patching it up. The colonel's hat's got a hole in it, so he came mighty close to shakin' hands with the devil. But that's all."

"We were lucky."

Remy nodded. "Very lucky. Maybe the fates, they are smilin' on us for a change."

Luke thought they had been pretty fortunate the whole trip, but he didn't point that out.

Colonel Lancaster said, "I don't know if there are any more Yankees in this area, but if there are, they're bound to have heard this battle. We need to get moving again quickly. Somebody move that old man's body out of the way."

"We could bury him, Colonel," Luke suggested.

Lancaster shook his head. "There's no time for that. Let's go. We'll all ride on the wagons until we catch up to our horses."

Luke thought it was likely the saddle mounts had stopped to graze somewhere along the trail. Once they were away from the sound of shots and the smell of powder smoke, they would have calmed down fairly quickly.

The boy had gone back to the shack and disappeared inside. Luke and Remy picked up the old man's body and carried it carefully off the trail. They had just returned to the wagons and climbed on when the youngster emerged from the cabin carrying an old squirrel rifle.

"You and your damned war!" he cried shrilly. "I hate all of you!" He started to lift the rifle.

Potter's revolver streaked out and blasted. The slug smashed into the boy's frail chest and lifted him off his feet as it drove him backward. Dust puffed up around him as he landed on the ground.

There hadn't been time for the other men to do anything. Lancaster turned to Potter and said in a horrified tone, "You shot that boy!"

"He was about to point a rifle at me," Potter said coolly as he reloaded the expended chamber. "Damned if I was gonna sit here and let him shoot me."

Luke hopped down from the wagon and walked over to pick up the rifle the boy had dropped. The youngster lay a couple feet away, staring sightlessly at the sky. Luke tried not to look at those open, empty eyes.

He checked the rifle and said in disgust, "I don't think this old relic would have even fired! You killed him for nothing, Potter."

Potter's shoulders rose and fell. "I didn't have any way of knowin' that, now did I?"

That was true, Luke supposed. He threw the squirrel rifle

aside. The boy and his grandfather lay dead on one side of the road, more than a dozen Yankees on the other. Once again Luke and his companions were surrounded by senseless death.

After all the things he had seen . . . all the things he had *done* . . . he wondered if by the time the war was finally over, he would have any soul left at all.

CHAPTER 9

The gold escort continued south, hoping the Yankees who'd ambushed them were the only ones on their trail. Luke thought it likely the women they'd encountered beside that creek had sent the soldiers after them.

Each day without an ambush or confrontation the Confederates became more aware the Yankees had other things to deal with, like the collapse of the Confederacy. The atmosphere of gloom and despair hung over the landscape like actual clouds. The air smelled of smoke, rotting flesh, and defeat.

It seemed to Luke like a month had passed since they left Richmond, but he knew it hadn't quite been two weeks. "We're getting close to Georgia now," he commented to Dale one day. "Have to be."

"I think you're right," Dale said. "What are you gonna do once we get where we're goin', Luke?"

"I guess that'll be up to the colonel. Maybe he has orders for what we're supposed to do next. If not, I guess I'll stay wherever the new capital is and try to do what I can to help." Luke shook his head. "No point in trying to go back to Richmond, even if we could get there."

"I got a feelin' you're right about that."

The trail entered a long, straight stretch between two mostly bald knobs. Luke frowned at the hills, thinking it would be another good spot for an ambush.

But when the trouble came, it popped up right in front of them through sheer bad luck. A Union cavalry patrol came trotting around a bend in the trail just beyond the knobs.

The Yankees regarded anybody who wasn't wearing the blue as an enemy. Sunlight winked on steel as the officer in charge of the patrol whipped his saber from its scabbard and shouted, "Charge!"

Just like that, the Confederates were in another fight, and there wasn't any good cover on either side of the road.

All they could do was shoot it out.

Luke brought his rifle to his shoulder, drew a bead on the officer leading the charge, and pressed the trigger. The rifle roared and bucked against his shoulder. Through the powder smoke stinging his eyes, he saw the Yankee topple off the galloping horse.

Their commanding officer's death didn't slow down the other cavalrymen. They kept moving forward, blazing away with pistols as they raced toward the wagons and the outriders.

Colonel Lancaster tried to wheel his horse around and gallop back to the cover of the wagons, but he jerked in the saddle as at least one bullet found him. A crimson stain bloomed on the colonel's shirt, as he galloped past the lead wagon.

Dale grunted in pain beside Luke, but Luke didn't have time to glance over and see how badly his friend was hurt. He had his revolver leveled at the charging Yankees. As he squeezed off his last two rounds, another cavalryman fell, taking his mount down with him. Another horse ran into the fallen animal and upended as well. The trail suddenly became a welter of flailing hooves and swirling dust.

The back of the charge was broken. Only three Yankees remained mounted. They whirled their horses and fled. A few final shots from the Confederates followed to speed them on their way.

Luke turned to Dale and found his friend clutching a bloody left shoulder. "How bad is it?"

"Don't know, but it hurts like hell," Dale replied through clenched teeth. "I'll be all right. See about Remy and Edgar."

Luke twisted on the seat to look back at the other wagon. Remy was reloading and seemed to be all right. He glanced up and gave Luke a brief nod to signify as much. Edgar waved to indicate he was unharmed, too.

Lancaster had galloped past both wagons before coming to a stop. Luke had a feeling the horse had been running blindly, that the colonel was no longer in control. He glanced back to where the horse had stopped. Lancaster was still mounted, sitting hunched over in the saddle.

Casey trotted his horse back to check on the officer. He put a hand on Lancaster's shoulder and leaned over to take a closer look at him. Then he turned and called to the others, "Hey, the colonel's shot to pieces!"

"Get him down from his horse," Luke said, "but be careful with him."

Casey frowned as if he didn't like the idea of Luke giving him orders, but he dismounted and reached up to take hold of Lancaster. Stratton got to them in time to swing down from his saddle and give Casey a hand.

They lowered Lancaster onto his back in the grass at the side of the trail. All the men gathered around him, even the wounded Dale Cardwell.

Lancaster was still alive. His eyes were open, and his mouth moved like he was trying to say something. He couldn't get the words out, though. Nothing came from his mouth except trickles of blood at each corner.

The colonel's shirt was so bloody it was hard to tell for sure, but it looked like the man had been hit at least three times. Clearly, the wounds were bad ones.

Luke figured Lancaster had only minutes to live, if that

long. He dropped to a knee beside him. "Colonel, can you hear me? Colonel!"

Lancaster managed to make a sound, but it was just a choked, incoherent moan. From the look in his eyes, he wasn't aware of anything except the pain that filled him.

"Colonel, listen to me!" Luke urged. "We need to know where we're going. Colonel, do you have a map? Can you tell me—"

"He can't tell you nothin', Jensen," Potter said. "He's next thing to dead, can't you see that? We're on our own now."

"Don't say that just yet," Luke snapped. "We can't give up—"

A grotesque rattle came from Lancaster's throat. When Luke looked at the colonel again, he saw that Lancaster's eyes were starting to glaze over.

"Well, he's sure enough dead now," Potter drawled, "and like I said, we're on our own. Question is, what are we gonna do?"

"Go check those Yankees and make sure they're all dead," Luke said as he reached over to close Lancaster's eyes. "Remy, patch up Dale's shoulder."

"*Oui.*"

"Then we'll get moving," Luke went on. "We can't afford to wait around. Three of those troopers got away. They'll go tell other Yankees what happened. We need to get off the trail and find a place to hole up for a while."

He glanced up. No one except Remy, who was tearing pieces off his shirt to bind up the wound in Dale's shoulder, had moved to do what he said. "Blast it, get moving."

"Hold on just a minute, Jensen," Potter said. "I don't recall anybody puttin' you in charge."

"Somebody's got to take over," Luke said. "Or would you rather stand around and argue about it until a whole company of Yankee cavalry shows up?"

Potter thought it over for a couple seconds, then shrugged.

"All right, we'll do what you say . . . for now. But this ain't settled."

Luke didn't expect it to be, but for the moment he would take what he could get. He said to Edgar, "Let's put the colonel's body in one of the wagons."

"Why not leave him where he lays?" Stratton suggested.

"Because I want to search him later and see if he's got any written orders or a map on him."

That answer satisfied the others, and they went about their business. All the fallen Yankees were dead except for a couple, and Casey didn't waste any time slitting their throats. Luke and Edgar carried Lancaster's body over to the second wagon and placed it alongside the crates containing the gold bullion. By that time, the crude job Remy had done of bandaging Dale's wound had stopped the bleeding.

"Somebody tie the colonel's horse behind the second wagon," Luke said. "We'll take it with us."

That done, they followed the trail for another half mile until Luke spotted a narrow path leading off into a thick stretch of woods. He was driving the lead wagon since Dale couldn't handle the team with a wounded arm and drove between the trees, calling back to Remy, "Once we're all off the trail, get a branch and wipe away our tracks as far back as you can."

Remy waved a hand in acknowledgment of the order.

The path was little more than a game trail. Trees and brush crowded in on the wagons from both sides. Branches clawed at the men. Several times the wagons' sideboards scraped against tree trunks, and Luke worried they would get stuck. Finally, they broke out into a small clearing. It was big enough to turn the wagons around and go back out the way they had come in, but it would be a challenge.

When Remy rode in a few minutes later, he said, "Not only did I wipe away our tracks, but I pulled some brush in front of the opening as well. If any Yankees ride by, they may not even notice a gap big enough for the wagons."

Luke nodded his approval. "That was good thinking.

Let's get the colonel out of the wagon so I can check his pockets."

"Robbin' the dead?" Potter asked mockingly.

"Checking for a map or orders, like I said before."

"You go right ahead. I ain't fond of handlin' dead men."

Neither was Luke, but he made himself do it. He searched all Lancaster's pockets but didn't find anything except a couple bloodstained letters from the colonel's wife. He didn't read them, tucking them back into Lancaster's pocket. He didn't have any right to intrude on the colonel's private life.

Since that search came up empty, Luke opened Lancaster's saddlebags next. He was luckier there, finding a leather dispatch case with a folded map inside. As the others gathered around, he spread the map on the ground and studied it. After a second, his finger poked a spot that had been circled. "Copperhead Mountain. That must be where we're going. There's probably a settlement nearby where the government's going to set up." He straightened as he folded the map. "That's where we're going, anyway."

Wiley Potter's voice was flat and hard as he said, "I'm not so sure you're right about that, Jensen."

CHAPTER 10

L uke stiffened. Somehow, he wasn't surprised by what Potter said or the thinly veiled threat in the words. "What are you talking about?"

"All you've got is a map," Potter said. "You don't know that this Copperhead Mountain place is where we're supposed to go."

"It's the only thing in the colonel's belongings that has a destination marked. I think we all know that's what it means."

"Maybe," Stratton said. "But we don't have to go there, now do we?"

"Lancaster's dead," Richards added. "The mission's over."

Luke shook his head. "What makes you think that? Just because we've lost our commanding officer, doesn't mean we don't still have our orders."

"Orders from who? Jeff Davis?" Potter laughed. "The president of a country that may not even exist by now? Hell, Richmond could have fallen the day after we left, for all we know!"

Edgar said, "Even if Richmond fell, the war's still going on. General Lee hasn't surrendered. The way those Yankees keep attacking us proves that."

"Edgar's right," Remy said. "Our responsibility still lies with the Confederacy."

Casey finally put into words what was uppermost in all their minds. He pointed at the wagons and exclaimed, "But there's all that gold just sittin' there!"

It had happened even faster than Luke thought it would. The temptation of that fortune in gold bullion had been there all along, of course. Lancaster's presence and the men's habit of taking orders had held it in check.

But Lancaster was gone, and all Potter, Stratton, Richards, and Casey could think of was how they could be rich men. All they had to do was forget about delivering the gold to Copperhead Mountain, take the wagons, and strike out on their own. If they headed west, they might be able to leave the war behind them. There had been battles between Union and Confederate forces out on the frontier, but not many.

Luke glanced right and left. Remy, Dale, and Edgar stood with him, as he had known they would. They faced the other four men across a short distance. No guns were drawn—yet—but everyone was tense and ready for trouble.

It might not be possible to reason with the others. That much gold had a way of making a man's brain not work as well as it usually did. But Luke was going to try. "Look, you know we're not going to let you take those wagons. That gold belongs to the Confederacy. If we do anything with it except deliver it where we're supposed to, we'll be thieves . . . and traitors."

Potter let out a contemptuous snort. "How can you betray a country that don't exist anymore?" he demanded.

"You don't know that."

"Hell, Jensen, you've got eyes! There's no way Richmond was able to hold out. The streets are probably full of Yankees by now. And if Lee *hasn't* surrendered yet, he's got Grant chasin' him across Virginia. It's only a matter of time until what's left of the army is cornered. Lee's not gonna fight to the death, and you know it. He'll surrender."

Luke suspected Potter was right about that. General Robert E. Lee cared too much about his soldiers to let them be slaughtered to the last man in a futile cause.

But that still didn't change anything. They had their orders.

"Forget it, Potter. From the looks of that map, we're not far from Copperhead Mountain. We can be there in another couple days. And that's where we're going with that gold."

"That's your final word?" Potter asked. Next to him, Casey nervously licked his lips, anxious to grab for his gun. So were Richards and Stratton.

From what Luke had seen of those men, they were probably faster on the draw than Dale and Edgar. He and Remy might be able to match them, but that wasn't good enough. If it came down to a fight, he and his friends would probably die.

Some of the others would die, too, but more than likely one or two of them would survive. Those survivors would be very rich men.

The ones who didn't make it would be dead, and that worry lurked in Wiley Potter's eyes. Potter didn't want to risk his own life to make somebody else rich.

That realization was confirmed a second later when Potter burst out, "Ah, the hell with it!"

"Wait a minute, Wiley," Stratton protested. "What do you mean?"

"I mean I don't feel like dyin' over this," Potter declared.

Casey looked stricken. "The Confederacy don't need that gold," he said with a whining note in his voice. "It oughta be ours!"

"A man can always get rich if he's smart enough," Potter responded. "But not if he's dead!"

Luke didn't relax and let his guard down. He didn't trust Potter, not for a second. It could be some sort of trick. "You'll go on to Copperhead Mountain with us?"

"I didn't say that," Potter replied. "Look, we've fought Yankees over and over again on the way down here. They're probably lookin' for us right now. Our luck's bound to run out sooner or later. I've had enough of this war, Jensen. I'm riding away. The rest of you do whatever you damned well please."

"In other words, you're deserting," Luke said in a hard voice.

Potter surprised him by laughing. "You think I care what you call it? You can't betray a country that doesn't exist, and you can't desert from an army that's probably surrendered by now. All I know is I'm done with it."

"Me, too," Stratton said.

"And me," Richards added.

Casey still looked like he wanted to shoot somebody, but he gave a grudging nod. "Yeah, I'll go along with the others. I reckon bein' alive is the best thing."

"So, Jensen," Potter said. "Is it settled . . . or is it going to be a fight?"

Luke glanced at his companions. Remy shrugged a little. Edgar gave him a tiny nod. Dale just looked like he was in pain from that wounded shoulder.

"Go ahead and get out of here, if that's what you want to do." Luke didn't bother trying to keep the scorn out of his voice.

"We're taking the horses."

"Go ahead. We've got the colonel's horse. Remy can ride it. I'll handle one wagon and Edgar the other."

Potter smirked. "Sounds like you've got it all figured out. You'll be a real hero when you get to Copperhead Mountain with that gold. That is, until the Yankees take it away from you and you see what a waste it all was."

"I'll know that I followed orders, anyway."

"Yeah, that'll buy you a lot." Potter jerked his head at his allies. "Come on. I want to put some distance behind us before any more blue bellies can catch up to us."

"Wiley, are you sure about this?" Stratton asked.

"I'm sure. We'll have other big chances later on. Stick with me, boys, and we'll all be rich sooner or later."

The others still didn't look happy about it, but they followed Potter's lead and mounted up. Potter took a small bag of supplies from one of the wagons and held it up to Luke, raising his eyebrows. Luke nodded for him to take it.

The four men didn't follow the path back toward the road. They struck out across country, soon vanishing in the thick woods.

"Deserters," Edgar said in disgust. "Lousy deserters."

"Maybe worse than that," Remy said. "You don't trust them, do you, Luke?"

"Not one bit. We'll keep our eyes open in case they double back and make a try for the gold."

"So now we have to worry about the Yankees *and* those four," Dale said. "Things don't get any easier, do they?"

Luke shook his head. "Hardly ever."

They buried Colonel Lancaster's body in the woods and stayed hidden in the little clearing all night. Several times Luke heard a lot of hoofbeats in the distance and thought it was likely the Yankees were hunting for them. None of the searchers came close to the wagons, though. Luke wondered if that was because they really hadn't gone very far from the site of the battle with the cavalrymen. The Yankees might have expected them to head on south as quickly as possible.

Nor was there any sign of Potter, Richards, Stratton, and Casey. Luke hoped the four men really had lit a shuck for the frontier. It would certainly make things easier.

By morning, Dale had developed a fever and lay stretched out under one of the wagons.

Luke looked at him, then at the others. "If we move him, we take a chance on him getting worse."

"We could stay here another day," Remy suggested. "Give the Yankees that much more time to get tired of lookin' for us."

That sounded like a pretty good idea to Luke. They continued lying low and took turns wiping Dale's face with a wet cloth to keep him cool as he tossed and muttered. It was all they could do for him.

The fever broke the next night. Dale was still weak, but a lot more coherent the morning after that. As he sipped a little broth Edgar had made from the salt pork, he said, "We gotta get movin' again. That gold needs to get to the new capital."

Luke had his doubts whether that new capital even existed, but on the chance that it did, they had to continue their mission. He nodded. "We'll hitch up the teams."

Dale was able to sit up and ride on the seat of the lead wagon next to Luke. Edgar handled the other wagon while Remy rode ahead to scout their route. He came back to report that the trail was clear.

"Lots of tracks, though, and they're pretty recent," Remy said. "There are still plenty of Yankees in these parts. Might be better if we started travelin' at night again."

"That won't be easy since we don't know exactly how to get where we're going," Luke said. "We've got the colonel's map, though. Maybe we can figure it out."

Late that afternoon, they had to leave the road hurriedly to avoid a cavalry patrol. Luke and Edgar managed to pull the wagons behind a hill before the blue-clad troopers rode past, but it was close.

"You're right," Luke told Remy. "We'll travel at night the rest of the way, starting tonight. We'll stay here and let the horses rest for a few hours, then try to put a few more miles behind us."

They made a cold supper from rations that had dwindled to almost nothing. For days, they had gotten by on about half the food they really needed. Luke's belly felt empty all the time. The trek wouldn't last much longer, he told himself, and then things would be better.

Remy did a little more scouting while it was still light and returned to tell the others, "There's a river about a mile from here. It's shallow, and there's a good ford. We shouldn't have any trouble gettin' across."

"And we can fill up our water barrels and canteens while we're at it," Edgar said.

That sounded like a good plan to Luke. When they had rested for a while and it was good and dark, they started the wagons rolling south again.

The moon hadn't risen yet when they reached the river, but Luke saw stars reflected in its placid surface. Remy rode out in front of the wagons so the others could see how deep the water was. Luke figured it was only about a foot.

"The bottom's good and solid," Remy said. "The only problem is that the bank on the other side is a little steep. It'll be a hard haul for the teams gettin' all that weight up to the top. But I reckon they can do it."

"All right, let's go." Luke slapped the reins against the backs of his team. The big draft horses leaned into their harness. Water splashed around the wheels as the wagon began fording the river.

Luke made the crossing without any problem and started up the grade on the far side as Edgar's wagon rolled out of the water behind him. Remy sat his horse to one side.

Suddenly, what felt like a sledgehammer slammed into Luke, low down on his back. He cried out in agony as the impact drove him forward. Dropping the reins, he slumped over and almost pitched off the seat to land under the hooves of the team. At the last moment he twisted his body and fell to the side, landing with stunning force beside the front wheel.

He had never felt such pain in his life. It swelled and burst into a fiery explosion that seemed as big and hot as the sun. As Luke lay there gasping for breath, he heard shots, heard men cry out. Remy cursed and gasped. Edgar roared in defiance, a bellow that was cut short by a flurry of gunfire.

They had been ambushed. The question was whether the bushwhackers were Yankees . . . or those damned deserting curs, Potter, Stratton, Richards, and Casey.

He got his answer a moment later when hoofbeats sounded close beside his head. Instinctively, he tried to jerk away from them, but his body wouldn't work anymore. All he could do was lie there and twitch.

"I don't hear you giving any orders now, Jensen," a man's harsh voice said.

Wiley Potter. Luke recognized the voice, even though he couldn't respond to it.

He thought his gun was still tucked in his waistband and tried to edge his hand toward it. A gun roared, and mud from the riverbank splattered in his face as the bullet tore into the ground beside his head.

"You're beat, Jensen," Potter said. "You might as well admit it. The other three are dead, and you soon will be. And that gold's goin' with us, just like it was supposed to all along. You stupid idiot, did you really think we were just gonna ride away and leave it?"

Luke was hurting too much to force his thoughts into any coherent order. He shifted a little, and an even more terrible wave of agony made him scream.

"Your back's busted," Potter went on. "That was a hell of a shot I made, if I do say so myself. You're gonna be a long time dyin', Jensen, and I'm going to sit right here on my horse and enjoy every minute of it. So you go ahead and scream. It's music to my ears."

"Wiley, we can't stay here too long." That was Stratton. "We need to take these wagons and get movin'. Why don't you just put a bullet in his head and be done with it?"

Casey laughed. "What fun would that be? I'm with you, Wiley. I want to listen to Jensen scream while he's dyin'."

Luke's mind cleared abruptly. He understood what they'd been saying and forced himself to cut short the agonized cries coming from his tortured throat. He wasn't going to give them the satisfaction.

But his resolve was short-lived, as the pain made him cry out again. Several of the deserters laughed, obviously enjoying Luke's torment.

They weren't going to have much longer to indulge their sadistic glee. A darkness that had nothing to do with night was closing in around Luke, washing over his mind like a black tide. *This is what dying feels like,* he thought in a final moment of clarity.

"He's dead," he heard Wiley Potter say.

That was all. After that, the darkness was complete.

BOOK TWO

CHAPTER 11

When Luke Jensen was ten years old, he fell out of a tree and broke his left arm. It hurt like blazes, and he couldn't hold back the tears as his pa set the bone and splinted the arm.

"No need to cry," Emmett Jensen had said. "That don't make the arm feel any better, does it?"

"Hell yes, it does!" Luke had yelled.

Emmett had laughed too hard to get on to him for cussing. Luke's ma took care of that later, fussing at him until he wished he'd broken his ears instead of his arm.

Luckily, Emmett had set enough broken bones that he knew what he was doing, so his oldest son's arm healed cleanly and Luke didn't suffer any loss of strength or movement in it. He never forgot how bad it hurt when it happened, though.

A couple years later, while getting some wood from the pile next to the back door of the Jensen cabin, he was stung on the right hand by the biggest scorpion he'd ever seen. It felt like somebody had shoved a dull knife through his palm.

The hand swelled up and got almost as red as a beet, and for a while the family worried that he would lose it. Emmett was prepared to cut the hand off if it meant saving Luke's life, but first, he rode up into the hills and brought back an old granny woman who scoured the countryside for plants, made a foul-smelling poultice out of them, and bound it onto Luke's hand.

Within a day the swelling started to go down and the redness went away. By the time a week had passed, the hand was back to normal and Luke couldn't even see the place where the scorpion had stung him.

He remembered what that had felt like, too, and took particular satisfaction in stomping every one of the ugly little varmints he saw after that.

The pain radiating from his back made breaking his arm seem like stubbing his toe. That scorpion sting was nothing more than a mosquito bite. Without a doubt, the current pain was the worst agony Luke had ever experienced in his life.

He wasn't sure how long he lay there, awash in suffering, before he realized the pain meant he wasn't dead.

His pulse hammered an insane rhythm inside his skull. He tried to force his eyes open, but couldn't do it. There wasn't enough strength in him even for a tiny task like that. All he could do was lie there and drag ragged breaths into his body.

After another unknowable length of time, he became aware of light striking his eyelids. He tried again to lift them, and succeeded.

Sunlight lay in a dappled pattern around him. Lying on his stomach on damp ground, his head was turned to the right, his left cheek pressed against the dirt. After a moment, he figured out the sun was shining down on him through some tree branches. Trying to make his brain work provided a welcome distraction from the pain.

He tried to remember how he'd gotten there. At first, everything up until that moment was a blank slate in his mind, but slowly the details began to fill in. He remembered the gold, the journey from Richmond, the friends who had been with him . . .

Then the ambush and Wiley Potter's sneering voice

telling him the others were dead and he was dying. In fact, he recalled Potter saying, "He's dead."

Potter had been wrong about that. Luke was too weak to move, but he sure wasn't dead. Not yet, anyway.

Since Potter had been wrong about him, maybe the bushwhacker had been wrong about the others, too. Luke yelled, "Remy! Dale! Edgar! Can any of you hear me?"

It was only when he heard the faint croaking sounds that he realized he wasn't yelling at all. He'd only thought that he was. *He* was the one making those incoherent noises. Finally, after what seemed like another hour, he struggled to get out the name, "R-Remy . . ."

He heard some birds in the distance, the wind stirring the branches in the trees, the tiny lapping sound of the river flowing nearby, but that was all.

He had to get up and look for them. He might still be able to save them.

The gold was gone. Luke knew that. Potter and the other deserters would have taken the wagons with them when they left him for dead, so Luke didn't waste time worrying about that. His only concerns were saving his own life and helping his friends if he could.

He needed to get up and see how badly he was hurt, but one thing at a time, he told himself. First he wanted to look around. He moved his hands enough to dig his fingers into the dirt and brace himself. Then, with a grunt of effort, he lifted his head.

A yell burst from him as even that much movement set off a fresh explosion of pain. He wanted to drop his head, close his eyes, and retreat back into the welcoming darkness.

Instead, he forced his head from side to side in small, jerking motions.

He couldn't hold back a sob as he saw Dale lying on the ground a few yards away. The young man's face was unmarked and his eyes were open, but flies were crawling around on them. He was dead, no doubt about it. His clothes were black with blood where he'd been shot.

Remy and Edgar had fallen in the other direction. Edgar's face was a hideous ruin where several shots had struck him, but Luke recognized his friend's burly build. Remy was disfigured as well, with most of his jaw shot away. The flies were feasting on their spilled blood, as well.

Luke groaned and let his head fall. There was nothing he could do for his friends, after all. Nothing he could do except save himself and maybe go after Potter and the others once the pain in his back got better.

He didn't know how long he lay there, stretched out on the riverbank. The earth turned and the sun moved in the sky, and he was no longer in the shade. When the heat began to bother him, he tried to heave himself up to hands and knees so he could crawl where it was cooler.

The muscles in his arms and shoulders bunched, and the upper part of his body lifted slightly, but that was all. Luke pushed on his hands again to move upward, but was unable to move high enough. He tried to press against the ground with his knees . . . and realized he couldn't *feel* his knees. He couldn't feel any part of his legs.

Horror washed over him. His body seemed to end at his lower back, where the bullet had struck him and the pain was so bad. Below that, however, nothing hurt. His legs might as well not have been there, and for one sickening moment, he believed they weren't. He thought Potter had sawed them off before leaving.

Slowly, Luke moved his right hand next to his hip. Breathing heavily against the pain, he twisted his neck and looked along his body. He couldn't see very well, but caught enough of a glimpse to know his right leg was still there.

He slumped down. The effort had made his heart pound crazily and left him breathless. As he gasped for air, he remembered a farmer back in Missouri named Claude Monroe, who'd been kicked in the back by a rambunctious mule. The accident busted something in Monroe's back, and after that

he was never able to walk again. He had lived for a couple
years, lying in bed or sometimes lifted into a chair, before
he'd taken an old flintlock pistol, carefully loaded and
primed it, and blown a hole right through his head.

He wouldn't have to do that, Luke thought as a hysterical
laugh worked its way up his parched throat. No, he would
die right where he was . . . on the riverbank . . . more than
likely. He knew from the terrible thirst gripping him that
he'd lost quite a bit of blood, and he might be losing more
all the time without being aware of it. The easiest thing in
the world would be to just give in to the pain that enveloped
him, and wait for death. So easy . . .

There was no dramatic moment, no stirring speech he
made to pull himself back from the brink of despair. It was
just that after a while he got so thirsty he thought he might as
well try to get a drink from the river. He moved his left arm
next to his left hip and cautiously looked under his arm to
see if his left leg was still there. It was. He pushed and
clawed at the ground in an effort to turn himself around.

When he got far enough around, the steep slope worked
against him, and before he knew what was happening, he
was rolling down toward the water, his useless legs flopping
loosely.

*So, I'm going to fall in the river and drown in a foot of
water.* As that thought flashed across Luke's mind he reached
out, caught hold of a root growing from one of the trees on
the bank, and stopped himself at the edge of the river.

He hung on to the root with one hand while he reached
out with the other and cupped it in the stream. When he
brought that hand to his mouth, the water he sucked out of
his cupped palm was the sweetest he'd ever tasted.

Thirst made him ignore the pain in his back. His movements grew frenzied as he drank. He missed sometimes and
splashed water over his face. It felt good.

Then his stomach lurched, and he spewed up all the water
he had managed to guzzle down. The spasm made him cry
out.

The sickness faded after a few minutes. Luke lay there a little longer and started drinking again, slower.

He kept it down.

When his thirst wasn't so desperate, he twisted around and looked up at the top of the riverbank again. In his condition, the slope seemed impossible for him to climb. He would be better off just staying close to the water, so he could get another drink later.

Making that decision was all he could manage. Closing his eyes, he rested his head against the ground, content to lie there and wait for . . . something.

What he got wasn't good. A short time later, it started to rain.

Luke hadn't noticed the sun going behind the clouds, hadn't been aware the day was growing dark and ominous with the approach of a storm. He had no idea what was happening until thunder suddenly boomed so loud it shook the earth underneath him.

Or was that artillery fire? He had felt the earth move plenty of times in Richmond as the Yankees pounded the city with their big guns.

No, definitely thunder, he thought as several large raindrops pelted the back of his head. In a matter of seconds, a torrent was sluicing down around him.

Luke lifted his head, tilted it back as much as he could, and shouted at the heavens, "Go ahead! Rain on me, damn you! After everything that's already happened to me, how much worse can this be?"

He wasn't sure if he actually bellowed out the words or just thought them, the way he'd thought he was calling his friends' names earlier. But either way, the sentiment was real.

Unfortunately, a few minutes later he realized his situation *could* get worse.

When he looked along the banks, he saw how they were washed out in places. That was why the root he'd grabbed was sticking out of the ground. It meant the river had a tendency to rise when it rained. If the marks on the bank were right, the water could come up higher than the place where he was sprawled.

But how long will it take to do that? he asked himself. *And how much will it have to rain before I'll be in danger?*

He couldn't answer those questions, but it was a downpour, no doubt about that. A real toad-strangler, they'd call it back home. All along the banks, miniature waterfalls were already forming as rain landed higher up and ran down to the river, raising its level drop by drop.

And there were millions of drops.

Luke started laughing again. By all rights, he should have been dead already. How many more times could he manage to dodge the reaper? When was his luck going to run out?

Soon, he thought. Soon.

The water would climb up his body until the current plucked him away from the bank and spun him out into the stream and sucked him under. Tomorrow his lifeless body would wash up somewhere downriver. He could see that grotesque image in his mind, plain as day.

But he wasn't going to give in to that fate without a fight. His father had made it clear to him at an early age that Jensens didn't have any back up in them. Don't go lookin' for trouble, Emmett had told him, but don't ever go runnin' away from it, either. And if the devil finds you, spit in his face.

Luke reached up the bank, dug his hand into the mud, and pulled.

The ground was wet and slick, but he clawed at it stubbornly, grabbed another root, dug in with his elbows, and shoved. He got his body turned so he was facing up the bank again instead of lying sideways on it.

Even if he'd been able to use his legs, it would have been difficult to crawl up that muddy slope. With only his arms to pull himself along, it was sheer torture. The burning pain in his arms and shoulders dominated the misery in his back.

Slowly, inch by agonizing inch, he pulled himself up the riverbank.

After what seemed like hours, when he was too exhausted to go on, he turned his head, looking under his arm, and realized he was only a couple feet higher than when he'd started out. He looked back along his body as best he could.

His feet were already in the water. The river had risen about a foot, and the current was running fast, which meant more and more water was coming down from upstream.

Gritting his teeth, Luke tried to haul himself higher. He made another few inches, maybe half a foot, and his strength deserted him again.

Maybe what he ought to do was try to roll over onto his back, he thought. Then the rain, which was still coming down with blinding force, might drown him before the river rose high enough to do the job.

The problem was, he was too weak to roll over.

Luke laughed. "You got me," he rasped. "I'm done for. Fought all I can fight. I'm sorry, Pa. Wish I could see you again. You and Ma and Janey and Kirby . . . but this is where it ends for me."

His head fell forward. Mud covered his face, clogged his nose, choked him. He coughed and fought free of it, his instincts refusing to let him die. The rain washed some of the muck from his eyes.

And he was able to see the slender fingers reaching down and wrapping around the wrist of his outstretched right hand. Thunder boomed again and lightning flashed.

Luke Jensen blinked in amazement as he rose up as best he could, carefully turned his head, and saw the face of the angel who had reached down from heaven to lift him from earth.

It was funny. He'd always figured when he died, he'd be headed in the other direction.

CHAPTER 12

"Damn it!" the angel yelled.

Confused, Luke blinked rainwater out of his eyes. He'd never gone to prayer meeting all that much, but he didn't remember any preachers he'd ever heard saying anything about angels cussing.

"Come on, mister!" the beautiful vision urged. "You weigh too much for me to lift you by myself. You gotta help me some!"

Understanding sunk slowly into Luke's brain. Despite the pretty face, it was no angel above him but rather a flesh-and-blood girl. She wasn't wearing heavenly robes and didn't have wings, either. She was dressed in tattered overalls, a woolen shirt, and a battered old black hat with rainwater streaming from the brim.

She tugged on his wrist. "Mister, can you hear me? The river's comin' up. If we don't get you off this bank, you're gonna drown."

After fighting on his own for what seemed like an eternity, the sheer fact that someone else was trying to save him filled Luke with gratitude and relief. That feeling was short-lived, though, because he realized she was right. "Can you . . . get help?" he croaked.

"No time!" she said. "This ol' river comes up mighty quick

when it rains like this. Goldang it, I told Grampaw I heard somebody yellin' last night!"

"You better . . . fetch him. Has he got . . . a horse or . . . a mule?"

"Yeah, but like I told you, there ain't enough time for that." She dug the heels of her bare feet into the bank and got hold of his wrist with both hands. As she hauled hard on his arm, she said through clenched teeth, "Can't you push . . . with your damned legs?"

Luke couldn't, and he didn't have a chance to explain it. Just then her feet slipped in the mud and she sat down hard as her legs went out from under her. With a startled cry she started sliding down the bank toward him.

She didn't go very far. His head butted her in the stomach and stopped her. Her thighs rested on his shoulders. She put her hands on the ground and pushed herself away from him.

"Dadblast it!" she cried. "Don't you go gettin' any ideas, mister!"

"The only idea I have . . . is not drowning," Luke said. "Let's . . . try again."

The girl scrambled up and took hold of his wrist again. Luke used his other hand to grasp one of the tree roots and pulled. The combined effort was enough to break him free of the sticky mud. He slid upward almost a foot.

"Hang on," Luke told her. "Let me . . . get hold of . . . another root."

She waited until he had a good grip, and then both of them grunted with the strain as they lifted his mostly dead weight. He wound up higher on the bank.

"Here we go," the girl urged. "We're gettin' it now."

They had made some progress, that was true, but Luke didn't know how much longer his strength would last. He was already drawing on reserves he hadn't known he possessed.

The rain was falling harder, turning the riverbank into a swamp. Knowing there was a risk he would slide back down and lose all the ground he had gained, he reached up to grasp another root and pull himself higher with the girl's help.

But the roots were about to run out, he saw with a sinking heart. The top of the bank was only about six feet above him, but it might as well have been six miles. The rest of the slope was nothing but slick mud.

"You've got to hang on here," the girl told him. "I'll go find a branch or something I can reach down to you!"

"You can't hold my weight," Luke said.

"I'll figure out a way. It's our only chance!"

Luke nodded his agreement and got a good grip on the last root. "Okay."

With obvious reluctance even though it was her idea, she let go of his wrist and clambered up the bank, slipping and sliding. When she disappeared over the top, he felt a sharp pang of loss. There was a chance he would never see her again, and for some reason that bothered him as much as the possibility that he was about to die.

He hung on to the root for dear life as the rain continued to pound down on him. The river was making a rumbling sound, and he wondered if the water was already plucking at his legs. He still couldn't feel anything below the waist.

The jagged end of a gnarled tree branch nearly poked him in the face. He looked up and saw the girl lying on top of the bank, extending the branch down toward him. All he could see of her was her head, arms, and shoulders.

"Grab it!" she called. "Pull yourself up!"

Luke let go of the root with one hand and grabbed the branch. "I don't want to pull you over!"

"You won't! I've got it! Now climb, damn it!"

Luke shifted his other hand to the branch. Its rough surface provided a pretty good grip. He looked up at the girl again, and she gave him an encouraging nod.

He didn't see how it was going to work, since she probably didn't weigh even a hundred pounds soaking wet, the way she was at the moment. But he tightened his hands and hauled hard on the branch, and to his surprise, his body followed. Reaching hand over hand, he continued pulling himself up.

When he glanced at the girl, he saw pain etched on her face. Supporting his weight was obviously painful. Not wanting to hurt her any longer, he summoned all his strength and energy and continued climbing up the branch.

When he was finally close enough, she reached out and grabbed his shirt, pulling hard. He added his efforts and surged up and rolled over the top of the bank. He came to a stop on his back and had to push himself onto his side to keep the rainwater from filling his nose and mouth.

"C-careful," she said. "After all that, we d-don't want you to drown now."

Luke blinked water out of his eyes and looked over at her. She still wore the soaked wool shirt, but she had taken off the overalls. The suspenders were tied around the trunk of a tree while one of the legs was tied around her ankle. That was why she'd been hurting, he realized. The strain of his weight had gone through her whole body, passing through her hands on the branch to her shoulders, along her body, and through her ankle.

When he turned his head, he saw the surface of the river racing along about three feet below the edge of the bank. He almost hadn't made it.

This girl, whoever she was, had saved his life.

"Th-thank you," he gasped out.

"Don't thank me yet," she said. "The river could still get out of its banks."

Her hands were scraped raw from the rough bark, he saw as she sat up. Rain washed away the blood seeping from the wounds.

"I'll fetch Grampaw and the wagon," the girl went on. "He's pretty strong for an old fella. We oughta be able to lift you into the wagon." She paused. "Your legs don't work at all, do they?"

Luke shook his head. "No, I can't even feel them. I was . . . shot in the back."

"Last night?"

He nodded wearily.

"Then that was you I heard hollerin'. I wanted to come see, but Grampaw wouldn't let me. He said to let the damn Yanks and the damn fool Rebs shoot each other, that it weren't nothin' to us either way."

Luke didn't know exactly what she meant, but it wasn't the time to discuss it.

The girl untied the overalls from her leg and scrambled to her feet. "You could have the decency to close your eyes, seein' as how I ain't got no pants on and I saved your life and all."

Incredibly, Luke felt himself smiling. "Yes, ma'am." He squeezed his eyes shut. "Could I ask you one more favor?"

"What's that?"

"Tell me your name."

She hesitated, then said, "Emily. Emily Sue Peabody."

"You sound like a good Georgia girl, Emily Sue Peabody."

"I am. Where are you from?"

"Missouri. My family has a farm up in the Ozarks."

"Then you must be a soldier, in spite of what you're wearin'. Otherwise you wouldn't be so far away from home."

"I was a soldier," Luke said. "But not any more."

That was true. The gold was gone, his friends were dead, and he had spent the past day on the razor's edge of death. It wouldn't surprise him one bit if he closed his eyes and opened them again to find himself in Hell.

"What's your name?" Emily asked.

"Luke Jensen."

"Well, I'd say that I'm pleased to meet you, Mr. Jensen, but right now that'd be a plumb lie. Now don't you move . . . Come to think of it, I guess you won't, will you?"

"Not likely."

"I'll be back quick as I can with the wagon. I'd take it kindly if you don't die in the meantime."

"I'll . . . try not to," Luke said as a new wave of exhaustion washed over him. His eyes closed. He heard the swift splashes as Emily hurried away over the wet ground.

Maybe it was his imagination, but he thought it wasn't raining quite as hard. Even if the downpour stopped, it wouldn't mean the danger was over. All the water that had fallen upstream still had to go somewhere. The whole area might flood. If it did, he would be helpless.

I'm pretty much helpless either way, he reminded himself. All he could do was lie there and wait for Emily to come back.

"Emily Sue Peabody," he murmured. It was a pretty name for a pretty girl.

Thinking about her made the pain not quite so bad.

CHAPTER 13

The sound of wagon wheels creaking brought Luke out of his stupor. Rain still fell, but it was definitely not pouring down as hard.

The wheels stopped, and he heard a thud as somebody jumped down from the wagon. Footsteps ran over to him.

"You ain't dead, are you, Mr. Jensen?" Emily asked.

He opened his eyes and lifted his head. "I'm . . . still here," he croaked.

Emily bent down to look at him. "Good." Then she turned her head to call, "He's still alive, Grampaw!"

"I'm glad to hear it," replied a voice cracked with age. "I'd hate to think you dragged me out in this rain for nothin'! My rheumatiz don't like this damp weather at all."

Luke looked past Emily and saw a man with long white hair and a drooping white mustache coming toward them. The years had bent him some, but he was still fairly tall and his shoulders were broad with strength. He reminded Luke of a thick-trunked old oak tree draped with moss.

"Let's roll him onto his back so I can get hold of him under his arms and drag him," the old man suggested.

"We can pick him up and carry him," Emily said. "I'll help you."

"No, the other way will be easier," her grandfather insisted.

"He said he'd been shot in the back. Draggin' him like that's liable to hurt him even worse."

The old man frowned. "You might be right about that," he admitted. "All right, get on that side of him. I can take most of the weight, but you'll have to support some of it."

"I've got it." Emily moved to loop both arms around Luke's right arm in a secure grip.

Her grandfather took Luke's left arm in the same fashion. "All right, you ready? Lift!"

With grunts of effort, they straightened, hauling Luke upright for the first time since the night before. Emily's feet slipped a little in the mud as the strain of his weight hit her, but she managed to keep her balance and didn't lose her grip on him.

"This'd sure be easier if you could walk, mister," the burly old-timer said, "but since you can't . . ."

Half dragging, half carrying him, they started toward the wagon, which Luke saw had a team of four rawboned mules hitched to it. They looked like pretty sorry specimens and the wagon wasn't much better. Every step the old man and Emily took sent pain jolting through him, but he gritted his teeth and didn't cry out. He recalled how he had screamed after Potter shot him, and the memory filled him with shame. He wasn't going to let himself act like that in front of Emily Sue Peabody and her grandfather.

That wasn't the only shame he felt. The knowledge that he had driven right into that ambush, had lost the Confederacy's gold, and gotten his friends killed had started to gnaw at him. He had known good and well there was a chance Wiley Potter and the others would double back and make a try for the bullion. For a couple days he had watched very closely for any signs of an ambush.

But he guessed he'd let his guard down, especially while he was concentrating on getting the wagon up the steep slope

of the riverbank. All it had taken was that moment of care-
lessness, and he had lost everything.

Well, not everything, he corrected himself. He was still
alive, even if just barely. Remy, Dale, and Edgar couldn't
say that much. The guilt Luke felt because of that ate at his
insides all the more.

When they reached the wagon, the old man said, "Mister,
you grab on to the sideboard and help hold yourself up
whilst Emily puts the tailgate down. Hop to it, girl."

Luke grasped the side of the wagon as tightly as he could.
When Emily had the tailgate lowered, they helped him
around to it and lowered him face down over the gate.
Luke's weight kept him there while they lifted the lower half
of his body and shoved him into the wagon bed.

That hurt like hell, too.

"I can see where the bullet tore his shirt," the old-timer
commented. "Looks like the rain washed out most of the
blood. Maybe it did the same for the wound. If it didn't, he'll
likely die of blood poisonin' in a day or two."

"Grampaw!" Emily said.

"Just tellin' you the truth of it," her grandfather said. "I'll
wager the fella's already thought of that his own self."

"I . . . have," Luke gasped from where he lay with the
side of his face pressed against the rough boards of the
wagon bed. "I appreciate you . . . trying to save my life anyway."

"It was the girl's idea," the old man said. "I got no use for
either side in this war. Haven't ever since it took my boy and
my two grandsons."

That explained the bitter undertone in the old-timer's
voice, Luke thought, as well as Emily's comment that her
grandfather didn't want to get involved in the Yankees and
the Confederates shooting each other. He thought he had already lost enough to the fighting, and he was probably right
about that.

Luke didn't consider himself a Confederate anymore, not

after the way he'd let down the cause by losing that gold. But it didn't really matter since, as Emily's grandfather had mentioned, he expected to die from his wound in the next few days.

He would worry about guilt when and if he survived.

"Might be a good idea if you was to climb up there with him and hold him as still as you can," the old man told Emily. "It's gonna be a rough ride, and bumpin' around's just gonna hurt him worse."

"You're right." She climbed into the wagon bed and sat down next to Luke. Her grandfather got on the seat and took up the reins, yelling at the mules and slapping them with the lines until they lurched forward into a walk.

The jarring motion sent fresh bursts of agony through Luke's body, just as the old-timer had predicted. His breath hissed between clenched teeth, but again he managed not to yell. Emily lay down beside him and put her arm around his shoulders, hanging on tightly to brace him against the wagon's rocking and bouncing.

He couldn't help being aware of the warmth of her torso pressed to his. If he responded to it, he didn't know it, but somehow it comforted him anyway. Gradually the pain eased a bit.

He didn't know how far it was to their destination or how long it took to get there, but finally the wagon came to a halt.

"We're here," Emily said. "This is our farm."

Luke felt the wagon shift as the old man got down from the seat. A moment later Luke heard the tailgate drop and felt himself moving. He knew the old-timer had taken hold of his feet to drag him out of the wagon, even though he couldn't feel the grip.

The rain had tapered off to a drizzle. It was late in the afternoon and darkness was coming on quickly, earlier than usual because of the overcast. As they lifted him from the wagon, Luke saw a rectangle of yellow light and recognized it as an open doorway. The glow from a lantern spilled out from the room beyond the door.

Emily and her grandfather wrestled him inside.

The old man said, "We better get him outta these wet duds, or he'll catch the grippe for sure. He don't need that on top of ever'thing else. I ought to take a look at that bullet hole in his back, too."

"You think you can help him, Grampaw?"

"You want me to, don't you?"

"Well . . . yeah, if you can."

"One thing I got to know first." The old man hung on to Luke's arm, but moved enough so he could peer into Luke's face. "Are the Yankees gonna come lookin' for you, mister? Is helpin' you gonna get me and my granddaughter killed?"

"The Yankees . . . don't know I exist," Luke whispered.

That might not be exactly true—there might still be patrols searching for eight or nine men with two wagons—but the Yankees would have no interest in a lone man with what was probably a mortal wound in his back. The bodies of Remy, Dale, and Edgar had surely washed downstream, Luke realized, and when they were found, likely they would be miles from there.

He figured Emily and her grandfather would be safe enough having him. If the Yankees had left them alone so far, they'd have no reason to bother them now.

"All right," the old man said. "I hope you're tellin' the truth. I'll hold him up, gal. Get a knife and cut them clothes off him. That'll be the easiest way to do it."

Luke was in too much pain to worry about the girl seeing him naked. Anyway, he'd seen her wearing nothing but that soaked woolen shirt, so he supposed turnabout was fair play, as the old saying went.

He heard the faint sound of a sharp blade cutting through fabric. His clothes fell away from him. A chill went through him, and he started to shiver.

"Get somethin' and dry him off," the old man said as he struggled to keep Luke upright. "Then we'll put him in my bunk."

Luke felt her drying his torso. When she moved around

behind him, he heard her sharp intake of breath. He figured she had spotted the wound low down on his back.

"It don't look too good, Grampaw."

"I wouldn't expect it to. Come on, we need to get him warmed up some."

Emily finished drying him, and they carried him over to a bunk. As they lowered him face first onto it, Luke heard a rustling sound that told him the mattress was stuffed with corn husks.

Even with nothing but a rough blanket covering it, it felt wonderful. He let his face sink into the softness.

His head jerked up a second later as something prodded into the wound in his back. His lips drew back from his teeth in a pained grimace.

"Looks like the bullet's still in there," the old man said. "It'll have to come out, but not now. The hole's already festerin' too much. Fetch me that jug o' corn."

"You don't need to get drunk, Grampaw," Emily said.

He snorted. "I ain't plannin' to drink it. It'll clean out that wound better'n anythin' else we got."

After hearing that, Luke knew what to expect. But he groaned anyway, a moment later, when the liquid fire of the corn liquor burned into his back and seemingly all the way through to the core of his being. Something poked into the wound again, probably the old man's fingers, he guessed.

That was confirmed when the old-timer said, "I can feel the bullet. Should be able to get it. But not yet. I'll dig it out in a day or two . . . if he's still alive."

"He'll be alive," Emily said. "I'm gonna see to that."

"Why in Tophet do you care so much whether this varmint lives or dies? You don't even know him."

"I know his name," Emily said softly. "That's enough for now."

The pain eased a little, and Luke let out the breath he had been holding. As the long sigh escaped him, his eyes closed.

Exhaustion caught up to him, crashing down like a hammer, and once again he knew nothing but darkness.

CHAPTER 14

When he woke up the next time, the only light in the room came from a small candle burned down to almost nothing. The dim glow was enough to reveal Emily sitting in an old rocking chair next to the bunk, dozing. Her eyes were closed.

Now that Luke got a better look at her, he saw that his initial impression had been right: she was beautiful. Her face showed lines that sorrow and hard work had put in it already, even though she was only around twenty years old, but that didn't detract from her beauty as far as he was concerned. Her thick dark hair was plaited into a single braid hanging over her left shoulder as she sat in the rocking chair. She had put on a clean shirt and a clean pair of overalls, maybe the only clothes she owned besides the ones she'd been wearing earlier.

Rough snores came from a long, bulky, blanket-wrapped shape in the bunk on the other side of the room. Luke recalled the bunk in which he lay belonged to Emily's grandfather, which meant the old-timer had claimed Emily's bunk while she slept in the chair.

Or maybe she had insisted on sitting up with him, he thought. That was certainly possible.

The pain in his back had receded to a dull throbbing. He

felt it with every beat of his heart, but was able to ignore it by focusing his attention on Emily.

Growing aware of his gaze somehow, her eyes opened, the initial flutter of eyelids as delicate as that of a butterfly's wings. She scooted forward in the rocker and leaned toward him. Quietly, she spoke. "You're awake. How do you feel?"

Before Luke could say anything, Emily shook her head. "You don't have to answer that. I'm sure you hurt like hell."

Incredibly, he felt his lips curving in a smile. In a voice that sounded rusty to his ears, he said, "I do."

"Then why are you smilin'?"

"Because I don't think I've . . . ever run across a young woman who . . . talks like you do."

She looked surprised, and Luke saw a pink tinge spreading slowly through her lightly olive skin. She was blushing, he realized.

"You mean the cussin'? I started doin' it for a reason. After . . . after we got word that my pa and my brothers wouldn't be comin' back from the war, I got worried that Grampaw would miss not havin' any other menfolks around, and since one of the things men seem to do a lot is cuss, I figured it might make Grampaw feel better if I was to do it. They all tried to watch their language around me while I was growin' up, what with me bein' the only gal in the place, but I heard enough. I can cuss up a storm when I want to."

"How did that . . . turn out for you?" Luke asked.

"To be honest, it spooked the hell outa Grampaw at first, but once he got used to it, I think he sorta likes it. And I got used to it, too, I reckon, so I don't hardly know I'm doin' it anymore. Sometimes when you're really mad or frustrated, it sure feels good to let loose with a few ripsnorters."

"Yes, I can . . . imagine."

Emily put a hand to her mouth and looked embarrassed again. "As bad as you must hurt, you must really feel like cussin'. You go right ahead if you want to, Mr. Jensen. It won't bother me none."

"That's all right. What I'd really like . . . is for you to call me Luke."

Emily thought it over and nodded. "I reckon I can do that. I've always been taught to be careful around fellas who were slick talkers, because my pa said there was only one thing they wanted, but I guess the shape you're in, I don't have to worry about that, do I?"

"Not hardly," Luke told her. "And even if I . . . wasn't hurt . . . my pa brought me up to be a gentleman."

"I can see that in your eyes," she said softly, nodding. She reached forward and lightly rested her hand on his forehead. "Oh, my Lord! You're burnin' up with fever."

Luke wasn't surprised. He had already known he felt chilled and lightheaded. He supposed the wound in his back had festered and blood poisoning had set in, just like Emily's grandfather had predicted.

"I'll wake Grampaw and see if there's anything he can do for you," she went on.

"There's . . . no need. Just get a wet cloth . . . wipe my face with it . . . That's about all . . . anyone can do for me."

"There's gotta be somethin' else!"

"There's not," Luke told her. "It's pretty much . . . out of our hands now."

He knew that was true. If the fever broke, he might have a chance. If it didn't, he would die. Simple as that.

And it might be better if the fever went ahead and took him, he thought. Emily and her grandfather could bury him and be done with it. They wouldn't have to run even the slight risk of the Yankees finding him and taking action against them.

Better for him, too, because he still couldn't feel his legs or anything below the waist, and he would rather be dead than a cripple. He wouldn't go back to the farm and be a burden to the rest of his family.

Emily got up for a moment and came back with a wet rag. She leaned down and swabbed it over his face. The cool touch felt wonderful.

Sometime while she was doing that, he passed out again. When he woke up, bright sunlight was slanting in through the cabin's open door.

"Huh. You ain't dead after all." That somewhat surprised statement came from Emily's grandfather, who had taken her place in the rocking chair beside the bunk.

Luke licked dry, cracked lips and husked, "I could use . . . something to drink."

"Yeah, you're pretty well wrung out, I expect. I'll fetch you a cup."

The old man came back with a dented tin cup. Luke took a sip of the clear liquid in it and promptly spit it out in an instinctive reaction.

"That's a waste of good corn, son," the old-timer said. "See if you can keep some of it down this time. You're gonna need it."

"What do you . . . mean by that?"

"I mean your fever may have broken for now, but that wound in your back's in bad shape. That Yankee bullet's got to come out if you're gonna have any chance of makin' it."

Two things were wrong with that, Luke thought. It wasn't a Yankee bullet that had laid him low, but rather one fired by a renegade Confederate. And he wasn't sure he wanted to have a chance of making it, not in the condition he was in.

But the hatred of giving up was bred deeply within him. "All right, give me another sip of that shine."

The old man chuckled. "Emily said you was from up in the Missouri Ozarks. I reckon you prob'ly know good corn liquor when you taste it." He held the cup to Luke's lips.

Carefully, Luke sipped the fiery stuff. His stomach rebelled against it, but he managed to keep it down. He drank enough that it affected him immediately and set his head to spinning. "You're going to . . . cut the bullet of me, aren't you?"

The old man nodded gravely. "That's the only thing to do. As soon as Emily gets back from the tradin' post to hold you down, we'll get started."

"Go ahead and . . . do it now," Luke urged. "I can . . . stay still."

"You don't know what you're sayin'. Even with that liquor in you, it's gonna hurt worse 'n anything you ever felt before."

"Look . . . Emily doesn't weigh enough . . . to hold me down . . . if I start bucking around. I'm going to have to . . . control it . . . whether she's here or not."

The old man rubbed his jaw as he frowned in thought. His fingertips rasped on the white stubble. "More than likely you're right about that," he admitted. "Might not make much difference whether the gal's here or not."

"I don't want her . . . to have to see it," Luke said. "Give me . . . a leather strap or something . . . to bite on."

"My razor strop'll do."

"And maybe . . . some more of that moonshine first."

"We can sure do that," the old man said.

A few minutes later, after several more swallows of the potent liquor, Luke's head was spinning even faster. He set his teeth in the leather strap and watched as the old man heated the long blade of a hunting knife in the fireplace until it glowed cherry red.

He carried the knife quickly back over to the bunk. "The wound's scabbed over, but I'll have to open it again so all the pus can get out. You ready?"

"Just . . . get it done," Luke said around the strap. He took a deep breath and closed his eyes.

The old man was right about one thing: it hurt worse than anything Luke had ever experienced. His teeth bore down on the leather and every muscle in his body turned tight and hard as an iron strap . . . every muscle he could still feel, anyway. The mingled stink of burned flesh and corruption filled the room. Luke groaned.

After what seemed like an eternity of torture, the old-timer exclaimed, "I got it!"

Some of the terrible pressure Luke had felt in his back

was released. The pain didn't slack off much, but any relief at all was a blessing.

He felt the old man wiping at his back with a rag. "You're bleedin' like a stuck pig, boy, but I reckon that's a good thing. Maybe it'll wash out all the festerin'. If you don't bleed to death first, that is."

The pain continued to recede. Luke's head slumped back to the bunk, and the leather strap slipped out of his mouth as his teeth released their grip on it. His pulse pounded inside his skull, and he breathed harshly and heavily.

"Grampaw, what in hell are you doin'?" That startled cry came from Emily. "My God, there's blood all over the place! You've killed him!"

"Take it easy, gal. He's alive. And I got that bullet outta his back."

"Is that why you sent me to the tradin' post?" she demanded. "So you could start cuttin' on him without me bein' here to stop you?"

"Shoot, I didn't even know he was gonna wake up. His fever broke, but it would've come right back if I didn't get that bullet out. Look there . . . that's healthy blood comin' out of him now. We can go ahead and stop it, and he can start gettin' his strength back."

Emily went closer to the bunk and bent down to peer at Luke's face. He saw her only vaguely through his pain and weariness.

"You mean he's gonna be all right?" she asked.

"I mean he's got a chance now," her grandfather told her.

But the biggest question, Luke thought just as he slipped back into unconsciousness, wasn't whether he would live or not.

The question was whether his legs would work . . . or whether he was going to be a cripple for the rest of his life, however long that was.

CHAPTER 15

The fever didn't come back. When Luke woke again, he was ravenously hungry, but able to eat only a few bites of the stew Emily fed him before it started to sicken him. He kept it down, though.

From talking to Emily, he found out it wasn't the day after she'd rescued him from the riverbank. As a matter of fact, three days had passed since that stormy afternoon.

"You were burnin' up with fever and out of your head most of that time," she told him as she sat in the rocker beside the bunk. "You kept ravin', but I couldn't make much sense out of most of it."

"What did I say? Did I talk about anybody in particular?"

"Oh, your ma and pa, of course. I'd expect that. And somebody named Kirby."

"My little brother," Luke said.

"And Janey."

"My sister."

"And Potter."

It was all Luke could do not to snarl in hatred. "He's not part of my family."

"I hope not, the way you were talkin' about him. Remember how I said I could cuss pretty good? Well, you had me beat all hollow while you were talkin' about that fella Potter."

"He's the man who shot me," Luke said. "He and his friends are deserters and renegades."

"Well, then, you've got good reason to be cussin' him. I figured somebody must've waylaid you and robbed you when I didn't find no horse anywhere thereabouts."

Luke waited a moment, then asked, "Did I talk about anything else?" He wanted to know if he had said anything about the gold while he was out of his head.

"Not really. There were some other names . . . Renny, somethin' like that?"

"Remy," Luke said. "A good friend."

"And Dale and Edgar. Who are they?"

"More friends." Luke didn't offer any further explanation. Their bodies must have been taken by the river before Emily found him, otherwise she would have asked him before now who those dead men were.

Just as well, he thought. He didn't want to tell her about the gold, about the way he had lost it and gotten his friends killed. That was a burden he was going to bear alone.

"Grampaw says it looks like that bullet hole in your back is healin' up better now," Emily went on. "I was sure upset with him when I came in and found that he'd been cuttin' on you, but I reckon he did the right thing."

"What's your grandfather's name?" Luke hadn't heard her call him anything except Grampaw.

"Linus Peabody," she told him.

"A fine name. I'm in his debt . . . and yours."

She shook her head. "You don't owe me nothin'."

"You saved my life. I would have died out there if it wasn't for you."

"It's my Christian duty to help folks in need."

"I wish more people felt like you about that," Luke said. "If they did, we might not have had this war."

"Grampaw says we didn't need to have it anyway. We never had no slaves and didn't want any. He tried to talk my pa and my brothers into not goin' off and fightin', but they said it was their duty because the Yankees had no right to invade us."

"They were right about that. I just wish it had never come to that point."

Emily sighed. "Wishin' don't do folks a lot of good, Mr. Jensen . . . I mean, Luke. If it did, there's a whole heap of things in the world that'd be different."

She was certainly right about that, Luke thought.

Because if wishing did any good, his legs would work again, and so far . . . they didn't.

It really hasn't been very long yet since my injury, he reminded himself several times that day . . . and the next and the next and the day after that.

By the time a week had passed, Luke's appetite had returned and so had some of his strength. He was able to sit up in the rocking chair with a pillow to cushion his wounded back, as long as Peabody and Emily helped him get there from the bunk.

But he still had no feeling in his legs, and when he sat there and stared at them and willed them to move, nothing happened. The legs remained limp and lifeless.

"I wish I could help you with the chores," Luke said at supper one evening. "You folks saved my life, you're feeding me, and I can't do a blasted thing to repay you."

"Nobody's asked you to repay nothin'," Peabody said.

"I know that, but I want to, anyway."

"Maybe the time will come that you can. You can't never tell."

Another couple days passed. Luke continued to get stronger. Peabody built him a bunk of his own, so he and Emily could return to their own beds. He checked the wound in Luke's back and changed the dressing on it, then proclaimed, "Looks like that hole's just about healed up, son. I got to admit, I didn't think it'd happen that way, but you must be durned near as strong as a mule . . . and stubborn as one, too."

Emily said, "Grampaw!"

But Luke threw back his head and laughed, which was something he hadn't done much of for a long time. "My pa used to say the same thing about me. The stubborn part, anyway. But the real reason I'm not dead is because you and Emily took such good care of me, Mr. Peabody."

"The gal wouldn't have it no other way," the old-timer said, which brought another blush to Emily's face.

Peabody went out to work in the fields, leaving Emily to finish cleaning up after breakfast before she joined him. With just the two of them to take care of the place, they both worked from dawn to dusk most days. They had gotten behind on the chores during the time they'd had to take turns looking after Luke, and knowing that added to his feeling he owed them more than he could ever repay.

A short time after leaving, Peabody hurried back into the cabin just as Emily was finishing up with the dishes. Luke saw instantly that the old-timer was upset about something.

Peabody didn't keep them in the dark about it. "Yankees comin'."

"Oh, dear Lord," Emily said. "How many?"

"Just a dozen or so . . . but that's plenty if they're lookin' for trouble." Peabody frowned at Luke. "You're sure they ain't huntin' you?"

"I don't see how they could be."

An old single-shot rifle Peabody used for hunting game hung on hooks attached to the wall. He took it down and checked its load.

"You don't want to start trouble," Luke warned him. "Not if there are a dozen of them."

"Don't plan on startin' it. But if they force me to it, I'll fight."

Luke thought swiftly. "How close are they?"

"About a quarter mile, I'd say."

"Put the rocker on the porch and help me into it. I'll hold the rifle in my lap, under a blanket."

"They'd be able to see it anyway," Emily said. "I have a better idea." She opened a cabinet and took out the Griswold and Gunnison revolver Luke had brought with him from Richmond.

He didn't know what had happened to his rifle, but the sight of the revolver lifted his spirits a little. Only for a moment, though. He recalled how wet the gun had gotten. "The charges in that are bound to be ruined."

"They were," Emily agreed, "until I cleaned it up and reloaded it."

"Where'd you get ammunition for that gun?"

"Bought it at the tradin' post the other day. I thought we might need it sometime."

Luke hoped that time hadn't come. Even with the revolver, he wouldn't be any match for a dozen Yankee cavalrymen, especially stuck in a rocking chair with useless legs.

But being armed was always better than being defenseless, so he held out his hand for the gun and slipped it into the pocket of the overalls he was wearing. It was a good thing Linus Peabody was a fairly big man. His clothes fit Luke without being too tight.

Peabody dragged the rocking chair onto the cabin's front porch, then he and Emily helped Luke get seated in it. She hurried back into the cabin to grab the blanket from the bunk, which she draped over the lower half of Luke's body.

It was the first time he'd been outside since the day of the storm. The air was warm and smelled good. It was a beautiful spring day.

At least, it would have been if it hadn't been marred by the sight of those Yankee troopers riding toward the cabin.

Peabody came out onto the porch holding the rifle. He said to Emily, "Get back inside, gal. And don't come out no matter what happens."

"You know damn good and well I ain't gonna do that, Grampaw."

"Blast it. For once in your life, do what I tell you!"

Emily looked angry and upset, but she said, "I'll be right inside," and moved back through the door.

Luke put his right hand under the blanket, slipping the revolver out of his pocket and gripping it tightly as he watched the Yankees ride closer. He had to fight down the impulse to yank out the gun and start blazing away at the enemy.

Or are they the enemy anymore? he suddenly asked himself. They were laughing and talking among themselves as they approached the cabin. They certainly didn't seem to be looking for trouble.

The officer in charge of the patrol, a lieutenant judging by his insignia, heeled his horse into a trot and rode ahead of the others. He came up to the cabin with the others trailing behind him and reined in. With a friendly nod, he touched a finger to the brim of his hat. "Good morning, gentlemen. Does one of you own this farm?"

"I do." Peabody's voice was flat and hard.

"Then I'd like to ask your permission to water our horses."

Peabody took one hand off the rifle and jerked a thumb toward the north. "River's about half a mile that way. Plenty of water there."

"Oh," the lieutenant said. "I didn't know that. I'm not that familiar with the area. We're obliged to you for the information. We'll just water our horses at the river."

"That's a good idea." Peabody stood stiffly, both hands tight on the rifle again.

The Yankee officer hesitated, then said, "Sir, you *have* heard the news, haven't you?"

"What news?"

Luke had a hunch he knew what the answer was going to be even before the lieutenant spoke.

"The war's over, sir," the young officer said. "General Lee offered his surrender to General Grant nearly three weeks ago at a place up in Virginia called Appomattox Courthouse."

Luke closed his eyes. He'd been right.

And Potter and the others had been right, too, about the Confederacy collapsing. They hadn't been traitors, after all.

Just murdering, back-shooting rogues.

"The fighting is all over," the lieutenant went on. "There's no need for you and your son to worry, sir. We're all countrymen again."

Peabody didn't correct the man about Luke being his son. He just said, "The river's up yonder."

The lieutenant nodded. "We'll be going, then. Good day to both of you, and thank you again."

The cavalrymen rode around the cabin and headed north. Luke listened to the sound of their hoofbeats fading as Emily came out of the cabin.

"I'm sorry, Luke," she said.

"About the war being over?" He shook his head. "Don't be. I'm not. I knew that was how it was going to turn out. Better to have it end before more good men were killed for no reason."

"Amen to that," Peabody said.

Luke took the revolver from under the blanket and handed it to Emily. "I guess you can put that away again."

"All right." She hesitated, then said, "Luke . . . what are you gonna do now?"

He looked up at her and realized he had no idea.

CHAPTER 16

L uke balanced himself on the crutches, reached into the bag he held, and slung grain onto the ground for the chickens clustering around him. The fowl went after the stuff with their usual frenzied enthusiasm.

He draped the bag's strap over his shoulder, got a good grip on the crutch handles so he could turn himself around, and stumped back toward the cabin.

Emily came out onto the porch before he got there. "I was gonna feed the chickens," she told him with a grin.

"No need," Luke said. "I took care of it."

"There's just no stoppin' you, is there?"

"Not when it's something I can do." He changed course, angling toward the side of the house where the big stump they used for splitting firewood stood. The ax leaned against the stump, handle up.

"What are you fixin' to do now?" Emily asked.

"You said you needed some wood for the stove," Luke explained.

"I didn't say you had to split it!"

"I don't mind." He reached the stump and propped the right-hand crutch against it. With only a small amount of awkwardness, he picked up a piece of wood from the pile beside the stump and set it upright in the middle. Then he took hold of the ax and lifted it one-handed.

"You're gonna miss and cut your leg off one of these days," Emily warned.

"No great loss," Luke said.

"Unless you bleed to death!"

Luke swung the ax above his head and brought it down in a precise stroke, splitting the cordwood perfectly down the middle. He used the ax to brush the two pieces off the stump, leaned the ax against it, and picked up another piece of wood to split.

Emily blew out her breath and shook her head in exasperation. "You are the most stubborn man I ever saw, Luke Jensen."

And that was a good thing, Luke thought, otherwise he'd probably be dead. The wound he had suffered a few months earlier would have killed him.

The late summer sun blazed down, and it didn't take Luke long to work up a sweat. His damp linsey-woolsey shirt clung to his back. He lifted his arm and sleeved beads of perspiration off his face.

When he'd first started shaving himself again, rather than relying on Emily to do it, he'd been shocked at the gaunt, haggard face looking out at him from the mirror. That man looked at least ten years older than he really was, Luke thought.

Since then his features had begun to fill out some, and he thought he looked more like himself. Most of the time, the strain of what he had gone through painted a rather grim expression on his face. When he laughed, though, he didn't feel quite as ugly. *Still ugly, mind you,* he told himself, *just not as much.*

Recently he had stopped shaving his upper lip and let his mustache grow. It gave him a certain amount of dignity, in his opinion, and Emily didn't seem to mind. How she thought about things had taken on a lot of importance during the months he had spent on the Peabody farm.

She came down from the porch to gather up the chunks of wood he had split. "Breakfast is ready. Come on inside and eat."

She didn't have to tell him twice, and she didn't have to help him up the steps. He made it just fine with the crutches.

He had carved them himself, putting quite a bit of time and effort into it. He'd wanted the crutches to be as comfortable as possible, since it looked like he'd be using them for quite a while. Some of the feeling had started to come back into his legs, enough that he could get around a little with the help of the crutches, but he was still pretty helpless. He didn't let himself think too much about how long that might go on. He still held out hope that one day his legs would work again, the way they were supposed to.

Because of that, he'd asked Emily to help him exercise the muscles in them. He knew it wasn't fair to place that extra burden on her, but she didn't object. He had seen what happened to Clyde Monroe back home. Doing nothing after his injury had made him worse. Luke wasn't going to give up like that . . . which led right back to that stubbornness Emily had accused him of.

He fed the chickens and gathered eggs and split wood and hoed the vegetable garden and shucked corn. Anything he could do sitting down or balanced on one crutch, he would do. The work put thick slabs of muscle back on his arms and shoulders and back.

He was damned if he was going to be useless. He would die first.

Emily and her grandfather had both asked him if he wanted to send a letter to his family back in Missouri letting them know he was alive. Luke only had to think about it for a second before he shook his head.

After failing the Confederacy and his friends, he didn't want his pa and Kirby finding out about that. One day, if what he planned came about, he would return home, but not until he had done the job he had set out for himself.

Once his legs worked right again, he was going to track down Potter, Stratton, Richards, and Casey and kill each and every one of them. He knew he probably wouldn't be able to recover the gold they had stolen—there was no Confederacy to return it to, anyway—but at least he could even the score for what they had done to Remy, Dale, and Edgar.

And to him.

Then and only then, when he had reclaimed at least a vestige of his honor, would he return to his family. Until then it was better to let them think he was dead, even though they would mourn him.

It had to be that way. On his darkest nights, he admitted to himself there was a very strong possibility he would never walk normally again, no matter how much he tried. In that case, he would live out his life on the Peabody farm, unless Emily and her grandfather kicked him out.

The way he and Emily had started to feel about each other, he didn't think that was likely.

And yet that thought tortured him, too. Emily might be falling in love with him—Lord knew he'd been in love with her pretty much from the moment he first saw her and mistook her for an angel—but was it fair for him to saddle her with a cripple for a husband? He wasn't even sure he could be a real husband to her, although lately he'd begun to feel some stirrings that told him it might be possible.

Feeling *anything* below the level of the wound in his back was a good sign. The bullet wound was completely healed. A pale, ragged scar was the only sign of it that remained. Luke hadn't seen the scar himself, of course, but Emily had described it for him. He could move around now without feeling even a twinge in his back.

He clumped over to the table Emily had set for three people. Setting one of the crutches aside, he gripped his chair and lowered himself into it.

Emily poured coffee for him and set a plate of flapjacks, bacon, and eggs in front of him. They ate fairly well, because the Peabody farm had escaped most of the damage and destruction inflicted by the Yankees when they rampaged through the area a year earlier.

As she sat down opposite Luke, Emily said, "Grampaw told me he's goin' to town today, if you need anything."

The settlement of Dobieville was about five miles down the road. A trading post was closer to the farm, but Linus Peabody refused to do any business there since a Yankee carpetbagger had taken it over a month earlier when the previous owner had been unable to pay his taxes.

Luke shook his head. "I can't think of anything. Unless he can pick me up a new pair of legs."

Emily frowned across the table at him. "I thought you promised to stop sayin' things like that."

"Sorry," he muttered.

"I know you think you got to walk again, Luke, and I don't blame you for feelin' that way, I really don't. But you don't have to. Not . . . not for me, anyway. It ain't gonna change the way I feel about you."

Suddenly the food in front of him didn't seem so appetizing. He didn't want to have this discussion. Of course, it was his own fault for bringing it up.

He looked at the plate. "We don't need to talk about this. It won't change anything, anyway."

His voice sounded harsher than he intended. He didn't look up at Emily, afraid he would see hurt in her eyes.

"All right," she said. "Let's just eat."

Linus Peabody came in a few minutes later. He'd been in the barn, tending to the mules, the milk cow, and the hogs. If he sensed the tension between Luke and Emily, he had the good sense not to say anything about it as he sat down. "Did Emily tell you I'm goin' to town this mornin', Luke?"

"She did, but there's nothing I need right now."

"I was thinkin' you might want to go with me."

Luke frowned in surprise. "To Dobieville?"

"Yep. Actually, I thought we might all go. Been stuck here on this farm all summer."

Luke glanced at Emily and caught a glimpse of excitement on her face.

She hurriedly covered it up. "I don't need nothin' in town, Grampaw."

"Yes, you do. You need to see somebody 'sides a pair of ugly ol' galoots like me and Luke."

"Neither of you is ugly," she protested.

"There's no point in arguing with the facts," Luke said with a smile. "Neither of us is going to win any prizes for being good-looking, are we, Linus?"

The old-timer cackled. "The judges'd have to be plumb blind if we did!" Peabody nodded. "So it's settled. After we eat, we'll all load up in the wagon and head for town."

CHAPTER 17

Luke had to have some help doing it, but he managed to climb into the back of the wagon. From there he was able to use his arms to pull himself to the front, just behind the seat. Peabody settled down on the seat next to Emily to handle the team.

Despite what the old man had said, Luke had a hunch there was more to this trip into Dobieville than Peabody let on. He didn't press the issue, though, as the wagon rolled across fields and along narrow, tree-shaded country lanes toward the settlement.

It was a good test of how well his back actually had healed. The wagon wasn't in the greatest shape, and its ride was pretty rough, even on level ground. But he didn't feel any pain in his back, and that was encouraging.

The mules didn't get in any hurry. The trip to town took more than an hour. Luke was tired by the time they got there, but he still wasn't hurting.

Dobieville had a wide main street running for several blocks between businesses, along with a couple side streets lined with houses. The steeples of the Baptist and Methodist churches stuck up above the trees on the edge of town. Some of the businesses had been burned when the Yankees came through, but Dobieville had gotten off with less destruction than many Southern settlements.

Several of the businesses that had been burned were being rebuilt, Luke saw as Peabody sent the mules plodding along the street with the wagon rolling slowly behind them. The sounds of hammering and men calling to each other as they worked filled the air.

But Luke sensed something was wrong about what he was hearing, and after a moment he realized what it was. When the workers raised their voices to talk, it wasn't in the slower, softer drawl of Southerners, but rather the hard, brisk tone of folks from up north.

Those were Yankees rebuilding those businesses.

Carpetbaggers.

He had heard Peabody talking about greedy opportunists from up north swarming in all over the South. He saw for himself what was going on. It wasn't just the carpenters. Men in derby hats and gaudy tweed suits and cocky grins strolled along the town's boardwalks, cigars clenched at jaunty angles in their teeth. All Luke had to do was look at them to know they were Yankees.

The true citizens of Dobieville knew it, too. Luke saw the glances filled with resentment, anger, and fear the townsfolk cast toward the newcomers.

Blue-uniformed soldiers lounged here and there. Yankee troopers stood in every block, not necessarily doing anything, but their mere presence was a bitter reminder that the Confederacy had been defeated and the Southern states had been forced back into the union at gunpoint, after the spilling of rivers of blood.

Peabody brought the wagon to a halt in front of Connally's General Store. He turned on the seat and said to Emily, "Go on inside, gal. I'll join you in a minute."

"What about Luke?" she asked.

"I'm all right sitting back here. It's too much trouble for the two of you to help me down and then back up again."

"No, it's not," she argued. "You came to town so you could see something different from the farm."

"And so I can." Luke smiled. "I can see just fine from right where I am."

"Oh, all right." Emily climbed down from the wagon. "But if you change your mind, we can get you out of there and you can use your crutches."

"I know," Luke assured her.

She still looked a little puzzled, but she went on into the general store. Peabody sighed and turned more on the seat to say quietly, "I wanted a chance to talk to you while Emily ain't around, Luke."

"I thought that might be the case. What's wrong, Linus?"

Peabody let out a disgusted snort. "What's wrong? Just look around you, son!"

"You're talking about all the Yankees?"

"Soldiers and carpetbaggers alike. They've moved in like a swarm of locusts!"

"What did you expect? We lost the war. They can do whatever they want now."

"They could treat us with some respect," Peabody said as fierce anger edged into his voice. "Instead they've just bulled their way in, run folks off, took over businesses . . . What you're lookin' at, son, is the beginnin' of something that may turn out to be even worse 'n the war itself."

"I don't see how that could be possible."

"You just hide and watch," Peabody said. "Them Yankees got the idea they can waltz in, grab what they want for themselves, and grind the rest of the South into dust under their heels. And they'll laugh at us while they're doin' it."

That was probably right, Luke thought. That was exactly what the carpetbaggers intended to do, and they had the Yankee troops to back them up on it. "Why did you want to show me this?"

"Because there's gonna come a time when we may have to fight for what's ours. So far the Yankees ain't come anywhere near the farm, but one of these days they're liable to. And I don't intend to just let 'em take it away from me."

"You didn't support the war," Luke said. "They should leave you alone."

Peabody waved a gnarled hand. "This ain't about the war anymore. It's about greed, pure and simple, and the chance for a bunch of no-good skunks to grab what ain't theirs."

"And you want to know if I'll stand with you against them?" Luke couldn't keep the dry, acid tone out of his voice.

"I'm just sayin' you may have to make a choice," Peabody snapped. "Legs or no legs."

Luke sighed and nodded. "You're right, Linus. I'm sorry. I appreciate you bringing me to town today and showing me what we may be facing. It's always best to know when trouble's coming."

"That's what I thought."

"And as for whether or not I'll be with you when that trouble comes . . . you ought to know the answer to that. You saved my life, you and Emily . . ."

"I know how you feel about her, too," Peabody said. "I've seen the way she's started lookin' at you lately. I ain't sayin' that I like it—"

"I'm not exactly the man you had in mind for your granddaughter. I know that."

"Maybe not, but you're a good man, Luke." Peabody clapped a hand on Luke's shoulder and squeezed. "I know that, too." He wrapped the team's reins around the brake lever. "Now, I'm gonna go and help Emily pick up a few supplies. Sure you'll be all right out here?"

Luke nodded. "I'll be all right."

"Okay." Peabody jumped down from the wagon and went inside the store.

Luke looked around at the bustling settlement. If it hadn't been for the presence of the Yankees, he would have said Dobieville was well on its way to recovering from the war already.

Unfortunately, under the surface, the truth was that Dobieville was well on its way to being gutted by the carpetbaggers.

Peabody was worried their greedy reach would extend outside the settlement, Luke mused. The old-timer was probably right about that. Even though the prospect worried Luke, too, he didn't see what an old man, a girl, and a cripple could do to stop the arrogant outsiders who now held power in the South.

Peabody wanted to fight if the carpetbaggers came for his property, and he wanted Luke to fight with him. If it came down to that, Luke knew he wouldn't turn his back on the two people who had saved his life. But if that happened, there was a very good chance he and Peabody would wind up dead, leaving Emily alone and defenseless . . .

Or else she would take up arms, and the Yankees would kill her, too.

Maybe the best thing to do, Luke thought suddenly, would be to pack up and leave at the first sign of any Yankees trying to take over the farm. It would mean running from trouble, which stuck in his craw worse than anything. Peabody would probably feel the same, but it might be the only way to save their lives.

The frontier was a big place, with lots of room for folks to settle and start new lives. Luke thought maybe he could even swallow his pride and return home to the Ozarks, taking Emily and her grandfather along with him.

He took a deep breath. No use getting ahead of himself. At the moment, things were all right. Maybe they'd be lucky and it would stay like that.

As he mused, a couple Yankee soldiers came along the boardwalk toward the general store. They stopped and propped their shoulders against one of the posts holding up the awning in front of the store. One of the troopers, a wiry little man with dark hair, glanced at Luke and then looked away, obviously uninterested in him.

The taller, brawnier soldier, with bushy side-whiskers

and a thatch of straw-colored hair sticking out from under his forage cap, fastened a cool, appraising stare on Luke.

Keeping an eye on them without drawing attention to himself, Luke tried to ignore them.

A short time later, Emily and her grandfather came out of the store. She was carrying a crate of supplies, while Peabody had a bag of flour slung over his shoulder. As they moved to place the supplies in the back of the wagon, the big trooper straightened from his casual pose.

"Hey, Reb"—he directed the harsh words at Luke— "what kind of man sits by and lets a girl and an old geezer do all the work?"

Peabody turned toward the soldier and snapped, "Who you callin' an old geezer, sonny?"

Emily put a hand on her grandfather's arm and asked the soldier, "Just leave us alone, why don't you?"

"I wasn't talking to either of you." The Yankee soldier pointed at Luke. "I was talking to that big strapping specimen of Southern manhood." A grin stretched across his rough-hewn face. "But I guess he's like the rest of those Johnny Rebs . . . just a lazy coward."

Emily forgot about being reasonable. Even as Luke started to say, "No—", she put herself in the trooper's face. "Shut your mouth, you big, stupid, Yankee tyrant."

The man's eyes widened in surprise. He brought his hand up to slap her and growled, "You foul-mouthed little Rebel slut! I'll—"

Luke grabbed the crutch from the wagon bed beside him and drove the tip of it into the soldier's midsection as hard as he could. He put plenty of the strength in his arms and shoulders behind the punch.

The trooper cried out in pain and stumbled back a step, tripping on a loose board in the porch. He sat down hard, gasping for breath, the blow had been so strong.

His companion acted swiftly, unsnapping the holster at his waist and pulling out a revolver. He eared back the hammer as he raised the gun and pointed it at Luke's face.

CHAPTER 18

Luke knew in that instant how close he was to dying. He had reacted instinctively when Emily was threatened, and it looked like that reaction was going to cost him his life.

But before the little Yankee could pull the trigger, a voice asked sharply, "What's going on here?"

The soldier's gaze darted past the wagon toward a man who had come along the street from the other direction. The short Yankee hesitated, licking his lips. "This Reb just attacked Private Packard, Mr. Wolford."

The newcomer strode past the wagon to confront the soldiers. "It looked to me more like he was defending this young woman. Packard was about to strike her, wasn't he?"

"Beggin' your pardon, sir, but you didn't hear what she called him."

"Nor do I care," Wolford replied. "A man who acts like he's going to hit a lady deserves whatever he gets. And I'm confident Colonel Morrison would agree with me." He used the walking stick he carried to point at the bigger soldier. "Now put that gun away, help Private Packard to his feet, and both of you move along."

The little trooper took a deep breath, obviously reluctant to follow the civilian's orders. But Luke could tell he was afraid not to do what Wolford said. After a couple seconds the soldier holstered his revolver and turned to extend a hand to his companion. "Come on, Packard. We got things to do."

Packard had gotten his breath back, but his face was pale. Anger made twin spots of red glow on his cheeks. He brushed aside the other soldier's hand and climbed to his feet on his own.

"This ain't any of your business, Wolford—"

"Come on," the smaller soldier urged. "Let it go." He got hold of Packard's sleeve and tried to drag him away.

Packard didn't want to, that much was clear. He glared darkly at Luke, who saw a promise in the man's eyes that the skirmish wasn't over. But the soldier turned and stalked off along the boardwalk, his shorter compatriot hurrying to keep up with him.

Wolford turned to Luke, Emily, and Peabody and smiled ingratiatingly. "I'm sorry about that unpleasantness. Unfortunately, too many soldiers haven't gotten it through their heads yet that the war is over." He put out a hand to Peabody. "Vincent Wolford."

The man's accent marked him as being from somewhere in New England. He was about forty, with a lean face, dark hair, and thick, salt-and-pepper side-whiskers. His suit was a subdued blue, and he wore a black beaver hat.

Wolford wasn't just a carpetbagger, Luke thought. He was a *boss* carpetbagger.

Peabody hesitated, clearly not wanting to shake hands with any Yankee, but Wolford had kept the little soldier from shooting Luke. After a moment, he took Wolford's hand and clasped it briefly. "Linus Peabody."

"It's a pleasure to meet you, Mr. Peabody." Wolford smiled at Emily. "And this is your granddaughter, I expect? I can see the resemblance."

"My name's Emily. I ain't much on shakin' hands with Yankees, though."

Wolford smiled. "That's all right, Miss Peabody. A perfectly understandable attitude, considering all the upheavals that have taken place. Believe me, I know what you're going through."

Luke didn't believe that for a second. Wolford had the smooth look of a man who had always been rich and gotten whatever he wanted.

"Or perhaps it's not Miss Peabody," Wolford went on as he turned to Luke. "Are you the lady's husband, sir?"

"That's Luke—"

"Luke Smith. I'm a friend of the family, that's all."

"I see." Wolford glanced at Luke's legs and the crutch still in his hand. "You were wounded in the war?"

"That's right."

"A terrible shame."

Luke was aware that Emily and her grandfather were looking at him curiously, no doubt wondering why he had given Wolford a false name. Without much thought, it had popped out of his mouth. He'd been brooding a lot lately— about the stolen gold and the deaths of his friends—and hated to think the name Jensen would ever be linked to such a shameful failure. That probably had something to do with it.

And the fact he instinctively didn't trust Vincent Wolford.

"Colonel Morrison, the commander of the troops in this area, is a good friend of mine," Wolford went on. "I'll have a word with him and ask if he could order his men to treat the citizens with a bit more respect. After all, we're all partners now in rebuilding the South. If we're going to work together, we should get along, shouldn't we?"

"We don't want trouble with anybody," Peabody said, which didn't really answer Wolford's rhetorical question.

"Of course not." The man smiled and lifted a hand to the brim of his beaver hat. "Well, good day to you folks."

As Wolford strolled away, Peabody climbed quickly to the wagon seat and told Emily, "Get on the wagon, girl. We're gettin' outta here."

The old-timer turned the vehicle around and got the

mules headed back toward the farm. Peabody muttered under his breath about how they shouldn't have come to Dobieville today in the first place.

Emily turned around to lean over the back of the seat. "You shouldn't have got mixed up in that, Luke. That big, dumb Yankee never would've been able to hit me. I'm too fast for the likes of him."

Luke shifted on the wagon bed. "Maybe so, but it's bad enough I had to sit by while you and Linus loaded the supplies. You can't expect me to do nothing while that soldier attacked you."

"You almost got yourself killed, that's what you did."

Luke couldn't argue with that.

"If that slick-talkin' Yankee carpetbagger hadn't come along, that mean little varmint would've blowed your head off."

"More than likely," Luke admitted with a sigh.

"And what was that business about callin' yourself *Smith*?" Peabody asked. "Have you been lyin' to us all along, son? Are you some sort of criminal on the run from the law?"

"No," Luke answered without hesitation. "Absolutely not. I may not have told you quite everything, Linus, but I give you my word, nobody's looking for me, lawman or otherwise."

Peabody nodded. "Reckon I can accept that. Just like I can accept it's your business what you call yourself."

"Well, it may take me some gettin' used to, after callin' you Jensen all this time." Emily paused. "Just don't get yourself killed on account of me, Luke Smith or Jensen or whatever the hell name you want to use."

Luke laughed. "I'll certainly try not to."

When they got back to the farm, Emily and her grandfather helped Luke down from the wagon before they unloaded the supplies. He stood at the back of the vehicle on his crutches and said, "If you want to drape that flour sack over my shoulder, Linus, I might be able to carry it in."

"There ain't no need of that," Peabody said. "You don't have to prove anything to us, Luke."

"That's right." Emily turned away from the tailgate with the crate in her hands. "You already do plenty to help out around—

Oh!" she cried out as the heavy crate slipped from her grasp and fell on Luke's right foot.

Luke took a sharp breath.

"Hell and damnation!" Emily exclaimed. "Oh, Luke, I'm so sorry! I didn't mean to drop that on you. It must've—"

He smiled as she stopped short in what she was saying. "Must have hurt? Only a little. That's one thing I don't have to worry about."

Looking flustered, Emily picked up the crate. "Well, when we get inside, I want to take a look at your foot anyway. You could be hurt and not even know it."

"I suppose you're right," Luke said.

A few minutes later, he was sitting in the rocking chair. Emily knelt in front of him and took off his boot and sock. There was a red mark on the top of his foot where the crate had landed, but no blood. Emily poked around on the spot.

Luke blinked.

"Doesn't feel like any bones are broken." Without looking up, she pulled his sock back onto the foot. "You were lucky."

"That's me. Lucky Luke Smith."

Emily snorted.

After they ate a hasty midday meal, Emily and Peabody went out to work in the fields, leaving Luke sitting in the rocker. When he was sure they were gone, he put his hands on his thighs and squeezed as hard as he could, working the muscles. He had succeeded in covering up his reaction so Emily and her grandfather hadn't noticed it, but it had hurt like blazes when that crate fell on his foot, the most sensation he had felt in one of his feet for a long time. And it had been repeated when Emily poked at the site of the injury.

It excited him as no pain ever had.

He stared at his legs, willing them with every fiber of his being to move, but all he could summon up were a few twitches.

He slumped back in the rocking chair, suddenly breathless and exhausted. *That might be the most my legs will ever move,* he told himself. But his heart soared inside him, anyway. For the first time in months he had real hope again.

Hope that someday he might be able to have the things he most wanted . . .

Emily.

And vengeance.

CHAPTER 19

Over the next few days, Luke struggled against the impatience he felt as he looked for another sign that his legs might be improving. Any time he was alone at the cabin, he moved them as much as he could, sometimes unconsciously straining his other muscles until he was breathing hard and sweat popped out on his face. He rubbed his legs and then pounded on them in frustration when they failed to respond as much as he wanted them to.

One day he lifted himself out of the chair with his crutches, then let them fall to the sides in the hope he could force himself to stand.

He fell on his face.

And struggled hard to push himself up with the crutches to get back in the chair.

He didn't give up. He worked at it every day and would continue as long as it took.

He didn't say a word about his efforts to Emily or her grandfather. If he failed—again—he didn't want them to know about it. There would be time enough later to fill them in if he was successful in learning to walk again.

Emily continued to exercise the muscles in his legs, massaging and working them back and forth.

Several days after his fall she noticed a change. "It may

be my imagination, Luke, but it seems to me like your legs are getting stronger rather than weaker."

"Really? Well, that's good, isn't it?"

"Yeah, real good. I knew it was just a matter of time before you started healin' up."

He thought she was just trying to be encouraging, but maybe she was more right than she knew. Whenever Emily and her grandfather weren't around and Luke was on his crutches, he let more of the weight of his body rest on his legs.

At first they had buckled, but as the days went on he was able to stiffen them and partially support himself more than he could before. He still didn't say anything to Emily or her grandfather. Hope and resolve filled him, but he was wary.

One evening while Emily was inside cleaning up after supper, Luke sat in the rocker on the porch and the old man sat on the steps. Peabody filled his pipe and lit it, then said quietly enough that Emily wouldn't overhear, "I spotted some fellas on horseback watchin' the place today."

Luke tensed, hearing the worry in the old-timer's voice. "Soldiers?"

"Nope. Civilians. I didn't get a very good look at 'em, but I could tell that much."

"What do you reckon they wanted?"

Peabody shook his head. "Don't know, but Bud Harkness come by today and talked to me. Bud's got the next farm over. He says there's some problem with the taxes and he might lose his place."

"Didn't he pay them?"

"He did . . . but the judge the Yankees put in charge of such things says that Bud didn't pay enough. It's a blamed lie . . . but he's a judge."

"What's this fellow Harkness going to do?" Luke asked.

"What *can* he do? He can stay and fight, or he can leave." Peabody puffed on the pipe for a second or two in silence, then went on. "Bud's got five kids and another on the way. He can't afford to get himself killed."

"So he's going to pack up and leave?"

"I expect so. That's the smart thing to do."

"If they're after his place . . ."

"This one's next in line," Peabody said, his voice heavy. "That's who I think was watchin' us today. Somebody who works for the varmint who's got his eye on this place."

"You happen to know who that is?"

Peabody turned his head to look at Luke in the fading light.

"Wolford."

The answer didn't surprise Luke. Vincent Wolford had stepped in to help them that day in Dobieville when they'd had the trouble with the soldiers, but he had seen through the man's slick façade to the predator underneath. Weighing his words carefully, Luke said, "Maybe Harkness has the right idea. There's Emily to think of—"

"You mean you think we should run, too?" Peabody snapped. "That ain't the way you sounded the last time we talked about this, son."

"I know. I just don't want anything bad to happen to Emily."

"You think I do? But you got to remember this . . . gettin' her to leave wouldn't be easy. This land . . . well, look at it this way. When her pa and her brothers went off to fight, they figured they were doin' it to protect our home. This land. Emily still sees it the same way. She'll feel like she has to defend it, too, just like they did."

Luke understood that. He felt the same way about the Jensen farm in Missouri. So would his pa and Kirby.

There was no good answer. None at all.

Emily appeared in the doorway behind them, drying her hands on a cloth. "What are the two of you talkin' about so serious-like?"

"Who says we're talkin' serious?" her grandfather said. "I was just tellin' Luke a joke."

"I didn't hear anybody laughin'."

"That's because I ain't got to the funny part yet." Peabody turned to Luke. "So then the farmer says, 'You're all mixed up, mister. That there's my prize hog.'" He slapped a hand on his thigh and hooted with laughter.

Luke threw back his head and laughed, too, even though on the inside he had seldom felt grimmer.

Using the crutches, Luke lifted himself from the chair and stood beside the table. He took a deep breath and let go of the crutches, allowing them to fall to the sides like he had done before. As they thumped on the floor, he stood with his hands spread, trying to balance himself.

He didn't fall immediately. He felt the weight on his legs, felt the muscles struggling to support him. But they began to give out, and he had to slap his palms down on the table to hold himself up. Even that was progress, he thought as his pulse pounded in his head. He hadn't collapsed. Yes, he was leaning on the table, but he was still standing.

A footstep sounded on the porch.

Luke turned his head toward the door, and as he did so, his legs folded up underneath him. He tried to catch himself on the table, but wound up lying on the floor between the chair and the table.

Emily came in and saw him there. "Damn it all to—" She stopped herself. She had been trying to stop cursing so much lately.

He thought maybe she had decided it wasn't ladylike . . . as if acting more like a lady might have become more important to her.

She rushed over to him and bent to take hold of him. "Lord have mercy, Luke, what happened? How did you manage to fall?"

"Don't worry about that," he snapped, furious at himself for letting her distract him. "Just help me up."

He saw the quick flash of hurt in her eyes and wished he

could call back the sharp words, but they were already out there. He couldn't do a thing about them except add in a softer tone, "Please, Emily."

As she lifted him, he reached up and grabbed hold of the table. With it to support him, she was able to get him back into the chair.

"I'll pick up your crutches."

He held out a hand to stop her. "I can get them. Thank you."

She looked at him with a slight frown. "Were you trying to walk, Luke? I've told you, I don't care about that, not for me. I want it for you, but it's not going to make any difference how I feel—"

"Of course it makes a difference. It's bound to." Luke frowned at her.

"No," she said as she leaned closer to him. "I swear to you, it doesn't. I'll prove it to you."

Before he could stop her, she lowered herself onto his lap, her arms clasped around his neck, and her mouth pressed hungrily to his.

Luke bit back a groan of mingled despair and desire. His arms went around her. She was such a little bit of a thing, yet the curves of her body were those of a woman. Her lips worked urgently against his, their taste sweet and hot.

As he held her and kissed her, he felt something, no doubt about that.

She did too. Pulling back slightly, her eyes widened. He was about to apologize, but a pleased glow sprang to life in her eyes. "See, Luke," she whispered. "I told you it didn't matter."

She kissed him again, then slid out of his arms and stood up.

"Grampaw might be comin' in any time, so we'll save our sparkin' for later."

Luke nodded. After everything Linus Peabody had done for him, he didn't want to offend the old-timer.

Peabody hurried in a short time later, all right, as Emily had predicted. He wore a worried expression on his face, and it quickly became obvious the last thing on his mind was who was sparking his granddaughter. "There's a buggy and some riders comin'." He reached for the rifle hanging on the wall near the door.

"Yankee soldiers again?" Emily asked, her body tensing as she stood next to the stove where she had started supper.

Peabody shook his head as he checked to make sure the rifle was loaded.

"Nope. It's that fella Wolford, and unless I miss my guess, the men he's got with him are hired guns."

CHAPTER 20

"Get my revolver," Luke told Emily.

"What're you thinkin' about doin'?" She looked at her grandfather. "What are the both of you thinkin' about doin'?"

"Nothin' we don't have to," Peabody told her. "Could be Wolford just wants to talk. If he does, I'll listen to him. Won't do him any good, but I'll listen."

"Is this about the folks who have been losin' their farms to the carpetbaggers?"

Peabody frowned. "You know about that?"

"How the hell could I *not* know about it?" Emily blurted out. "It's the only thing folks all over this part of the country are talkin' about!"

"I need my revolver," Luke said again. He was trying to stay calm, but the same tense feelings he had experienced before every battle were going through him. He might soon be fighting for his life, and the lives of Emily and her grandfather as well.

But that wasn't exactly likely, he told himself, not just yet, anyway. From what Peabody had said about Wolford's attempt to take over Bud Harkness's farm, the carpetbagger was using quasi-legal means in his land grabs, relying on corrupt judges and what passed for the law under Yankee occupation.

Wolford would have hired guns in reserve, though, and if he couldn't get what he wanted peacefully, he would use force to take it. Luke had no doubt about that.

He looked intently at Emily until she sighed and went to the cabinet where the Griswold and Gunnison revolver was kept. She took it out and brought it over to Luke. "I can use this gun."

He held out his hand. "You need to stay inside."

A quick flash of anger lit up her eyes. "Luke—"

"Luke's right," Peabody said. "You stay in the house, girl, like you did when the Yankees came."

"Men!" she said in exasperation. "You're the most stubborn critters on God's green earth!"

Luke stuck the revolver in the pocket of his overalls and grasped his crutches. "That's because we're raised by women to be that way." With a smile, he lifted himself to his feet.

She still looked mad, but rested a hand on his arm for a second. "Don't start trouble with them."

"I don't intend to start trouble with anybody," Luke assured her. He didn't say anything about finishing it, if things came down to that. He looked out through the door Peabody had left open. "Here they come."

"Be careful," Emily whispered to Luke. "We just . . ."

She didn't finish, but he knew what she meant. They had just admitted how they felt about each other. She didn't want him going and getting himself killed.

Luke didn't want that, either. He nodded to show her he understood as much.

Peabody went out onto the porch. Luke followed him, moving fairly easily on the crutches. He wished he could have walked out there bold as brass, but that was something for the future if his legs continued to improve.

With a clatter of hoofbeats and wheels, Vincent Wolford

drove his buggy up to the cabin and brought the vehicle to a halt, reining in the two fine black horses pulling it. Luke found himself wondering who those horses used to belong to, and how Wolford had gotten his hands on them. He was willing to bet the carpetbagger hadn't bought them fair and square.

Three men on horseback accompanied Wolford. As they reined in, Luke studied them. Back home he had seen Jayhawkers from Kansas on several occasions, and these men reminded him of those ruthless guerrillas.

One wore a derby and a flashy eastern suit. He was big, with broad shoulders and a rough-hewn face dominated by a rusty handlebar mustache. His hands were huge, with knobby knuckles broken more than once in various brawls. He wasn't carrying a gun that was visible, but Luke figured there was probably a revolver in a shoulder holster under that tweed coat.

The other two riders were dressed more like frontiersmen in boots, work clothes, and broad-brimmed hats. They wore their guns out in the open, carrying holstered pistols on their hips. They had rugged, hard-planed faces and cold eyes.

Luke knew all three men were probably killers, paid by Vincent Wolford to enforce his will and help him take what he wanted. They would be fast on the draw. If Linus Peabody raised his rifle, one or more of the gunmen would drill him before he got a shot off.

Luke was pretty handy with a gun, but knew he wasn't a match for those three. Not with the Griswold and Gunnison stuck in his pocket. If he had a regular gun rig and a pair of revolvers, he might manage to down a couple, maybe all three, but they would get lead in him, too.

It wasn't going to come to that. He couldn't allow the carpetbaggers to kill him and Peabody, leaving Emily at their mercy.

"Take it easy," he said under his breath to Peabody. "Stay calm."

The old man nodded, but the tense way he stood and the urgency with which he gripped the rifle told a different story. He was ready to fight. He *wanted* to fight.

Luke levered himself forward on his crutches, putting himself between Peabody and the buggy. He nodded to Wolford. "Howdy. What brings you out here from town?"

"Mr. Smith, isn't it?" Wolford asked with that phony smile of his, without getting down from the buggy. "I came to speak with Mr. Peabody there. I have a business proposition for him."

Peabody moved up even with Luke. "I ain't interested in doin' business with the likes of you."

"You should hear me out," Wolford said. "That's just a smart rule of thumb. Always listen to the other fellow's proposal. You never know when he might offer something you want."

Peabody glared darkly at the visitors, but after a moment he nodded. "I'll listen. I don't reckon it's very likely you got anything I want, though."

"You might be surprised. What I'm proposing, Mr. Peabody, is that I take this farm off your hands for a very reasonable price."

"Why in blazes would I want to sell?" Peabody snapped.

"Well, the market for cotton, tobacco, and other crops is very depressed right now. You can't hope to make very much for them."

"We'll get by," the old man said.

"Yes, perhaps, but you can do even better somewhere else. I hear people are having phenomenal success migrating to the frontier. There are millions of acres out there just ripe for the taking."

"This is my home. I've lived on this land all my life, and my pa lived here before me. I intend to stay until the Good Lord calls me home."

Wolford's smile didn't budge, but Luke thought he saw impatience growing in the man's eyes.

"You can do that," Wolford said, "but you'd still be wise to sell out to me. If you don't want to leave, you can always stay and work the land on shares."

"Why in the Sam Hill would I want to do that?"

"You wouldn't have all the worries of dealing with the new government. I'd handle all that. You could just work the land the way you always have."

"While you rake in all the profits?" Peabody asked.

"Not all of it. You'd still get by, as you put it." Wolford's voice finally hardened as he went on. "You don't seem to understand, Mr. Peabody, that things have changed around here. It's not the same as it was before the war, and it never will be again. Different people are running things now. I happen to be well acquainted with Colonel Morrison and Judge Blevins, and although I may be speaking out of turn here, I know they're going through all the records and un-covering a number of cases where insufficient taxes were paid on properties in this area."

"You mean you're gonna grab folks' land by claimin' they owe taxes they really don't," Peabody said.

The big eastern tough in the derby glared and edged his horse forward. "Don't you talk to Mr. Wolford like that, you old Rebel," he warned.

Wolford lifted a hand. "Take it easy, Joe. I'm sure Mr. Peabody didn't mean to cast any aspersions."

"What I'll cast is you offa my land," Peabody said. "I paid my taxes, and can't nobody say otherwise!"

"Yes, but you paid them to the Confederates who were in charge here at the time." Wolford shook his head as if he were genuinely regretful. "There's no way of knowing where all that money went, but it isn't in the county's coffers like it's supposed to be. Unfortunately, in order to fund the new government, a new taxation schedule will have to be put in place—"

"Why don't you call it what it is?" Peabody broke in. "Stealin', plain and simple!"

"I'm just trying to help." Wolford leaned over slightly on

the buggy seat to look past Luke and Peabody. "Isn't that your granddaughter I see just inside the door?" He raised a hand to his hat. "Good day to you, Miss Peabody. You're looking as lovely as ever."

"You leave Emily outta this—" Peabody began, but she stepped onto the porch and confronted Wolford and his gunmen, too.

"We don't want your so-called help, mister." Her eyes blazed with fury.

She counseled restraint, Luke thought, but her emotions got the better of her and she couldn't practice what she preached.

"You'd better turn that buggy around and get off our land, right now!"

"Or what? An old man and a cripple will run us off?" The gunman leaned over in his saddle and spat. "I don't think so."

"Please, Howell, there's no need for unpleasantness." Wolford smiled at Emily again. "I think if you'd just give me a chance, Miss Peabody, you and I could be good friends. If you were to help persuade your grandfather to be reasonable, why, I can see all sorts of benefits in it for you. A girl as beautiful as you should have some of the finer things in life, the sort of things a man like me could give you—"

"So I could be some sort of backwoods harlot for you?" Emily turned toward her grandfather and reached for the rifle. "Gimme that gun."

Luke saw the three hired killers grow tense in their saddles and knew the situation was teetering perilously close to violence. Under the circumstances, the outcome of that wouldn't be good for him and his friends.

He moved between the Peabodys and the unwelcome visitors and said in a loud, hard voice, "That's enough."

"Do you speak for these people, Mr. Smith?" Wolford asked with a sneer.

"I speak for myself, and this is what I've got to say, Wolford." Luke looked right into the man's eyes. He didn't like taking his attention off the others, but knew they wouldn't act unless Wolford ordered them to. "If there's trouble here today, you'll be sorry. I'll see to that personally."

"That's mighty big talk for a man on crutches." The eastern tough called Joe sneered.

Luke let go of the right-hand crutch, letting it fall behind him, and moved his hand so it wasn't far from the butt of the revolver sticking out of his pocket. "I only need one to balance on," he told Wolford, making it clear as he could. If any gunplay broke out, Luke was going to draw that revolver and kill Wolford, no matter what else happened. He might die, and Emily and her grandfather probably would, too, but Wolford would die first.

Luke was going to see to that.

Reading the deadly message in Luke's steady gaze, fear flared in the carpetbagger's eyes. An instant later, it was replaced by smoldering anger.

But the fear was still there, underneath, and Luke knew it.

"All right," Wolford snapped. "I was just trying to be generous. I thought perhaps we could consider ourselves friends and neighbors, Mr. Peabody. But if you'd rather this . . . this unreconstructed Rebel speak for you—"

"Smith's right," Peabody said. "We've heard enough. You and your boys need to git."

Wolford lifted the reins. "We'll be going, then. Perhaps I was wrong, Mr. Peabody. Perhaps you won't lose your farm"—he paused—"but don't count on it."

With that, he turned the team and sent the buggy rolling away from the cabin. The three gunmen lingered a moment, giving Luke hard, murderous stares before they wheeled their horses and followed Wolford.

"I ain't countin' on nothin'," Peabody said, "except that this trouble ain't over."

Luke knew the old-timer was right about that.

CHAPTER 21

Wolford had been so angry when he drove away Luke wouldn't have been surprised if problems started cropping up right away. But several days passed with no sign of the carpetbagger or his hired guns.

Linus Peabody reported the Harkness family on the neighboring farm had packed up and moved away, abandoning the place because they couldn't pay the exorbitant taxes being demanded by the Reconstruction government. Another worried neighbor had come by the farm and told Peabody about it, adding that the sheriff was going to auction off the Harkness farm in Dobieville on Saturday.

Luke knew Vincent Wolford would win that auction at a rock-bottom price. And he would probably get some of the money back from the sheriff and the judge in the form of a kickback.

The idea of Emily going out to work in the fields with her grandfather worried Luke. If Wolford's gunnies showed up, intent on causing trouble, Peabody wouldn't be able to protect her. In his current condition, Luke couldn't watch over them, so he made up his mind the best thing for him to do was improve as much and as quickly as he could.

With that determination goading him on, he worked with his legs for long hours each day while Emily and her grandfather were gone. He put more and more weight on his own muscles, forcing them to move and carry him, not just support him.

Back and forth across the cabin's main room he shuffled endlessly, using the crutches. Eventually he was able to take a step, then several steps, without touching the floor with the crutches, although he held them ready to catch himself if he fell.

Those efforts made his legs ache almost intolerably, but he welcomed the pain, even embraced it. To have his legs hurt was so much better than to have them feel nothing at all.

By the time a week had passed since Wolford and his gunmen had shown up at the farm, Luke was able to take actual steps as he walked across the room, no longer sliding his feet in a shuffling manner. He left the crutches behind and walked on his own; something that had seemed utterly impossible a few months ago. His gait was slow and halting, to be sure, and he told himself with a wry smile that he was a long way from being able to dance a jig, but he was getting there.

He was getting there, all right, and it was the best pain he had ever felt, although he sometimes had to bite his lip to keep from crying out when Emily massaged his legs.

It wasn't long before she noticed the change in his legs. "These muscles are definitely harder and stronger than they were. You're gonna walk again one of these days, Luke. You just wait and see."

"Thanks to you, I am," he told her. Without the way she had kept him going through his darkest days and nights, and without the determination his fear for her safety gave him, he might not have ever walked again. Soon he was going to be ready to reveal his secret to her.

A little later, when Peabody caught a moment alone with him, the old-timer said, "I spotted them fellas who work for Wolford watchin' the place again today."

Luke hated to hear that, but he wasn't surprised. He had

known better than to hope Wolford would give up on getting his hands on the farm. Even worse was knowing the man wanted to get his hands on Emily. He had hinted as much when he visited the farm, and Luke had seen the unmistakable lust in the carpetbagger's eyes when Wolford looked at her.

"Why don't I start going out to the fields with you and Emily during the day?" Luke had discarded that idea a week earlier but was beginning to think it might work.

"On your crutches?" Peabody asked with a frown.

"No, you can help me climb into the wagon, and I'll sit up there and keep an eye on things while you're working. We can take along the rifle and my revolver. I can handle a gun just fine."

Peabody scratched his stubbly jaw and shrugged. "That ain't a bad idea."

The next day they put it into practice, even though Emily was insistent on knowing why Luke was coming with them.

"Wolford's men have been watchin' us again," Peabody admitted.

"Oh, them? Shoot, I saw them before. They don't scare me."

"Well, they scare me, and they ought to scare you, too," Peabody insisted. "They're bad men, and the fella they work for is even worse. We got trouble on the horizon."

It was even closer than they suspected.

With help from Peabody and Emily, Luke climbed to the wagon seat and they went out to the fields. He wished he could help them harvest the late summer corn crop. Unfortunately, his legs weren't yet steady enough. Instead, he scanned the surrounding countryside for any sign of Wolford's men without spotting them.

The sound of shots made Emily cry out in alarm and Luke twist around on the seat to peer toward the cabin.

The shots continued from that direction as Emily and Peabody dropped what they were doing and ran to the wagon. Peabody scrambled up to the seat and jerked the reins loose from the brake lever while Emily practically threw herself into the back. Even the normally stubborn mules sensed something was wrong. They broke into a run as Peabody headed them toward the cabin.

Breathing hard, Emily leaned over the back of the seat between the two men. "What are they doin'?" she asked anxiously. "What's all that shootin' about?"

"We'll know in a minute." Luke gripped the rifle tightly. It was only a single-shot weapon, but the revolver in his pocket was fully loaded.

The shooting stopped before they came in sight of the cabin. As they did, Luke caught a glimpse of several riders galloping away from the place. They were already too far off for him to make out any details, but he was willing to bet they were the three hired guns who worked for Vincent Wolford.

"No!" Emily cried as her grandfather wheeled the wagon into the open area between the cabin and the barn. Limp, bloody bundles of feathers were scattered around on the ground. The chickens had been blasted to pieces. In the pen over by the barn, the hogs lay motionless in the mud.

Emily leaped out of the wagon and ran into the barn. When she came back a moment later, tears were running down her cheeks. "They killed the milk cow, too. Looks like they just shot everything that moved."

"Why in blazes would they do that?" Peabody asked furiously. "It aggravates the hell out of me, but losin' those animals ain't enough to ruin the farm."

"This is just the opening gambit," Luke said. "Think of it as a warning. Wolford wants to let you know it'll get a lot worse if you don't give him what he wants."

"Never! I'm goin' to town and swearin' out a complaint against the varmints! The sheriff's got to do somethin'. He's supposed to uphold the law around here."

"The sheriff works for Wolford and that judge of his and the rest of the Yankees," Emily said bitterly. "He's not gonna do anything, Grampaw."

"We don't know that. If nobody ever speaks up, nothin' will change around here!"

The old-timer was right about that, Luke supposed. But like Emily, he didn't think complaining to the law would do any good. They would never know if they didn't try, though. "We'll all go to Dobieville. Maybe round up some of your friends and neighbors who've had trouble with the carpetbaggers and take them with you. If more people are speaking up, the men in charge will have a harder time ignoring them."

Peabody nodded. "That's a good idea."

"Not as good an idea as goin' to town and shootin' that snake Wolford for tellin' his men to do this," Emily said.

It might come to that, Luke thought, *but we have to try reason first . . . then bullets.*

Peabody spent the rest of the day visiting his neighbors and putting together a delegation to complain to the sheriff in Dobieville. The killing of his livestock wasn't the first such outrage in the area. Barns had burned down mysteriously, crops had been trampled on dark nights, wells had been fouled, and cattle had been run off.

Nor would that harassment stop, Luke thought. In fact, he expected it to escalate into outright violence in fairly short order. Wolford and the other carpetbaggers were not patient men.

The farmers rendezvoused outside of town and rode in on mules and in wagons and buggies. Some of them walked. A few had brought their wives and children with them, something Luke thought probably wasn't wise. A group about forty strong converged on the sheriff's office.

Their arrival in town stirred up enough of a commotion that the lawman heard them coming. He stepped out onto the porch of his office to wait for them. He was a middle-aged man with thinning brown hair and a mustache. A gun belt was strapped around his waist, and he carried a shotgun in addition to the holstered revolver.

"Fella's name is Royce Wilkes," Peabody explained to Luke as they approached in the wagon. "Used to be a deputy here, but he was too fond of corn liquor. The old sheriff ran him off. When the war was over, the Yankees put him back in office and gave him the sheriff's job. He's local, but he's in the back pocket of them no-good carpetbaggers."

Wilkes had the shotgun cradled in his left arm. He held up his right hand for silence and called, "All right, what the devil's goin' on here?"

Everyone in the group turned to look at Linus Peabody. He had talked them into coming, and they regarded him as their spokesman.

"Sheriff, we're all here to lodge complaints against Vincent Wolford and those fellas who work for him," Peabody said. "I beg pardon of the ladies in earshot of my voice, but Wolford's men have been raisin' hell hereabouts, and it's gotta stop."

"You know for a fact that what you're sayin' is true, Linus?" Wilkes asked.

"I do," Peabody replied with a forceful nod. "They came out to my place yesterday and shot all my chickens and hogs and my milk cow. We seen 'em ridin' off after they done it."

Luke and Emily nodded. In reality the riders had been too far away for a positive identification, but there was no question in Luke's mind that Wolford's men were responsible.

"Well, that's a mighty serious charge," Wilkes said.

Another man in the crowd said, "That ain't all they've done. My barn burned down last week, and I know good and well somebody set that fire. I rode into town and told you all about it, Royce."

"You did," Wilkes said, "but you also told me you didn't see who done it."

"It had to be Wolford's men! You know that!"

"I'm a lawman," Wilkes boasted, his chest puffing out

pompously. "I got to have proof. And somebody thinkin'
they saw something ain't proof."

"Are you callin' us liars?" Peabody demanded.

"I'm sayin' maybe you were mistaken."

Luke suggested, "Why don't you at least ask Wolford
about it? See if he can account for the whereabouts of his
men yesterday when Mr. Peabody's livestock was being
slaughtered."

Wilkes shook his head stubbornly. "I ain't gonna bother
an important man like Mr. Wolford—"

"It's no bother," a new voice said.

Everyone swung around to look. The crowd parted, and
Vincent Wolford himself sauntered up to the porch.

"I heard there was a gathering of some sort and decided
to come see for myself what it was about," Wolford went on.
"I'd be glad to answer any questions you have for me,
Sheriff."

"I don't have any questions," Wilkes said.

"I do," Peabody snapped. "Did you send your men to kill
my livestock, mister?"

Wolford gave a solemn shake of his head. "Of course not,
Mr. Peabody. Why in the world would I do a thing like
that?"

"To try to run me off so you can grab my land!"

"I wanted to make you a fair offer for your land, but you
wouldn't even consider it," Wolford said. "As far as I'm
concerned, our business is over."

"Where were your men yesterday morning?" Luke asked.

"Burnett, Howell, and Prentice?" Wolford shrugged.
"I'm not sure. I don't keep track of their whereabouts every
hour of the day. As long as they do the jobs I give them,
that's all I really care about."

"Did you give them any jobs yesterday?"

"As a matter of fact, I didn't." Wolford smiled. "I didn't
even speak to them. So you see, even if there was anything
to these ludicrous accusations—and I assure you, there
isn't—I can't be held responsible for them."

Wilkes nodded. "Looks like that clears it all up. Sorry to bother you, Mr. Wolford."

"Oh, it's no bother, Sheriff, I assure you. All I want to do is carry on my business and get along with my neighbors."

Wilkes turned back to the farmers. "You've said your piece, now it's time for all of you to go back home and stop botherin' folks."

"Are you runnin' us out of town?" Peabody asked. "Don't we still have a right to go where we please?"

"No, you don't," Wilkes snapped. "Gatherin' up in mobs like this is against the law. So if you don't break it up and leave, it'll be my duty to arrest you . . . and I'll get the soldiers to help me, if I need to."

"You'd better do what he says, Linus," Luke told the old-timer.

"You mean let them get away with it?" Emily asked.

"Getting arrested isn't going to help anything."

Peabody scowled darkly, but he said, "All right, we'll go. But this ain't over, Sheriff. We'll get justice somehow."

"You step out of line and you'll be sorry," Wilkes warned.

With a lot of angry muttering, the crowd turned to leave town. As the wagon rolled past the last buildings, Emily said, "Like I told you, nothin's gonna change."

"At least Wolford knows we're on to him," Peabody said. "He's the one who's really to blame for everything."

"And all he's gonna do is laugh at us," Emily said as her shoulders slumped in despair.

If that's all that happens, Luke thought, *then they might be lucky.* Wolford's smooth façade had never budged, but he had to be angry that the farmers had banded together to complain about his tactics. Luke wouldn't be at all surprised if he decided to teach them a lesson.

And if he did, it would be a painful one. Luke was sure of that.

CHAPTER 22

Emily was cool toward Luke on the ride back to the farm and for the rest of the day. He wasn't sure why she was upset with him, unless it was because he had talked her grandfather out of setting off a showdown in town. Maybe she didn't understand he didn't want anything to happen to her . . . or maybe she did, and that just made her angrier.

Whatever the reason, she didn't have much to say to him around her grandfather, and they didn't get a chance to talk alone. Luke turned in knowing nothing was settled and the situation was likely to get worse before it got better . . . if it ever did.

Sometime during the night he came awake instantly, smelling smoke. It was too strong to be coming from the fireplace or the stove. He sat up. No lights burned inside the cabin, but a flickering red glow came through the cracks around the front door and through the thin curtains hung over the windows.

The barn was on fire. It was the only explanation that made sense.

And he knew it hadn't caught fire by itself.

"Emily!" he shouted. "Linus! Wake up!"

Peabody bolted from his bunk. Emily bolted from hers and cried out in alarm. "Something's on fire!"

"The barn!" With his nightshirt flapping around his legs, Peabody grabbed the rifle from the chair where he had placed it to be handy and headed for the door.

When he flung it open, the garish red light from the blazing barn spilled into the cabin. He rushed outside with Emily right behind him.

Still struggling to get out of his bunk, Luke swung his legs to the floor and stood up, using the back of a nearby chair for support. He picked up his revolver off the chair and grabbed one of his crutches propped against the wall next to the head of his bunk.

Hoofbeats pounded outside. Someone shouted, and Peabody's rifle cracked.

"No, no," Luke panted as he hurried toward the door as fast as he could. He knew without having to think about it what had happened. To get back at Peabody for trying to organize the farmers against him, Wolford had sent his men to the farm to set fire to the barn.

And those killers were still out there, where they threatened Emily and her grandfather. That thought made Luke's blood run cold.

As he reached the porch, he heard Emily scream, "Grampaw!" In the garish light of the fire, Luke saw a man on horseback nearly run down Linus Peabody. The old-timer threw himself out of the way just in time, losing his balance and sprawling on the ground. The rider wheeled his horse around and pointed a gun at Peabody as Emily ran toward her grandfather.

She leaped to shield him as the rider pulled the trigger. Luke fired at the same instant. Flame spat from the barrel of his revolver. The impact of the bullet jarred the man on the horse, knocking him forward.

"Emily!" Peabody cried out. "Oh, my God, Emily!"

Luke suddenly realized he was off the porch and didn't think about what he did next as he cast the single crutch aside and broke into a stumbling run toward Emily and Peabody. The nightmarish glare of the fire revealed Emily's body lying stretched on the ground while her grandfather hovered over her.

Hoofbeats thundered again as two more riders lunged out of the jagged shadows cast by the firelight. The newcomers seemed intent on trampling them. Still stumbling, Luke raised the revolver and thumbed off two more shots. He didn't know if he hit either of the attackers, but they veered sharply away.

The man he'd wounded yelled, "I'm hit! We gotta get out of here!"

Luke recognized the eastern accent of the tough named Joe Burnett. The other two had to be Howell and Prentice. One of them snapped a couple shots at him, coming close enough for him to hear the bullets whine past his head, as the other grabbed the dangling reins of Burnett's horse and all three gunmen fled.

Pain flared through Luke's legs, but they continued to support him. Peabody looked up at him as he reached the old man's side, but he didn't seem to notice Luke was standing and moving around without the aid of the crutches.

"Emily's hurt!" Peabody cried. "When that no-good shot at me, she got in the way of the bullet!"

"How bad is it? Where's she hit?" Luke figured if he knelt down, he wouldn't be able to get back up again, so he made his voice urgent in an attempt to get through the fear and confusion that gripped Peabody.

It seemed to work, because the old-timer looked down, gently grasped Emily's shoulders, and rolled her onto her back. Luke caught a glimpse of blood on her nightclothes, but the stain appeared to be a small one, at least so far.

"I . . . I don't think she's hurt too bad," Peabody said after a moment. "Looks like the bullet just nicked her side."

Emily groaned.

"She's comin' to." Peabody continued to watch his grand-daughter.

Luke watched and listened for any sign of the gunmen doubling back. In the firelight, the three of them made good targets, he thought.

Not seeing further danger, he turned his attention back to Emily and Peabody. "You'll need to pick her up and get her back in the cabin. Can you clean that wound and put a dressing on it?"

"Yeah, I reckon I can." Amazement crept into Peabody's voice as he went on. "Luke, you're standin' up on your own! And you ran across there a minute ago! I saw you with my own eyes."

"Don't worry about that. Just take care of Emily."

"I will. What are you gonna do?"

"Something that somebody should have done before now," Luke said.

He didn't know how long his legs would keep working. It had taken the threat to Emily and her grandfather for them to move like they had a few minutes earlier. The mixture of fear, desperation, and rage had burned through him like the fire that was consuming the barn, a cleansing fire that forced muscles and nerves to work again the way they were supposed to. His movements were rusty and a little clumsy, but he could get around again, and didn't want to waste the opportunity.

Peabody was still strong, and Emily was a slip of a girl. He had no trouble picking her up and carrying her back into the cabin.

Luke followed. While Peabody tended to Emily, he got dressed, reloaded the Griswold and Gunnison, and went back outside. His face was impassive in the firelight despite the pain shooting through his legs with every step. The rest of those nerves were waking up again after their long sleep, he thought. If they kept working for a while longer, it would be enough.

He pocketed his revolver and walked over to the spot where he had wounded Joe Burnett. The man's revolver, a Colt Navy, lay on the ground where Burnett had dropped it. Luke picked up the gun, hefting it in his hand, and realized his ammunition would fit it. Both weapons would be fully loaded when he headed for town.

He frowned. How was he going to get there? The luckless mules had been in the barn, and so had the wagon. His legs were finally working again, but he couldn't walk all the way to Dobieville.

Shouts and hoofbeats made him swing around and raise both guns. The man riding up to the farm reined in sharply and threw his hands in the air. "Whoa!" he exclaimed. "Hold your fire, mister! I'm a friend!"

Luke recognized the newcomer as one of the men who had gone into town with them that morning. He thought for a second and recalled the man's name. "You're Thad Franklin, right?"

"Yeah." The man dismounted. "My place is a couple miles east of here. I saw the light from the fire and knew somethin' had to be wrong. Thought I'd better come see if I could help." He shook his head. "It's too late to save that barn, though."

"Maybe you and the others can help Linus rebuild," Luke suggested.

"Is he hurt? How about Emily?"

Luke jerked his head toward the cabin. "They're in there. Emily was wounded by the varmints who set the barn on fire, but I think she's going to be all right."

"There'll be more folks showin' up soon, I reckon. People always come to help when they see a fire."

"You can help right now," Luke said. "Give me your horse."

"My horse? What? Say, you're the fella who can't walk!" Franklin looked Luke up and down in confusion. "But you're standin' up now."

Luke lifted the Colt Navy and pointed it at Franklin, saying coldly, "I need your horse. I'll get it back to you, if I can. If I can't, you'll find it in Dobieville."

"Careful with that gun, mister! What're you gonna do?" Franklin's eyes widened as he realized the answer to his own question. "You're goin' after the men who did this?"

Luke used his free hand to take the reins out of Franklin's

fingers. "Sorry, but it's got to be done." He got his left foot in the stirrup and swung up into the saddle, clenching his jaw at the pain caused by mounting.

"You're crazy," Franklin said. "You can't fight those carpetbaggers. There are too many of 'em, and they got the Yankee army on their side!"

"I don't plan to fight all of them, just one in particular and the men he sent to do this."

"They'll kill you!"

"Probably. But I plan on sending them to hell ahead of me."

CHAPTER 23

Still burning brightly, the fire cast an orange glow into the sky behind Luke as he rode toward Dobieville. Being on a horse again felt good.

Despite his concern for Emily, he felt more alive than he had in a long time.

He hadn't had a chance to reload the Navy after all. Checking the gun's cylinder, he found that Burnett had fired only one round. The other five chambers were loaded. He had eleven shots.

It would have to be enough.

Regret gnawed at him. He hadn't taken the time to say good-bye to Emily and her grandfather. He knew they would have tried to talk him out of forcing a showdown with Wolford. Luke didn't trust himself not to give in to Emily's pleading and stay at the farm with her.

If he had stayed, things would continue to get worse. He didn't know if they would actually improve once Wolford was dead, but at least if the carpetbagger and his gunmen were gone they wouldn't be able to threaten anyone else.

The raiders had come very close to killing Emily, and that knowledge filled Luke with a rage overpowering every other emotion. Somebody had to take a stand against their evil.

He was the man.

Simple as that.

Luke had a good sense of direction and was able to find the settlement without any trouble. When he saw its lights, he reined in for a moment, thinking of the situation and what he should do next.

The three gunmen weren't that far ahead of him. He figured the first thing they would do was report to Wolford, so there was a good chance he could find them together. It would certainly make things easier if all four of his enemies were in one place.

That notion turned his thoughts to Potter, Stratton, Richards, and Casey. He'd had four enemies to deal with that fateful night, too, and it hadn't turned out well. But he'd been taken by surprise, even though he shouldn't have been, and tonight he'd be the one doing the surprising.

He shook his head and turned his thoughts back to the situation at hand. Wolford owned the North Georgia Land Company. Luke had heard talk about it and had seen the sign on a building in town, earlier, when the group of farmers came to talk to the sheriff. He nodded. It was the first place he would look for his quarry.

He used his heels to get the horse moving again. Dobieville was quiet. No reason for it not to be, Luke supposed. The citizens didn't know what had happened out at the Peabody farm. They would hear about it by morning. As he rode down the deserted streets they were blissfully ignorant.

That was about to change.

The saloons were open, and a light still burned in the general store, but most of the businesses along Main Street were dark, including the building that housed Wolford's office. It appeared to be locked up for the night.

A faint glow in the alley behind the place told a different story. Luke looked along the side of the building, saw that glow, and knew one of the windows in the rear was lit up.

He dismounted and his legs sagged for a second, forcing

him to grab the saddle horn and hold himself up. He straight-ened and looped the reins around the hitch rack in front.

Hoping his muscles wouldn't betray him at the worst possible moment, he drew both revolvers from his pockets and started down the narrow passage beside the building. His gait was awkward as he kept his legs rigid, but they got him where he was going.

Reaching the rear corner of the building, he edged around it carefully and saw the lighted window. It was raised a few inches to let in the night air.

As quietly as possible, he moved closer to hear what was being said inside.

". . . doctor," a man said harshly. "This bullet's gotta come out of me."

"If we fetch the doctor, there'll be questions about how you managed to get shot, Joe." That was Wolford's voice. "I'd rather not deal with the potential embarrassment."

"So you're just gonna let me die?" Burnett's voice was drawn thin with pain.

"Of course not. Harve can dig the bullet out, can't you, Harve?"

One of the other gunmen answered, "I reckon I can give it a try." He didn't sound too confident about it.

"And I have a bottle of whiskey right here," Wolford went on. "Take a nice healthy slug, Joe, and then Harve can clean the wound with it, too."

"I don't know about this." Burnett was clearly reluctant to trust his fate to the medical skills of his fellow hired gun.

"You're being well paid to take risks," Wolford snapped, losing his patience. "And you didn't even manage to kill the old man like I told you to."

"That's not my fault," Burnett replied, a whine creeping in his tone. "I told you, boss, the girl jumped right in front of my gun just as I pulled the trigger."

"Yes, well, if she's dead, that's going to be very regret-table . . . for her and for you. I mean to have her, along with her grandfather's farm."

Luke's hands tightened on the guns, wanting to burst in there and start shooting. But it wasn't quite the right moment yet. He needed to wait just a little longer.

"Here's the whiskey," Wolford said.

Luke heard the glugging sound as the wounded man took a healthy swallow of the liquor.

Wolford went on, "You can lie down here on my desk, Joe. Thurman, you hold him down while Harve removes that bullet."

Murmurs of agreement came from the men.

Luke waited as he listened to them moving around.

Burnett let out a yelp. "Damn it, boss, at least give me somethin' to bite down on!"

"All right—"

Now, Luke thought.

While they were all gathered around the desk with their attention focused on the crude surgery he took a couple steps and rammed his shoulder against the building's back door. The flimsy lock gave under the impact and the door flew open.

Luke stumbled over the threshold, catching his balance as he brought up the guns in his hands. "Hold it!" he yelled. "Nobody move!"

They ignored the command and moved, all right. Luke had figured they would. But he had given them a chance to surrender, so his conscience was clear.

One of the gunmen—he still didn't know which one was Prentice and which one was Howell—whirled away from the desk and tried to claw out the gun holstered on his hip. Luke shot him in the face with the Griswold and Gunnison. The .36 caliber slug destroyed the man's nose and plowed into his brain, driving him backward over the desk, where he fell on top of the wounded Burnett.

The second gunman cleared leather, but before he could raise his gun, let alone get off a shot, a slug from the Colt Navy in Luke's left hand ripped into his throat. The man spun around in a half turn, blood from severed arteries spraying across the expensive rug on the floor of Wolford's private office.

Roaring in rage, Burnett shoved the dead man off himself and plucked the man's Colt from its holster. Even wounded, he had the strength to lunge up off the desk.

Luke fired both guns into Burnett's chest. The double impact lifted the big easterner off his feet and dumped him onto the desk again.

A pocket pistol went off with a small popping sound, and Luke felt something lance into his left shoulder. It wasn't much worse than a bee sting, but he knew he'd just been shot. He knew, as well, Wolford had shot him, because the other three men in the room were already dead.

Wolford fired again as he darted for the door leading into the front part of the building. Luke ducked, which gave the carpetbagger time to flee from the private office. As Luke straightened, he fired again and stomped into the bigger, darkened room after Wolford.

Wolford's gun went off again. Luke spotted the little tongue of flame from the muzzle as he heard the slug whine past his ear. He snapped a shot in return. Wolford cried out.

With Luke pursuing him inexorably, Wolford didn't have time to unlock the front door. He took the only way out, throwing himself against the front window. Glass shattered and sprayed as he burst through it and sprawled on the boardwalk outside.

Luke kept moving. His legs hadn't betrayed him so far, and miraculously, he was still alive. His quick reflexes and speed with a gun had saved him, but the job wasn't done yet.

He stepped through the broken window onto the boardwalk as Wolford tried to scramble away. Wolford screamed for help.

"Should've thought of that before you sent those men out to the Peabody farm tonight," Luke told him.

"You . . . you can't be doing this!" Wolford gasped as he scrambled to his feet. "You can't even walk!"

"Seems that I can." Luke shot the carpetbagger's left leg

out from under him, the bullet shattering the kneecap into a million pieces. "But you can't."

Wolford collapsed and clutched his bleeding, ruined knee as he screamed. Luke aimed carefully, since the man was writhing around, and blasted apart Wolford's other knee.

"Drop that gun!" a man yelled over Wolford's shrieks of agony. "Drop it right now!"

Luke glanced over and saw a hatless, nightshirt-wearing Sheriff Royce Wilkes pointing a shotgun at him.

Luke lined the Griswold and Gunnison's barrel on Wolford's forehead and eared back the hammer. His thumb was all that kept it from falling. "You can blast me to hell, Sheriff, but you can't pull those triggers fast enough to keep me from killing Wolford."

The carpetbagger realized how close he was to death, and screamed, "Don't shoot him, Sheriff! Don't shoot him!"

Wilkes held off, but the slight tremor of the shotgun's twin barrels showed how much he wanted to pull the triggers. "Listen here, mister, you'd better put that gun down. Otherwise you'll die here."

"So will this murderer," Luke said, "and I think I'm just fine with it if that's what it takes to rid the world of him."

"I . . . I never murdered anybody!" Wolford gasped. "Oh, God! Somebody help me!"

"You're beyond help from God or anybody else," Luke growled. "And you paid those gunmen of yours to go out to the Peabody farm, burn down the barn, and murder Linus Peabody. I heard you say that yourself, just a few minutes ago."

"Why . . . why would I . . ." Wolford couldn't go on. He lay whimpering in pain.

"Because with her grandfather dead, you thought Emily would have no choice but to turn to you," Luke continued. "You thought I didn't represent any threat. You were wrong on both counts. Even if you'd killed Linus and me, Emily would have wound up cutting out your heart. Trust me on that, Wolford."

"You . . . you're crazy."

"Am I? Sheriff Wilkes, why don't you ask Mr. Wolford if he sent his men to kill Linus Peabody?"

The shotgun was still trembling in Wilkes' hands, but it seemed to be from fear. "I don't want any part of this. I'm supposed to enforce the law—"

"Then arrest Vincent Wolford. Arrest him for murder and see to it he's tried, convicted, and hanged. And if you do that, then maybe, just maybe, there's still some hope for this country after all."

"Mr. Wolford?" Wilkes said, clearly uncertain what he should do.

"What does it matter?" Wolford suddenly cried. "Of course I sent my men to get rid of that stubborn old geezer! He's just a Rebel! We beat them! We won! We can do anything we want to them!"

"There's still supposed to be some law—"

"Not for Rebels!"

"We're still Americans," Luke pointed out. "Isn't that one of the so-called reasons you Yankees fought the war in the first place?"

Wolford let out a shriek of rage and hatred and pushed himself up from the boardwalk with his left hand. His right flung up the little pistol. "Go to hell!" he screeched.

"You first." Luke lifted his thumb. The revolver roared and bucked in his hand, and the bullet smacked into Wolford's forehead, hammering the back of his skull down on the planks. The gun fell out of Wolford's hand, unfired.

Luke expected to feel a double load of buckshot smash into him, ending his life.

Instead, he realized that other than the echoes of his shot dying away, the street was quiet.

He looked over at Wilkes. The sheriff had lowered the shotgun. Maybe it had something to do with the crowd of townspeople surrounding him. They had been drawn by the shots and the screaming, and probably had heard Wolford's confession. It was possible a lot of them didn't like the way

Wilkes had been doing the Yankees' bidding. He had to be worried the crowd would turn on him, if he shot Luke.

"The . . . the soldiers will be coming from their camp," Wilkes stammered out.

"When they get here, you can tell them some criminals have been executed," Luke said.

"There was no trial—"

"More than they deserved. Wolford got to speak his piece." Luke nodded at the crowd. "All these people heard it."

"There's gonna be warrants sworn out on you—"

"Fine." Luke tucked the Colt Navy away, but kept the Griswold and Gunnison in his hand as he stepped down carefully from the boardwalk. The horse he had ridden into town was only a few steps away. It looked like he wasn't going to be able to return the mount to Thad Franklin after all. If he could, later on he would send some money to the man to pay for the horse.

"I thought you couldn't walk," Wilkes remarked.

"It seems that I can," Luke said again.

"Old Peabody and his granddaughter . . ."

"They're all right. Emily was wounded, but I don't think it's bad."

"Then Wolford's men didn't murder anybody after all."

"Not for lack of trying," Luke said. "And there's no telling what other crimes they're guilty of, or how many men they've killed."

"You're the killer," Wilkes said, his voice shaking. "A cold-blooded killer!"

"In that case, Sheriff," Luke said quietly, "I think you'd do well to stay out of my way." He put his foot in the stirrup and swung up onto the borrowed horse. Or stolen horse, if you wanted to look at it that way, he thought.

Part of him couldn't believe he was still alive, or his legs were still working. But that was the case, and he had learned to deal with things the way they were, not the way he wished they could be.

Wilkes was right. The law would probably come after him. He could never go back to the Peabody farm. It would bring down more trouble on their heads, trouble they didn't need.

One thing had to be left perfectly clear before he rode away. Raising his voice so he addressed the townspeople as much as the sheriff, he said, "Emily Peabody and her grandfather had nothing to do with what happened here tonight! I did it on my own, and the law has no reason to bother them for this or anything else! I'm counting on the good people of this community to make sure that's understood! *I* did this!"

"We don't even know your name, mister," one of the townies called out.

"It's Smith. Luke Smith."

With that, Luke jammed his heels into the horse's flanks. People scrambled to get out of his way as he galloped out of the settlement. The darkness at the edge of town swallowed him.

It swallowed Luke Smith . . . because Luke Jensen was dead. He had died the night the Confederate gold was stolen. His ma and pa, Kirby, and Janey would never know he was a failure and a fugitive.

The swift rataplan of hoofbeats in the night faded and then was gone.

BOOK THREE

CHAPTER 24

1870

An icy wind clawed at Luke through the sheepskin coat he wore as he brought his horse to a stop in front of the squat roadhouse. Settlers' homes and most businesses on the almost treeless Kansas plains were built of sod because it was too expensive to have lumber freighted in. Any grass on the thatched roofs was dead. It was late autumn.

He was glad he'd found the place perched on the bank of a narrow creek with ice forming along its edges. No other human habitation was in sight for miles around on the open plains. At least he'd have somewhere to spend the night out of the frigid weather.

His legs sometimes gave him trouble when it was cold. Usually he got around just fine, as if he'd never been injured, although it had taken months to regain his full strength. The wound in his shoulder was minor and had healed quickly, but his legs had given him trouble for a long time. Every so often the old ache was there, deep in his muscles, and it was worse when the temperature dropped.

Other old aches bothered him more, like the knowledge that he had failed the Confederacy and his friends, and the fact that he had ridden away without saying good-bye to Emily.

At least he knew she and her grandfather were all right.

A few months after leaving Georgia, he'd been tending bar in a little East Texas town when none other than Sheriff Royce Wilkes had walked into the saloon where Luke worked. Former Sheriff Royce Wilkes was more accurate, because as it turned out, Wilkes had been run out of town, just like when he'd been a deputy.

Luke dismounted and tied his horse at the rack with half a dozen others. He glanced at the gray sky. Sleet or snow would probably fall later, but for now there was just the cold wind and the fading light. He shuttered in the cold, remembering that long ago meeting with Wilkes.

As he came up to the bar, his eyes widened in shock as he recognized Luke. "Smith!" His hand dropped toward the gun on his hip.

Luke reached under the bar and rested his hand on the stock of the sawed-off shotgun the owner kept on a shelf there. "I wouldn't do that, Sheriff. There's a Greener pointing at you under here."

Wilkes moved his hand well away from his gun and muttered, "Sorry. And I ain't a sheriff no more. Haven't been since not long after you left Dobieville."

"What happened?"

Wilkes' mouth twisted bitterly. "Everybody in the damned county raised hell with Judge Blevins and Colonel Morrison about how Wolford tried to have Linus Peabody killed. That old man's well-liked around those parts. Morrison and the judge tried to brush it off. Blevins swore out a warrant for your arrest on murder charges. But I said I wasn't gonna go after you, so they booted me from the job."

"That's a shame," Luke said. "A man shouldn't lose his job for doing the right thing . . . for once."

"You don't know what it was like back there when the

Yankees came in." Wilkes scowled and shrugged. "Or I reckon maybe you do, since you were there. Anyway, the Yankees didn't want me anymore, and the townsfolk didn't have any use for me to start with, so I thought I might as well come on out here to the frontier and see what I was missin'. So far it ain't been a hell of a lot."

Luke asked, "Do you know how Emily is?"

"She was fine when I left. She wasn't hurt bad that night. In fact, she started lettin' Thad Franklin's boy Jess start courtin' her."

Luke drew in a breath. Hearing that hurt, but at the same time he was glad Emily wasn't sitting around and pining away. He wasn't worth her being unhappy.

"What about those murder warrants?"

Wilkes shrugged again. "They're still in effect, I guess, but nobody's gettin' in any hurry to serve them. I reckon there's a good chance that if you stay out of Georgia, nobody's even gonna bother lookin' for you."

Luke hoped that was true. He had spent the first three months looking over his shoulder, even as he worked his way west, taking whatever odd jobs he could find.

"I see you're still up and walkin' around," Wilkes went on.

"Yeah, my legs are a lot better."

"You're a lucky man. How about a beer?"

Luke nodded and reached for a mug. "I can do that."

Wilkes had his drink and left. Luke was relieved, knowing Emily was all right. Maybe she would marry the Franklin boy and settle down to have a long, happy life, Yankees or no Yankees.

It was still on Luke's mind when he left the saloon that night and started back to the shabby little room he rented a block away.

The soft scrape of a footstep behind him was all the warning he had . . . or needed. As he twisted, his hand streaked to the Colt Navy tucked in his waistband. He never went anywhere without being armed. One of his revolvers was always in easy reach, even when he was sleeping.

The gun came out with blinding speed. The muzzle flash from the other man's gun bloomed in the darkness. Luke's revolver crashed. A man cried out and reeled from the mouth of the alley Luke had just passed, collapsing in the muddy street.

He knew, even before he snapped a lucifer to life with his thumbnail, the man he'd just killed was Royce Wilkes. He'd been nursing a grudge against Luke ever since leaving Georgia, and when fate had brought the two of them together again, the moment was inevitable.

And it was a damned shame, Luke thought. Back in Dobieville, Wilkes had acted like a real lawman for a moment, but ultimately, doing the right thing had brought him to a violent end.

The former sheriff was responsible for bushwhacking him, though, so Luke wasn't going to lose any sleep over killing the man. Nor was he going to stay around. He didn't need the attention or the trouble. Before anyone came to see what the shooting was about, he hustled to his room, rounded up what little gear he had, got his horse from the shed behind the boarding house, and lit a shuck, heading west again.

In the years since, he had continued to drift, never staying in one place for too long. He had driven a freight wagon, worked as a shotgun guard on a stagecoach run, tended bar, and even worked as a clerk in a store more than once, although he hated that job. Sometimes he sat in on a poker game and usually came out ahead. He had made enough money to send some back to Thad Franklin for the horse, a mount he had traded in on a better one in San Antonio. He owned a decent saddle, a Winchester rifle, and a gun belt and holster in which he carried the Colt Navy. He kept the Griswold and Gunnison either in his saddlebags or tucked in his waistband. He picked up books wherever he could find them and spent most of his nights reading.

It wasn't much of a life, but it was what he had.

The vague idea of going to Denver had struck him, and the way he lived, he didn't spend much time thinking about what he was doing next. He just did it. So he'd set out across Kansas, not figuring on the late autumn storm that was sweeping down across the plains from Canada. He might have to hole up at the roadhouse for a while before continuing his endless journey.

The first thing that struck him as he stepped inside the sod building was the silence. He'd expected some talk and raucous laughter from the patrons, maybe the clatter of coins tossed onto a table as somebody anted up in a poker game, or the clink of a whiskey bottle against a glass.

Instead, once he swung the door closed behind him and cut off the long, hard sigh of the wind, he didn't hear anything.

Then the sound of harsh breathing came to his ears.

The low-ceilinged, windowless room was lit only by a couple dim and flaring lamps, and the air was thick with smoke and shadows. Luke's eyes adjusted quickly to the gloom, and took in the scene before him.

A couple young men who looked like they might be cowboys up from Texas sat at one of the crude, rough-hewn tables scattered around on the hard-packed dirt floor. Another man in an overcoat with a flashy but well-worn suit underneath it sat alone at another table. Luke pegged him as a gambler.

Three men in shaggy, buffalo hide coats had a woman pinned up against the bar, which consisted of planks laid across several whiskey barrels. Long-haired and unshaven, they were about as shaggy as the buffalo that had provided their coats. They turned their heads to glare at Luke.

A few feet away, on the other side of the bar, a skinny, bald-headed man stood, looking nervous. He probably owned the place, Luke thought.

The young cowboys looked a little scared, too. The gambler's face was impassive, but that didn't mean much. Tinhorns made their living by not letting their faces give anything away.

To the room at large, Luke said in a mild voice, "Don't mind me. I'm just looking for a place to get out of that blue norther that's blowing in."

One of the hardcases shrugged and started to turn away, and Luke thought that was the end of it. But the woman said, "I know you."

Luke hadn't gotten a good look at her. He'd seen enough soiled doves in his travels, taking what comfort he could from them when he had to. She tried to step out of the half circle of men around her, and the lamplight hit her face, revealing the curly blond hair, the face that was still pretty despite the hard lines settling in around the eyes and mouth, and the little dark beauty mark near the corner of that mouth.

Luke stiffened. He remembered her, too. It was hard for him to forget somebody who had pointed a shotgun at him. The most vivid memory was of her standing in a shallow creek in wet, skimpy undergarments, but it was followed closely by the mental image of her threatening him and his companions with that scattergun. "Tennessee. Or maybe Georgia."

Before the woman could respond, one of the hardcases put a grimy hand on her chest and shoved her back against the bar. "Mind your own business, mister," he snarled.

"Oh, I intend to," Luke said. "But I'd appreciate it if you wouldn't treat the lady quite so rough, friend."

The blonde said, "They're gonna do a lot worse than that." Her voice rose a little as she tried to control the fear she obviously felt. "They're going to kill us all, once they're through having their fun. These are the Gammon brothers."

The name didn't mean anything to Luke, but he said, "I see."

One of the hardcases said, "Hey, Cooter, you think this fella could be that U.S. marshal who's been on our trail?"

"I don't know, Ben." The man squinted across the room at Luke. "But it don't really matter, does it?"

As soon as the hardcase said that, Luke knew the woman was right. The three of them planned to kill everybody and loot the place before they rode off. They'd probably keep the blonde alive the longest, figuring she could help keep them warm until the storm blew over.

Luke didn't take his eyes off the outlaws, but he asked the cowboys, "You fellas from Texas taking a hand in this?"

"Mister, all we got are rifles, and they're outside on our horses," one of the young punchers said.

"We just came in for a drink," the other added miserably. "Now we'd just like to get out of here alive."

"How about you, Ace?" Luke asked the gambler.

"The deck was stacked against me . . . until now."

The hardcase who had spoken first yelped, "Hellfire, Cooter, they're gonna draw on us!"

Luke told the Texans, "You boys hit the floor *now!*"

CHAPTER 25

Moving fast but not rushing, Luke palmed the Colt smoothly from its holster. At the same time, his left hand twisted at the wrist, grasped the butt of the Griswold and Gunnison sticking up from his waistband, and pulled that gun, too.

He wished the blonde wasn't standing right by the bar where a stray bullet could hit her, but most of the time a man couldn't choose the fights that came to him. All he could do was try to stay alive.

The outlaws swept aside the long buffalo coats and grabbed for their guns. They were fast, but Luke was faster. They had just cleared leather when his guns began to roar.

He shot the one called Ben first, triggering the Colt twice and slamming the slugs into the man's body, hoping two shots would be enough to put the big man down.

The bullets slammed Ben back against the bar and knocked some of the planks loose. Luke fired his left-hand gun at Cooter and saw the man stagger.

To Luke's left, the gambler's pistol cracked, but the third outlaw had his gun leveled and jerked the trigger twice, sending return shots at the tinhorn.

Luke pivoted and used the Griswold and Gunnison on the third brother while he sent two more slugs from the Colt into

Cooter's slumping form. The third man was hit, but he still stood tall and straight and fired at Luke, who felt the hot breath of the bullet as it whipped past his ear.

Something flashed in the lamplight, and the third Gammon brother made a gurgling, gasping sound. Bright red blood flooded from his neck, which the blonde had opened almost from ear to ear with a single backhanded swipe of the straight razor she held in her hand. The man dropped his gun and pawed at his neck, but there was nothing he could do to stop the bleeding. He collapsed onto his knees and then pitched forward on his face to lie motionless as a crimson puddle formed on the dirt floor beneath his head.

Cooter and Ben were both down. So was the gambler, and so were the two cowboys, although they lifted frightened faces to look around as the shooting ended. Luke saw the proprietor peeking out from behind one of the whiskey barrels where he had taken cover.

Luke said to the blonde, "Why don't you step away from those men, ma'am, so I can make sure they're dead?"

"The one I cut is, you can count on that. Looks like just about all the blood he had in him has leaked out."

"It never hurts to make sure." Luke approached the fallen outlaws with both hands still filled with revolvers and toed them over onto their backs. In all three cases, sightless eyes stared up emptily at the low ceiling.

"Told you," the blonde said.

One of the cowboys had gotten up to check on the gambler. "This fella's hurt bad."

Luke tucked away the Griswold and Gunnison but kept the Colt in his other hand as he went over and knelt beside the gambler. The man's white shirt was dark with blood under his once-fancy vest.

"Sorry," Luke said.

"D-don't be," the gambler managed to say. "I knew it was . . . a game of chance . . . when I took cards . . . It's just the way they were . . ." He wasn't able to finish as his eyes went glassy.

"That's right," Luke said, even though the tinhorn couldn't hear him anymore. "It's just the way they were dealt." He looked up at the blonde. "You know his name?"

"I don't have any earthly idea. He just rode in a while ago, like the rest of you. Those cowboys were first, then him, then the Gammons. Then you."

Luke stood up, reloaded the Navy, and introduced himself. "Luke Smith."

"I'm called Marcy."

"Pleased to make your acquaintance . . . again." He noticed the razor she had used to cut the throat of the third Gammon brother was nowhere to be seen. She'd probably slipped it back into a hidden pocket in her dress. "I take it these are some of the local bad men?"

"They're bad, all right. They've robbed, raped, and murdered their way across half of Kansas and Nebraska."

"Then the world's better off with them dead."

"I reckon. The world really would've been better off if they'd been put in gunnysacks and drowned when they were babies."

Luke couldn't help smiling. "A bit bloodthirsty, aren't you?"

"Men like that deserve it," Marcy said, prodding one of the bodies with the toe of her boot.

Luke turned to the Texas cowhands. "How about giving me a hand dragging them out?"

The proprietor spoke up from behind the bar. "As cold as it is, there's liable to be wolves around tonight. If you put the bodies outside—"

"Then these three will finally serve a purpose in nature, won't they?" Luke looked at the gambler. "We'll put this fellow in the shed where the wolves can't get at him. Maybe the ground won't be frozen too hard in the morning to dig a grave."

* * *

The proprietor told Luke his money wasn't any good as long as he was there. Since Luke's funds were running a little low, he didn't argue, and enjoyed the beer, the bowl of stew, and the chunk of hard bread the man brought to his table once the bodies of the dead men had been tended to.

Marcy came over and sat down at the table with him, bringing a glass of whiskey with her. "What happened to those fellas who were with you the last time I saw you?"

"Four of them are dead," Luke said. "I don't know about the other four."

He had kept his eyes and ears open while he was drifting, hoping he might run across something or somebody who could put him on the trail of Potter and the others, but so far he hadn't had any luck. He had no idea where to start searching, so he asked questions about them and waited and hoped. "You haven't seen any of the others since then, have you?"

She shook her head. "You're the first one, Luke."

He swallowed some of the beer from his mug and smiled. "I appreciate you not shooting me that day."

"Don't think I didn't think about it," she said solemnly. Then a faint smile tugged at her lips, too.

"You're about as hardboiled as a lady can be, aren't you?"

"Who the hell said I'm a lady? And do you know any other way for a woman to survive out here? We've got to be tougher than all you men. We just can't let you see it."

Luke grinned and lifted his beer. "To toughness."

She clinked her glass against his and nodded. "To toughness."

After they drank, he said, "What happened to the other women who were with you that day?"

"Turnabout's fair play on that question, eh?" She shrugged. "Damned if I know. Some of them are dead, and the others are scattered. Just like your friends, I reckon."

"The ones who are left alive aren't my friends," Luke said, his smile disappearing.

Marcy regarded him shrewdly for a moment and then nodded. "It's like that, is it?"

"It is."

"Well, then, I don't know whether to hope you find them or not."

"Why's that?" Luke asked.

"Because there's four of them and one of you, and I hate to see any man I let into my bed without payin' get himself killed."

Luke's eyebrows rose a little. "You're going to let me into your bed without paying?"

"Let me finish this drink"—Marcy lifted her glass—"and then we'll see."

Luke and Marcy spent the night in one of the small rooms partitioned off at the back of the roadhouse. Wrapped up in blankets and each other, they stayed warm enough despite the icy wind howling outside.

When Luke woke up in the morning, she was gone, but he smelled coffee brewing and hoped he would find her in the main room. He sat up and dressed quickly. Pushing the curtain aside, he stepped out of the tiny room and saw Marcy standing at the stove fully dressed with a blanket wrapped around her shoulders. Even inside the roadhouse, it was cold.

She looked up at him and smiled. "How do you feel?"

"Not bad." As he walked over to her his gait was a little awkward. His muscles had stiffened up some while he was asleep.

She noticed, and asked, "Something wrong?"

"Just an old injury. Nothing to worry about."

She nodded. "Yeah, I know all about those old injuries. The world's got a way of knockin' folks around, doesn't it?"

"It sure does," Luke agreed.

"Well, sit down somewhere. Coffee will be ready soon, and then I'll whip up some breakfast."

"You're the cook here, too?"

"That's right." Her smile was wry. "I have lots of different jobs."

While Luke was sitting there, the two young cowboys came in from outside. They had spent the night at the roadhouse, too, and Luke figured they'd been out to check on the horses, all of which had been put in the shed behind the building along with the body of the gambler.

"Mornin', Mr. Smith," one of the youngsters greeted him. "Got something here for you." He lifted a gun belt with double holsters. The walnut grip of a revolver stuck up from each holster.

"We took 'em off one of those Gammon brothers when we dragged the carcasses outside last night," the other puncher explained. "Didn't see any point in armin' the wolves that were gonna drag 'em off."

"I see." Luke took the gun belt from the first cowboy. The holsters were reversed for a cross draw. He slid one of the guns from leather and recognized it as a Remington. *Fine weapon*, he thought. "What about the other two brothers?"

The cowboys grinned and pulled back their coats to reveal that they had taken the gun belts from those bodies, too.

"Those looked like the best guns, so we figured you deserved to have them, Mr. Smith. And the horses, too, if you want 'em."

"I'll take one horse as an extra mount," Luke said. "You fellows can get some good use out of the other two, I expect."

The punchers exchanged grins.

"We sure can," one of them said. "We was just about broke last night, 'cept for our saddles and our hosses. Now we got good guns and extra mounts. Reckon we're plumb rich!"

Luke wasn't sure he had ever been as young and carefree as those two Texas cowboys. If he had been, he couldn't remember it.

Marcy came over with the coffeepot. "You two sit down," she told the punchers. "Breakfast will be ready in a little bit."

They were all eating a short time later when the door opened again. Luke glanced up and saw a bulky figure silhouetted against the gray light of the overcast day. The first things he noticed were the rifle in the man's hand and the tin star pinned to his coat. He recognized it as a United States marshal's badge.

The man wore a thick sheepskin coat and had a broad-brimmed brown hat pulled down tight on his head so the wind wouldn't blow it away. His face was red, either from the cold, a close acquaintance with whiskey or both, and a close-cropped blond beard stuck out on his cheeks and chin.

Luke took a deep breath. He was still wanted on murder charges back in Georgia.

CHAPTER 26

"Good morning," the man said as he came into the roadhouse and swung the door closed behind him. "Mighty chilly out there to go with the dusting of snow."

"We have coffee if you want it, Marshal," Marcy said. "And grub."

The lawman slapped gloved hands together to warm them and grinned. "That sounds fine, ma'am. Nothing like hot food and drink to warm a man up."

Marcy stood and motioned with her head toward one of the empty tables. "Have a seat. I'll get you a cup and a plate."

"Much obliged."

The marshal went over to the table, set his rifle on it, pulled off his gloves, and dropped his hat next to them. He smiled at Luke and the two cowboys. "Morning, gents."

The punchers muttered greetings, but Luke said, "Good morning, Marshal."

"Deputy Marshal," the lawman corrected him. "Name's Jasper Thornapple."

When a man introduced himself, it was only polite to return the favor, and despite the rough environments in which he spent his life, Luke had come to pride himself on his manners. "I'm Luke Smith."

Thornapple didn't seem to recognize the name, but that didn't mean anything. Maybe he was just good at covering up his reactions.

"Teddy Young," one of the cowboys said.

"Burt Tuttle," the other puncher added.

"Pleased to meet you," Thornapple said.

Marcy set a cup of steaming coffee in front of Thornapple. "What brings you out here in the middle of nowhere, Marshal?"

Thornapple nodded his thanks for the coffee. "Well, I'm trailing some men."

Luke wasn't surprised by the answer.

"Cooter, Ben, and Carl Gammon. Reckon you've probably heard of them," the marshal added.

"I sure have." Marcy went back and sat down next to Luke.

"Or rather, I should say I *was* trailing them," Thornapple went on. "Came across a wolf pack about a mile east of here, having themselves a feast in a dry wash. There wasn't much left of the fellas they'd been after, but I'm pretty sure one of them was Cooter Gammon. He had a streak of white in his hair hard to miss. Since there were two men about the same size with him, I feel confident my boss can close the books on the Gammon brothers."

"Bad luck for them, being caught by a pack of wolves like that," Luke commented.

Thornapple took a sip of his coffee and nodded. "Especially when those wolves were carrying guns," he said with a shrewd smile.

The two cowboys couldn't stop themselves from flinching guiltily. Luke's face was like stone, though. "What do you mean by that?"

"I mean one of those skulls had a bullet hole smack-dab in the middle of its face. Somebody shot that Gammon brother before the wolves got at him. A well-deserved fate, I might add." Thornapple took another sip of coffee. "You folks have anything you want to tell me? Bear in mind I'm a federal lawman who doesn't cotton to being lied to."

"Mr. Smith didn't have any choice!" one of the punchers burst out. "He didn't have any choice at all. Those Gammons were worse 'n hydrophobia skunks. They were gonna kill us all!"

As soon as the words stopped tumbling out of the youngster's mouth, he turned a stricken face to Luke. "I'm sorry, Mr. Smith. I shouldn't 've said nothin'—"

Luke lifted a hand to stop the apology. "That's all right. I have a feeling Marshal Thornapple already had a pretty good idea what happened. He strikes me as a man who's been to see the elephant."

"There and back again," Thornapple agreed with a smile. "You killed all three of them, Mr. Smith?"

"Two of them, anyway, and I contributed to the third."

"I cut his throat," Marcy put in. "He probably would have died anyway, but I didn't see any harm in hurrying him along to hell."

"Nor would I, ma'am," Thornapple said. "In that case, I suppose the two of you will have to come to some sort of equitable arrangement concerning the division of the reward money."

"Reward money!"

"That's right, ma'am. Each of the Gammons had a thousand dollar bounty on his head."

Marcy leaned back in her chair, her eyes wide with amazement. "Three thousand dollars!"

"That's right. Come with me to Wichita, and I'll authorize payment. You can collect from the bank there."

Marcy looked over at Luke. "My God, we're rich! I never saw three thousand dollars in my life!"

Luke hesitated to say anything. He didn't fully trust Thornapple. Maybe the lawman was trying to trick him into going along to Wichita, where he would promptly place him under arrest.

Giving it more thought, that didn't seem likely. Luke could tell by looking at Thornapple the badge-toter had plenty of bark on him. If Thornapple wanted to make an arrest, he'd just do it instead of trying some fancy trick.

More than likely, Thornapple had never seen any of the wanted posters charging Luke with murder that had circulated back in Georgia.

"There's just one thing," Luke said slowly. "I'm not a bounty hunter."

"You killed three men with a price on their heads," Thornapple offered. "It's not like you have to file papers ahead of time or anything. That money is yours by rights, Mr. Smith."

Marcy looked even more excited. "We've got to do it, Luke. We've got to claim that reward."

He understood then how much it meant to her. She had spent her life struggling just to get by, enduring hardship and degradation. The tough times were starting to take a real toll on her.

Yet there was still a spark of dignity inside her, and a sense of determination that might allow her to make something better of her life if she just got the chance. The bounty money could give her that chance.

"All right," Luke finally agreed. "We'll go to Wichita with the marshal."

She threw her arms around his neck. "Thank you, Luke! You don't know what this means to me."

It meant he had inadvertently done something good for somebody. That wasn't enough to make up for past failures . . . but it was a start.

Thornapple nodded toward the holstered Remingtons and coiled shell belt still laying on the table where Luke and Marcy sat. "Nice looking guns. Whose are they?"

"They're mine." Luke reached out and pulled a gun out of the holster. *One more bit of bounty for killing the Gammon brothers,* he thought.

*   *   *

They split the reward money down the middle, fifteen hundred apiece. Marcy didn't think that was fair. She wanted to take five hundred for her part and give the rest to Luke, but he refused and insisted she take half.

They set aside an equal amount from each share, and got a room in the finest hotel in Wichita. For a week they ate in the best restaurants the town had to offer, drank champagne they had sent up from one of the saloons, and spent long hours together in bed.

After that week, pleasant though it was, Luke was so restless he couldn't stand it anymore.

He left the room early one morning while Marcy was still sleeping and walked to the livery stable where he was keeping his horses. He had just thrown his saddle on one of the animals when a voice asked, "Going somewhere, Mr. Smith?"

Luke looked around to see Marshal Jasper Thornapple standing in the open double doors of the livery barn with his shoulder propped casually against one of the jambs.

"Thought I might take a ride," Luke answered, assuming as casual an attitude as Thornapple.

"Did you tell the young lady good-bye?"

"Who said I wasn't coming back?"

Thornapple chuckled. "I've seen plenty of fiddlefoots in my time, Smith. Hell, I've been one. I know the look of a man who feels the call of distant trails."

Luke shrugged. "Marcy and I aren't really the sort for sentimental farewells."

"I have a hunch you might be wrong about how she feels . . . but it's none of my business, is it?"

"No, it's not."

"That's right, my business is hunting down lawbreakers. That line of work has given me a healthy curiosity about the people I meet."

Luke turned a little so he could move faster if he needed to reach for the Remingtons. He had started wearing the cross-draw rig, and wished he'd had more time to practice getting those irons out in a hurry. "Out here on the frontier, curiosity's generally considered to be not that healthy," he commented.

"Maybe not, but it's my job. So I sent some wires and did some checking. I wasn't surprised to find out that Luke Smith is a pretty common name."

"Lots of Smiths around," Luke said, his voice tight.

"The only one I came across that might be of some interest to a man like me was from Georgia. He was wanted for killing a land speculator and some hired guns about five years ago. *Was* wanted, Smith. That's important. The charges were dropped last year."

Luke's heart suddenly slugged hard in his chest. He wanted to believe what Thornapple was telling him, but it didn't seem possible it could be true. He managed to ask, "Why would they drop the charges in a case like that?"

"Because once the Reconstruction government was forced to let go of some of its power, the facts of the case came out. Turns out the land speculator was nothing but a carpetbagging thief, and evidence indicated he'd had men killed in order to grab their land. That particular Luke Smith can go back to Georgia without having to worry about the law anymore."

Luke drew in a deep breath. "That's a lucky break . . . for him."

The excitement he'd felt for a second had vanished. There was nothing waiting for him back in Georgia. Emily was probably married to Jess Franklin and raising a couple kids. Even if she wasn't, she wouldn't want to see him again. Not after he'd ridden off that night and never come back.

"I just thought you might be interested in hearing about that before you rode off," Thornapple went on. "Which way do you plan to head? West . . . or east?"

"I set out to go to Denver a while back," Luke said. "I suppose I still will."

Thornapple straightened and nodded. "Have a safe journey, then." He turned to head out of the livery.

Something occurred to Luke. "Marshal."

Thornapple stopped and turned back to Luke. "Yes?"

"Can I ask you if you've heard of some other men? While in your line of work, I mean."

Thornapple's brawny shoulders rose and fell. "Sure, go ahead."

"Wiley Potter. Keith Stratton. Josh Richards. Ted Casey."

For a long moment, Thornapple frowned in thought. Then he shook his head. "None of those names ring a bell, Smith. Should they?"

"I don't know. Thought it was possible."

"Well, I haven't heard of them. Sorry."

"That's all right. I'll catch up to them one of these days."

Thornapple lingered. "What do you plan to do with yourself?"

Luke thought about it for a second, then grunted. "Seems like there's good money in bounty hunting."

"Well . . . there's money in it. Some wouldn't call it good. Some folks call it blood money. And going after it is a good way to get yourself killed." Thornapple shrugged again. "But you saw that for yourself. Not every owlhoot has a price on his head as big as the bounties on the Gammon brothers. But some are even bigger."

"That's what I thought." Luke tightened the cinch on his saddle. "I'll be seeing you, Marshal."

"I wouldn't be a bit surprised," Thornapple said.

Luke didn't wave or even look back as he rode out of Wichita. He hoped Marcy was still asleep, snug and warm in that hotel room bed, dreaming of the new life she could make for herself with her share of the money. He hoped that when she woke up and found him gone, she wouldn't hate him.

But either way, he was going.

CHAPTER 27

Blood money, Thornapple had called it, and that turned out to be true.

As the years passed, Luke Smith saw a veritable lake of blood.

From the Rio Grande to the Canadian border, from New Orleans and the Mississippi River delta to San Francisco, Luke roamed, always on the trail of men with a price on their heads. Whether the bounty was big or small didn't really matter. Kill enough penny-ante owlhoots, as long as somebody was willing to pay for the carcasses, and the money added up.

Sometimes there were big kills, too, high-dollar rewards netting Luke enough cash that he wouldn't have to track down any more outlaws for a while if he didn't want to.

But what else was he going to do?

The face looking out at him from the mirror when he shaved became craggier, more weathered. The ordeal he had suffered at the end of the Civil War made him look older than his years, and the life he lived after that certainly didn't make him appear any younger. Those deep-set eyes had seen too much death and suffering to ever be innocent again.

His only consolation was the men he killed had it coming. They were robbers, rapists, arsonists, murderers.

He wasn't arrogant enough to consider himself some sort of avenging angel delivering justice. If he was working for any higher power, it was Lucifer, reaping more souls to be plunged, screaming, into the depths of Hades.

Luckily, there were a few moments of humanity here and there, or he might have gone insane.

Deadwood, 1877

The gold rush that had caused the town to spring into existence a year earlier had dwindled away as mining syndicates and corporations moved in and, for the most part, replaced the individual prospectors who had sunk shafts in the sides of the gulches all around the settlement. It still had its rough edges, though, and enough vice to attract men from all over, including those on the run from the law.

Luke rode in on the trail of a man named Robert Fescoe, who had killed a bank teller during a robbery down in Yankton. Fescoe was reported to be heading west , and Luke hoped the fugitive paused long enough in Deadwood to get drunk and find himself a whore.

Those two things didn't sound that bad to Luke, either, although he wasn't one to indulge his baser appetites indiscriminately. However, a man couldn't just sit and read during all his spare time.

He stopped at a livery stable, and as he turned his horse over to the hostler, he asked, "Have you seen a tall, skinny fellow with a half-moon-shaped scar on his chin?" Luke was grateful for the outlaw's scar because it made him easy to describe.

The hostler frowned in thought and shook his head. "Can't say as I have, mister."

"He would have ridden in within the last day or two," Luke added.

"Nope. Sorry."

"Is this the only livery stable in town?"

The hostler chuckled. "I wish it was. I'd make a lot more

money that way. No, there are three or four more. Maybe the hombre you're lookin' for left his hoss at one of them."

"Maybe so." Luke flipped a five-dollar gold piece to the man, who caught it deftly. "That ought to cover my bill for a while . . . and buy your discretion if you happen to see the man I'm looking for."

"If you mean I won't say nothin' to him about you lookin' for him, you're danged right about that. I'll even come see if I can find you."

"I'd be much obliged," Luke told him. "Meanwhile, what's the best place in town to get a drink?"

The hostler scratched his beard-stubbled jaw. "Well, there's the Bella Union. It's pretty nice. Or the Gem, which ain't as nice, but their whiskey is good and they got some fine whores. Folks tend to get shot there from time to time, though."

"An all-too-common occurrence."

"Or there's a new place you could try. It's called the Buffalo Butt."

Luke had to laugh. "What a name for a saloon!"

"Yeah, I don't know why the gal who owns it decided to call it that. *She* don't look like a buffalo's hind end, I can tell you that for dang sure. She's one of the prettiest gals in Deadwood, I'd say."

"Well, that certainly sounds intriguing. I'll give it a try." Luke lifted a hand in farewell and left the livery stable.

It didn't take him long to find the Buffalo Butt Saloon. Despite the crude name, it appeared to be a well-furnished and successful establishment, sitting at an intersection with its bat-winged entrance right at the corner so it was easily visible from both streets.

Luke pushed the batwings aside and stepped in with his usual caution. A man in his line of work never knew when he might run into an old enemy, although most of the men Luke tried to take into custody put up a fight and wound up dead.

A long mahogany bar ran down the left side of the room,

with gambling layouts to the right and tables in between. At the far end of the room was an open area where people could dance and a small stage for performers, which was empty at the moment. Men sat at about half the tables, drinking, and the bar was pretty busy, too, although there were plenty of open spots. A couple poker games were going on, and the click and clatter of a roulette wheel mixed with the sounds of talk and laughter. Luke liked the looks of the Buffalo Butt, inelegant moniker and all.

A staircase next to the stage led up to the second floor. If the place was like most saloons, the girls who worked downstairs delivering drinks also worked upstairs delivering something else. Luke glanced at the women moving around the room. Unlike some saloon girls, they were fully dressed in nice gowns cut low enough to reveal the swells of their breasts. Luke might have tried to single out one of them for his attentions later, but a man at a nearby table tilted his head back to look up and said, "Lord have mercy, who's that?"

Luke instinctively followed the direction of the man's gaze. His breath caught in his throat and he stiffened as he saw a woman standing at the railing on the second floor balcony, looking down at the room. She wore a dark red dress tight enough to reveal her splendid figure, and a thick mass of curly blond hair spilled around her shoulders.

Luke knew her instantly. Marcy hadn't changed much in the seven years since he'd ridden away from Wichita, leaving her in that hotel room.

He saw her suddenly clutch the railing and knew she had recognized him, too. He started toward the stairs, weaving among the tables, as she came along the balcony. He went up the stairs as she came down, and they met halfway, embracing with a desperate urgency as their mouths met.

"Aw, hell!" That disappointed exclamation came from the man who Luke had heard speak when he entered the saloon. "Looks like she's already took."

Luke and Marcy kissed for a long moment, and Luke felt the dull emotional pain that dogged his steps flow out of him. The unexpected reunion was like being plunged into a clean, icy mountain stream.

Then Marcy pulled back a little, lifted her hand, and pressed the barrel of a derringer against the side of his head. "Damn you, Luke Smith. I ought to put a bullet in your brain."

Most of the time, if somebody pointed a gun at him, he reacted violently. He suppressed that urge and smiled instead. "You'd probably be justified. I knew you'd be upset that I left you in Wichita. On the other hand, you appear to be doing well for yourself."

He remembered what the liveryman had said about the owner of the Buffalo Butt being one of the prettiest women in Deadwood. Wherever Marcy was, she would fall into the category. "This is your saloon, isn't it?"

"What if it is?"

"You wouldn't be the owner of a successful business if you hadn't gotten a start from your half of that reward money, would you?"

She let out a snort. "That shows what you know. I used that money to buy an interest in a whorehouse in Wichita. Then it burned down and I lost everything. I had to start over. But by then I'd learned I was pretty good at running things. It took me a while, but I'm doing all right again."

"I'm glad to hear it," Luke said. "Now, if you're not going to pull the trigger on that popgun, I'd appreciate it if you took it away from my head. It might go off by accident."

"I don't do *anything* by accident."

As Marcy lowered the derringer and let its hammer down carefully, Luke became aware the saloon had gone deathly quiet. He supposed someone had noticed her holding a gun to his head and pointed it out, and as the news spread, everyone stopped what they were doing to watch.

Marcy kissed Luke again, and someone let out a cheer, breaking the silence. Customers returned to their drinking and gambling, filling the saloon with noise once more.

Marcy took Luke by the hand and led him upstairs so they could get reacquainted properly.

* * *

That evening, Luke sat with Marcy at her private table in the rear corner of the saloon's main room. One of her bartenders had brought supper over from the dining room of the Grand Central Hotel. It was the best food in the Black Hills, she had explained, and Luke had to admit she was probably right. The roast beef was as good as any he'd had in a long time.

As they ate, washing down the food with sips of fine wine, they talked about everything that had happened since they'd seen each other last.

"I don't have much to tell," Luke told her. "I'm a bounty hunter, have been ever since that run-in with the Gammon brothers."

"I know. I've heard talk about you from time to time. You have quite a reputation." Marcy smiled. "Did you know I named this place after the Gammons?"

"I wondered how come you called it the Buffalo Butt."

"In those buffalo coats, they were as ugly and smelly as buffalo rumps."

"I can't disagree with that," Luke said.

"Even though I didn't want to admit it to you this afternoon, I reckon that was when my life started to change for the better. So I felt like I ought to commemorate the occasion."

Luke thought about it and decided the name was appropriate after all. He lifted his wineglass. "To the good that can come from ugly, inelegant things."

"I'll drink to that." Marcy clinked her glass against his, and he thought her eyes had a meaningful, mischievous twinkle in them as she looked at him.

He *was* ugly and inelegant, he thought. He had so much blood on his hands he could never wash it off, even if he tried.

But he had done some good in his life, too. He had saved Emily and her grandfather from Vincent Wolford. If the carpetbagger had lived, he wouldn't have stopped going after them until he got what he wanted.

And Luke had helped Marcy escape a life that would have eventually killed her if she hadn't gotten out of it. Some people might consider owning a saloon in a frontier town like Deadwood to be pretty disreputable, but those folks just didn't know how low people really could sink. Marcy was better off. He was sure of it.

"What are you going to do now?" she asked.

"I thought I'd have another glass of this surprisingly good wine," he replied with a smile.

"No, I mean with your life. Blast it, Luke, you know that."

He poured the wine and set the bottle aside. "I'll keep doing what I've been doing. I don't see any reason to change now. I'm not sure I *could* change, even if I wanted to."

"I did," Marcy said.

"You wanted to."

"Wouldn't you like to have a normal life? Maybe a business? Like . . . half interest in a saloon?"

He saw the hope in her eyes and knew it would be kinder to dash it right away, rather than letting it linger and grow. He shook his head. "I'm not going to settle down. I can't. Now that I know you're here, I might try to drift this way more often—"

"Don't put yourself out on my account." Her expression turned cold, like a blue norther blowing down across the plains.

"You don't understand. I can't be who you want me to be, Marcy, but knowing that I have a friend somewhere . . . well, it might make those cold nights out on the prairie a little easier to bear."

She wasn't going to give in easily. "I'll think about it." Her voice and body remained stiff with disappointment and anger.

Luke lifted his glass to her. "That's all I can ask."

* * *

She came to him that night seemingly as passionate as ever, but he sensed she was holding something back. His declaration that he would be riding on had changed whatever had been between them.

And how could it fail to do so? he asked himself, regretting it had happened.

Later, as Luke was dozing off with Marcy's head pillowed on his shoulder, he heard her whisper, "If you run out on me in the morning without saying good-bye again, I'll hunt you down and kill you."

He laughed softly and promised, "I'll be here."

He was sound asleep when his instincts took over and warned him. Maybe it was the faint creak of a floorboard, but whatever the reason, his eyes snapped open and caught a flicker of movement in the shadows of the room.

Reacting with the speed that had saved his life many times, Luke shoved a startled Marcy out of bed and rolled the other way. With a boom like a crash of thunder, a shotgun went off, twin gouts of flame erupting from its barrels.

Luke snatched up the Remington he had left lying on a chair right beside the bed and thumbed two shots just above the muzzle flash from the scattergun. Momentarily deaf from the shotgun's roar, he couldn't hear if his target cried out or dropped the weapon.

Keeping himself low to the ground, he crept forward. After only a couple steps, Luke tripped on something and stumbled. He put his left hand out to catch himself and it landed on something hot and sticky. He pulled it back and lashed out with the revolver, thudding against something soft.

"Get a light on," Luke told Marcy, hoping none of the buckshot had winged her.

A lucifer flared to life. He squinted against the glare, his eyes adjusting as she lit a lamp on the table beside the bed. Light filled the room and revealed Luke kneeling beside a gaunt man with a scar shaped like a half-moon on his chin.

The would-be killer's chest was a bloody mess from the two slugs that had torn through it.

"Who is he?" Marcy asked. "Do you know him?"

Luke heard the question, indicating his hearing had come back. He shook his head. "We never met, but I know who he is. His name's Fescoe. I've been on his trail for a while. Somebody must have told him I was in town looking for him, so he asked around until he figured out where he could find me. Thought he'd get me off his trail permanently."

Luke was going to have a talk with that liveryman, who had obviously double-crossed him.

Marcy put her hands on her hips. "My bed's ruined from that shotgun blast, and he's getting blood on the rug, too."

Luke stood up. "I'll send you money for the damages once I've gotten the reward. I'll have to ride back down to Yankton to collect."

"But you won't be coming back?"

"Not for a while. Not after this."

"I've seen men die before, you know. I've even had them try to kill me."

"Death doesn't follow you around, though. Not like it does with me."

Marcy sighed as one of the bartenders pounded on the door and called out to see if she was all right.

"I can't decide if you're the best man I know, Luke Smith, or just a sorry SOB."

Luke walked to the chair by the side of the bed and slipped the Remington back into the holster. "It's a good question. I don't know the answer myself."

CHAPTER 28

Even though his visit to Deadwood had a more bitter-sweet ending than he would have preferred, Luke took some good memories away from there. He knew Marcy was not only still alive but thriving, and that eased one of the worries he had carried around with him for years. He made himself a promise to drift up to the Black Hills every now and then to visit her and hoped the next time they met, she would still be glad to see him.

The next year, in the summer of 1878, he was in Santa Fe when he saw another familiar face across a crowded cantina. He picked up his mug of beer and made his way across the room until he reached the table where a thick-bodied man with graying fair hair and beard sat nursing a glass of tequila.

"Hello, Marshal," Luke said to Jasper Thornapple.

The two of them had crossed trails several times over the years. Luke had turned over to Thornapple a few fugitives he'd captured and sometimes it was sheer coincidence how they met. The frontier, for all its vastness, could sometimes seem like a small place.

The lawman looked up with a pleased smile. "Luke! I

was hoping I'd run into you again one of these days. I've got some news for you." Thornapple gestured for Luke to have a seat at the table. "Heard about it from another deputy marshal."

Luke settled down into the chair. "What kind of news?"

"Remember a long time ago, the first time we met up in Kansas, you asked me about four men?"

Luke stiffened. "You mean Potter, Stratton, Richards, and Casey?"

"Those are the ones. You never found them, did you?"

Luke frowned but didn't say anything. His mind was too full of bitter memories. He had looked for the four men who had betrayed him, betrayed their country, murdered his friends, nearly killed him, and stolen the gold. As much as he roamed, as many people as he met during his travels, he had thought it was inevitable that he would pick up their trail.

But instead he had run into stone wall after stone wall. Nobody knew the men he was looking for. Maybe they were all dead already, he often told himself, but never really believed that. It was as if fate had conspired with those four no-good deserters to keep them safe from his vengeance.

Finally, in a quiet voice, he told Thornapple, "No, I never found them. To tell you the truth, after a while I quit looking so hard." He looked at the marshal, his pulse quickening. "Do you know where they are?"

"I do," Thornapple said, then dashed Luke's hopes. "They're in the ground. They're all dead, Luke."

A strange feeling washed through Luke. It wasn't disappointment, really, or even relief, but rather an odd, hollow mixture of the two. He wanted them dead, but he took no real satisfaction from knowing that they were.

"What happened to them?" he asked Thornapple, although he didn't really care.

"They were killed up in Idaho Territory a while back, at a settlement called Bury. The name turned out to be fitting. They started the town and ran everything in the area. Ran roughshod over everybody in those parts, too. A gunfighter calling himself Buck West rode in and raised hell. Wound up killing all of them. Turns out that wasn't really West's name at all. He was really a fella named Smoke Jensen."

The surprise Luke had felt at hearing his enemies were dead was nothing compared to the shock that went through him upon hearing his family name. It had been so long since he'd used the name Jensen it seemed like he had always been Luke Smith.

Despite that, he had never forgotten his family. Sometimes it was hard to remember what his ma and pa had looked like. They might both be dead. Probably were. And Janey and Kirby would be grown. He might pass them on the street and never know them.

But who in blazes was Smoke Jensen?

Luke shook his head. "I haven't heard of him."

"No reason you would have," Thornapple said. "There were wanted posters out on him for a while, especially while he was calling himself Buck West, but from what I hear there are no charges against him now."

"Did you ever see him?"

Thornapple shook his head. "Nope. Supposed to be a big, sandy-haired fella who's really fast with his guns. He'd have to be, because from what I've heard, not only did he kill those men you were looking for, but he and some old mountain man friends of his wiped out a small army of hired killers who worked for Potter and the others, too. It was a full-fledged war up there."

Kirby had ash-blond hair, Luke recalled. If he'd grown big enough, he might fit the description of Smoke Jensen. But why in the world would he have taken that name?

Why not? That wry thought crossed Luke's mind. I *took a different name, and for a good reason, didn't I? Maybe Kirby did, too.*

"You know where he is now?"

"Jensen?" Thornapple shook his head. "No idea. The way I heard it, he rode away from Bury with some good-looking gal he met up there, and they never came back. Do you want to find him?"

"I thought I might look him up. Thank him for doing my job for me."

"I had a feeling you had a score to settle with those hombres you asked about," Thornapple said. "Well, it's done, so you can forget about it now."

"I suppose so." Luke drank down the rest of his beer and set the empty mug on the table. Inside he felt as empty as that mug.

He continued to ride, drifting from one place to another. Over time that feeling faded. Glad Potter and the others were dead, Luke would have liked to have been the one to pull the trigger and send them to hell, but nobody ever said life was fair. Justice had caught up to them, and he had to be satisfied with that. He had other killers to hunt down and bring in. But as he went about it, he kept his ears open and learned everything he could about the man called Smoke Jensen.

Smoke was said to be fast with a gun, mighty fast. Maybe the slickest on the draw in the entire West. Luke heard stories about some of the battles Smoke had had with a wide assortment of outlaws and cold-blooded killers, and Smoke always emerged triumphant.

But those who had met him, without fail, said Smoke Jensen was no arrogant, vicious gunman, but rather a stalwart friend, a decent man, and a loving husband to his wife Sally. They had a successful ranch somewhere in Colorado called Sugarloaf, and judging by all the stories Luke heard about the man, Smoke wanted to live a peaceful life and never went out looking for trouble.

He sure didn't back down from it, though, and just about the worst mistake anybody could ever make was to threaten one of Smoke's friends or relatives. That was a mighty quick way to wind up dead.

Yes, Smoke Jensen sounded like the sort of man Luke would be proud to know, but despite what he had told Thornapple, he never made any attempt to find Jensen. Maybe the famous gunfighter really was his little brother Kirby, or maybe he wasn't, but either way, he figured Smoke wouldn't want a bloody-handed bounty hunter showing up on his doorstep claiming to be kinfolk. Luke felt sure if any of his family had even thought about him during the long years since the end of the Civil War, they must have assumed he was dead.

Because of that, whenever Luke was in Colorado, he was always careful to steer well clear of the Sugarloaf Ranch and the nearby town of Big Rock, the same way that he had never returned to the Ozarks of southwestern Missouri. It was entirely possible there weren't any Jensens left back there, but he didn't want to take that chance.

It was better for Luke Jensen to just stay dead.

He was in northern New Mexico Territory, in the town of Raton, with the Sangre de Cristo Mountains and Raton Pass looming to the north, when he heard a rumor that Solomon Burke and his gang had been spotted in the area.

Luke had been trailing Burke for a couple weeks, so he took a keen interest in what he heard and finally located the old-timer who was the source of the rumor. He bought the man a drink in the High Hat Saloon and asked him about Burke.

The garrulous old man was glad to talk. "I seen 'em while I was out huntin' one day. I got me some diggin's up there, so I keep a pretty close eye on all the comin's and goin's thereabouts."

Luke didn't figure the old-timer's mining claim amounted to much, but that wouldn't stop him from being fiercely protective of it.

"I heard riders comin' and took cover in some trees," the wizened, bearded oldster continued. "Seen 'em ride right past me, no more 'n fifty yards away. I seen ree-ward dodgers on Burke with his picture on 'em before, so I recognized him right away. Had a couple o' big Mexicans with him, so I figured they had to be Hernandez and Cardona. I've heard mighty bad stories about them two. Don't know who all the other hombres were, but they was prob'ly Burke's regular bunch of owlhoots."

Luke didn't doubt that. "Could you tell where they were going?"

The old prospector hesitated, licking his lips, and Luke signaled for the bartender to bring another round. That got the old-timer talking again.

"I don't know for sure, no, but they rode on outta the valley where my diggin's are and over the pass into the next valley. They's an old abandoned cabin over there they could be usin' as a hideout, right on the banks of Bluejay Creek. I can tell you how to get there"—a shrewd look appeared on the man's whiskery face—"And I will, if you swear to give me a cut of the bounty you collect on 'em."

"How do you know I'm a bounty hunter?" Luke wanted to know.

"Well, you don't really look like a star packer, and I can't think of nobody else who'd be trailin' a bunch of hydropho-bia skunks like Solomon Burke and his gang. Gimme your word you'll cut me in?"

Luke nodded his agreement and then added, "If I come back alive, that is."

"Yeah, it's kind of a sucker bet on my part, ain't it? But here's how to get to that cabin . . ."

Luke had followed the old-timer's directions. The valley was a two-day ride from Raton. He thought he was still in New Mexico Territory, but up in the high country it was difficult to be sure. He might have crossed over into Colorado without realizing it.

Colorado . . . the place where Smoke Jensen lived. It wouldn't take but a few days to reach Big Rock, Luke mused as he trailed the Burke gang. He might be able to get a look at Smoke without having to introduce himself. Would he recognize his own brother, if that's who Smoke turned out to be?

That question still lurked in the back of Luke's mind as he dismounted and crept forward through some trees to spy on the old cabin where he thought the outlaws might be hiding.

Then bad luck cropped up again, as José Cardona, out hunting or taking a leak or just looking around, stumbled on him, tackled him, and tried to kill him. Nothing could ever just be easy. Not for Luke Smith.

He'd wiped out the gang, but he'd taken three bullets in return. His efforts to patch himself up hadn't done much good. He wound up passing out and crashing to the floor in the cabin.

Just like fifteen years earlier, when he'd been left for dead on the banks of a shallow river in Georgia, as blackness claimed Luke he was sure he would never wake up again, that it was the end.

BOOK FOUR

CHAPTER 29

Luke winced a little as light struck his eyelids. He turned his head away and felt something soft and smooth against his cheek. *A pillow? Light?*

He was alive. Like the other times over the years when he had come awake after being convinced he was going to die, he struggled to grasp the concept that he wasn't dead after all. Once again, his stubbornness had somehow kept him breathing . . . although he was sure he'd had help, too. Someone had found him in that cabin after he'd passed out from losing so much blood.

Wondering where he was and how much time had passed, he tried to open his eyes, but the light was too bright. *Sunlight,* he thought, but it didn't seem like he was outside. He didn't feel any wind. Moving his hands, he felt crisp fabric. He was lying on a mattress covered with clean sheets. So . . . he was in a bed, inside a house somewhere, and the sun was shining on him through a window.

Keeping his eyes closed, he turned his head back and heard a sweet sound that puzzled him. It reminded him of the music of a mountain stream.

It was music, all right, he realized. What he heard was a woman humming softly to herself.

His tongue felt twice as big as it should have as he licked

his dry, rough lips. He had to swallow a couple times before his throat loosened enough for him to speak. All he could manage was to rasp, "H-hello . . . ?"

"Oh, my!" the woman exclaimed.

Luke heard the rapid patter of her footsteps as she crossed the room. The mattress shifted a little, and he figured she had rested a hand there as she leaned over him. Even through his closed eyes he felt the light change as she came between him and the light, so he tried opening them again.

For the second time in his life, he found himself looking up at what seemed to be an angel. This woman was older than Emily Peabody had been, but she had the same sweet, dark-haired beauty.

She smiled. "You're all right. You've been wounded, but you're going to be just fine. You're among friends."

"F-friends?" Luke repeated, his voice weak. "I don't . . . have any friends."

That wasn't strictly true. He considered Jasper Thornapple to be a friend, and Marcy, too, of course. But Thornapple was nowhere around, as far as Luke knew, and he was a long way from Deadwood.

"You're wrong," the woman told him, still smiling. "Anybody who's in trouble has friends here." She straightened. "You just lie there and rest. I'll go tell Smoke you're awake."

Once again Luke felt a shock go through him. As the woman turned away she moved out of the sunlight, causing him to flinch as the brilliant rays fell on him again. But he was able to say, "Wait . . . Did you say . . . Smoke?"

She paused, still smiling down at him, although it was hard for him to see her with the light filling his eyes.

"That's right. Smoke Jensen. He's my husband. I'm Sally Jensen. You're on the Sugarloaf Ranch, near Big Rock, Colorado."

That was loco, Luke thought. Smoke Jensen's place was

days away from where he'd fought that battle with Solomon Burke and the rest of those outlaws. How in the world had he gotten to the Sugarloaf?

Someone had brought him, of course, he realized as he forced his brain to work and struggled to put his thoughts in order. But why had they brought him to the ranch of a man who might well be one of his relatives? How had they known?

"I'll be right back." Sally hurried out of the room, leaving a very confused Luke lying there.

He continued wrestling with his thoughts. He must have been unconscious for days since he was far north of where he'd been the last time he knew where he was.

Slowly, he became aware of something tight around his torso, and moved his hand to his chest. Someone had wrapped bandages around him. He moved his hand upward and discovered his shoulder was bandaged, too, and so was his arm. The wounds he'd received during the shootout had been tended to.

With a sigh, he tuned into his wounds. They ached, but not too bad. With the instincts of a man who lived somewhat like a wild animal, Luke knew he wasn't going to die from his injuries after all. For that, he could thank whoever had come along and found him in that old cabin.

Footsteps sounded in the hallway outside the room. Sally came back in, followed by a tall man with very broad shoulders. She stepped over and pulled the curtains over the window, shielding Luke's eyes from the bright light. "I'm sorry, I should have thought to close these before I left. The sun must be blinding you."

Luke was looking at the man who stood next to the bed, but cleared his throat and managed to squeak out a few words. "That's all right. The sun was warm. Felt good."

The man's face was too rugged to call handsome, although it was the sort of face women usually found attractive. The strong features were topped by close-cropped, ash-blond hair. In him, Luke saw both his mother and his father, the resemblance vivid enough to almost take his breath away.

He knew he was looking at his brother. He almost said Kirby's name, but stopped himself in time.

The man gave him a friendly smile. "Welcome to the Sugarloaf. Sally was afraid we were going to lose you, but I took one look at her and told her not to worry. I know a stubborn varmint when I see one."

"He ought to," Sally put in. "He sees one looking back at him from the mirror every morning."

The man chuckled. "I'm Smoke Jensen. This is my ranch."

"L-Luke. Luke Smith."

"Pleased to meet you. We'll shake and howdy later, when you're feeling better. Right now you need some rest, Mr. Smith. You lost a lot of blood. Stubborn or not, it's a miracle you survived the trip up here from the Sangre de Cristos."

"How . . . how did I . . ."

"How'd you get here?" Smoke asked. "An old prospector heard a bunch of shooting and decided to go investigate."

The old-timer had been trying to protect his potential payoff, Luke thought.

"He had a couple friends visiting him at the time," Smoke went on, "a pair of old mountain men. They all went looking and found you still alive in a cabin with a bunch of dead men outside. It must have been quite a battle."

Luke managed to nod slightly. "It was," he whispered.

"Anyway, you'd been shot up and were running a fever. You were out of your head and did a lot of ranting and raving while they were taking care of you. You mentioned my name several times, and those mountain men knew who I was. I have a lot of friends among those old-timers. They figured I might know you, and when they thought you were strong enough, they decided to bring you up here." Smoke paused and gave Luke an intent look. "*Do* we know each other, Mr. Smith?"

Luke forced himself to shake his head. "S-sorry. Never saw you before." Those words practically broke his heart. He knew he was looking at his own flesh and blood.

Nearly twenty years had passed since he'd seen his little brother, and he couldn't even acknowledge that. Kirby— Smoke—had built a fine life for himself. Why ruin that by admitting the shot-up stranger was really his disreputable, bounty-hunting failure of a brother?

Smoke frowned. "Then why were you talking about me while you were feverish?"

"Hell . . . I don't know. Like you said . . . I was out of my head. Maybe I heard somebody else talking about you . . . before I got shot. I know the name . . . You're some sort of . . . gunfighter."

"That's a reputation I never set out to get." Smoke's face settled into grim lines.

The moment passed quickly, and he smiled again. "Well, I suppose it doesn't really matter. What's important is that you're safe here, and your wounds are starting to heal. Now that you're awake again, you can concentrate on resting and getting better."

"Why would you . . . go to so much trouble for me?" Luke asked. "For a . . . stranger?"

Sally answered his question. "Nobody who needs help is a stranger on the Sugarloaf, Mr. Smith. That's just the way we are around here."

"I can't . . . pay you."

Smoke's face hardened again. "You don't know Sally and me, so we'll let that pass. Are you hungry?"

Luke suddenly realized he was ravenous. It had probably been quite a while since he'd had any solid food. "Yeah. I could . . . sure eat."

"I have a pot of stew on the stove downstairs," Sally said. "I'll bring some up to you, although it'll be mostly broth starting out."

"That sounds . . . mighty good, ma'am. I'm . . . obliged to you." Luke looked at Smoke. "And to you."

"*De nada*," Smoke said, then before he could go on, somebody knocked on the open door.

Luke cut his eyes in that direction and saw a tall, gangling cowboy standing in the doorway, holding a battered black hat in one hand.

Smoke looked toward the doorway and asked, "What is it, Pearlie?"

"Hate to bother you, Smoke, but Cal just rode in and told me somebody caved in a bunch of boulders on the Fortuna Ridge waterhole. Covered it up completely. We'll have to move the cows on that range, since they won't have any water."

"Could it have been a natural rockslide?" Smoke asked with a troubled frown.

"Didn't sound like it from what Cal said. He told me he rode up to the top of the ridge and found a place where a bunch of horses stopped this mornin'. He figured some of Baxter's men dabbed their loops on one of them boulders and used their horses to start it rollin'. That's all it would've took. But you can ride up there and take a look for yourself, if you want."

Smoke shook his head. "I trust Cal's opinion. He's a good hand, even if he is pretty young. But there's no way of knowing it was Baxter's men who ruined the waterhole."

"We don't know they were the hombres who took them potshots at us the other day, or ran off that jag of cattle, but who else could it be? You got any other enemies around here right now?"

"Simeon Baxter claims he just wants to be neighbors with us."

Pearlie let out a disgusted snort, then glanced at Sally. "Sorry for almost sayin' what I almost just said," he apologized.

"Don't worry about it," Sally told him with a smile. "I was probably thinking the same thing about Simeon Baxter. All I had to do was look at the man to know he can't be trusted . . . and I think you know that, too, Smoke. You just want to give him the benefit of the doubt."

"Yeah, well, that's starting to wear a little thin," Smoke admitted. "Pearlie, tell the boys to saddle up. We're going to take a ride over to the Baxter spread."

"Now you're talkin'," Pearlie said with undisguised enthusiasm. "I'll tell 'em to oil up their smoke poles, too."

"We're not going to ride in shooting."

"No, but we may have to ride out that way."

Smoke didn't dispute that speculation.

Luke saw the worried glance Sally directed in her husband's direction as Pearlie hurried away down the corridor.

"Is this going to turn into another range war, Smoke?" she asked.

"I hope not. I've had my fill of those, and I know you have, too. But I'm not going to let Simeon Baxter bull his way in and take over. You know me better than that."

"Yes. I do."

"And you wouldn't want me to be like that, anyway." Smoke went to her and kissed the thick dark hair on top of her head.

"No, I don't suppose I would," she agreed. "But I wish you'd be careful, anyway."

"Always," Smoke said with a grin. He hugged her and then hurried out after Pearlie.

"Sounds like . . . you folks have some trouble around here," Luke acknowledged.

"It's nothing for you to worry about, Mr. Smith," she assured him. "Just some range hog who moved in recently. He's got the loco idea in his head that he can bully Smoke Jensen."

"Sounds like . . . a pretty foolish thing to do."

"It is." Sally sighed. "I just hope this isn't the time Smoke's luck finally changes."

"It's not . . . luck." Luke knew it was the Jensen blood. The sheer determination to do the right thing and stand up for yourself. He had failed in that respect so long ago, and he'd been trying to make up for it ever since. He could take another step on the long road back . . . if he could strap on his guns and stand beside his brother as Smoke faced down this trouble.

But that wasn't possible, at least not at the moment. Luke had lost too much blood, been unconscious for too long, grown too weak. All he could do was lie there and regain his strength.

When he was stronger, he could offer to help Smoke with his troubles. He wouldn't have to reveal who he really was. He'd just be a grateful stranger returning a favor.

Time enough for that later. He could barely keep his eyes open.

Sally recognized his weariness. "I'll bring you some of that stew later, Mr. Smith. I think you need to rest a bit more before you eat."

"Maybe . . ." Luke murmured, trying to fight off the exhaustion threatening to wash over him. Realizing he couldn't, he gave in and let it claim him.

His last thought was that he wasn't passing out. It wasn't unconsciousness, it was good honest sleep. Healing sleep—just what he needed.

And when he woke up next time, he would be that much closer to being able to help his brother.

CHAPTER 30

The stew Sally Jensen brought up to him tasted as good as it smelled, Luke discovered after the delicious aroma roused him from his slumber. It seemed to possess some magical power, as well, he decided, because after one bowl of it, he felt strength coursing back into his body.

She sat in a chair beside his bed and fed him, and when the bowl was empty, Luke asked, "Did your husband get back from talking to that fellow Baxter?"

Sally had been smiling and cheerful when she came into the room, but a shadow passed over her face at his question. Luke didn't like that he had caused her distress, but he needed to know what was going on.

"They talked," Sally said. "Baxter denied having anything to do with the trouble we've been having. From the way Smoke sounded, it was pretty tense between them for a few minutes, but there was no shooting."

"That's good. Range wars usually don't work out well for either side."

"I know that. Sometimes you have to stand up and fight for what's yours, though. I know that, too."

Luke couldn't argue with her. Earlier, the exact same thought had crossed his mind. He said carefully, "I've heard stories about your husband, Mrs. Jensen. I would think a man would have to be pretty foolish to come in and try to hog Smoke Jensen's range."

"Some men are so arrogant they think they can have whatever they want," she replied with a shrug. "Baxter has plenty on his payroll who are fast with their guns. Smoke just has our ranch hands, although Pearlie had a reputation as a gunman, too, before he gave that up to be Sugarloaf's foreman."

"How did Smoke leave it with Baxter?"

"With a warning that nothing else had better happen."

Luke thought that was unlikely. He knew what Sally meant about the arrogance of some men driving them on, even when the smart thing to do would be to back off. He counted on the outlaws he hunted having the same attitude. They could usually be goaded into doing something stupid that would give him a chance to bring them down.

Sally changed the subject, saying she wanted to check the dressings on Luke's wounds. He let her do so, feeling a little bit embarrassed about having his sister-in-law poking around his body. She didn't know they were related, and he didn't tell her.

"Everything looks fine," she announced when she was finished. "Those old mountain men who found you probably had plenty of experience patching up bullet wounds. They took good care of you and put you on the road to recovery."

"How long do you think it'll be before I'm up and around?"

"Not long," she assured him. "It's mostly just a matter of getting your strength back." Sally hesitated. "I noticed a terrible scar on your back . . ."

"An old war wound," Luke said, trying not to sound too curt but making it clear he didn't want to talk about it.

"Smoke was too young for the war, but just barely. His father and brother fought in it, though."

Luke's interest quickened. "Did they make it through?"

"His father did . . . but he was killed not long afterward by some men responsible for the death of Smoke's brother

Luke during the war." She cocked her head to the side as she looked down at him. "You have the same name as him."

Luke suddenly worried that he had probed too much. "There are plenty of men around named Luke."

"Of course there are."

Even though he knew he probably shouldn't, he risked another question. "What happened to those men? The ones responsible for the deaths of Smoke's pa and brother?"

"Smoke found them."

The flat sound of Sally's answer told Luke all he needed to know. Jasper Thornapple's information had been correct. Smoke had settled that long-standing score.

Only it was worse than Luke had ever known. From what Sally had just said, Potter and the others were responsible for the death of his father as well. The confirmation that Emmett Jensen was dead, and had died violently at the hands of trash like that, was like a knife inside Luke for a second.

"Good riddance, I'd say," he forced out.

"Yes, indeed," Sally agreed. She brightened. "You get some more rest now. Let that stew do its work."

"I'll do that," Luke promised. He leaned his head back against the pillows and closed his eyes. He owed a debt to Smoke Jensen for killing those four no-good thieves. He would find a way to pay that debt, he promised himself.

Even if it had to be as Luke Smith.

A couple nights later, Smoke brought him a cup of coffee and a plate of bear sign. Luke was glad to see him. After being unconscious for so long, once he began to get his strength back he wasn't nearly as sleepy.

"Need me to break pieces off this and feed 'em to you?" Smoke asked as he settled down in the chair beside the bed.

"I think I can handle a pastry." Luke sat up, moved the pillows behind him, and then proved it by taking one of the doughnuts off the plate.

"You sound like a cultured man, Smith."

Luke managed not to laugh. "Far from it. I just have a taste for reading. I suppose I've picked up a few things from that. Most of my life has been spent about as far from what people would consider culture as you can imagine."

"I have some books downstairs. Would you like me to bring a few of them up here for you?"

"That would be very much appreciated," Luke said.

"In the meantime, you can tell me about all those dead men scattered around the place where my friends found you."

Luke smiled. "You've been wanting to ask me about that ever since I woke up, haven't you?"

"That old prospector said they were outlaws. Somebody named Solomon Burke and his gang. Supposed to be pretty bad hombres. Did you kill all of them by yourself?"

"Seemed like the thing to do, especially since they were trying to kill me at the time."

"If they were using that place for a hideout, that means they didn't ambush you. It was the other way around, wasn't it?"

"I was hunting them, yes," Luke admitted with a nod. "I was after the bounty on them." He had to laugh. "I'll bet that old pelican claimed it for himself, though."

"I wouldn't be surprised," Smoke said. "So you're a bounty hunter."

"That's right."

"There was a time I had a price on my head." Smoke shrugged. "But I suppose a fella's got to do whatever is necessary for him to get by."

"I don't blame you for not being fond of the idea of having a bounty hunter under your roof. For what it's worth, all the men I've gone after were bad sorts, the kind of men who really need to be behind bars or six feet under."

"As far as you know," Smoke said.

Luke inclined his head in acknowledgment of that point. "I believe I'm right, but no one knows everything about the other people in this world."

"That's true. For example, you strike me as the sort of man who has secrets of his own, Smith."

Luke didn't like the turn in the conversation. "You already know all that's worth knowing about me, Jensen."

It sounded odd to him, saying his own name like that.

"I'm not sure," Smoke said. "There's something about you . . . something I can't put my finger on. I feel like I ought to know you. Are you sure we've never met?"

"Positive." Luke hoped he kept the tension out of his voice. "I know who you are, but I never heard the name Smoke Jensen until a couple years ago." That was true, as far as it went.

Smoke made a face. "I never asked for a reputation as a gunfighter. I just wanted to be left alone. But then I found out some men had done my family wrong—skunks who had to be dealt with—and I set out to do it. I'd already met an old mountain man named Preacher. He taught me how to handle a gun. Taught me everything worth knowing that my pa hadn't already taught me. Along the way I got married to a fine woman, even had a son, but some other evil lowlifes took that family away from me. I met a young fella named Matt Cavanaugh and took him under my wing the way Preacher did with me. Matt's the same as my brother now, even goes by the name Matt Jensen. Then Sally came along—" Smoke stopped and shook his head.

"I don't know why I started going on about all of that. You're not interested in my checkered past, as they say in the dime novels. But it might be boring enough to help you sleep."

"I wasn't bored," Luke said honestly. In fact, he had a hard time keeping the emotion out of his voice. Hearing about his brother's life stirred up a lot of feelings inside him. He wished he had gone home after the war, that he had been at Kirby's side when trouble came to call. Things might have turned out completely different.

But he hadn't been able to return. He'd been a wanted

fugitive, and didn't know Kirby—Smoke—had gone through the same sort of ordeal for a while.

All that was behind them. Luke couldn't think of a single reason why he couldn't tell Smoke who he really was.

And suddenly that was exactly what he wanted to do. *I've been a damned fool all these years,* he told himself.

As soon as Thornapple told him the gunfighter named Smoke Jensen had killed Potter, Stratton, Richards, and Casey, Luke should have gone looking for him and found out the truth. That blasted prideful stubbornness of his had stolen two more years out of his life, two years he could have spent with his brother . . . or at least knowing he had a brother.

The coffee and the bear sign were forgotten. Luke wasn't sure exactly how he would go about it, but it was long past time for the truth to come out.

And it might have, if fate hadn't chosen that moment for the sudden, harsh sound of gunfire to fill the night.

CHAPTER 31

Smoke was on his feet instantly, blowing out the lamp on the bedside table and stepping to the window to flick back the curtain so he could look out without being silhouetted. "Masked raiders shooting up the place," he snapped, dropping the curtain.

Luke opened his mouth to say he wanted to help, but it was too late. Smoke was through the doorway and gone, leaving Luke sitting in the bed listening to the sounds of battle as gunmen attacked his brother's ranch.

Not while I can do anything about it, by God, Luke thought as resolve stiffened his muscles. Especially since his revolvers were within reach.

Earlier, he had asked Sally where his guns were. She'd tried to tell him not to worry about that, but he had persisted, learning his gun belt and the twin Remingtons were in a wardrobe at the side of the room, along with his clothes. His Winchester was downstairs.

He didn't think he could handle stairs, but he could get to his revolvers. He pushed the covers aside, swung his legs out of bed, and stood up.

A wave of dizziness swept through him. He fought it off as his eyes adjusted to the moonlight filtering through the curtains. Tightly bandaged as he was, he found he could move around without his wounds hurting too much. Wearing only those bandages and the bottom half of a pair of long underwear, he made his way to the wardrobe and opened it.

It had been too long, he thought as his hands closed around the smooth walnut grips of the guns. For a decade and a half, the weapons he carried had been the closest friends he had. That might not be true anymore—he had a brother again—but it still felt mighty good to heft the Remingtons as he turned around and walked back to the open window.

The night breezes were tainted with the acrid bite of powder smoke as Luke thrust the curtains aside and looked out. Riders with bandannas tied over their faces galloped through the open area between the ranch house and the bunkhouse. The guns in their hands spat flame and lead as they sent shots in both directions.

Return fire came from the Sugarloaf's defenders, but they were heavily outnumbered. Luke figured there were at least thirty raiders in the yard.

He could improve the odds a little, he thought as he thrust the right-hand Remington out the window, drew a bead on one of the riders, and fired. The masked man rocked back in his saddle and had to drop his gun and grab the saddle horn to keep from toppling off his mount.

One low-down sacker out of the fight, Luke told himself. He eared back the Remington's hammer and shifted his aim to another of the masked men.

He got off several rounds, dropping a couple more men, before the raiders noticed the shots coming from the second floor window of the ranch house. A few twisted in their saddles and flung their guns up to fire in that direction. Luke was forced to reel back from the window as glass shattered and bullets whipped through the opening.

He waited until the barrage stopped and then moved forward again, kneeling at the window so the wall gave him some cover. It looked thick enough to stop most bullets.

Still galloping back and forth, the raiders continued their

barrage, but the deadly accurate fire of the defenders was starting to take a toll. Luke added to it by triggering both revolvers and spraying bullets among the marauders. Gunthunder rolled from the Remingtons.

The masked killers finally had enough. The one who seemed to be in command wheeled his horse and yelled, "Let's get out of here!"

Those still mounted—some badly wounded—followed him as he galloped off into the darkness, leaving seven or eight bodies scattered on the ground.

Luke didn't stand up immediately. He didn't want to catch a final wild slug thrown through the shattered window.

Also, he was tired. When he was sure they were all gone, he placed his left-hand gun on the floor and used that hand to brace himself as he leaned forward and drew in several deep breaths. The bandages around his midsection prevented him from breathing too deeply, but he did the best he could.

The door opened behind him. Sally Jensen stood in the doorway, wearing a nightdress and a coat slung around her shoulders. "Mr. Smith! Are you all right?"

Luke looked back over his shoulder at her, noticing immediately the rifle in her hands. He figured she had been right in the middle of the fight downstairs. "I'm fine."

Feeling a little stronger, he picked up the gun and pushed himself to his feet.

"Smoke said he thought he heard shots coming from up here. You really shouldn't have gotten out of bed."

"After all you folks have done for me, I wasn't going to just lie there while you were under attack," Luke argued. "That's not the way I'm built."

Sally smiled. "I know. We haven't been acquainted for long, Mr. Smith, but you remind me a little of my husband. He can't turn his back on a fight, either."

It was the Jensen blood, Luke thought, but he couldn't say that. Instead he asked, "Was anybody hurt?"

Sally's smile was replaced by a look of grim anger. "We're fine in here, but Smoke's gone out to the bunkhouse to see about the men. I'm worried some of them were wounded."

Luke became uncomfortably aware that he was standing in his underwear with a pair of empty guns in his hands. He wasn't sure which of those things bothered him more. He didn't think the masked raiders would double back and launch another attack, but the possibility couldn't be ruled out entirely. First things first, he decided. "I'd better reload. Just in case."

"No, what you'd better do is get back in that bed and let me check your dressings. I want to make sure none of your wounds have broken open again."

Luke thought about it for a second, then chuckled. "I always try not to argue with a woman, especially one holding a loaded rifle."

"That's a good policy," Sally told him, smiling again.

He was back in bed and she had taken a look at his bandages, determining that none of the wounds were bleeding again by the time Smoke came into the room with a Colt in his hand. Sally turned toward him with a worried frown on her face.

"Two men were killed," Smoke reported. "Steve Rankin and Charlie Moss."

Sally cringed. "Oh, no. What about the wounded?"

"A bullet busted Phil Weston's arm. Other than that just some nicks and scratches." Smoke's face was set in hard, bleak lines. "But they killed two men who rode for me, and I'm not going to let Baxter get away with that."

"You don't know they were Baxter's men," Sally maintained.

"Yes, I do. I took a look at the bodies of the men they left behind. I remember seeing all of them at Baxter's place when I was over there a couple days ago."

"Then you can go tell Monte about it and let the law handle this," Sally suggested.

Smoke shook his head. "I'll send a rider to Big Rock to-morrow to tell Monte what happened, but Pearlie, the rest of the men, and I will be heading for Baxter's ranch."

Sally opened her mouth, and for a second Luke thought she was going to argue with her husband. But then she nod-ded. "You're right, Smoke. We need to stomp our own snakes."

Smoke grunted. "Damn right we do." His expression eased a little as he looked at Luke. "Are you all right, Smith?"

Luke nodded. "I'm fine."

"You were burning some powder up here, weren't you? I heard the shots."

Luke grinned. "Like I told your wife, I owe you folks too much to sit by and do nothing. If you'll let me borrow a horse, I'll ride over to Baxter's with you in the morning for the showdown."

"Oh, now, I don't think that would be a good idea at all," Sally protested. "You're not in good enough shape to ride yet, Mr. Smith."

"I agree with Sally," Smoke added. "But I appreciate the offer. I'm obliged to you for taking a hand tonight, too. You're probably responsible for some of those men we downed."

Luke knew he was, but didn't say anything. He'd never been one to boast.

Smoke went on. "You just keep recuperating. I'll handle Baxter."

Luke nodded. "All right." He looked at Sally. "I'd be obliged, though, if you'd bring my gun belt over here. I sure don't like having empty guns." He smiled. "Gives a man the fantods."

Pearlie, Calvin Woods, and the rest of the Sugarloaf hands were so upset about the deaths of their friends that they had wanted to charge over to Simeon Baxter's ranch right away and settle the score. But Smoke had decided to wait for daylight, thinking Baxter might have an ambush set up for them.

He mentioned that reasoning to Luke early the next morning, before dawn actually, when he stopped by Luke's room.

"That's good thinking," Luke agreed. "I've ridden into more ambushes than I should have, just because I was too eager or too careless. Gunfighting is almost as much about thinking as it is about shooting."

"You sound like a man speaking from bitter experience," Smoke commented.

"Is there any other kind?"

Smoke hefted the rifle he had carried into the room. "I brought your Winchester up. I don't expect you to need it, but I thought you might feel better having it close at hand."

Luke smiled. "Thanks. You'd better not put it on the bed, though. Mrs. Jensen wouldn't like it if you got gun oil on her sheets."

"Wouldn't be the first time," Smoke said with a grin as he placed the rifle on the floor next to the bed. He didn't look like a man who was about to ride off and fight a battle to the death with a ruthless enemy. But like Luke, life on the frontier had taught Smoke how to live in the moment.

"Still wish I was going with you," Luke said.

"I know that." Smoke stuck out a hand. "And I appreciate it."

They shook. Again, Luke wished he could tell Smoke who he really was, but he had decided that could wait. Smoke already had enough on his mind without the shock of finding out the brother he had thought to be dead for the past fifteen years was really alive.

"Sally will be up with some breakfast in a little bit." Smoke lifted a hand in farewell and left the room.

Luke looked at the holstered revolvers and coiled shell belt on the table beside the bed, then pushed the covers back and swung his feet to the floor. He stood up, feeling a lot steadier than he had the night before. Getting back into action seemed to have had a bracing effect on him.

With the approach of dawn, the sky outside was lighter. He went over to the wardrobe, opened it, and could see his clothes hanging on hooks inside the wardrobe. As he pulled on the black shirt and buttoned it up he realized it was clean. Sally had cleaned and patched his clothes. He took the black trousers off the hook, braced himself with one hand on the wardrobe and hung the pants as low as possible with his other hand. Gingerly, he put one leg, then the other into the pants and pulled them up around his hips.

He picked up his boots and clean socks from the floor of the wardrobe and carried them to the chair. Carefully, he lowered himself down. Taking a big breath, he crossed one leg over the other and pulled on a sock. He grimaced. One sock, and he needed to rest before crossing the other leg and pulling on the other sock. It had taken more effort than he had anticipated. After another moment or two, he stood and stuck his feet into his boots. It wasn't easy, but he managed without doing any damage to his wounds.

Being dressed made him feel even better, but he wasn't *fully* dressed yet, he thought with a wry smile as he turned toward the bedside table. He picked up the cross-draw rig and buckled it on.

A footstep sounded at the doorway. "What in the world are you doing, Mr. Smith?" Sally stood with her hands on her hips.

Luke turned toward her. "I was thinking I might come downstairs for breakfast for a change."

"I'm not sure that's wise."

"I've got to get up and start moving around again sometime. The sooner I do, the sooner I'll get better."

She gave him a stern look for a moment, then shook her head and laughed. "I've seen Smoke act exactly the same way, and arguing with him never did any good, either. I swear, if I didn't know better—" She stopped short, and a puzzled frown came over her face.

To keep her from thinking too much, Luke said hurriedly, "If you'd just pick up that rifle and hand it to me . . . I'm not sure I'm ready to do a lot of bending yet."

"All right." She went over to the bed, picked up the Winchester, and gave it to him. "You want your hat, too? It's in the wardrobe."

"A gentleman doesn't wear his hat indoors. I know I may not look like one, but I strive for a certain standard of civilized behavior."

"No offense, Mr. Smith, but you're an odd man."

"So I've been told."

Keeping the rifle in one hand and the other on the wall for support, Luke followed Sally down the stairs. As they reached the kitchen, he heard the sound of numerous horses leaving the ranch.

Her face tightened at the sound. Smoke and the other men were riding off for the showdown with Simeon Baxter and his hired gunmen. She knew her husband was going into danger, but what woman ever truly got used to it?

Sally brought Luke a cup of coffee and a plate of flapjacks, bacon, and eggs, and he dug in with gusto. His appetite had come back as strong as ever, and Sally's good cooking had already put some meat back on his bones.

As he ate, he asked, "Did Smoke get any sleep last night?"

"Not much," Sally admitted. "He was upset about the men who were killed. He was up early this morning, well before dawn, digging graves for them in the little graveyard we have here on the ranch. Pearlie went out to help him, but Smoke would have done it by himself."

"He's a good man," Luke said.

"The best I've ever met, by far," Sally agreed. "And I thank God every day that the two of us found each other."

Luke would have liked to think he had something to do with the way Smoke had turned out, but that wasn't likely. Kirby had been only twelve years old when Luke went off to war, so he hadn't had much chance to mold the boy into the man he had grown up to be. Their father had more to do with

that, along with the old mountain man called Preacher. Luke
hoped to hear a lot more about him before his visit to the
Sugarloaf was over.

And it was only a visit, no doubt about that. Even if he
told Smoke the truth and Smoke invited him to stay at the
ranch, Luke knew that wasn't going to happen. Smoke sure
as hell didn't owe him a home, and after all the years of
drifting, Luke didn't think he was even capable of settling
down.

After breakfast, he said, "I think I'll go sit out on the
front porch for a while, and take the rifle with me. I believe
the sun might be good for me."

"You're probably right. I'll clean up in here, and then I
might come out and join you." Sally paused, then added,
"I'm really curious about something, Luke . . . but we can
talk about that later."

He frowned as he made his way to the porch. He had an
idea what Sally wanted to talk about, and it wasn't a conversation he wanted to have just yet. Not until he'd discussed it
with Smoke, anyway.

She might not give him any choice, though, he thought as
he carefully sat down in one of the rocking chairs on the
porch and slowly cocked his right ankle on his left knee.
After the way she had taken care of him, he didn't think he
could bring himself to lie to her.

His head was so full of those thoughts he almost didn't
notice the wink of sunlight on something metal in the trees
about two hundred yards away from the ranch house. But
his instincts still worked and shouted a warning to him. He
hadn't stayed alive by ignoring what his gut told him.

He threw himself forward, landing on the porch on his
knees, just as a rifle cracked in the distance. He felt the
wind-rip of a bullet passing close beside his car.

CHAPTER 32

Two hundred yards was too far for a handgun, so Luke drew his rifle and fired a shot in the direction of the hidden rifleman, aiming high so the bullet would carry a little farther. Ignoring the pain lancing through his side, he rolled toward the doorway as another shot blasted. He didn't want the wound on his side to break open and start bleeding again, but that pain was better than being a sitting duck.

The slug struck the rocking chair he'd been sitting in, and a chunk of wood flew off the back of it.

"Mr. Smith!" Sally cried as she jerked the door open. "Luke!"

He dived at her, tackling her around the knees and taking her down as a bullet plowed into the door. They scrambled farther into the house, and Luke kicked the door closed behind them.

"Luke!" Sally gasped. "I heard shots! What—"

A rumble of hoofbeats sounded outside, and Luke knew Smoke had miscalculated . . . and so had he. Neither had realized Baxter's attack on the ranch the night before was just a feint. Baxter had counted on some of his men being killed, and on Smoke recognizing them. He'd been trying to goad Smoke into rushing over to the neighboring spread and taking most, if not all, of the Sugarloaf crew with him.

"It's Baxter," Luke told Sally in a taut, grim voice. "He's come for you. He figures with you as his prisoner, Smoke won't have any choice but to do what Baxter tells him."

"Men have tried that before," Sally informed him. "Smoke killed them. He'll kill Baxter."

"More than likely," Luke agreed as the rush of hoofbeats came to a stop outside the house. "If I don't kill him first." He jerked his head toward the stairs. "Get up there. I'll stop them."

"You're one man against two dozen, and you're wounded!" Sally protested. "You can't—"

"Go!" Luke told her as he climbed to his feet. He didn't have anything to lose, making him more dangerous than any number of men Baxter could muster.

Sally didn't understand that. She stood up beside him, and suddenly threw her arms around him and came up on her toes to brush a kiss across his gaunt cheek. "Luke," she whispered, "I don't know how it's possible, but I think I know—"

"Just go," he cut in, "while you still can."

A man shouted orders outside. The gunnies knew Baxter wanted Sally alive, but they also knew at least one man with a gun was inside. Luke figured they wouldn't come in shooting for fear of hurting her, but they would rush the place, counting on the force of numbers to overwhelm any opposition.

Sally squeezed his arm and turned to run to the stairs. As she started up, Luke faced the door, squaring himself to the opening and bracing his feet. He had both guns drawn and pointed at the doorway, waiting grimly to start their thunderous song.

He didn't have long to wait. Something crashed against the door and it flew open. Hard-faced men with guns in their hands rushed into the room, and at the sight of the tall, lean man dressed in black waiting for them, they raised the weapons to open fire.

They were too late. The revolvers in Luke's hands were already spouting flaming death.

As it always did at such moments, everything else faded away for Luke. The world receded until there was nothing left in the universe except him and the men he was trying to kill . . . the men who were trying to kill him. The roar of guns was like the bellow of great primordial beasts, the clouds of powder smoke rolling through the room like the eruption of ancient volcanoes, and the blood flowing the bright crimson of man like going all the way back to the dawn of time.

Luke didn't feel the smash of bullets like he expected. He was still on his feet and fighting, and that was all that mattered to him. Men fell before his guns like wheat before a scythe.

Vaguely, he became aware of shots pealing out from other places. There seemed to be a battle going on *outside* the ranch house, as well as a rifle blasting somewhere close by.

Suddenly, as the hammers of both Remingtons clicked on empty chambers, only one enemy faced him, a tall, burly man with a rough-hewn face and silver hair under a black Stetson. The man's clothes were better and more expensive than those of the others, and Luke had a hunch he was facing Simeon Baxter.

That was confirmed a second later when the man pointed a fancy, nickel-plated revolver at Luke and yelled, "I don't know who you are, you lousy interloper, but you've ruined all my plans! Now you're gonna die, you and that skirt both!"

Luke glanced over and realized Sally was standing beside him, holding the Winchester. "I'm empty. You?"

"Me, too." But she was smiling, unafraid.

Luke realized why when a powerful voice bellowed from outside, "Baxter!"

The would-be cattle baron whirled around. A shot blasted from his gun, soaring harmlessly into the air, and was answered by a pair of crashing reports from a Colt. The bullets drove Baxter through the doorway and spilled him onto his back, almost at the feet of Luke and Sally. He writhed in pain, pawing at his chest with blood welling through his fingers, and ended up on his side looking up at Luke. "Who . . . who are you?" he gasped.

Smoke appeared in the doorway. "His name's Luke Jensen. He's my brother."

Baxter's head sagged back, an ugly rattle came from his throat, and he died.

Normally the first thing Luke did when he held empty guns was reload them, but he was just too tired. He slid both guns back into their holsters and looked himself over, expecting to see more blood on his clothes. It was a shock to realize he didn't seem to be hit. With all the lead that had been flying around the room, he didn't see how it was possible, but he didn't feel any new pains, just a dull ache in his side from that old wound.

Smoke pouched his iron and rushed across the room to draw Sally into his arms. He cupped a hand behind her head and kissed her. "Are you all right?" he asked when he lifted his mouth from hers a moment later.

"I'm fine . . . thanks to Luke. Smoke, he's—"

"My brother. I know. I can't figure out how it's possible, but there's no doubt in my mind." With his arms still around Sally, Smoke turned his head to look at Luke. "All I had to do was see him standing there with the dead men he'd killed defending you heaped at his feet, and I knew." He shifted so that he could hold out a hand to Luke. "Welcome home . . . brother."

Luke didn't hesitate. Reaching out, he clasped his brother's hand.

Pearlie and the other hands had dragged the corpses out of the living room and dumped sand on the floor to soak up the blood. Cleaning it all up was going to take awhile.

In the kitchen, Smoke filled Sally and Luke in on what had happened after he left the ranch. "I figured out what

Baxter was up to when we were about halfway to his ranch. We turned around and got back here as fast as we could, with me kicking myself for being a damned fool the whole way."

"You were upset about your men being killed last night," Luke said. "It's understandable you wanted to have a show-down with Baxter."

"And that's what he was counting on." Smoke shook his head. "I'm just glad we got back in time."

"So am I," Luke said with a wry smile. "I didn't have enough bullets to kill all of Baxter's men."

"Maybe not, but from the sound of it I expected to find a small army trying to fight them off inside the house, not just the two of you."

"Luke did most of it." Sally gave credit where credit was due. "I never saw anybody handle guns like that, Smoke . . . well, nobody but you, that is."

"It's a skill that seems to run in the family." Smoke took a sip of his coffee and fixed Luke with an intent look across the table. "I heard you were killed fighting Yankees in the wilderness, and then told later you were murdered by those varmints who stole that shipment of Confederate gold. What's the real story, Luke?"

"I suppose if anyone has a right to hear it, it's you." Luke looked away. "Some of it's not too pretty, though."

"I want to know anyway."

"Of course."

For the next half hour, Luke told them everything that had happened since that fateful night in Richmond with the Yankee artillery pounding away at the city. He didn't leave out anything. When he was finished, he glanced at Sally and saw tears shining in her eyes.

"You considered yourself a failure because those terrible men ambushed you?" She wiped at a tear.

"They stole the gold I was supposed to protect. They killed my friends."

"And they nearly killed you! My God, Luke, that wasn't your fault. You could have gone back home to your family."

He shrugged. "I saw it differently." He knew from the look in Smoke's eyes that his brother understood.

"That wasn't all. I was wanted for murder in Georgia."

"Well, that just wasn't right," Sally declared. "You were only trying to protect that girl and her grandfather."

"Yes, but I figured I'd caused enough trouble for them."

"*You* didn't cause the trouble." Sally was starting to sound a little exasperated with him. "You saved them from it!" She blew out her breath and shook her head. "You stiff-necked Jensen boys! Matt's the same way, and he's not even a blood relative. You all think you have to be perfect and that you can never let anybody down."

"Well, that's something to aspire to, isn't it?" Smoke asked with a faint smile.

"Maybe . . . but it's not human." Sally took Smoke's hand, then reached across the table and clasped Luke's hand, too. "At least the two of you are back together, after all these years. Now I understand why you seemed so familiar to me, Luke. Even though you and Smoke don't look that much alike, I was seeing him in you. I knew there was something special about you all along."

"That's nice to hear," he told her as he squeezed her hand.

"And you have a home again at last," Sally added.

Luke didn't say anything. Glancing at Smoke, he saw the knowledge in his brother's eyes and realized Smoke knew he wasn't going to stay on permanently. Luke could never adjust to that sort of life. The wanderlust was just too strong in him.

Anyway, he still had outlaws to hunt down.

But not right away.

At that moment, he was content to sit in a quiet kitchen with his family and know that, while the place would never be his home, it was as close to one as he would ever come.

EPILOGUE

Three weeks later, on a cool morning with streamers of fog hanging around the mountain peaks in the distance, Luke saddled the fine horse Smoke had insisted was his and led the animal out of the barn, leading a pack horse behind him. He had thought he might be able to slip away from the ranch without anybody noticing until he was gone, but he supposed that was too much to hope for.

Smoke stood waiting for him. "You don't have to go, you know."

"Yeah, I do." Luke checked the cinches one more time. "I've been talking to Monte Carson, and he tells me that Badger McCoy was spotted up in Laramie a few days ago."

Monte Carson was the local sheriff in Big Rock, and he had a whole desk drawer full of wanted posters he had let Luke look through.

"Badger McCoy," Smoke repeated.

"Train robber. The reward's only eight hundred dollars, but I have a hunch I can get more out of the railroad if I'm able to recover some of the loot McCoy's stolen, too."

"So you're bound and determined to go on risking your life hunting down fugitives?"

"It's what I do," Luke said. If anybody could understand that, it was Smoke.

After a moment, Smoke nodded. "Sally won't be happy you didn't tell her good-bye."

Luke shook his head. "Not good at that."

"I know. I'll try to explain it to her. And I'll tell her you promised to come back. You will, won't you? I want you to meet Preacher and Matt."

"I'd like that." Luke put out his hand. "Next time."

"Next time," Smoke agreed as he shook hands.

Luke swung up into the saddle, but before he could ride away, Smoke went on, "There's one more thing."

"What's that?"

"Forget about calling yourself Luke Smith. You've got a name. You should use it."

Luke frowned. "You really want people to know me as Luke Jensen? A bounty hunter?"

"You're a good man and you're my brother." Smoke looked up at Luke. "That's all I care about. Jensen's a proud name, and I think you should wear it."

Luke thought about it for a moment and then nodded. "All right. If that's what you want, I can do that."

"Good. So long, Luke."

Lifting a hand in farewell, Luke turned his horses and rode out of the ranch yard.

"Don't forget!" Smoke called after him. "You always have a home here if you want it!"

Luke waved, but didn't look back as he rode north. *Home*, he thought. He hadn't had one of those for a long, long time. The idea would take some getting used to.

But it was a pretty thing to think about. It surely was.

TURN THE PAGE FOR AN EXCITING PREVIEW!

MONTANA

**Two Families. Six Generations. One Stretch of Land.
A Bold New Saga Centuries in the Making.**

*An exciting new series from the bestselling Johnstones cele-
brates the hardworking residents of Cutthroat County: the
ranchers who staked their claims, the lawmen who risked
their lives, and the descendants who carried their dreams
into the twenty-first century.*

Bordered by the Blackfeet Reservation to the north and
mountain ranges to the east and west, Cutthroat County is
seven-hundred glorious square miles of Big Sky grandeur.
For generations, the Maddox and Drew families have ruled
the county—often at odds with each other. Today, Ashton
Maddox runs the biggest Black Angus ranch in the country,
while County Sheriff John T. Drew upholds the law like his
forefathers did over a century ago. A lot has changed since
the county was established in 1891. But some things feel
straight out of the 1800s. Especially when cows start disappearing from the ranches. . . .

Intrigued, a local newsman digs up the gun-blazing tale of
the land-grabbing battles fought by Maddox's and Drew's
ancestors. Meanwhile, their present-day descendants face a
new kind of war that's every bit as bloody. When a rival
rancher's foreman is found shot to death, Ashton Maddox is
the prime suspect. Sheriff Drew is pressured into arresting
him, in spite of a lack of evidence. So the two families decide to do what their forefathers did so many years ago:
join forces against a common enemy. Risk their skins
against all odds. And keep the dream of Montana
alive for generations to come . . .

National Bestselling Authors
William W. Johnstone and J.A. Johnstone

MONTANA

On sale wherever Pinnacle Books are sold.

Live Free. Read Hard.

PROLOGUE

From the May issue of *Big Sky Monthly Magazine:*

By Paula Schraeder

The bestselling T-shirt for tourists at Wantlands Mercantile in Basin Creek has an image of a colorful trout in the center circle and these words:

**WELCOME TO
CUTTHROAT COUNTY**
*We're Named
After Montana's
State Fish*

But on the back is the image of a tough-looking, bearded cowboy wearing an eyepatch and biting down on a large knife blade, with these words below:

But <u>WATCH</u> Your Back

Yes, this is Cutthroat County, all 1,197 square miles, according to the U.S. Geological Survey's National Geospatial Program, with 31.2 of those square miles water. The county's population is a healthy 397, according to the 2020 U.S.

Census Bureau, though, the sunbaked, silver-headed lady working the counter at Wantlands Mercantile when I dropped in on a windy but wonderfully sunny June afternoon told me:

"Oh, 'em guvment volunteers mighta missed a coupla dozen or so. Folks live here cause they've lived here all their lives. Or they come because. . . ."

I waited. Finally, I had to ask, "Why do folks come here?"

"To hide," she said.

Having been in Cutthroat County for three days, I know there must be roughly 1,130 square miles (not including the 31.2 water miles) for anyone to hide. The accompanying map on the double-truck should make that obvious.

It seems like a good place to hide.

Getting to Basin Creek isn't easy. I left Billings early in the morning in my Toyota Camry, winding through plenty of Big Sky country, and after hitting the turnoff north at Augusta, I drove and drove and drove, with nothing to see but pastures and open country.

Aside: A truck driver at a Great Falls coffeeshop on my way back home laughed when he heard my story.

"Was it at night?" he asked.

"No, sir," I told him.

"You should drive through there at night. It's like you're in a [expletive] bowl." He sipped his latte. "Liked to've sent me to the looney bin a time or two."

Back to my trip: Finally, reaching a crossroads store, I stopped for coffee and confirmation.

"Is this the right way to Basin Creek?" I asked the young Native man who rang me up.

"Yes." He took my money.

He must have read the skepticism on my face. Then he smiled, tilted his head north, and confirmed: "Just keep going that way," he said, "and drive till you reach the end of the earth."

Cutthroat County is bordered by the Blackfeet Indian

Reservation on the north, the Ponoka (Elk) Mountains to the east, the Always Winter mountain range on the west, and U.S. Highway 103 on the south. If you are driving to Glacier National Park or the Canadian entry point at Milk River City, it's a good idea to take your potty break here. Maybe top off the gas tank, as well. (That crossroads station I stopped at on the drive north has no gasoline for sell; and I did not have courage enough to use the outhouse.) There are only two gas stations in Cutthroat County, and both are in Basin Creek.

"That's not exactly true," I am later told.

"Roscoe Moss has a pump at Crimson Feather [a community of four trailers and a ranch far to the east of where owner Garland Foster has brought in wind turbines]. At least when the Conoco truck—there's a refinery in Billings, you know—remembers to stop on the first of the month. Course, old Roscoe's prices are higher than a loan shark's interest rates, and his pump is slower than spring getting here."

The speaker, a handsome man of slightly above average height, dark hair flecked with gray, and the darkest eyes I've ever seen, pauses to sip coffee—black (his third cup since I've been interviewing him)—and appears to be counting the other gas pumps.

"And most ranchers and mining companies have their own pumps," he continues. "Though some stopped after they had to dig up their old pumps and haul them away. EPA thing, if I remember right." His smile is disarming. "But you're too young to remember leaded gasoline."

He does not appear to be flirting. But he sure is charming.

"If you run out of gas, there's a pretty good chance that someone will top you off with enough to get you to East Glacier. Maybe as far as Cut Bank."

This disarming man is John T. Drew, Cutthroat County sheriff. Drew is one of those fellows *who've lived here all their lives.*

"Well," he politely corrects, "if you don't count four-and-a-half years in Bozeman." He points to the Montana State

University diploma—criminal justice—on the wall to the right of the window overlooking the county courthouse grounds.

Those four and a half years might be the only period of time when any Drew male has not dined, slept and worked in Cutthroat County since long before Cutthroat County was carved out of Choteau County in 1891.

The first Maddox to set foot in Cutthroat County was a mountain man—*seven, eight, nine generations ago?*

Drew smiles and shrugs. "I've never figured the math." He nods at the diploma. "Math's why it took me an extra semester to get that sheepskin on the wall."

"Do people hide here?" I ask.

"People escape here," he says, the smile still warm. "Tourists come here to flyfish for cutthroat trout—or to pick up one of those T-shirts Maudie sells by the scores during peak season. The three-hundred and ninety-seven folks who call this patch of heaven home live here because they love it. Because this country's in their blood. The air's clean. The water's pure. And if you don't mind a whole lot of winter most years, it's a good place to call home."

Sixty years ago, Cutthroat County made national headlines for being the last of the Old West towns. The sprawling Maddox Ranch, now headed by Ashton Maddox, was likened to the Ponderosa of TV's *Bonanza,* and the county sheriff—yes, John Drew's grandfather—was called a real Matt Dillon, the character played by James Arness in the long-running western series *Gunsmoke.*

Tourists from across the world flocked to Cutthroat County not just to go trout fishing in America but to see the Wildest Wild West. A Montana state tourism guide raved about four guest ranches—three of which boasted to be real, working ranches—and a restored historic hotel. Two stables offered guided horseback rides along the county's myriad peaks, valleys, and creeks. A plan was to turn part of the long abandoned railroad tracks, originally laid in the 1890s, into an Old West tourism train complete with a coal-powered locomotive and mock gunfights and train robberies.

That boom lasted, maybe, slightly less than a decade.

A few years later, Cutthroat County, and especially Basin Creek, got statewide attention—and a joke on *The Tonight Show* [though I have been unable to confirm; there's no video on YouTube]—as a speed trap.

Drew laughs at that memory. "Well, the town speed limit was thirty-five, and my daddy did not like speeders. Maybe because his daddy preferred riding a horse than driving that Ford Galaxy. We have Ford Police Interceptor SUVs now, by the way. But we're getting some pressure from the state to move to hybrids. And if we get another electric charging unit, we might go for that. But that's up to the county. And the annual budget."

Today, no 1890s train runs through Basin Creek. There aren't even any iron rails anymore. And there is only one electric-charging station in the county, at my motel, though the Wantlands Mercantile is investigating the costs and reliability of adding one in the next two years. The restored historic hotel burned down twenty-five years ago. Now the site's home to the cinder-block Wild Bunch Casino, where cowboys, sheepherders, townspeople, and a few passing tourists drink beer and play video poker, video keno, video blackjack, video slots, while Chuckie Corvallis serves up food.

Today's special: A $7.99 Tater-Tot Casserole.

I opt for coffee and the soup of the day, cream of mushroom, probably straight from a can.

There's a No Smoking sign on the outside door.

But Chuckie Corvallis is lighting a new filterless Pall Mall with the one he just burned down to almost nothing.

"It's my place," he says when he notices my questioning, healthy-lung face. "I own this place. I can smoke if I wanna. Nobody else can. Ain't my law. It's the [expletive] feds."

(By the time our interview is over, I have to race back to my motel room, shower twice, and find a laundromat to rid my clothes of tobacco stink.)

"What happened to Basin Creek?" I ask Corvallis.

"The [expletive] government. [Expletive] feds. [Expletive expletives]. Folks stopped carin' 'bout their country. Hippies. Freaks. Now it's the [expletive expletives] and their [expletive] ignoramus politics. [Expletive] 'em." He pulls hard on his cigarette and blows smoke. "Pardon my [expletive] French."

Both stables have been paved over. On one sits my quaint motel.

Things, however, are changing in Basin Creek.

A month before my arrival, newcomer Elison Dempsey announced his candidacy for Cutthroat County sheriff—a position that has been held almost exclusively by Drews since the county's founding. Dempsey heads the Citizens Action Network, a quasi-military vigilante group—MSNBC said there is nothing "quasi" about C.A.N.—and Dempsey has been getting plenty of press, statewide, regionally, and nationally.

Elison Dempsey is tan, clean-shaven, with his dark hair buzzed in crew-cut fashion, and white teeth. He looks like he might have been an Olympic track star or boxer. Smiling after I tell him that, he corrects me:

"I might have done well in the biathlon. I'm a great skier, downhill or cross-country. Out here, it's good to be able to ski. Winters can be long, and skiing sure beats snow-showing when it's forty below zero. But I am an excellent marksman. Rifle. Shotgun. Forty-five automatic."

The Colt .45 is holstered on his hip. The rack behind him in his massive four-wheel-drive Ford carries a lever-action Winchester, a twelve-gauge pump shotgun, and a lethal-looking assault rifle, perhaps an AK-47. I don't know. And I don't want to ask.

"I do have a concealed carry permit," he assures me when he notices my focus on the automatic pistol. "You can ask our soon-to-be ousted sheriff." He chuckles. "All the members of C.A.N. have concealed carry permits, too. But as you can see, we *conceal* nothing."

Dempsey has volunteered to take me on a tour of Cutthroat County. His truck gets eight miles a gallon, he says, but tells me not to worry. The gas container in the bed of the Ford looks like it could refill an aircraft carrier.

"The problem here," he says as he slows down and pulls off the road, "is that two men run this county." He nods at a gate on the left. The arched sign above the dirt road reads:

Maddox Cattle Company

An encircled M—a brand well recognized across Montana—hangs just below the company's name.

"There's one of them. Ashton thinks he's God," Dempsey says. "Maddoxes have been gods here for too long. "Maddoxes and Drews. It's time for someone to put both of those gods in their place."

He's wearing a camouflage T-shirt that appears painted to his chest and upper arms. It's not a tourist T-shirt from Wantlands Mercantile, but a red, white, and blue Citizens Action Network T-shirt.

Cutthroat County
C.A.N.!
We
WILL!
Citizens Action Network

He flexes his muscles and grins those white teeth.

"And I happen to be Zeus, Hercules and Apollo rolled into one."

For the record, Ashton Maddox declined my multiple interview requests.

"Who's the other god?" I ask.

He snorts. "You just spent a couple hours with him in the sheriff's office. You know that. For more than a century—two centuries really—this county has been all Drew and all Maddox. I'm here to change that. And I will. For the better."

Several miles up the road, we turn onto another two-track. An hour later, I'm thinking:

No one's going to find my body. Ever!

Dempsey stops, rolls down his window, and nods at a ramshackle building that I figure is abandoned.

"Here's another problem nobody seems to want to fix."

I stare at the house, if that's the right word. One wall is made of strawbales. The rest, that I can see, appear to be made of anything and everything someone could throw together. Wooden crates. Driftwood. Broken two-by-fours. Cans. Cinderblocks. Dirt. The window—singular—is apparently made of Coke bottles and Mason jars.

"Someone lives there?" I finally ask.

"If you call that living," Dempsey answers.

I'm about to ask what someone who lives here does? Maybe this is a line camp for Ashton Maddox? Then I remember the lady at Wantlands Mercantile.

They hide.

"You've heard of folks wanting to live off the grid?" Dempsey asks.

"Sure, but . . . ."

"You can't get further off the grid than Cutthroat County—and fifteen miles off the highway." He shifts the gear into first and we pull away.

"He's not so bad. I mean, he likely paid money for four or five acres. Land's cheap here. This ain't Livingston or Missoula. And if he's registered to vote, I like him. He can vote for me come November. I don't care what party he belongs to. See, I'm running as an independent. I like all folks—those who don't break the law, I mean. So . . . Maybe he grows a little grass. Does some illegal trapping. There's a good crick four miles northeast. Poaches a pronghorn or takes an elk out of season. I don't know. Maybe he's like you. Wants to be a real writer. A real Louis L'Amour."

I let him know: "I am a *real* writer."

A half hour later, he stops again.

"Here's another problem," he says, pointing at another rundown trailer home. "The dude that lives here is a poacher. See, that good-looking deputy that Drew got himself, she was pulling a deer that got hit by a tourist on the way back from Glacier, pulling it off the road, and this dude comes by in that Jap rig and asks if he can take the deer carcass. Deputy Mary Broadbent let him. That's illegal.

"This isn't deer season. She broke the law. Broadbent, I mean. When I heard of it, I told Drew. He didn't do a thing. So I called Trent, the local game warden here. He didn't do a thing. Because if Ashton Maddox isn't ruling Cutthroat County, John T. Drew is."

We drive back to the main highway, and head back to Basin Creek. When we see two hitchhikers, Dempsey swears, blows the horn, and floors the rig, sending the lean man and tall woman jumping over the ditch and almost falling against the barbed-wire fence.

"That's another problem," Dempsey says after he stops laughing. "Blackfeet Indians keep coming down here, taking jobs away from folks who live here and want to work."

I don't bring up the fact that Cutthroat County covers what once was Blackfeet country and that anyone has the right to work anyplace in America.

He has to slow down when we find ourselves behind a semi hauling cattle.

"And there's the final biggest problem in Cutthroat County I am to fix once I send John T. Drew to pasture," Dempsey says.

I smell cattle manure over diesel.

"You won't believe this, lady, but this spring, we had a report of rustling here. Cattle rustling. Just like you'd see in an old movie on Channel Sixteen."

"Rustling?"

He nods, then names his suspects, but I leave them out of this article because my editor and publisher have a policy that they don't want to be sued for libel.

Elison Dempsey says he has reached out to George Grimes, a noted Texas Ranger recently retired, and asked Grimes—the subject of last year's action movie titled *Beretta Law*—to join C.A.N. as a stock detective. But, he says he fears the fee George Grimes demands is far more than C.A.N. can afford.

Grimes could not be reached for comment.

"Is rustling why Garland Foster put up wind turbines on his ranch?" I ask.

"Foster is a fool," is all Dempsey says. "He won't vote for me. But he'll be the only one."

When I reach Garland Foster by telephone, he laughs when I ask for a response to being called a fool.

"Been called worse, little lady," he says.

Foster, who still reaps millions from his Florida condos and myriad business interests in Texas, many Great Plains states and in Mexico, Central and South America, moved from southern Texas after the death of his wife four years ago.

Dempsey isn't the only person who has criticized Foster.

"Ashton Maddox hates my guts," Foster says with another chuckle. "But it's not my fault that his grandaddy had to sell off part of that big ol' Circle M spread during the Great Depression. I just happened to have a few million bucks to spend and thought Montana would sure beat the heat in Florida, Texas, and Mexico. I didn't know a blasted thing about Sacagawea Pasture when I paid cash for eleven sections [7,040 acres] of real estate."

Sacagawea Pasture, according to legend once property of both Maddoxes and Drews, has a name that dates to the 1840s—but the Maddox and Drew names go back even further in Montana lore and legend and actual history.

So why, I ask, is a longtime cattle rancher turning to wind turbines?

"More sheep than cattle," he corrects. "Least for the past five-six years. But wind turbines don't smell like cattle or sheep, and while beef and wool prices fluctuate, the wind always blows in this country."

"What about rustling?" I ask.

Foster laughs. "Nobody's rustled one of my turbines yet."

But back in town, John T. Drew confirms that there have been one report of rustling on a small ranch, and he and his deputies (both of them, though one, Denton Creel, when I am visiting is in Billings on personal leave) are investigating. "Not to sound like a fellow running for public office, but I cannot comment further because this is an active investigation."

There's that disarming smile again.

"Elison Dempsey says he has offered his Citizens Action Network volunteers to help with your investigation," I tell him.

He nods. "Elison Dempsey says lots of things. Offers a lot of things. Most of them I ignore. No, I reckon I ignore anything Dempsey says. But I did tell him and some of his C.A.N. folks that they are welcome to volunteer for the county's search and rescue team."

There's a lot of country for hikers, hunters, and anglers to get lost in, he explains, and a lot of his time as county sheriff is spent searching and rescuing, not citing speeders who think all Montana highways are *Autobahns*.

I ask about Mary Broadbent, the game warden, and the deer given to a so-called squatter.

"Deputy Broadbent told that man that he could have the deer as long as he told the game warden about it the next morning," Drew says. "Which he did." He smiles. "No sense in letting good deer meat rot when it could feed a family for a week. I'm partial to backstrap myself."

That is confirmed by Ferguson C. Trent of the state Department of Fish, Wildlife and Parks. Not the backstrap part. But the part that the taker of the deer did call Officer Trent about taking the road kill for many suppers.

He stares at me. "This place can still be the frontier."

I ask about Mary Broadbent, who, like Ashton Maddox, declined to talk to me for this article.

The smile is gone, and the eyes again harden. "She's a good deputy."

Then I look around the office. I keep looking.

"You look confused, Miss Schraeder," the sheriff says politely.

I look because I am. "Do you have a dispatcher? I mean, where do calls come in. If you're patrolling how do you—"

"Nine-one-one calls go to Glacier County—Cut Bank. Those are relayed here." The smile returns. "We're small. But we are efficient."

"Do you think you'll win reelection?"

"That's up to the voters."

"Are things changing in Cutthroat County?" I ask.

"Nothing ever stays the same," Drew says, and the look on his face tells me he's OK with change—unlike some Westerners I've interviewed over the years. "We've never been on CNN or *Face the Nation* or NPR till recently. That takes some getting used to. But if that brings us some tourist dollars—and we thank *Big Sky Monthly Magazine* for sending you here—that won't hurt us.

"Just remind your readers that we indeed have speed limits. If you speed here, you'll get pulled over. And fined. And if you commit a major crime, there's one thing you need to know."

"What's that?"

There's that smile again. "The judge might not be in town for some time. Our jail holds ten comfortably. But it's like any jail anywhere. It loses its uniqueness after a few hours."

The jail is in the basement of the combination county courthouse and town hall, a rectangular two-story building of limestone that is dwarfed by Basin Creek's biggest structure, a leaning wooden granary next to the old depot in what is called Killone Memorial Park.

Abe Killone was a rancher, and the man who paid for the construction of the county courthouse out of his own pocket, who was murdered on the streets of Basin Creek in 1917.

The first floor holds the county library (the entire eastern wing, except for the bathrooms) and several rooms labeled

STORAGE, and town-related government offices (or desks)—
mayor (Sabrina Richey), tax assessor (Henry Richey) and
the constable, though Derrick Taylor likes to call himself the
town marshal. Taylor isn't in this afternoon because it's
Wednesday. His hours are the same as the county's justice of
the peace, 9 a.m.-noon Mondays, 1-4 p.m. Thursdays. Other
kiosks are scattered across the western side of the dark
building for the school superintendent, clerk and recorder,
while the county's road department, treasurer and assessor
have their own offices. Though none is in this afternoon.

"They keep the important stuff downstairs," librarian
Phyllis Lynne tells me. "So people don't have to walk up
those stairs."

Don't worry. The building is ADA compliant. An eleva-
tor is at the far corner, completed in 1992 and, county manager Dan O'Riley tells me, "runs like it was put in in 1492."

O'Riley's offices are upstairs, along with Sheriff Drew's,
the three elected county commissioners (who are responsible for the hiring of all non-elected county officers, including the county coroner, county attorney but not the sheriff).
Cutthroat County went to a county commissioner manage-
ment style in 1948.

Commissioners (chairwoman Grace Gallagher, Sid Prit-
chard and Mack—"Yes, it's my real name-wanna see my
birth certificate?"—McDonald) are the commissioners.

The courthouse covers most of the second floor of what's
officially called the Cutthroat County Courthouse/Basin
Creek Municipal Building, even if the court is hardly used—
for trials, anyway. Town hall meetings are sometimes held
here, and the public school, three years ago, put on a presen-
tation of *Inherit the Wind.*

The clerk, James Alder, says the last criminal case tried
was six months ago. "Connie Good Stabbing stole a truck to
get back to the rez. Well, she said she borrowed it. Dom
Purcell pressed charges. But they reached a plea deal while
the jury was deliberating. So everybody was happy. The ju-

rors got paid for their time, Connie had to paint the Catholic church here in town and pay Malone a 'rental fee' and reimburse him for gas."

I stare at him, and expect to wake up in front of an *Andy Griffith* rerun on MeTV.

"It's not always this tame," John T. Drew says when I find my way back to his office. "And this is a long way from Mayberry."

There have been four deaths over the past eighteen months, two in traffic accidents (neither involving alcohol), and one hiker who met up with a bear in the Ponoká range, and, this past December, a cowboy on Garland Foster's ranch, while working alone, apparently was killed in what the coroner called "a horse wreck."

The coroner, George J. White, by the way, does not live in Cutthroat County. He resides in Harve, Hill County seat and "a bit of a haul" from Basin Creek. The county attorney lives in Choteau, Teton County seat and "not as far away as Harve," attorney Murdoch Robeson tells me over the phone, "but it sure ain't close."

"Does that work?" I ask Dan O'Riley, who's standing in the doorway to the sheriffs office.

"It has to. Lawyers can't make a living in Cutthroat County. Coroners don't have much to do here, either."

So why is Elison Dempsey talking about the need for his Citizens Action Network in a town and county like this?

Dempsey told me that Cutthroat County needs a change and that a lot of illegal activity goes unreported.

O'Riley laughs. "Most illegal activity goes unreported everywhere, Miss. But how much illegal activity do you think you can find in a county of fewer than four hundred people?"

But Dempsey also said he would reopen the investigation into the death of one of those traffic accidents. A single-car accident that claimed the life of forty-nine-year-old Cathy Drew, wife of Sheriff John T. Drew.

Disgusted as this makes me, I have to bring that up to the

charming sheriff because those charges have been flying around the state—and on some cable news networks—since Mrs. Drew was found in her overturned Nissan Rogue on U.S. Highway 103 between 12:30 and 4:15 a.m. on Friday, December 3, 2021. She was rushed to a Missoula hospital and pronounced dead on arrival.

Drew sighs. "U.S. Highway, so Montana State Police troopers were the primary on that. They handled the investigation. Best guess is that she swerved, overcorrected. I'm a cop. I don't like best guesses. I'd like to know for sure what happened. But I have gotten mighty sick of Elison Dempsey and one of these days, he's going to wish he kept his mouth shut."

Dan O'Riley quickly changes the subject. "You read enough history books on Montana and you'll come across lots of names that you'll still find on the list of registered voters."

"Like Drew and Maddox?" I ask.

"More than that," O'Riley says. "My ancestors came here in 1881. But I'm a newcomer. You don't read anything about Dempseys."

"There you have it," Elison Dempsey yells when I meet him at the Busted Stirrup Bar in Basin Creek. "If your roots don't go back to fur trappers and cattle rustlers and Indian killers, you got no right to live in Cutthroat County. That's what I'm fighting. That's why I'm running for sheriff. And that's why the truth will come out and I will be elected."

Yet, when I leave my motel, and drive down Main Street, I see Sheriff John T. Drew getting out of his Interceptor in front of the county-town courthouse. I stop, roll down the window, and thank him for all his help.

His eyes are mellow again, and he leans against the passenger door.

"You're welcome back anytime, Miss Schraeder."

"You haven't read my story yet."

His grin widens and his eyes twinkle. "And, most likely, I won't. No offense. I just don't like reading about me or

Drews or Maddoxes. Got enough of those yarns grow-
|ing up."

Well, we heard the stories, too, read the novels, some so-
called histories, and heard the schoolground rhymes even
when I was a child.

> *Pew Pew*
> *Marshal Drew*
> *Killed a Maddox*
> *Times Thirty-two*
> *Pew Pew*
> *Marshal Drew*

"Drive safe," the sheriff says, tips his hat, and steps back.
"And watch your speed. Remember what I told you. A person can wait a long time before the judge comes to town."

I make sure when I return to Billings that I don't go a hair
over thirty-five miles per hour as I drive out of Basin Creek,
and I keep my Camry at sixty-five, just to be safe, as I head
out of Cutthroat County, the last frontier in Montana, but a
frontier that is rapidly changing.

DAY ONE
THURSDAY

CHAPTER 1

After opening the back door, Ashton Maddox stepped inside his ranch home in the foothills of the Always Winter Mountains. His boots echoed hollowly on the hardwood floors as he walked from the garage through the utility room, then the kitchen, and into the living room.

Someone had left the downstairs lights on for him, thank God, because he was exhausted after spending four days in Helena, mingling with a congressman and two lobbyists—even though the Legislature wouldn't meet till the first Monday in January—plus lobbyists and business associates, then leaving at the end of business this afternoon and driving to Great Falls—for another worthless but costly meeting with a private investigator—and crawling back into his Ford SUV, to spend two more hours driving, with only twelve on the interstate, then a little more than a hundred winding, rough, wind-buffeted miles with hardly any headlights or taillights to break up the darkness. And having to pay constant attention to avoid colliding with elk, deer, bear, Blackfoot Indian, buffalo, or even an occasional moose.

Somehow, the drive from Basin Creek to the ranch road always seemed the worst stretch of the haul. Because he knew what he would find when he got home.

An empty house.

He was nothing short of complete exhaustion.

But, since he was a Maddox, he found enough stamina to switch on more lights and climb the staircase, clomp, clomp, clomp to the second floor, where his right hand found another switch, pushed it up, and let the wagon wheel chandelier and wall sconces bathe the upper storm in unnatural radiance.

The grandfather clock, still running, said it was a quarter past midnight.

His father would have scolded him for leaving all those lights on downstairs, wasting electricity—not cheap in this part of Montana. His grandfather would have reminded both of them about how life was before electricity and television and gas-guzzling pickup trucks.

When he reached his office, he flicked another switch, hung his gray Stetson on the elkhorn on the wall, and pulled a heavy Waterford crystal tumbler off the bookshelf before making a beeline toward the closet. He opened the door, and stared at the mini-icemaker.

His father and grandfather had also rebuked him for years about building a house on the top of the hill. "This is Montana, boy," Grandpa had scolded time and again. "The wind up that high'll blow you clear down to Coloradie."

Per his nature, Ashton's father had put it bluntly:

"Putting on airs, boy. Just putting on airs."

What, Ashton wondered, would Grandpa and Daddy say about his having an icemaker in his closet? Waste of water *and* electricity!

Not that he cared a fig about what either of those hard rocks might have thought. They were six feet under now. Had been for years. But no matter how long he lived, no matter how many millions of dollars he earned, he would always hear their voices.

Grandpa: *The Maddoxes might as well just start birthin' girls.*

Daddy: *If you'd gone through Vietnam like I did, you might know a thing or two.*

He opened the icemaker's lid, scooped up the right number of cubes, and left the door open as he walked back to the desk, his boot heels pounding on the hardwood floor. Once he set the tumbler on last week's Sunday *Denver Post,* which he still had never gotten around to reading, he found the bottle of Blanton's Single Barrel, and poured until bourbon and iced reached the rim.

Grandpa would have suffered an apoplexy had he knew a Maddox paid close to two hundred bucks, including tax, for seven hundred and fifty milliliters of Kentucky bourbon. Both his grandpa and father would have given him grief about drinking bourbon anyway. As far back as anyone could recollect, Maddox men had been rye drinkers.

The cheaper the better.

"If it burns," his father had often said, "I yearns."

He sipped. Good whiskey was, he thought, worth every penny.

Now he crossed the room, glass still in his hand, till he reached the large window. The heavy drapes had already been pulled open—not that he could remember, but he probably had left them that way before driving down to the state capital.

They used to have a cleaning lady here. One of the hired men's wife, sweetheart, concubine, whatever. But that man had gotten a job in Wyoming, and she had followed him. And now . . . with Patricia gone . . . Ashton didn't see any need to have floors swept and furniture dusted.

He debated closing the drapes, but what was the point? He could step outside on the balcony. Get some fresh air. Close his eyes and just feel the coolness, the sereneness of a summer night in Montana. Years ago, he had loved that— even when the wind come a-sweepin' 'cross the high plains. Grandpa had not been fooling about that wind, but Ashton Maddox knew what he was doing, what the weather was like, when he told the man at M.R. Russell Construction Company exactly what he wanted, and exactly where, he wanted his house.

Well, rather, where Patricia wanted it.

Wherever she was now.

He stood there, sipping good bourbon and feeling rotten, making himself look into the night that never was night. Not like it used to be.

"You can see forever," Patricia had told him on their first night up here, before Russell's subcontractor had even gotten the electricity installed.

He could still see forever up here. Forever. Hades stretching on from here north to the Pole and east toward the Dakotas, forever and ever and ever, amen.

The door opened. Boots sounded heavy on the floor, closing, a grunt, the hitching of jeans, and sound of a hat dropping on Ashton's desk.

"How was Helena?" foreman Colter Norris asked in his gruff monotone.

"Waste of time." Ashton did not turn around. He lifted his tumbler and sipped more bourbon.

"You read that gal's hatchet job in that rag folks call the *Big Sky Monthly?*"

"Skimmed it. Heard some coffee rats talking about it at the Stirrup."

"Well, that gal sure made a hero out of our sheriff." Ashton saw Colter's reflection in the plate-glass window. He held a longneck beer in his left hand. "And made Garland Foster sound like some homespun hick hero, cacklin' out flapdoodle about cattle and sheep prices and how wind's gonna save us all." Colter lifted his dark beer bottle and took a long pull.

Ashton started to raise his tumbler, but lowered it, shook his head, and whispered: "'. . . while beef and wool prices fluctuate, the wind always blows in this country.'"

The bottle Colter held lowered rapidly. "What's that?"

"Nothing." Now Ashton took a good pull on bourbon, let

some ice fall into his mouth, and crunched it, grinding it down, down, down.

"Thought you said you just skimmed that gal's expose." The foreman frowned. Colter Norris never missed a thing: a sign, a clear shot with a .30-.30, a trout's strike, or a half-baked sentence someone mumbled.

Raising the tumbler again, Ashton held the Waterford toward the window. "He didn't put up those wind turbines," he said caustically, "because of any market concerns." He shook his head, and cursed his neighboring rancher softly. "He put those up to torment me. All day. All night."

A man couldn't see the spinning blades at this time of night. But no one could escape the flashing red warning lights. Blinking on. Blinking off. On and off. Red light. No light. Red light. No light. Red light. Red . . . red . . . red . . . red . . . all night long, all night long till dawn finally broke. There had to be more wind turbines on Foster's land than that skinflint had ever run cattle or sheep.

Ashton turned away and stared across the room. Colter Norris held the longneck, his face showing a few days' growth of white and black stubble and that bushy mustache with the ends twisted into a thin curl. The face, like his neck and wrists and the forearms as far as he could roll up the sleeves of his work shirts, were bronzed from wind and sun, and scarred from horse wrecks and bar fights. The nose had been busted so many times, Ashton often wondered how his foreman even managed to breathe.

"You didn't come up here to get some gossip about a college girl's story in some slick magazine," Ashton told him. "Certainly not after I've spent three hours driving in a night as dark as pitch from Helena to here by way of Great Falls."

"No, sir." The man set his beer next to the bottle of fine bourbon.

"Couldn't wait till breakfast, I take it." Ashton started to bring the crystal tumbler up again, but saw it now contained nothing but melting ice and his own saliva.

"I figured not." Few people could read Colter Norris's

face. Ashton Maddox had given up years ago. But you didn't have to read a cowboy's face. The voice told him everything he needed to know.

This wasn't some hired hand wrecking a truck or ruining a good horse and had been paid off, then kicked off the ranch. It wasn't someone who got his innards gored by a steer's horn or kicked to pieces by a bull or widow making horse.

Frowning, Ashton set the glass on a side table, walked to the window, found the pull and closed the drapes. At least he couldn't see those flashing red lights on wind turbines now.

He walked back and made those cold blue eyes meet Colter Norris's hard greens.

"Let's have it," Ashton said.

The foreman obeyed.

"We're short."

Ashton's head cocked just a fraction. No punch line came. But he had not expected one. Most cowboys Ashton knew had wickedly acerbic senses of humor—or thought they did—but Colter Norris had never cracked a joke, hardly even let a smile crack the grizzled façade of his face. Still, the rancher could not believe what he had heard.

"We're . . . *short?*"

That rugged head barely moved up and down once.

Ashton reached down, pulled the fancy cork out of the bottle, and splashed two fingers of amber beauty into the tumbler. He didn't care about ice. He drank half of that down and looked again at his foreman.

No question was needed.

"Sixteen head. Section Fifty-four at Dead Indian Pony Creek." He pronounced creek *crick,* as did many Westerners.

The map hung on the north-facing wall, underneath the bearskin, and Ashton took his glass and rising anger to the modern map hanging on the paneling. Colter Norris left his empty longneck on the desk and followed, but the foreman had to know better than point.

Ashton Maddox knew his ranch, leased and owned, better than anyone living. He found it quickly, pointed a finger wet from the tumbler, and then began circling around, slowly, reading the topography and the roads.

"You see any truck tracks?" he asked.

"No, sir. Even hard-pressed, a body'd never get a truck into that country 'cept on our roads. What passes for roads, I mean. Our boys don't even bring ATVs into that section. Shucks, we're even careful about what horses we ride when working up there."

Ashton nodded in agreement.

"Steers?" he asked. "Bull or . . . ?"

"Heifers."

"Who discovered they were missing?"

"Dante Crump."

The head bobbed again. Crump had been working for the Circle M for seven years. He was the only cowboy Ashton had ever known who went to church regularly on Sundays. Most of the others were sleeping off hangovers till Mondays. A rancher might question the honesty of many cowboys, but no one ever accused Dante Crump of anything except having a conscience and a soul.

Ashton kept studying the map. He even forgot he was holding a glass of expensive bourbon.

Colter Norris cleared his throat. "No bear tracks. No carcasses. The cattle just vanished."

"Horse tracks?" Ashton turned away from the big wall map.

The cowboy's head shook. "Some. But Dante had rode 'cross that country—me and Homer Cooper, too—before we even considered them cattle got stoled. So we couldn't tell if the tracks were ours or their'n's."

"Do we have any more cattle up that way?" Ashton asked.

"Not now. Dante went up there to bring them up to the summer pasture. We left fifty down there in September. Found bones and carcasses of three. About normal. Dante brought down thirty-one. So best I can figure is that sixteen got rustled."

"Rustled." Ashton chuckled without mirth. The word sounded like something straight out of an old Western movie or TV show.

"Yeah," the foreman said. "I don't even never recollect your daddy sayin' nothin' 'bout rustlers."

"Because," Ashton said, "it never happened." He let out another mirthless chuckle. "I don't even think my grandpa had to cope with rustlers, unless some starving Blackfoot cut out a calf or half-starved steer for his family. And Grandpa had his faults, but he wasn't one to begrudge any man with a hungry wife and kids." He sighed, shook his head, and stared at Colter Norris. "You're sure those heifers aren't just hiding in that rough country."

The man's eyes glared. "I said so," was all he said.

Which was good enough for Ashton Maddox now, just as it had been good enough for Ashton's father.

"Could they have just wandered to another pasture?"

"Homer Cooper rode the lines," the foreman said. "He said there was no fence down. Sure ain't goin' cross no cattle guards, and the gates was all shut and locked."

They studied one another, thinking the same thought. An inside job. A Circle M cowboy taking a few Black Angus for himself. But even that made no sense. No one could sneak sixteen head all the way from that pasture to the main road without being seen or leaving sign.

"How?" Ashton shook his head again. "How in heaven's name . . . ?"

Colter Norris shrugged. "Those hippies livin' 'cross the highway on Bonner Flats will say it was extraterrestrials."

He said that without a smile, and it probably wasn't a joke. In fact, Ashton had to agree with the weathered cowboy.

The *Basin River Weekly Item* had reported cattle turning up missing at smaller ranches in the county, but Ashton had figured those animals had probably just wandered off because the ranchers weren't really ranchers, just folks wealthy enough to buy land and lease a pasture from the feds for grazing and have themselves a quiet place to come to and get a good tax break on top of that. Like that TV director or producer or company executive who ran buffalo on his place and had his own private helicopter. There were only two real ranchers in Cutthroat County now, though Ashton would never publicly admit that Garland Foster was a real rancher. He'd been a mostly a sheepman since arriving in Cutthroat County, and now he was hardly even that.

He looked at the curtains that kept him from seeing those flashing red lights all across Foster's spread.

"How did someone manage to get sixteen Black Angus of our herd out of there? That's what perplexes me." He moved back to the map, reached his left hand up to the crooked line marked in blue type Dead Indian Pony Creek, and traced it down to the nearest two-track, then followed that to the ranch road, then down the eleven miles to the main highway.

"Without a truck or trucks. Without being seen?"

Colter Norris moved closer to the map. Those hard eyes narrowed as he memorized the topography, the roads, paths, streams, canyons, everything. Then he seemed to dismiss the map and remember the country from personal experience, riding a half-broke cowpony in that rough, hard, impenetrable country in the spring, the summer, the fall. Probably not the winter, though. Not in northern Montana. Not unless a man was desperate or suicidal.

The head shook after thirty seconds.

"I can take some boys up, see if we can find a trail," Colter Norris suggested.

Ashton's head shook. He had forgotten about a wife who had left him. He had dismissed a fruitless trip to the state capital and then for an even more unproductive meeting in a Great Falls coffeeshop with a high-priced private dick.

"No point in that," Ashton said. "They stole sixteen head of prime Black Angus because we were sleeping. Anyone who has lived in Montana for a month knows you might catch Ashton Maddox asleep once, and only once, because I'll never make that mistake again. They won't be back there. Any missing head elsewhere?"

"Nothin' yet," Colter Norris replied. "But I ain't got all the tallies yet."

He remembered the bourbon, and raised the tumbler as he gave his foreman that look that needed no reinterpretation.

"I want those tallies done right quick. Because there's one thing in my book that sure hasn't changed since the eighteen hundreds. Nobody steals Circle M beef and gets away with it."

Visit our website at
KensingtonBooks.com
to sign up for our newsletters, read
more from your favorite authors, see
books by series, view reading group
guides, and more!

BOOK | CLUB
BETWEEN THE CHAPTERS

Become a Part of Our
Between the Chapters Book Club
Community and Join the Conversation

Betweenthechapters.net